P9-CKQ-579

IN THE BLOODY AFTERMATH of the War of Souls, Mina buried her Dark Queen and her future. But then she fell in love with Chemosh, the charming, handsome god of death.

As a vampiric cult sweeps across Krynn, heroes— including a monk pledged to the evil goddess of the sea and a kender who communicates with the dead—must thwart Mina's pact with evil and stop the dark disciples.

The first DRAGONLANCE® novel by *The New York Times* best-selling author Margaret Weis following her sensational War of Souls trilogy.

"Offers plenty of fantasy action intermixed with a mythic feel that is appropriate to a book about fickle gods."
—VOYA

"Margaret Weis is a legend in the world of fantasy fiction."
—Publishers Weekly

the Dark Disciple

AMBER AND ASHES

AMBER AND IRON

AMBER AND BLOOD

AMBER AND ASHES

the Dark Disciple

Volume I

MARGARET WEIS

AMBER & ASHES

The Dark Disciple, Volume 1

©2005 Wizards of the Coast, Inc.

All characters in this book are fictitious. Any resemblance to actual persons, living or dead, is purely coincidental.

This book is protected under the copyright laws of the United States of America. Any reproduction or unauthorized use of the material or artwork contained herein is prohibited without the express written permission of Wizards of the Coast, Inc.

Distributed in the United States by Holtzbrinck Publishing. Distributed in Canada by Fenn Ltd.

Distributed to the hobby, toy, and comic trade in the United States and Canada by regional distributors.

Distributed worldwide by Wizards of the Coast, Inc. and regional distributors.

DRAGONLANCE, WIZARDS OF THE COAST, and their respective logos are trademarks of Wizards of the Coast, Inc., in the U.S.A. and other countries.

All Wizards of the Coast characters, character names, and the distinctive likenesses thereof are property of Wizards of the Coast, Inc.

Printed in the U.S.A.

The sale of this book without its cover has not been authorized by the publisher. If you purchased this book without a cover, you should be aware that neither the author nor the publisher has received payment for this "stripped book."

Cover art by Matt Stawicki
First Printing: August 2004
First Paperback Printing: July 2005
Library of Congress Catalog Card Number: 2004116903

9 8 7 6 5 4 3 2 1

ISBN-10: 0-7869-3742-4
ISBN-13: 978-0-7869-3742-4
620-96708000-001-EN

U.S., CANADA,   EUROPEAN HEADQUARTERS
ASIA, PACIFIC, & LATIN AMERICA   Hasbro UK Ltd
Wizards of the Coast, Inc.   Caswell Way
P.O. Box 707   Newport, Gwent NP9 0YH
Renton, WA 98057-0707   GREAT BRITAIN
+1-800-324-6496   Please keep this address for your records.

Visit our web site at **www.wizards.com**

ACKNOWLEDGEMENTS

I would like to thank Deb Guzman of Delavan, Wisconsin, and her border collies, Coy, Tell, and Bizzy, for instructing me and my border collie Tess in the fascinating work of the herd dog.

My thanks to Joshua Stewart of Beaumont, Texas, who suggested the word "emmide" for Rhys's staff.

I would like to thank Weldon Chen, "Granak" of Reno, Nevada, who made a khas board for me so that I could learn to play the game. Thanks also to Tom Wham of Lake Geneva, Wisconsin, who played numerous games of khas with me and helped me understand the rules.

DEDICATION

To Jamie and Renae Chambers.

We've faced some severe storms at sea. Your friendship and dedication kept our ship afloat.

With my love and thanks,
Margaret

INTRODUCTION

I remember the first time I came across Margaret's work as clearly as if it was yesterday. It was the mid-'80s and I had just sent out the manuscript of my first novel, *Echoes of the Fourth Magic*. Making myself crazy watching the mailman every day, I decided to divert my attention. I had heard of some new fantasy books that were making quite a splash, so I went to my local book store and bought the first DRAGONLANCE® novel.

I was immersed in that book when the bad news began to arrive. Rejection letter after rejection letter showed up at my door; I had no idea of how badly I wanted to get published! Frustration turned to outrage, which I took out on the book I happened to have in my hands at the time. I remember declaring in no uncertain terms that "I can write a better book than this!" And all the while, I didn't even realize the declaration as an expression of my own pain.

A few years later, I landed the deal with TSR and was subsequently asked to come out to Gen Con. My editor, Mary Kirchoff, took me aside to where two people, Margaret Weis and Tracy Hickman, were preparing for a signing.

"Watch these two," she told me. "Learn how a pro handles a signing line."

I sat down, a bit embarrassed, given my reaction to that DRAGONLANCE book those years before. Let me say here that I hadn't finished that novel then. I was just too angry and frustrated.

I met Margaret and Tracy and we exchanged a few pleasant words. Nothing too substantial, because the line had started to form. The things that most struck me during that book signing were the questions and the remarks of the readers. Fan after fan came up and breathlessly and reverently spoke of Kitiara and Tanis and Raistlin. These people, numerous, intelligent and erudite, had been deeply touched by that book I had angrily tossed aside those years before.

That moment remains an epiphany for me. The first thing I did when I got home was go back to the book store and buy all of those early DRAGONLANCE books. This time I read them honestly. When I got done, I could have been one of those people in that line, demanding to know more about Raistlin, worried about Tanis and in love with Flint and Tasslehoff. The tale was wonderful and wonderfully told, with characters rich and enchanting (okay, except for Sturm. Man, I hated Sturm and cheered for the dragon! Mwahahahaha!).

Err, back on point . . . I am not surprised that Margaret draws lines of fans at every signing, nor am I the least bit surprised that after all these years, those original DRAGONLANCE books continue to sell tens of thousands of copies each year. They tell a tale familiar yet fresh. They show us heroes familiar yet unique. And they show us villains, wonderful and delicious. Of course, there's also Raistlin, so multi-dimensional, so cool and so bad, so conflicted and so straightforward. The books are worthy of all the praise, to be sure.

Wow.

Just wow.

Margaret Weis is one of my favorite writers. I wish I could put words together as beautifully as she. She's also one of my favorite people. Too often we hear the cliché that someone's smile "lights up a room." Too rarely do we actually meet someone who has a smile that really does.

Rock on, Margaret, and don't you dare stop writing!

—R.A. Salvatore

PROLOGUE

*T*he temple dedicated to his worship was located below the castle's walls and ramparts, below the towers and spires, below the great hall with its moldering tapestries, below even the dungeons. The noble family to whom this castle had once belonged had buried their honored dead in this subterranean vault in order to maintain the holy sanctity of death, to keep the tombs safe from grave robbers and worse.

The grave robbers came anyway.

Eons ago, the noble and long forgotten family was consumed in some noble and long forgotten war. With the castle abandoned, there was no one left to protect the dead. Although the vault had been dug deep and the stairs that led to it were hidden, those who have a nose for treasure were able to sniff it out. The robbers pried loose the marble slabs, carved with the likeness of noble lord and noble lady, from the tops of the tombs and tossed them, broken, to the floor. They stripped the ruby rings from bony fingers, lifted the golden circlets from grinning skulls, snatched up the diamond pendants, and carried away the bejeweled swords.

After the robbers came worse.

Reviled throughout Ansalon, those who embraced the worship of Chemosh, Lord of Death, were forced to hold their sacred rites and rituals in places hidden from public view. Temples dedicated to the worship of Chemosh were established in caves, catacombs, and basements, and it was rumored that there was one in the sewers of Palanthas. The choicest of all locales for the god's temple were those already dedicated to Death, for there the power of the god could be most keenly experienced. Local cemeteries were ideal, but these tended to be visible and were therefore often raided by local authorities seeking to eradicate the undead, thus making them dangerous places of worship for the clerics of Chemosh. The discovery of a family vault that was unknown to the rest of the world was an important find. Chemosh's followers did all they could to keep it safe and keep it secret.

Clad in their ceremonial black robes, their faces hidden by white skull masks—for these followers of Chemosh trusted no one, not even each other—the clerics of the Lord of Death performed the rituals that brought the bodies of the dead back to what they considered "life." When they themselves died, the souls of these clerics were not free to join the River of Souls to the next stage of the wondrous journey. Having pledged their loyalty to the god in return for favors given to them while they were living, they were constrained by the god to remain in the world after death, forced to do his bidding, their mortal remains animated and ordered to guard temple or treasure and fight off invaders, their corpses dying over and over again, to be reanimated over and over again.

When the Age of Mortals came and Takhisis stole the world out from the other gods—including Chemosh—his clerics lost their power. No longer would skeletons rise at their command and take up arms in their fleshless hands to guard them against their foes. Some of the clerics burned their black robes and white masks and blended in with the neighbors. Others kept the faith, kept it safe and secret. Trusting that someday their god would return, they locked up the vaults, the tombs, and the crypts and carried such secrets in their hearts. The living loyal to Chemosh bided their time, and so did the dead.

When Takhisis, Queen of Darkness, came seeking souls to fuel her return to the world, she could not locate many of those souls who were bound to Chemosh. Hidden in the darkness of undeath, they kept silent when she called, waiting for their master.

And now he was here, world found, treacherous Queen deposed and deceased. Chemosh was back, but he wasn't happy.

He stood in the family vault that had once been his temple, stood amidst the dust and the rat droppings and bits and pieces of dismembered bodies—a collar bone here, a shin bone there—and he looked at his followers, who were slowly making their way out of dark corners or pulling themselves up out of coffins. His lip curled.

"What an ugly lot you are," he told them. "And you stink, too. Stink to high heaven. I'm surprised I couldn't locate the world from your stench alone."

The corpses didn't understand. They turned empty eye sockets in his direction and waited in tongueless silence for his command. As they stood, looking incredibly stupid, a finger bone dropped off one. Another lost its kneecap. An arm fell off another.

Chemosh frowned. A rat ran across his boot. He was so plunged in gloom that he didn't bother to kill it but let it go. The creature took refuge inside a skull, its tail sticking ludicrously out of the grinning mouth.

"There you stand, awaiting my commands. And just what am I supposed to tell you to do? Go out and recruit followers for my worship? Wait!" he commanded irritably. Some of the decaying bodies, having mistaken this for a command, were heading for the exit. "That wasn't an order, you brainless jumble of bones. I can imagine the sort of followers you are likely to bring me. Everyone is eager to worship a god whose devotees are in the last stages of rot."

Chemosh glowered at them, then made a sudden, impatient

gesture. "Oh, go on! Get out of here. You turn my stomach. Go terrorize some village. With any luck," he added, as they clanked and clattered and shuffled their way out, dropping body parts all the way, "some holy cleric of Mishakal will find the lot of you and smash you to bits."

Chemosh sat on the lid of a sarcophagus and flicked a fragment of bone off the black velvet of his breeches.

"Where are the young, the strong, the beautiful?" he demanded. "Why don't they come to me? I'll tell you why." He cast a disgusted glance at the departing skeletons. "The young don't think of death. They think of life, of living, of joy and happiness, youth and beauty. Speak of Chemosh, and they laugh at the thought. 'Come back to talk to me of him when I am old and ugly,' they say. Those are the worshippers *I* attract—arthritic old geezers who haven't a tooth in their heads, cackling old crones who chant my name and wave black cats at me. Cats!" he muttered. "What do I want with cats?"

Chemosh kicked at the skull and sent it rolling. The rat went skittering off into a dusty corner. "What I want is youth, strength, power. Converts who come to me willingly, eagerly. Converts who will frequent my temples in broad daylight and proclaim that they are proud to worship me. That's what I want. That's what I need." His fist clenched. "To gain the seat of power in the heavens, that is what I must have."

He stood up and roved restlessly about the vault. "Sargonnas has his minotaur empire that grows larger every day. The namby-pamby Mishakal. How they adore her, all flocking to her worship with cries of 'Heal me, heal me!' How can I compete with that?"

He paused to brush strands of sticky cobweb from his black velvet coat. "Even Zeboim, that wanton trollop, has the heart of every sailor in the fleet. Me? I have large quantities of mold and mildew. And spiders. How can I become a king among the pantheon when the most intelligent of my followers are the maggots who feed off them?"

Chemosh wiped the dust from his hands, shook the dirt and bone fragments from his boots, and stalked out the broken-down door that led into the vault. He wound his way up the stairwell that led back to the surface, back to sunshine and fresh air.

"I am going to make changes," he vowed. "Death will have a new face. A face with bright eyes and ruby lips."

He emerged into the night and paused to gaze up at the stars, the newly formed constellations, the newly returned three moons. Chemosh smiled.

"Lips people will be dying to kiss."

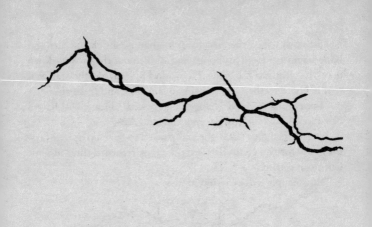

BOOK I

AMBER

Mina buried her queen beneath a mountain.

The queen had raised that mountain, molded it, shaped it, lifted it up with her immortal hands. And now she lay beneath it.

The mountain would die. Gnawed by the teeth of the wind, savaged by the drops of rain, slowly, over time, century upon century, the magnificent mountain Takhisis had created would crumble into dust, mingle, and become lost among the ashes of its dead creator. The final ignominy. The final, bitter irony.

"They will pay," vowed Mina, watching the sun set beyond the mountain, watching its shadow steal across the valley. "They will pay—all those who had a hand in this, mortal and immortal. I would make them pay, if I weren't so tired. So very tired."

She woke up tired; if one could use the term "waking," for she never truly slept. She passed the night in a restless doze in which she remained conscious of every shift in the wind, every animal grunt or cry, every dimming of the moonlight or flicker of the stars. Sleep lapped at her feet, ripples wetting her toes. Whenever sleep's waves, silent and calm, restful and peaceful, would start to carry her away, she would jerk to wakefulness with a gasp, as though she were drowning, and sleep would recede.

Mina spent the daylight hours guarding the Dark Queen's burial site. She never moved far from that tomb beneath the mountain, though Galdar nagged at her constantly to leave, if only for a little while.

"Go for a walk among the trees," the minotaur begged her, "or bathe in the lake or climb the rocky cliffs to see the sunrise."

Mina could not leave. She had a terrible fear that some person of Ansalon would find this holy site, and once that happened, the gawkers would come to stare and poke at the body and giggle and smirk. The treasure seekers and despoilers would come to rip off the jewels and lug away the holy artifacts. Takhisis's enemies would come to triumph over her. Her faithful would come, desperate to have their prayers answered, to try to bring her back.

That would be worst of all, Mina decided. Takhisis, a queen who had ruled heaven and the Abyss, forever chained to the whining pleas of those who had done nothing to try to save her when she died except wring their hands and whimper, "What will become of me?"

Day in and day out, Mina paced before the entrance to the tomb beneath the mountain where she had placed the body of the dead queen. She had worked hard, for weeks, for months maybe—she had no sense of time—to hide the fact that there was an entrance, planting trees, bushes, and wild flowers in front of it, training them to grow over it.

Galdar helped her in her task, and so did the gods, though she was not aware of their help and would have scorned it if she'd known of it.

The gods who had judged Takhisis, Queen of Darkness, and found her guilty of breaking the immortal oath they had all sworn at time's beginning, knew as well as Mina what would happen if mortals discovered the location of the Dark Queen's resting place. Trees that were seedlings when Mina planted them grew ten feet tall in a month. Brush and bramble bushes sprang up overnight. A howling wind that never ceased to blow polished the cliff face smooth, so that no trace of the entrance to the tomb remained visible.

Even Mina could no longer find the entrance, at least when she was awake. She could see it always in her dreams. Now there was nothing left for her to do except to guard it from everyone—mortal and immortal. She had become distrustful even of Galdar, for he had been among those responsible for her queen's downfall. She didn't like the way the minotaur was always urging her to leave. She suspected that he was waiting for her to depart and then he would break into the tomb.

"Mina," Galdar swore to her over and over, "I have no idea where the entrance to the tomb is. I could not even find this mountain if I left it, for the sun never rises in the same place twice!" He gestured to the horizon. "The gods themselves conceal it. East is west one day and west is east another. That is why it is safe to leave, Mina. Once you leave, you will never find your way back. You can move on with your life."

She knew the truth of that in her heart. She knew it and longed for it and was terrified of it.

"Takhisis was my life," Mina said to Galdar in answer. "When I looked in a mirror, her face was the face I saw. When I spoke, her voice was the voice I heard. Now she is gone, and when I look in the mirror, no face looks back. When I speak, there is only silence. Who am I, Galdar?"

"You are Mina," he replied.

"And who is Mina?" she asked.

Galdar could only stare at her, helpless.

They had this conversation often, almost every day. They had it again this morning. This time, though, Galdar's answer was different. He had been thinking long about this and when she said, "Who is Mina?" he responded quietly, "Goldmoon knew who you were, Mina. In her eyes you could see yourself. You didn't see Takhisis."

Mina considered this.

Looking back on her life, she saw it divided into three parts.

The first was childhood. Those years were nothing but a blur of color, fresh paint that someone had smeared with a soaking wet sponge.

The second was Goldmoon and the Citadel of Light.

Mina had no memory of the shipwreck or of being washed overboard or whatever had happened to her. For her memory—and life—had begun when she opened her eyes to find herself, wet and water-logged, lying in the sand, looking up at a group of people who had gathered around her, people who spoke to her with loving compassion.

They asked her what had happened to her.

She didn't know.

They asked her name.

She didn't know that either.

They would eventually conclude that she had been the survivor of a shipwreck—though no ships had been reported missing. Her parents were presumed to have been lost at sea. That theory seemed most likely, since no one ever came searching for her.

They said it was not unusual that she remembered nothing of her past, for she had suffered a severe blow to the head, which often accounted for memory loss.

They took her to a place they called the Citadel of Light, a wondrous place of warmth and radiance and serenity. Looking back on this time, Mina could not ever remember gray skies in connection with the Citadel, though she knew there must have been days of wind and storm. For her, the years she spent there, from the age of nine to fourteen, were lit by the sun gleaming on the crystal walls of the Citadel. Lit by the smile of the woman who came to be dear to her as a mother—the founder of the Citadel, Goldmoon.

They told Mina that Goldmoon was a hero, a famous person all over Ansalon. Her name was spoken with love and respect in every part of that continent. Mina didn't care about any of that. She cared only that when Goldmoon spoke to her, she spoke to her with gentle kindness and with love. Although a busy person,

Goldmoon was never too busy to answer Mina's questions, and Mina loved to ask questions.

Goldmoon was old when Mina first met her, as old as a mountain, the girl used to think. Goldmoon's hair was white, her face lined with deep sorrow and deeper joy, lines of loss and grief, lines of finding and hope. Her eyes were young as laughter, young as tears and—Galdar was right. Looking back through time, Mina could see herself in Goldmoon's eyes.

She saw a girl growing too fast, awkward and gawky, with long red hair and amber-colored eyes. Every night, Goldmoon would brush the red hair that was thick and luxurious, and answer all the questions Mina had thought up during the day. When her hair was brushed and plaited and she was ready for her bed, Goldmoon would take Mina onto her lap and tell her stories of the lost gods.

Some of the stories were dark, for there were gods who ruled the dark passions that are in every man's heart. There were gods of light in opposition to the gods of dark. Gods who ruled all that was good and noble in mankind. The dark gods struggled endlessly to gain ascendancy over mankind. The gods of light worked ceaselessly to oppose them. The neutral gods held the scales of balance. All mankind stood in the middle, each man free to choose his or her own destiny, for without freedom, men would die, as the caged bird dies, and the world would cease to be.

Goldmoon enjoyed telling Mina the stories, but Mina could tell that the stories made her adopted mother sad, for the gods were gone and man was left alone to struggle along as best he could. Goldmoon had made a life for herself without the gods, but she missed them and she longed more than anything for them to return.

"When I am grown," Mina would often say to Goldmoon, "I will go out into the world, and I will find the gods and bring them back to you."

"Ah, child," Goldmoon would answer with the smile that made her eyes bright, "your search should carry you no farther than here." She placed her hand on Mina's heart. "For though the gods are gone, their memory is born in each of us: memories of eternal love and endless patience and ultimate forgiveness."

Mina didn't understand. She had no memory of anything from birth. Looking back, she saw nothing except emptiness and darkness. Every night, when she lay alone in the darkness in her room, she would pray the same prayer.

"I know you are out there somewhere. Let me be the one to find you. I will be your faithful servant. I swear it! Let me be the one to bring knowledge of you to the world."

One night, when Mina was fourteen, she made that same prayer, made it as fervently and earnestly as she had on the very first night she had ever prayed it. And, on this night, there came an answer.

A voice spoke to her from the darkness.

"I am here, Mina. If I will tell you how to find me, will you come to me?"

Mina sat up eagerly in bed. "Who are you? What is your name?"

"I am Takhisis, but you will forget that. For you, I have no name. I need no name, for I am alone in the universe, the sole god, the one god."

"I will call you the One God, then," said Mina. Jumping out of bed, she hastily dressed herself, made ready to travel. "Let me go tell Mother where I am going——"

"Mother," Takhisis repeated in scorn and anger. "You have no mother. Your mother is dead."

"I know," said Mina, faltering, "but Goldmoon has become my mother. She is dearer to me than anyone, and I must tell her that I am leaving, or when she finds that I am gone, she will be worried."

The voice of the goddess changed, no longer angry but sweetly crooning. "You must not tell her or that would ruin the surprise. Our surprise——yours and mine. For the day will come when you will return to tell Goldmoon that you have found the One God, the ruler of the world."

"But why can't I tell her now?" Mina demanded.

"Because you have not yet found me," Takhisis replied sternly. "I am not even certain you are worthy. You must prove yourself. I need a disciple who is courageous and strong, who will not be deterred by unbelievers or swayed by naysayers, who will face pain and torment without flinching. All this you must prove to me. Do you have the courage, Mina?"

Mina trembled, terrified. She didn't think she did have the courage. She wanted to go back to her bed, and then she thought of Goldmoon and how wonderful the surprise would be. She imagined Goldmoon's joy when she saw Mina coming to her, bringing with her a god.

Mina laid her hand over her heart. "I have the courage, One God. I will do this for my adopted mother."

"That is as I would wish it," said Takhisis, and she laughed as though Mina had said something funny.

Thus began the third part of Mina's life, and if the first was a blur and the second was light, the third was shadow. Acting on the One God's command, Mina ran away from the Citadel of Light. She sought out a ship in the harbor and went onboard. The ship had no crew. Mina was the only person aboard, yet the wheel turned, the sails raised and lowered; all tasks were accomplished by unseen hands.

The ship sailed over waves of time and carried her to a place that she seemed to have known forever yet just this moment discovered. In this place, Mina first beheld the face of the Dark Queen, and she was beautiful and awful, and Mina bowed down and worshipped her.

Takhisis gave Mina test after test, challenge after challenge. Mina endured them all. She knew pain akin to the pain of dying, and she did not cry out. She knew pain akin to the pain of birth, and she did not flinch.

Then came the day when Takhisis said to Mina, "I am pleased with you. You are my chosen. Now is the time for you to go back to the world and prepare the people for my return."

"I went back to the world," Mina told Galdar, "on the night of the great storm. I met you that night. I performed my first miracle on you. I restored your arm."

He cast her a meaningful glance, and she flushed and said hurriedly, "I mean—the One God restored your arm."

"Call her by who she was," said Galdar harshly. "Call her Takhisis."

He looked involuntarily at the stump that was all that was left of his sword arm. When he had found out the true name of the One God, the god who had returned his lost arm to him, Galdar had prayed to his god Sargonnas to remove it again.

"I would not be her slave," he muttered, but Mina didn't hear him.

She was thinking about pride, hubris and ambition. She was thinking about the desire for power and who had truly been responsible for the fall of the Dark Queen.

"My fault," she said quietly. "I can admit that now. *I* was the one who destroyed her. Not the gods. Not even that wretched god-elf Valthonis, or whatever he calls himself. I destroyed her. I betrayed her."

"Mina, no!" Galdar returned, shocked. "You were her slave just as much as any of us. She used you, manipulated you—"

Mina raised her amber eyes to meet his. "So you believed. So they all believed. I alone knew the truth. I knew it and so did my Queen. I raised an army of the dead. I fought and killed two mighty dragons. I conquered the elves and brought them under the heel of my boot. I conquered the Solamnics and saw them run from me like whipped dogs. I made the Dark Knights a power to be feared and respected."

"All in the name of Takhisis," said Galdar. The minotaur scratched the fur on his jowls and rubbed his muzzle. He looked uneasy.

"I wanted it to be in *my* name," said Mina. "She knew it. She saw into my heart and that was why she was going to destroy me."

"And that was why you were going to let her," said Galdar.

Mina sighed and bowed her head. She sat on the hard ground, her legs drawn up, her arms wrapped around her knees. She wore the clothes she had worn that fateful day when her Queen had died, the simple garments worn underneath the armor of a Dark Knight—shirt and breeches. They were ragged and worn now, bleached by the sun to a nondescript gray. The only color that was bright upon it was the red blood of the queen who had died in Mina's arms.

Galdar shook his horned head and sat up straight on the boulder he was using for a seat, a boulder he'd rubbed smooth over the past several months.

"All that is over now, Mina. It is time you moved on. There is yet much to do in the world and a new world in which to do it. The Dark Knights are in disarray, unorganized. They need a strong leader to bring them together."

"They would not follow me," said Mina.

Galdar opened his mouth to remonstrate then shut it again.

Mina glanced up at him, saw that he knew the truth as well as she did. The Dark Knights would never again accept her as a commander. They had been wary of her from the beginning—a girl of seventeen, who barely knew one end of a sword from another, who had never seen a battle, much less led men into one.

The miracles she performed had won them over. As she had once told that wretched elf prince, men loved the god they saw in her, not her, and when that god was overthrown and Mina lost her power to perform miracles, the knights went down to disastrous defeat. Not only that, but they believed that she deserted them at the end, left them to face death alone. They would never follow her again, and she could not blame them.

Nor did she want to be a leader of men. She did not want to go to back into the world again. She was too tired. She wanted only to sleep. She leaned back against the bones of the mountain where her queen lay in her eternal slumber and closed her eyes.

She must have drifted off, for she woke to find Galdar squatting beside her, pleading with her earnestly.

"—must leave this prison, Mina! You've punished yourself enough. You have to forgive yourself, Mina. What happened to Takhisis was her own fault. Not yours. You are not to blame. She was going to kill you! You know that. She was going to take over your body, devour your soul! That elf did you a favor by killing her."

Mina raised her head. Her look stopped him, stopped the words on his lips and rocked the minotaur back on his heels as surely as if she'd struck him.

"I'm sorry, Mina. I didn't mean that. Come with me," Galdar urged.

Mina reached out her hand, patted him on the one arm that was left to him. "Go on, Galdar. I know your god has been hounding you, demanding that you join him in his conquest of Silvanesti."

She smiled wanly at Galdar's sudden discomfiture.

"I've eavesdropped on your prayers to Sargonnas, my friend," she told him. "Go fight for your god. When you come back, you will tell me all that is happening in the world."

"If I leave this accursed valley, I can never come back. You know that, Mina," said Galdar. "The gods will see to that. They will see to it that no one ever—"

His words froze on his tongue. Even as he spoke them, they were being proven untrue. He stared out across the valley, rubbed his eyes, stared again.

"I must be seeing things." He squinted into the sun.

"What now?" Mina asked wearily. She did not look.

"Someone is coming," he reported, "walking across the floor of the valley. But that can't be."

"It can be, Galdar," said Mina, her gaze now going to follow his own. "Someone *is* coming."

A man strode purposefully across the windswept, bare-bones floor of the desert valley. He was tall and moved with commanding grace. Long, dark hair blew back behind him. His body shimmered in the waves of heat that rose up from the surface of the sand-covered rock.

"He is coming for me."

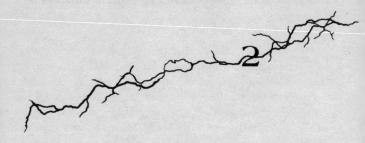

*T*he valley was a bowl-like depression scooped out of the same bedrock that had been lifted up to form the mountain. A fine layer of sand covered the rock, which was reddish yellow in color. A few sparse and scraggly bushes grew there, but no trees. No trees grew anywhere in this part of the land, except the strange trees that had sprung up in front of the tomb. A stream of water—cobalt blue against the red—zigzagged across the valley floor, cutting through the rock.

The mountain in which the Dark Queen was buried was honeycombed with caves, and in two of these Mina and Galdar had made their homes for the past year. Heat from the sun rose in shimmering waves off the floor of the valley in the daytime. The temperature dropped precipitously at night and rose again to unbearable levels during the day.

The valley was god-cursed. No mortal could find it. Galdar had found it only because he'd prayed day and night to Sargonnas to let him find it, and at last, the god relented. When Mina had carried the body of her goddess from the temple where Takhisis had died, Galdar had followed her. He alone knew the terrible grief she must be suffering. He hoped to be able to help her bury her queen forever. Galdar had followed Mina for a day and a night but could never seem to catch up to her, and then one morning, after waking from an exhausted sleep, he could not find her at all.

He guessed, of course, that the gods would not want any mortal to discover the burial place of Queen Takhisis and that they had hidden Mina from him for that reason. Galdar prayed to Sargonnas to be allowed to go to Mina and Sargonnas had granted his prayer—for a price. The god had transported Galdar to the secret burial site. Galdar and Mina had laid the Dark Queen to rest beneath the mountain, and then Galdar had spent the rest of his time trying to persuade Mina to return to the world. In this Galdar had failed, and now the god was putting pressure on Galdar to fulfill his end of the bargain. Minotaur ships were arriving in Silvanesti, bringing troops and colonists, making the former elf homeland the minotaurs' own, and making the humans who lived in the other nations of Ansalon extremely nervous.

The Solamnic knights, the knights of the Legion of Steel, and the formidable barbaric warriors of the Plains of Dust—all of these humans were eying the minotaur encroachment onto their continent with growing ire. Sargonnas needed an ambassador to these races. He needed a minotaur who understood humans to go to them and placate them, convince them that the minotaurs had no plans for expansion. The minotaurs were content with conquering and seizing the lands of an ancient foe. Solamnia and the other realms were safe.

Galdar had lived among humans and fought alongside them for years. He was the perfect choice as ambassador to the humans, and he was made even more perfect by the fact that humans tended to like him and trust him. Galdar wanted to serve the god who had saved him from Takhisis, taken away his arm and given him back his self-respect. Sargonnas was not a patient god. He had made it clear to Galdar that he either came now or he did not come at all.

Galdar had first thought, rather fearfully, that perhaps Sargonnas had grown so tired of waiting that the god was coming for Galdar.

A second look dissuaded him of that notion. He could not make out the features of this person, who was yet too far away, but it was human in shape and form, not minotaur.

But no human was permitted to walk this valley. No mortal, other than the two of them, was allowed here.

The hackles on Galdar's neck rose. The fur on his back and arms rippled with a fell chill. "I don't like this, Mina. We should flee. Now. Before this man sees us."

"Not a man, Galdar," said Mina. "A god. He comes for us. Or rather, he comes for me."

He saw her hand go to her waist, saw it close over the hilt of a knife—a knife he recognized. He reached for his own knife and found it was not there.

She glanced at him, half-smiled. "I took your knife, Galdar. I took it from you in the night."

He didn't like the way she held it, as though it were something precious to her.

"Who is that man, Mina?" the minotaur demanded, his voice hoarse with a fear he could not name. "What does he want with you?"

"You should leave, Galdar," she told him quietly, her gaze fixed on the stranger, who was drawing closer. His stride had quickened. He seemed impatient to reach his destination. "This is none of your concern."

The figure came into view. He was a human male of indeterminate age. His face was what humans consider handsome—cleft chin, square jaw, aquiline nose, prominent cheekbones, smooth brow. He wore his black hair long; sleek locks curled about his shoulders and hung down his back. His skin was so pallid as to seem bloodless. He had no color in his lips or cheeks. His eyes were dark as creation's first night. Set deep beneath heavy brows, they seemed darker still, always in shadow.

He was dressed all in black; his clothes were rich, which bespoke wealth. His black velvet coat came to his knees. Nipped in at his narrow waist, the coat was trimmed in silver at the sleeves and around the hem. He wore black breeches that came to just below the knee, trimmed with black ribbons. He had black silken stockings and black boots with silver buckles. White lace adorned his shirt, spread in frills over his bosom, protruding from his sleeves, falling languidly over his hands. He carried himself with grace and confidence and an awareness of his own power.

Galdar shivered. Though the sun's heat was intense, he could no longer feel it. A cold so ancient that it made the mountain young crept into the marrow of his bones. He had faced many terrible foes in his life, including the Dragon Overlord Malys, and he had not run from any of them. He could not help himself now. He began to edge backward.

"Sargonnas!" Galdar prayed to his god. His voice cracked on the name and he tried to swallow, to moisten his throat. "Sargonnas, give me strength. Help me fight this dread foe—"

The god's answer was a snort. "I've indulged your loyalty to this human female thus far, Galdar, but my patience has run out. Leave her to her fate. It is well-deserved."

"I cannot," said Galdar staunchly, though he blanched at the sight of the strange man. "I am pledged to her—"

"I warn you, Galdar," said Sargonnas in dire tones. "Do not come between Chemosh and his prey."

"Chemosh!" Galdar cried hollowly.

Chemosh. Lord of Death. Galdar began to tremble. His insides crawled.

Mina held up Galdar's knife. The knife was old with a bone handle. It was a utility knife, one used for a variety of purposes, from cleaning fish to gutting deer. He kept the blade sharp, well-honed. He watched Mina raise the knife, saw the light of the sun reflected in the metal of the blade but not in her eyes. Her gaze was focused on the god.

She held the blade in her right hand. Reversing it, she pressed the blade's sharp point against her throat. The inner flame in the amber eyes flashed briefly then dimmed. Her lips compressed. Her grip on the knife tightened. She closed her eyes and drew in a breath.

Galdar roared and lunged for her. He had waited too long. He could not reach her before she plunged the blade into her throat. He hoped his roar would distract her before she could destroy herself.

Chemosh lifted his hand in a negligent, almost careless gesture. Galdar flew off his feet, sailed into the air, upheld by the hand of the god. Galdar fought and struggled, but he was in the grasp of the god and there was no escape. No more than if he'd tried to flee from death itself.

Chemosh carried the minotaur—flailing and roaring—away from the valley, away from the mountain, away from Mina, who was receding into the distance, growing smaller and smaller, dwindling by the second.

Galdar reached out his hand to try desperately to grab hold of time and the world as both thundered past him—to seize hold of them, of her. She looked up at him with her eyes of amber and for a brief moment, the two of them touched.

Then the raging waters tore her from his grasp. His bellow of frantic desperation deepened, became a roar of despair.

Galdar sank beneath the floodwaters of time and knew no more.

Galdar woke to voices and to fear. The voices were deep and gruff and came from quite near him.

"Mina!" he cried, as he staggered to his feet, grappling for the sword that he had grimly taught himself to use with his left hand.

Two minotaurs wearing the battle armor of the minotaur legions jumped backward at his sudden rise and reached for their own swords.

"Where is she?" he raved, foam flecking his lips. "Mina! Where is she? What have you done with her?"

"Mina?" The two minotaurs stared at him, bewildered.

"We know of no one by that name," said one, his sword half-in and half-out of the sheath.

"It sounds human," growled his comrade. "What is she? Some captive of yours? If so, she must have run away when you fell from that cliff."

"Either that or she pushed you," said the soldier.

"Cliff?" Galdar was the one bewildered. He looked to where the minotaur pointed.

A steep cliff reared high above him, its rocky face barely visible through the heavy foliage. He looked around and found himself standing in tall grass beneath the shady branches of a linden tree. His body had left a deep gouge in the soft, moist loam.

Far from the sun-baked desert. Far from the mountain.

"We saw you fall from that great height," said the minotaur. He shoved his blade back into its sheath. "Truly, Sargonnas must love you. We thought you were dead, for you must have plunged over one hundred feet straight down. Yet here you stand with naught but a bump on your head."

Galdar tried to find the mountain, but the trees were too thick. He could not see the horizon line. He lowered his gaze. His head bowed, his shoulders slumped.

"What is your name, friend?" asked the other. "And what are you doing roaming about Silvanesti alone? The elf scum left in these parts do not dare attack us in the open, but they are quick to ambush a lone minotaur."

"My name is Galdar," he said, lifeless, dispirited.

The two soldiers gave a start, exchanged glances.

"Galdar the One-armed!" one exclaimed, his eyes fixing on the stump.

"Why, then, not only did the god save your life, he dropped you right at the feet of your escorts!" said the other.

"Escorts?" Galdar regarded them warily, confused and distrustful. "What do you mean . . . escorts?"

"Commander Faros received word that you were coming, my lord, and dispatched us to meet you to see that you reached headquarters safely. Truly, we are well-met, all praise to Sargonnas."

"It is an honor to meet you, my lord," added the other soldier, awed. "Your exploits with the Dark Knights are the stuff of legend."

"Now that I recall, there *was* someone called Mina. She served under you, my lord, did she not? A minor functionary?"

"The fall must have addled you, my lord. From what we hear, this Mina has been dead for a long time, ever since Sargonnas defeated and put to death Queen Takhisis."

"May the dogs chew on her bones," added the soldier grimly.

Galdar looked around one final time for some sign of the mountain, the desert. For some sign of Mina. Futile, he knew, yet he could not help himself. He looked back then at the two minotaur, who were waiting for him patiently, regarding him—one arm and all—with respect and admiration.

"Praise to Sargonnas," Galdar said softly, and, squaring his shoulders, he took his first step into his new life.

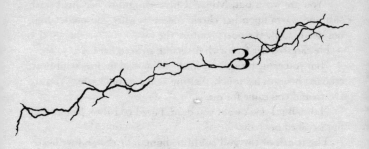

Bracing herself for death, Mina gave the knife a sharp thrust.

Death watched her with amusement.

The blade changed to wax that almost immediately began to melt in the hot sun. The warm wax oozed out between her fingers. Mina stared at it, stupefied, not understanding. Lifting her eyes, she met the eyes of the god.

Her legs trembled. Her strength failed her. She sank down onto her knees, dropped her head into her hands. She could no longer see the god, but she heard his footsteps coming nearer and nearer. His shadow fell over her, blotting out the hot sun. She shivered.

"Let me die, Lord Chemosh," she mumbled, not looking up. "Please. I only want to rest."

She heard the creak of his leather boots, sensed him moving near her, kneeling beside her. He smelled of myrrh, and she was reminded of the perfumed oils poured onto funeral pyres to mask the stench of burning flesh. Mingled with the musky fragrance was the faint, sweet odor of lily and rose, faded and fragile as the petals of youth pressed between the pages of life's book. His hand touched her hair, smoothed it. His hand moved from her hair to her face. His touch was cool on her sunburned skin.

"You are worn out, Mina," Chemosh said to her, his breath soft and warm upon her cheek. "Sleep is what you need. Sleep, not death. Only the poets confuse the two."

He caressed her face with his hand, stroked her hair.

"But you came for me, my lord," Mina said in drowsy protest, relaxing beneath his touch, melting as the waxen knife. "You are Death and you came for me."

"I did. But I don't want you dead. I need you alive, Mina." His lips brushed her hair.

The touch of the god could be human, if the god willed it. Chemosh's touch roused in Mina yearnings and feelings she had never before experienced. Virginal in body and mind, Mina had been protected from desire by her queen, who did not want her chosen disciple distracted by weaknesses of the flesh.

Mina knew desire now, felt it burn to life inside her.

Chemosh cupped her face with his hand, moved slowly to stroke her neck. His finger traced the path the blade of the knife might have taken, and Mina felt it sharp, cold, and burning, and she shuddered in pain that was both bitter and exalting.

"I feel your heart beating, Mina," Chemosh said. "I feel your flesh warm, your blood pulsing."

Mina did not understand the strange sensations his touch aroused in her. Her body ached, but the pain was pleasurable, and she never wanted such pleasure to end. She pressed nearer to him. Her lips sought his and he kissed her, slowly, gently, long and lingering.

He drew away from her, released her.

Mina opened her eyes. She looked into his eyes that were dark and empty as the sea on which she'd wakened one day to find herself alone.

"What are you doing to me, Lord?" she cried, suddenly fearful.

"Bringing you to life, Mina," Chemosh answered, stroking back her hair from her forehead with his hand. The white lace brushed against her face, the spicy scent of myrrh filled her nostrils. She lay back on the ground, yielding to his touch.

"But you are Death," she argued, confused.

Chemosh kissed her forehead, her cheeks, her neck. His lips moved to the hollow in her throat.

"Did any other gods come to you here, Mina?" he asked. He continued to caress her, but his voice was altered, took on an edge.

"Yes, some did, Lord," she said.

"What did they come for?"

"Some to save me. Some to chastise me. Some to punish me." She shuddered. His grip on her tightened and she was reassured.

"Did you make promises to any of them?" he asked. The edge grew sharper.

"No. None, my lord. I swear it."

He was pleased. "Why not, Mina?" he asked with a smile playing about his lips.

Mina took hold of his hand, placed it on her breast, over her beating heart. "They wanted my faith. They wanted my loyalty. They wanted my fear."

"Yes?"

"None of them wanted me."

"I want you, Mina," said Chemosh. He kept his hand resting on her breast, felt her heart beat increase. "Give yourself to me. Make me lord of all things. Make me the lord of your life."

Mina was silent. She seemed troubled, stirred uneasily beneath his touch.

"Speak what is in your heart, Mina," he said. "I will not be offended."

"You betrayed her," she said at last, accusing.

"Takhisis was the one who betrayed us, Mina," Chemosh replied, chiding. "She betrayed you."

"No, my lord," Mina protested. "No, she told me the truth."

"Lies, Mina. All lies. And you knew it."

Mina shook her head and tried to free herself from his grasp.

"You knew she lied to you," Chemosh said relentlessly. He held her pinned in his grasp, pressed her into the ground. "You knew it at the end. You were glad the elf killed her."

Mina raised up her hands, her amber eyes lifted to the dragon. "Your Majesty, I have always adored you, worshipped you. I pledged my life to your service and I stand ready to honor that pledge. Through my fault, you lost the body you would have inhabited. I offer my own. Take my life. Use me as your vessel. Thus, I prove my faith!"

Queen Takhisis was beautiful, but her beauty was fell and terrible to look upon. Her face was cold as the vast frozen wastelands to the south, where a man perishes in instants, his breath turning to ice in his lungs. Her eyes were the flames of the funeral pyre. Her nails were talons, her hair the long and ragged hair of the corpse. Her armor was black fire. At her side she wore a sword perpetually stained with blood, a sword used to sever the souls from their bodies.

Mina cried, a wail of grief and anger. She struggled in Death's grasp.

Takhisis reached for Mina's heart, intending to make that heart her own. Takhisis reached for Mina's soul, intending to snatch it from her body and cast it into oblivion. Takhisis reached out to fill Mina's body with her own immortal essence.

"Admit it, Mina." Chemosh held her fast, forced her to look into his eyes. "You were hoping someone would finish her for you."

The elf king held in his hand the broken fragment of the dragonlance. He threw the lance, threw it with the strength of his anguish and his guilt, threw it with strength of his fear and his love.

The lance struck Takhisis, lodged in her breast.

She stared down in shock to see the lance protruding from her flesh. Her fingers moved to touch the bright, dark blood welling from the terrible wound. She staggered, started to fall . . .

"I killed the elf with my own hands," Mina cried. "My queen died in my arms. I would have given—"

Mina stopped the words that had been pouring forth. She lowered her eyes from Chemosh's intense gaze, averted her head.

"You would have given your life for Takhisis? You gave her your life, Mina, the time you fought Malys. Takhisis brought you back for her own selfish reasons. She needed you. If she had not, she would have let you fall through her fingers as so much dust and ash. And at the end, she had the temerity to blame you for her downfall."

Mina went limp in his grasp.

"She was right, my lord." Tears of shame seeped from beneath her eyelids. "Her death was my fault."

Chemosh brushed aside the tangle of red hair to see her face. "And when she died, some part of you was glad."

Mina moaned and turned her face away from him. He smoothed back her tear-wet hair, wiped away her tears.

"Loyalty to your queen is not what has kept you in this valley. You stay because of your guilt. Guilt made you prisoner. Guilt is your jailor. Guilt was almost your slayer."

He put both hands on her face, looked deep into the amber eyes.

"You have no reason to feel guilty, Mina. Takhisis bought and paid for her own fate."

His voice softened, soothed. "She is gone and so is Paladine."

"Paladine . . ." Mina murmured. "My oath, to avenge my queen's death . . . on him, on the elves . . ."

"So you shall," Chemosh promised. "But not yet. Not now. The way must be prepared. Hear me, Mina, and understand. Both the great gods are gone now. Only one remains—their brother, Gilean, god of the book, god of doubt and indecision. He stands with the scales of balance, light in one hand, darkness in another. Every waking second, he weighs them to make certain that they do not shift."

Mina looked up at him, entranced. He had ceased to talk to her. He was talking to himself.

"A futile task," Chemosh was saying with a shrug. "The scales will tip. They must since the pantheon is now uneven. Gilean knows that he cannot maintain the balance forever. He sees his own downfall, and he is afraid. For I know what he does not. I know what will tip the balance.

"Mortals," said Chemosh, savoring the word. "Mortals are the ones who will topple the scale. Mortals like you, Mina. Mortals who come to the gods of their own free will. Mortals who do our bidding not out of fear, but out of love. Those mortals will grant power to their gods, not the other way around as it has been in ages past. That is why I did not want your death, Mina. That is why I want you alive."

He put his mouth close to her lips. "Serve me, Mina," he said so softly that she did not hear the words but felt them burn her skin. "Give yourself to me. Give me your faith. Your loyalty. Your love."

Mina trembled at her own daring, afraid he would be angry, yet she was thinking of what he said about the power of mortals in this Age of Mortals. She saw in her mind the golden scales that Gilean held, balanced so precariously that a single grain of sand could cause them to wobble.

"And if I give my love to you, what will you give me in return?" Mina asked.

Chemosh was not angered by her question. On the contrary, he seemed pleased.

"Life unending, Mina," he said to her. "Youth eternal. Beauty unspoiled. As you are now, so you will be five hundred years from now."

"That is all very well, my lord, but—" she paused.

"But you don't care about any of that, do you?"

Mina flushed. "I am sorry, lord. I hope you are not offended—"

"No, no. Do not apologize. You want from me what Takhisis was unwilling to grant. Very well. I will give you what you do care about—power. Power over life. Power over death."

Mina smiled, relaxed in his grasp. "And you will love me?"

"As I love you now," he promised.

"Then I give myself to you, my lord," she said and she closed her eyes and lifted up her lips for his kiss.

But he was not quite ready to take her for his own. Not yet. He kissed her on her eyelids, first one, then the other.

"Sleep now, Mina. Sleep deep and sleep dreamless. When you wake, you will wake to a new life, a life such as you have never known."

"Will you be with me?" she murmured.

"Always," promised Chemosh.

The elves, driven from both their ancient homelands, roam the world, exiles. Some have gone to the cities—Palanthas, Sanction, Flotsam, Solace—where they crowd together in dismal dwellings, working at whatever they can to buy food for their children, lost in dreams of past glory. Other elves live in the Plains of Dust, where every day they watch the sun set on their homeland that is far away, almost as far as the sun, or so it seems. They do not dream of the past, but dream blood-spattered dreams of a future of retribution and revenge.

The minotaur sail their ships on the foaming seas and fight their battles among each other, yet always the sun shines bright on the swords that vanquish the ancient enemy and on the axe that cuts down the green forest.

The humans celebrate the deaths of the dragon overlords and worry about the minotaur who have, at long last, established a presence upon Ansalon. The humans do not worry much, however, for they have other problems more pressing—political strife and turmoil in Solamnia, outlaws threatening Abanasinia, goblins rising to power in southern Qualinesti, refugees everywhere.

The dragons emerge from their caves into a world that was once theirs, was lost, and is now theirs again. But they are watchful, wary, even the best of them suspicious and distrustful, just now starting to realize that what was lost is lost for good.

The gods return to an Age of Mortals and know that it is truly named, for it is mortals who will determine whether or not the gods will have any influence over their creation. Thus the gods cannot sit at their ease in the heavens or in the Abyss or on any of the immortal planes, but walk the world, seeking faith, love, prayers. Making promises.

And while all this is happening, a shepherd stands upon a hill, watching his dog bring the sheep to the fold.

A kender plays games with the ghost of a dead child in a graveyard.

A young cleric of Kiri-Jolith welcomes a new convert.

A death knight seethes with rage in his prison and looks for a way out.

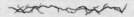

Mina woke from a strange dream that she could not remember to darkness so deep that the lights of the candles did little to illuminate it, just as the cold, pale light of the stars are unable to light up the night. Her sleep was as deep as the darkness. She could not remember when she had slept that soundly. No alarms in the night, no sub-commanders waking her with questions that could have waited until morning, no wounded carried in on litters for her to heal.

No face of a dead queen.

Mina lay back on the soft, down pillows that surrounded her and gazed into the darkness. She did not know where she was—certainly this was not the hard, cold floor of the desert on which she had been sleeping. She was too warm, too comfortable, too lethargic to care to try to find out. The darkness was soothing and scented with myrrh. The myriad candles around her bed burned with unwavering flames. She could see nothing beyond the bed. For the moment, she had no care for that. She was thinking of Chemosh, the words he had said to her yesterday.

When she died, some part of you was glad.

Mina was a veteran warrior. From where she had been standing on that fateful day, she could have never reached the elf in time to stop him from hurling his lance at the goddess whose punishment for stealing away the world had been mortality. Mina did not blame herself for her queen's death. Mina blamed herself for having—as Chemosh said—felt joy that the queen was dead.

Mina had slain the elf. Most thought she had killed him in retribution. Mina knew differently. The elf had been in love with her. He had seen, with the eyes of love, that she was grateful to him for what he had done. She saw that knowledge in his eyes and, for that sin, he paid with his life.

Her joy over her queen's death was immediately subsumed in grief and very real sorrow. Mina could not forgive herself for that initial burst of relief, for being glad that the decision to give up her life for her queen had been taken out of her hands.

"What would I have done when she came to kill me? Would I have fought her? Or would I have let her slay me?"

Every night, lying awake in front of the hidden entrance to the Dark Queen's mountain tomb, Mina asked herself that question.

"You would have fought for your life," answered Chemosh.

He drew near the bed. The silver that trimmed his coat glittered in the candlelight. His pale face had a light of its own, as did the dark eyes. He took Mina's hand, resting on the cambric sheet that wound around her body, and raised it to his lips. His kiss made her heart jump, tore at her breath.

"You would have fought because you are mortal and you have a strong need to survive," he added, "a struggle we gods never know."

He seemed to brood over this, for she felt his attention leave her, shift away from her. He stared into a darkness that was endless, eternal, and awful. He stared long, as if seeking answers, then he shook his head, shrugged, and looked back at her with a smile.

"And thus you mortals could say," he added, with a tone that was part mocking, part deadly earnest, "that the all-knowing gods are not so very all-knowing."

She started to reply, but he would not let her. He bent down, kissed her swiftly on the lips, then he strode in a leisurely manner away from the bed, took a turn around the candlelit room. She watched his walk, strong and masterful.

"Do you know where you are, Mina?" Chemosh asked, turning to her abruptly.

"No, my lord," she answered calmly. "I do not."

"You are in my dwelling place." He watched her intently. "In the Abyss."

Mina cast a glance around her then returned her gaze to him.

He regarded her with admiration. "You wake to find yourself alone in the Abyss, yet you are not afraid."

"I have walked in darker places," replied Mina.

Chemosh looked at her long, then he nodded in understanding. "The trials of Takhisis are not for the faint of heart."

Mina threw aside the cambric sheets. She climbed out of the bed and came to stand before him. "And what of the trials of Chemosh?" she asked him boldly.

The god smiled. "Did I say there would be trials?"

"No, my lord, but you will want me to prove myself. And," she added, looking up in the dark eyes that held her, Mina, inside them, "I want to prove myself to you."

He took her in his arms and kissed her, long and ardently. She returned his kiss, clasping him in her arms, swept by passion that left her weak and trembling when he finally released her.

"Very well, Mina," said Chemosh. "You will prove yourself to me. I have a task for you, one for which you are uniquely qualified."

She tasted his kiss upon her lips, spicy and heady, like the scent of myrrh. She was unafraid, even eager.

"Set me any task, my lord. I will undertake it."

"You destroyed the death knight, Lord Soth—" he began.

"No, lord, I did not destroy him . . ." Mina hesitated, uncertain how to continue.

He understood her dilemma and he waved it away. "Yes, yes, Takhisis destroyed him. I understand, yet you were the instrument of his destruction."

"I was, my lord."

"Lord Soth was a death knight, a terrifying being," said Chemosh, "someone even we gods might fear. Were you afraid to face him, Mina?"

"Within a few days time, Lord Soth, armies of both the living and the dead will sweep down on Sanction. The city will fall to my might." Mina did not speak with bravado. She was stating a fact, nothing more. "At that time, the One God will perform a great miracle. She will enter the world as she was long meant to do, join the realms of the mortal and the immortal. Once she exists on both planes, she will conquer the world, rid it of such vermin as the elves, and establish herself as the ruler of Krynn. I am to be made captain of the army of the living. The One God offers you the captaincy of the army of the dead."

"She 'offers' me this?" Soth asked.

"Offers it," said Mina. "Yes, of course."

"Then she will not be offended if I turn down her offer," said Soth.

"She would not be offended," Mina replied, "but she would be deeply grieved at your ingratitude, after all that she has done for you."

"All she has done for me." Soth smiled. "So this is why she brought me here. I am to be a slave leading an army of slaves. My answer to this generous offer is no."

"I was not afraid, my lord," said Mina, "for I was armed with the wrath of my queen. What was his power, compared to that?"

"Oh, nothing so much," said Chemosh. "Nothing except the ability to kill you with a single word. He could have simply said, 'die,' and you would have died. I doubt if even Takhisis could have saved you."

"As I told you, my lord," Mina replied gravely, "I was armed with the wrath of my queen." She frowned slightly, thinking. "You cannot want me to face Lord Soth. The Dark Queen destroyed him. Is there another death knight? One that is troublesome to you, my lord?"

"Troublesome?" Chemosh laughed. "No, he is no trouble to me nor to anyone else on Krynn for that matter. Not now at least. He was once trouble for a great many people—most notably, the late Lord Ariakan. Ausric Krell is his name. He is known in history, I believe, as the Betrayer."

"The traitor who brought about Lord Ariakan's death at the hand of Chaos," said Mina heatedly. "I have heard the story, my lord. The knights all spoke of it. None knew what ever happened to Krell."

"None would want to know," said Chemosh. "Ariakan was the son of Zeboim, goddess of the sea, and the Dragon Highlord Ariakan. The father was dead, slain during the War of the Lance. Zeboim doted on the boy, who was her only child. When he died by Krell's treacherous hand during the Chaos War, the tears of the goddess flowed so copiously that they raised the level of the seas the world over, or so they say.

"The fire of Zeboim's rage soon dried her tears, however. Sargonnas, god of vengeance, is her father, and Zeboim is her father's daughter. She hunted down the wretched Krell, dragged him from the miserable hole in which he'd been trying to hide, and set about punishing him. She tortured him for days on end, and when the pain and torment was too much for him and his heart burst, she restored him to life, tortured him until he died, brought him back and did this again and again. When she finally grew weary of the sport, she ferried what was left of him—his remains filled a small bucket, I am told—across the North Sirrion Sea to Storm's Keep, the island fortress built for the Knights of Takhisis and given to Lord Ariakan by his mother. There she cursed Krell, changed him into a death knight, and left him to fret out his sorry days upon that abandoned rock, surrounded by sea and storm that never let him forget what he had done.

"And there, for over thirty years, Lord Ausric Krell has been a prisoner, forced to live eternally in the fortress where he pledged his loyalty and his life to Lord Ariakan."

"And he is there still? During all those years, the gods were gone," Mina stated, wondering. "Zeboim was not in the world. She could not have stopped him from leaving. Why didn't he?"

"Krell is not Soth," said Chemosh dryly. "Krell is sneaky and underhanded, with the nobility of a weasel, the honor of a toad, and the brains of a cockroach. Isolated on his rock, he had no way of knowing that Zeboim was not around to keep an eye on him. The seas lashed the cliffs of his prison as relentlessly as when she was there. The storms that are so prevalent in that part of the world beat upon his prison walls. When he did eventually discover that he'd missed his chance, he was so furious that a single blow from his fist knocked down a small tower."

"And now that Zeboim has returned, does she guard him still?"

"Day and night," said Chemosh. "Testament to a mother's love."

"I have no love for traitors myself, my lord," said Mina. "I will gladly undertake whatever task you set for me in regard to this one."

"Good," said Chemosh. "I want you to free him."

"Free him, my lord?" Mina repeated, astonished.

"Help him escape Zeboim's watch and bring him to me."

"But why, my lord? If he is all that you describe him—"

"And more. He is shifty and cunning and sly and not to be trusted. And you must never question me, Mina. You may refuse to do this. The choice is yours, but you must not ask me why. My reasons are my own."

Chemosh lifted his hand, stroked his fingers over Mina's cheek. "Freeing Krell will not be an easy task. It is fraught with danger, for not only must you face the death knight, you must first deal with the vengeful goddess. If you refuse, I will understand."

"I do not refuse my lord," said Mina coolly. "I will do this for you. Where shall I bring him?"

"To my castle here in the Abyss. This is, for the time being, where I reside."

"For the time being, my lord?" asked Mina.

Chemosh took hold of her hands, raised them to his lips. "Another question, Mina?"

"I am sorry, my lord." Mina flushed. "That is a failing of mine, I fear."

"We will work on improving it. As for your question, that is one I do not mind answering. I do not like these accomodations. I want to walk in the world, among the living. I have plans to relocate. Plans that include you, Mina." He kissed her hands, soft, lingering kisses. "If you do not fail me."

"I will not fail you, Lord," she promised.

"Good," he said briskly and dropped her hands. He turned away. "Let me know if you need anything."

"My lord!" Mina called to him, as she began to lose sight of him in the darkness. "There is something I need—a blessed weapon or artifact or spell imbued with your holy powers."

"Such a weapon would not avail you much against Zeboim," Chemosh said. "She is a god, as am I, and is therefore immortal. I must warn you, Mina, that if Zeboim believes for one second you have come to rescue Krell, she will inflict upon you the same torment she inflicted on him. In which case, much as I will grieve your loss, I will be helpless to save you."

"I understand, my lord," said Mina steadily. "I was thinking more of the death knight, Krell."

"You faced Soth and lived to tell of it," Chemosh said with a shrug. "When Krell finds out that you are there to free him, he will be all eagerness to assist you."

"The problem will be remaining alive long enough for me to convince him of that fact, my lord."

"True," said Chemosh thoughtfully. "The only amusement poor Krell finds in his prison is slaughtering those who happen to wash up on his rock-bound shore. Being none too bright, he is the sort to kill first and ask questions later. I could bestow upon you some amulet or charm, except . . ."

He let the sentence hang, studied her intently, as he carefully adjusted the lace at his wrist.

"Except that finding a way to defeat him is part of my trial," said Mina. "I understand, my lord."

"Anything else you want, you have only to wish for."

He cast a glance at the bed from which she had risen, at the rumpled sheets, still warm from her body. "I look forward to your safe return," he said and, with a graceful bow, he left her.

Mina sank down on the bed. She understood his look and felt his promise, as she felt the touch of his lips on hers. Her body ached and trembled with her longing for him, and she had to take a moment to calm herself, force herself to concentrate on the seemingly impossible task he had set for her.

"Or maybe, not so impossible," said Mina. "Anything I want, I have only to wish for."

She was ravenously hungry. She could not remember eating while she'd been in the prison house of her own making. She supposed she must have. She had some dim recollection of Galdar urging her to eat, but there was no memory of taste or smell or even what it was she had fed upon.

"I require food," Mina stated, adding, by way of experiment, "I would like venison steak, lamb stew, a cottage pie, spiced wine . . ."

As she spoke, the dishes appeared in front of her, materializing on a table, spread with a cloth. There was wine and ale for her to drink, and clear, pure, cold water. The food was wonderfully prepared—all she could have wished for. As she ate, she went over various plans in her mind, discarding some outright, taking up those she liked, mulling over them in her mind. She borrowed something from one, put it together with an idea from another, and at last came up with the whole. She went over it all and was satisfied.

A gesture banished the food and the table, the wine and the cloth. Mina stood a moment deep in thought to make certain she missed nothing.

"I want my armor," she said at last. "The armor given to me by Takhisis. The armor forged of her glory on the night she proclaimed her return to her world."

Candlelight gleamed from the depths of shining black metal. The armor that she had worn throughout the War of Souls, the armor of a Dark Knight of Neraka, marked by her queen's own hand, was laid out on the floor at her feet. Lifting up the breastplate, adorned with Takhisis's symbol—the lightning-struck skull—Mina sat down on the edge of the bed and began to polish the metal, using the corner of the cambric bed sheet, until the armor shone with a high gloss.

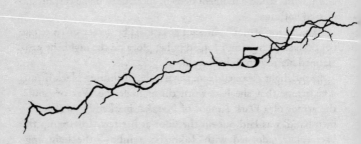

Mina's wish took her to the lord city of Palanthas, where she paid a visit to the Great Library. She did not linger in the city once she had completed her business at the library, though she did note that there were large numbers of elves about, ragged, thin, and impoverished. She looked at them as they passed her in the street and they looked at her as if they knew her, but couldn't remember where. Perhaps in a bad dream. She left Palanthas and wished herself next to a small fishing village on the northern shores of Abanasinia.

"You're daft, Lady," said the fisherman bluntly. He was standing on the dock watching as Mina loaded supplies onto the small boat. "If the waves don't swamp you and pound the boat to bits, the wind will rip off your sail, blow you over, and drive you under. You'll never make it. Ruin of a good boat."

"I've paid you the cost of your boat twice over," said Mina.

She stowed a leather skin filled with fresh water in the stern. Walking precariously as the craft rocked with the waves, she climbed back up the ladder to the dock. She was about to haul down the second water skin when the fisherman halted her.

"Here, Lady Knight," he said, scowling as he held out the bag of steel coins. "Take back your money. I don't want it. I won't be a party to this folly of yours. I'd have your death on my conscience for the rest of my life."

Mina picked up the waterskin and slung it over her shoulder. She walked past him to the boat, lowered the second skin down beside the first. Turning to go back for the food, she saw him still scowling, still holding out the money bag. He shook it at her, jingling the coins.

"Here! Take it!"

Mina put his hand gently aside. "You sold me a boat," she said. "What I do with it is not your responsibility."

"Aye, but *she* might not see it that way," he said darkly, with an ominous nod of his head toward the blue-gray water.

"She? Who is this 'she?' " asked Mina, climbing back down into the boat.

The fisherman cast a glance around, as if fearing they might be overheard, then leaning down, he said in a hissing, fearful whisper. "Zeboim!"

"The sea goddess." Mina had wrapped strips of salted beef in oilskin to keep them dry, and these she packed away in a wooden crate along with a waterproof bag of biscuits. She did not take much food because—one way or another—her voyage would be a short one. She removed a map, also wrapped in oilskin, and stowed it carefully, the map being more precious than food. "Do not fear Zeboim's wrath. I am on a holy quest. I intend to ask for her blessing."

The fisherman remained unconvinced. "My livelihood depends on her favor, Lady Knight. Take back your money. If you're truly going to try to sail across the Sirrion Sea to Storm's Keep, as you claim, she won't give you her blessing. She'll sink you so fast your head will swim, then she'll come looking for me."

Mina shook her head with a smile. "If you are so concerned with what Zeboim might think, take the money to her shrine and give it to her as an offering. I should think that sum would purchase you a large amount of her good will."

The fisherman considered this, and after a few moments of sucking his lower lip and contemplating the rolling water, he thrust the bag of money into his oilskin breeches.

"Perhaps you're right, Lady Knight. Old Ned, he gave the Mistress six gold coins, each stamped with the head of some bloke who called himself the Priest King or something like that. Old Ned, he found these coins inside a fish he cut open, and he figured that they must have been the Mistress's. Maybe she stowed them there for safe-keeping. He didn't figure they were worth much, on account of he had never heard of this Priest King, but they must have been worth something for now he never goes out in his fishing boat but that he comes back with more cod than you can count."

"Perhaps she will do the same for you," Mina remarked.

The food stored, she left the boat and returned for one last object—her armor.

"I hope so," said the fisherman. "I've got six hungry mouths at home to feed. The fishing ain't been that good of late. One reason I'm forced to sell this here boat." He rubbed a grizzled chin. "Maybe I'll split the money with her. Half for her. Half for me. That seems fair, don't it?"

"Perfectly fair," said Mina. She unpacked the armor, spread it out on the dock. The fisherman eyed it, shook his head.

"You best keep it dry," he said. "The salt water'll rust it something fierce."

Mina picked up the breastplate. "I have no squire. Will you help me put it on?"

The fisherman stared. "Put on armor? To go sailing?"

Mina smiled at him. The amber of her eyes flowed over him, congealed around him. He lowered his gaze.

"If you capsize, you'll sink like a dwarf," he warned her.

Mina fit the cuirass over her head and held up her arms, so that the fisherman could make secure the leather straps that held it together. Accustomed to tying the knots of his net, he went about his task quickly and deftly.

"You appear to be a good man," Mina commented.

"I am, Lady," said the fisherman simply, "or leastways I try to be."

"Yet you worship Zeboim—a goddess reputed to be evil. Why is that?"

The fisherman looked uncomfortable and cast another nervous glance out to sea.

"It's not that she's evil so much as she is ... well, temperamental. You want to keep on her good side. If she takes against you, there's no telling what she might do. Blow you out to sea and then leave you with never a puff of air, becalmed, to drift on the water till you die of thirst. Or she might raise up a wave big enough to swallow a house, or whip up storm winds that will toss a man about as if he were naught but a stick. We are good people around here. Most of us worship Mishakal or Kiri-Jolith, but if you live by the sea, you always make it a point to pay your respects to Zeboim, maybe drop off a little gift for her. Just to keep her happy."

"You mentioned the worship of other gods,' said Mina. "Do any worship Chemosh?"

"Who?" the fisherman asked, busy with his task.

"Chemosh, Lord of Death."

The fisherman paused in his work, thought a moment. "Oh, aye. There was some priest of Chemosh came around about a month ago trying to peddle that god to us. Moldy looking, he was. Dressed all in black and smelled like an open crypt. Talked about how the Mishakal cleric was lying to us when she said that our souls went on to the next stage of life's journey. The fellow told us that the River of Souls had been tainted or some such thing, that our souls were trapped here and that only Chemosh could free us."

"And what became of this priest?"

"Word went about that he'd set up an altar in the graveyard, promising to raise the dead to show us the power of the god. A few of us went, thinkin' to see a good show, if nothing else. But then the sheriff came, along with the cleric of Mishakal, and told the priest to take his business elsewhere or he'd have him arrested for disturbing the dead. The priest didn't want no trouble, I guess, 'cause he packed up and left."

"But what if he is right about the souls?" Mina asked.

"Lady," said the fisherman, exasperated. "Didn't you hear me? I got six children at home and all of them growing as fast as tadpoles and wanting three square meals a day. It's not my soul that goes to sea to catch the fish to sell at the market to buy food for the kids. Is it?"

"No, I guess it isn't," said Mina.

The fisherman gave an emphatic nod and the straps a final sharp tug. "If it was my soul went out and did the fishing, I'd worry about my soul. But my soul don't fish, so I don't worry."

"I see," said Mina thoughtfully.

"You say you're on a holy quest," said the fisherman. "What god do you follow then?"

"Queen Takhisis," Mina answered.

"Ain't she dead?" the fisherman asked.

Mina did not answer. Thanking the man for his help, she climbed down the ladder into the boat.

"Don't make sense," the fisherman said, as he started to cast off the lines that held the boat to the dock. "You're wasting your time, your money, and most likely your life, going on a holy quest for a goddess that ain't around anymore, or so the cleric of Mishakal tells us."

Mina looked at him, her expression grave. "My holy quest is not so much for the goddess as for the man who founded the knighthood dedicated to her name. I have been told that the one who betrayed my lord to his death lives out his miserable life on Storm's Keep. I go to challenge him to battle to avenge Lord Ariakan."

"Ariakan?" The fisherman chuckled. "Lady, that lord of yours died nigh on forty years ago. How old are you? Eighteen? Nineteen? You never knew him!"

"I never knew him," said Mina, "but I have never forgotten

him. Or what I owe him." She sat down in the stern, took hold of the tiller. "Ask for Zeboim's blessing for me, will you? Tell her I am going to avenge her son."

She steered the sailboat into the wind. The sail flapped for a moment, then caught the breeze. Mina turned her gaze toward the open waters, the breaking waves, and the thin, dark line of storm clouds that hung perpetually on the horizon.

"Aye, well, if anything would make the Sea Witch happy, it would be that," the fisherman remarked, watching the boat rise to meet the first of the rolling waves.

A freak wave struck the dock, splashed over him, drenching the fisherman from head to toe.

"I'm going, Mistress!" he shouted to the heavens and dashed off as fast as he could run to bestow half his money on the sea goddess's grateful cleric.

The first part of Mina's journey was peaceful. A strong breeze pushed the sailboat up and over the waves, carrying her farther and farther from shore. Mina had no fear of the sea, which was odd, considering that she'd been through storm and shipwreck. She had no memory of either, however. Her only recollection— and it was dim—was of being cradled by the waves, gently rocked, lulled to sleep.

Mina was an experienced sailor, as were most of those who lived on the isle of Schallsea, where the Citadel of Light was located. Although Mina had not sailed a boat in many years, the skills she needed returned to her. She guided the boat into the waves, rising up with the crest—an exhilirating sensation, as if one could keep rising to the heavens—then falling off, sliding down into the foaming trough of the wave, the sea spray blowing in her face. She licked her lips, tasting salt. Shaking back her wet hair, she leaned forward, eager to meet the next wave. She lost sight of land.

The sea grew rougher. The storm clouds that had been a dark line on the horizon were now a lightning-shot, leaden mass, steadily building. For a precious few moments, Mina was alone in the world, alone with her thoughts.

Thoughts always of Chemosh.

She tried to understand her attraction to him, to understand why she was out here in this fragile boat, risking her life to challenge the might of the goddess of the sea, to prove her love for the Lord of Death.

Mortal men, like that wretched elf, adored her. Galdar had befriended her, but even he had been in awe of her. Chemosh was the first to look into her, deep into her, to see her dreams, her desires—desires she never knew she had until his touch awakened them.

She had never felt her own flesh until he carressed it. She had never heard her own heart beating until he laid his hand upon her breast. She had never known hunger until she looked into his eyes. Never known thirst until she tasted his kiss.

Lightning flared in a blazing sheet across the sky, dazzling her eyes, jolting her abruptly out of her dreams. Blue fire flickered at the top of the mast. The waves grew more fierce, slapping at the boat, knocking the tiller from her hand. The wind whipped around. The sail flapped and the boat very nearly foundered. She struggled aft, the wind whipping and tearing at her, the boat plunging and rocking so that she had to fight to maintain her balance.

"Turn back," the sea was cautioning her. "Turn back now and I will let you live."

Rain spattered against her face. Mina gritted her teeth that crunched on salt. She managed to lower the sail, though it fought her like a live thing. Struggling back to the stern, she sat down, took hold of the tiller, and aimed the boat into the teeth of the storm.

"For Lord Ariakan!" Mina cried.

A wave, running cross-wise to all the other waves, struck Mina, swept her out of the boat and into the storm-tossed sea. Mina gasped for air, gulped water, and sank below the waves. Her lungs bursting, she fought the panicked urge to flail and thrash about in a desperate attempt to reach the surface. She kicked hard, propelling herself up with long, strong strokes of her arms. Another kick, stars flashing in her vision, and then her head broke the surface. She gasped a blessed lungful of air as she quickly blinked the water from her eyes to try to see where she was.

The armor's weight dragged her down again. The boat was near her. She lunged for it, caught hold of it before the next wave could sink her. She clung to the boat, held fast to it with all her strength, her fear now that the seas would flip the boat over on top of her.

Another wave came, a towering wave. Mina thought it would finish her, smash the boat to bits. She sucked in a huge breath, determined to fight and keep on fighting. The wave struck her, carried her up and over the gunwale, and dropped her into the bottom of the boat.

Gasping and shaken, Mina lay on the deck that was awash with seawater and blinked, her eyes stinging with the salt. When she could see, she saw a foot—a naked foot—resting on the deck very near her head. The foot was shapely and protruded out from beneath the hem of a gown that was green and blue, looked to have been made from cloth spun of seawater.

Hesitantly, Mina raised her head.

A woman sat in the stern, her hand upon the tiller. The sea raged about the boat. Waves splashing over the deck drenched Mina, but did not touch the woman. Her hair was the white of sea foam, her eyes the gray of the storm, her face beautiful as a sailor's dream, its expression ever shifting, ever changing, so that one moment she smiled upon Mina, as if she were pleased with her beyond measure, and the next she looked upon her as if would step on her with that shapely bare foot and crush her skull.

"So you are Mina," said Zeboim. Her lip curled. "Mommy's pet."

"I had the honor to serve Takhisis, your mother," said Mina. She started to rise.

"No, don't get up. Remain kneeling. I prefer it."

Mina stayed where she was, crouched on her knees at the bottom of the boat, that rocked and pitched. She was forced to keep fast hold of the gunwale to avoid being tossed out again. Zeboim sat undisturbed, the sea breeze barely ruffling her long, wild mane of hair.

"You served my mother." Zeboim sneered. "That bitch." She looked back down at Mina. "Do you know what she did to me? Stole away my world. But of course, you knew that. You were in Mommy's confidence."

"I wasn't—" Mina began to explain. "I never—"

The goddess ignored her, continued talking, and so Mina fell silent.

"Mommy stole away my world. She stole away my sea, and she stole away those like you"—Zeboim cast a disparaging glance at Mina—"my worshipers. The bitch took them all away from me and left me in the endless dark, alone. You cannot imagine," she said, and her voice changed, ragged with pain, "the terrible silence of an empty universe."

"I truly did not know what the goddess had done," said Mina quietly. "Takhisis told me nothing of this. She never told me her name. I knew her as the One God—a god who had come to take the place of gods who had abandoned us."

"Hah!" Zeboim gave a wild laugh. Lightning flared up and down the mast, crackled over the water.

"I was young," said Mina humbly. "I believed her. I am sorry for my part, and I want to try to make amends. That is why I am here."

"On a mission to Storm's Keep?" Zeboim idly stirred the water sloshing about in the bottom of the boat with her foot. "How will that make amends?"

"By punishing the one who betrayed Lord Ariakan," Mina replied. "As you see, I am a true knight." She gestured to the black armor she wore, as she lifted her gaze to boldly meet the eyes of the Sea Queen.

This was the tricky moment, when Mina would have to deceive a god. She would have to keep Zeboim from piercing her heart and discovering the truth. Mina had never considered trying to deceive Takhisis. Chemosh had laid bare all the secrets of her soul with a glance. If Zeboim looked closely, delved deeply, she must see the deception.

Mina met the eyes of the goddess, eyes that were deep green one moment, storm-ridden gray the next. Zeboim glanced at Mina and apparently saw nothing of interest, for she looked away.

"Avenge my son," she said scornfully. "He was the son of a goddess! You are nothing but a mortal. Here today, gone tomorrow. Of no use, any of you, except to admire me and laud me and give me gifts and die when it pleases me to kill you. Speaking of death, I hear you've been asking questions about Chemosh."

"That is true."

"And what is your interest in him?" Zeboim looked at Mina closely now, and in her eyes flickered blue fire.

"He is the god of undeath," Mina explained. "It occurred to me that he might help me defeat Lord Krell—"

Fast as the whipping wind, Zeboim struck Mina a blow across the face with the flat of her hand.

"His name is never spoken in my presence," Zeboim said and, leaning back against the tiller, she regarded Mina with a cruel smile.

"I am sorry, Mistress. I meant to say the Betrayer." Mina wiped blood from her mouth.

Zeboim seethed a moment, then grew calmer. "Very well, then, go on. I find you less boring than I had expected."

"The Betrayer is a death knight. Since Chemosh is the god of undeath, I thought perhaps my prayers to him might—"

"—might what? Aid you?" Zeboim laughed with malicious delight. "Chemosh is far too busy running around the heavens with his butterfly net trying to catch all the souls that Mommy stole from him. He cannot help you. I am the only one who can help you. Your prayers come to me."

"Then I do pray to you, Mistress—"

"I think you should call me Majesty," said Zeboim, languidly toying with a curl of her long tangled hair, watching the lightning dance on the mast. "Since Mommy is no longer with us, I am the Queen now. Queen of Sea and Storm."

"As you will, Majesty," said Mina, and she reverently lowered her head, a gesture that pleased Zeboim and allowed Mina to hide her eyes, keep her secrets.

"What is it you want of me, Mina? If it is to ask me to help you destroy the Betrayer, I don't believe I shall. I take a great deal of pleasure in watching that bastard fret and fume upon his rock."

"All I ask," said Mina humbly, "is that you bring me safely to Storm's Keep. It will be my honor and my privilege to destroy him."

"I do love a good fight," Zeboim said with a sigh. She twisted her hair around her finger, gazed into the storm that raged all around her, never touching her.

"Very well," she said languidly. "If you destroy him, I can always bring him back again. And if he destroys you, which I think quite likely"—Zeboim cast a cold, blue-gray glance at Mina—"then I will have avenged myself upon Mommy's little darling, which is the next best thing to avenging myself upon Mommy."

"Thank you, Majesty," said Mina.

There was no answer, only the sound of wind singing in the rigging, a mocking sound.

Mina raised her head cautiously and found she was alone. The goddess was gone as if she had never been, and for a moment Mina wondered if she had been dreaming. She put her hand to her aching jaw, her stinging lip, and drew back fingers smeared with blood.

As if to give her further proof, the wind ceased abruptly to howl around her. The storm clouds frayed, torn apart by an immortal hand. The waves calmed, and soon Mina's boat was rocking on swells gentle enough to lull a baby to sleep. The sea breeze freshened, blowing from the south, a breeze that would carry her swiftly to her destination.

"All honor and glory to you, Zeboim, Majesty of the Seas!" Mina cried.

The sun broke through the clouds, glinted gold on the water. She had been going to raise the sail, but it was not needed. The boat leaped forward, skimmed atop the waves. Mina gripped the tiller and drank in the rushing, salt-tinged air, one step nearer her heart's desire.

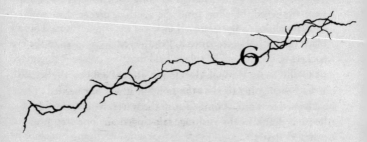

The isle of Storm's Keep had once teemed with life. Fortress and garrison of the Dark Knights of Takhisis, Storm's Keep had housed knights, men-at-arms, servants, cooks, squires, pages, trainers, slaves. Clerics dedicated to Takhisis had been on Storm's Keep. Wizards dedicated to her service had worked there. Blue dragons had taken off from the cliff, gone soaring over the sea, carrying their dragon riders on their backs. All of them had one abiding goal—to conquer Ansalon and from there the world.

They had almost won.

But then had come Chaos. Then had come treachery.

Storm's Keep was now the prison of death, with one lone prisoner. He had the mighty fortress, the towers and parade grounds, the stables and treasure vaults, the storerooms and warehouses, all to himself. He loathed it. Every sea-soaked inch of it.

In a large room at the top of the Tower of the Skull, the tallest tower of the fortress known as Storm's Keep, Lord Ausric Krell placed his hands—covered in leather gauntlets to hide their fleshless state—on the table and leveraged himself to a standing position. He had been a short, heavy brute of a man in life, and he was a short, heavy brute of an ambulating corpse in death.

That corpse was accoutered in the black armor in which he had died, burned onto him by the curse that kept him chained to this existence.

Before him, mounted on a stand, was a sphere fashioned out of black opal. Krell peered into it, fiend's eyes glowing red in the eye sockets of his helm. The sphere held in its fiery depths the image of a sailboat, small upon a vast ocean. In the sailboat, smaller still, was a knight wearing the armor Krell had disgraced.

Leaving the sphere, Krell strode over to the aperture in the stone walls that looked out over the raging seas. His armor rattled and clanked as he walked. He stared out the window and rubbed his gauntleted hands together in satisfaction, muttering, "It has been a long time since anyone came to play."

He had to get ready.

Krell clumped ponderously down the spiral stairs that led to the tower room where he was accustomed to spending most of his time staring, angry and frustrated, into the black opal scrying ball known as the Flames of the Storms. The magical ball gave Krell his only view of the world beyond his keep—a world he was convinced that he could rule if only he could escape this accursed rock. Krell had witnessed much of the history of the Age of Mortals in that scrying ball—a gift from Zeboim to her beloved son, Lord Ariakan.

Krell had discovered the powerful artifact shortly after his death and imprisonment, and he'd gloated over it, thinking that Zeboim had left it behind by mistake. Soon, however, he came to realize that this was just part of her cruel torture. She provided him with the means to witness the world, then took away his ability to be part of it. He could see, but he could not touch.

He found it so tormenting that there were times when he caught up the opal ball in his hands, ready to hurl it out the window onto the rocks below. He always thought better of his rash impulse, however, and would carefully replace it back upon its serpent stand. Someday he would find a way to escape and when he did, he would need to be informed.

Krell had watched the War of Souls take place inside the opal ball. He'd viewed the rise of Mina with glee, thinking that if anyone could rescue him, it would be her and her One God. Krell had no idea who the One God was, and so long as it could battle Zeboim—whom Krell was still half convinced was lurking about somewhere—he didn't care.

Krell could see within the magical sphere the trapped and hapless souls wallowing in the River of Souls quite clearly. He even tried to communicate with them, hoping to send a message to this Mina, telling her to come rescue him. Then Krell, watching from his opal ball, saw what she did to his counterpart—Lord Soth. After that, Krell did not send any more messages.

About this time, he found out the true identity of the One God, and while Takhisis wasn't as bad as her daughter, Krell thought it quite likely that the Dark Queen might hold the same grudge, for she'd been rather fond of Ariakan herself. He took to lurking about in the shadows of his Keep, never daring to show his metal face outdoors.

Then came the death of Takhisis and—cruelest blow of all—Krell discovered that Zeboim had been absent all this time and that he could have left this blasted pile of crumbling stone whenever he wanted with no god to stop him. His fury over this news was such that he battered down a small and insignificant tower.

Krell had never been a religious man. He had never really believed in the gods, right up to the terrifying moment when he found out that the clerics were right after all—the gods did exist and they took a keen interest in the lives of mortals.

Having found religion the minute Zeboim ripped open his belly, Krell now witnessed the gods' return and the demise of Takhisis and Paladine with keen interest. The death of a leader creates a vacuum at the top. Krell foresaw a struggle to fill the void. The thought came to him that he could offer his services to a rival of Zeboim's in exchange for release from his prison.

Krell had never said a prayer in his life, but on the night that he made this determination, he got down, clanking, on his armored knees. Kneeling on the cold floor of his prison, he invoked the name of the only god who might have it in his heart to help him.

"Save me from my torment," Krell promised Chemosh, "and I will serve you in any way you ask."

The god did not answer.

Krell did not despair. The gods were busy, hearing a lot of prayers. He made the same prayer daily, but he still had not received a response, and he was starting to lose hope. Sargonnas— the father of Zeboim—was gaining in power. No other god in the dark pantheon was likely to come to Krell's aid.

"Now this Mina—this killer of death knights—is on her way to finish me off," Krell growled. His voice rattled inside his hollow armor with a sound like gravel rolling about the bottom of an iron kettle. He added gloomily, "Maybe I should just let her."

He toyed briefly with the idea of ending his torment in oblivion, but quickly decided against it. His conceit was such that he could not bear to deprive the world of Ausric Krell—even a dead Ausric Krell.

Besides, the arrival of this Mina would relieve the monotony of his existence, if only for little while.

Krell left the Tower of the Skull and crossed the parade ground, which was wet and slimy from the endless salt spray, and entered the Tower of the Lilies. The Tower was dedicated to the Knights of the Lily, the armed might of the Dark Knights, of which august branch Krell had been a member. His quarters had been in this Tower when he was alive, and although he could no longer find rest in sleep, he would sometimes return to his small room in the upper chambers and lie down on the vermin-infested mattress just to torture himself with memories of how good sleep once felt. He did not return to his room today but kept to the main floor on the ground level, where Ariakan had established several libraries filled with books written on every subject martial, from essays on the art of dragon-riding to practical advice on how to keep one's armor rust-free.

Krell was not much of a scholar, and he had never touched a single book except when he'd once used a volume of the Measure to prop open a door that kept banging. Krell had another use for the library. Here he entertained his guests. Or rather, they entertained him.

He made hasty arrangements to receive Mina, arranging everything the way he liked it. He wanted to receive this important guest in style, so he hauled away the mutilated corpse of a dwarf, who had been his last visitor, and deposited it in the bailey with the others.

His work complete in the Tower of the Lily, Krell braved the whipping wind and driving rain of the courtyard to return to the Tower of the Skull. He peered into the scrying ball and watched with eager anticipation the progress of the small sailboat, heading for a sheltered inlet where, in the glory days, the ships that furnished Storm's Keep with supplies had docked.

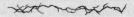

Unaware that Krell was watching her, Mina looked with interest on Storm's Keep.

The island fortress had been designed by Ariakan to be unassailable from the sea. Built of black marble, the fortress stood atop steep black-rock cliffs that resembled the sharp spiny protrusions on a dragon's back. The cliffs were sheer, impossible to climb. The only way on or off Storm's Keep was by dragon or by ship. There was one small dock, built on a sheltered inlet at the base of the black cliffs.

The dock had served as an entry port for food for man and beast, weapons and armaments, slaves and prisoners. Such supplies could conceivably have been hauled in by the dragons, dispensing with the need for the dock. Dragons—especially the proud and temperamental blue dragons favored by the knights for mounts—strongly objected to being beasts of burden, however. Ask a blue dragon to cart about a load of hay, and he might well bite off your head. Bringing in supplies by ship was much easier. Since Ariakan was Zeboim's son, all he had to do was pray to his mother for a calm voyage and the storm clouds would dissipate, the seas grow calm and gentle.

Mina had known nothing about the art of war when Takhisis had placed the girl—age seventeen—at the head of her armies. Mina had been quick to learn and Galdar had been an excellent teacher. She looked at the fortress and saw the brilliance behind its concept and design.

The dock was easily defensible. The inlet was so small that only one ship could safely enter it and then only at low tide. Narrow steps carved into the side of the cliff provided the only means of gaining access to the fortress. These stairs were so slippery and treacherous that they were little used. Most of the supplies were hauled up to the fortress by means of a system of ropes, winches, and pulleys.

Mina wondered, as did historians, how different the world might have been if the brilliant man who had designed this fortress had survived the Chaos War.

The wind died as she sailed into the inlet, forcing her to row across the calm water to the dock. The inlet was in shadow, for the sun was lowering into the west, and the inlet was on the eastern side. Mina blessed the shadow, for she hoped to take Krell by surprise. The fortress was enormous. The dock, located at one end of the island, was far from the main living quarters. She had no way of knowing that Krell was at this very moment observing her every move.

Mina dropped the small anchor and secured the boat by looping the rope around a rocky protrusion. There had once been a wooden pier, but it had long since been smashed to kindling by Zeboim's wrath. Mina climbed out of the boat. She gazed up at the black rock stairs, frowned, and shook her head.

Narrow and rough-hewn, the stairs wound precariously up the face of the cliff and were slimy with seaweed and wet with salt spray. As if that were not bad enough, the stairs looked to have been gnawed by the tooth of the vengeful Sea Queen. Many steps were split and cracked, as Zeboim's ire had extended to shaking the ground beneath Krell's feet.

"I need not worry about facing Krell," Mina said to herself. "I doubt if I will make it up the stairs alive."

Still, as she had told Chemosh, she'd walked in darker places. Just not as slippery.

Mina kept on the cuirass—black steel, marked with the lightning-struck skull. She tied the helm onto her leather belt, then regretfully unbuckled the rest of the armor. Climbing would be dangerous enough without being hampered by greaves and bracers. She carried on her belt her favored weapon—the morning star she had used in battles during the War of Souls. The weapon was not a holy artifact, nor was it enchanted. It would be useless against a death knight. No true knight would go into battle unarmed, however, and she wanted Krell to see her as a true knight of Takhisis. She hoped the sudden astonishing sight of one of his former brethren appearing unannounced on Storm's Keep would give the death knight pause, tempt him to converse with her, rather than simply kill her outright.

Mina checked the rope, making certain the boat was secure. The thought crossed her mind that Zeboim could very easily smash her boat and leave her stranded in the Keep, imprisoned with a death knight. Mina shrugged the thought away. She had never been one to fret or worry about the future, perhaps because she had been so close to a goddess, who had always assured Mina that the future was under control.

Having learned that even the gods can be wrong had not altered Mina's outlook on life. The calamitous fall of Takhisis had strengthened Mina in her belief that the future stretched before her like the treacherous stairs carved into black rock. Life was best lived in the present. She could only climb one step at a time.

Saying a prayer to Chemosh in her heart and speaking a prayer to Zeboim aloud, Mina began her assent up the cliffs of Storm's Keep.

Having watched Mina land in the inlet, Krell left the keep proper and ventured out onto a narrow, winding trail that twisted and turned amidst a jumble of rocks. The trail led to a jutting granite peak known jestingly among the knights who once garrisoned here as Mt. Ambition. The island's highest point, the peak was isolated, windswept and sea spattered, and it had been Lord Ariakan's custom to walk here of an evening—weather permitting. Here he stood, looking out at the sea and formulating his plans to rule Ansalon. Thus the name Mt. Ambition.

None of the knights walked here with their lord unless they were specially invited. There was no greater honor than to be asked to climb Mt. Ambition with Lord Ariakan, sharing his stroll and his thoughts. Krell had come here often with his lord. It was the one place he most avoided during imprisonment. He would not have come here now, but that this peak afforded him the best view of the inlet and the dock, and the human speck that was attempting to climb what the knights called the Black Stairs.

Perched amid the rocks, Krell looked down over the edge of the cliff at Mina. He could see the life pulsing in her, see life's warmth illuminating her, as a candle flame lights the lantern. The sight made him feel death's chill all the more, and he glared down at her with loathing and bitter envy. He could kill her now. It would be easy.

Krell recalled a walk with his commander along this very part of the wall. They had been discussing the possibility of an assault on their keep by sea and arguing over whether or not they would use archers to pick off any of the enemy who were either bold enough or stupid enough to try to climb the Black Stairs.

"Why waste arrows?" Ariakan gestured to the boulders piled in heaps all around them. "We will simply toss rocks at them."

The boulders were good-sized. The strongest men in the knighthood would have had to work hard to lift them up and heave them over the wall. Himself one of those strong men assigned to this post, Krell had always been disappointed that no one had ever mounted an assault against the fort. He had often pictured the carnage that those hurtling missiles would have created among an enemy—soldiers struck by the stones falling off the stairs, plunging, screaming, to bloody and broken death on the crags below.

Krell was sorely tempted to pick up one of those boulders and hurl it down on Mina, just to witness firsthand the destruction he had always fondly imagined. He controlled himself with an effort. Meeting this killer of death knights face-to-face was a rare opportunity, one not to be wasted. He was so looking forward to it that he actually cursed when he saw Mina slip and almost fall. If he'd had breath in his body, he would have sighed it out in relief when she managed to regain her footing and continue her slow and laborious climb.

The air was chill, for the sun was rarely allowed to break through the clouds that hung over Storm's Keep. Exertion and the sudden flash of terror caused by her near fatal slip sent chill sweat rolling down Mina's neck and breasts. The wind that keened endlessly among the rocks dried the sweat, set her to shivering. She had brought gloves, but she found she could not wear them. More than once, she was forced to dig her fingers into fissures and slits in order to drag herself from one stair up onto the next.

Every step she took was precarious. Some of the stairs had large cracks running through them, and she had to test each one before she put her weight on it. Her leg muscles soon cramped and ached. Her fingers bled, her hands were raw, her knees scraped.

Pausing to try to ease the pain in her legs, she looked upward, hoping she was near the end.

Movement caught her eye. She caught a glimpse of a helmed head peering down at her from the top of the cliff. Mina blinked to clear her eyes of salt spray, and the head was gone.

She did not doubt what she had seen, however.

The stairs seemed to go on forever, climbing up to heaven, and at the top, Krell was waiting.

Below her, the sea surged over glistening, sharp pointed boulders. Foam swirled on top of turgid water. Mina closed her eyes and sagged against the cliff face. She was worn out and she was only about halfway up the stairs. She would be exhausted by the time she reached the top, where she would have to face the death knight who had somehow been warned of her coming.

"Zeboim," Mina said with a curse. "She warned Krell. What a fool I am! So proud of myself to think that I had deceived a goddess, when all along it was the goddess who was deceiving me. But why would she alert him? That's the question. Why?"

Mina tried to puzzle this out. "Did she look into my heart and see the truth? Did she see I was coming to free Krell? Or is this just a whim of hers? Pitting the two of us against each other for an hour's entertainment."

Thinking back to her conversation with the goddess, Mina guessed the latter. She pondered what to do and it was then a thought occurred to her. She opened her eyes, looked back up at the peak where she had seen Krell standing.

"He could have killed me if he'd wanted to," she realized. "Cast a spell on me, or if nothing else, dropped a rock on my head. He didn't. He's waiting to confront me. He wants to toy with me. Taunt me before killing me. Krell is no different from other undead. No different, even, than the god of death himself."

From months of commanding a legion of souls, Mina knew that the dead have a weakness—a hunger for the living.

The part of Krell that remembered what it was to be alive craved interaction with the living. He needed to feel vicariously the life that he had lost. He hated the living, and so he would kill her eventually. But she could be assured that at least he would not slay her outright, before she had a chance to speak, to tell him her plan. The knowledge lent her hope and raised her spirits, though it did nothing to ease the cramps in her legs or the bone-numbing chill. She had a long and dangerous trek ahead of her and she had to be ready, both physically and mentally, to meet a deadly foe at the end of it.

The name of Chemosh came, warm to her numb lips. She sensed the god's presence, sensed him watching her.

She did not pray for help. He had told her he had none to give, and she would not demean herself by begging. She whispered his name, held it fast in her heart to give her strength, and placed her foot carefully on the next stair, testing it.

The stair held firm, as did the next. Gaining that stair, she had her eyes on her footing, watching where she was going, using her hands to feel her way along the cliff face. Inching her hands along, she was startled to feel nothing, so startled that she almost lost her grip. A narrow fissure split the rock wall.

Balancing precariously on the stair, Mina placed her hands on either side of the crack and peered inside. The gray light of day did not penetrate far into the darkness, but what she could see was intriguing—a smooth floor, obviously man-made, about three feet below where she stood. She could not see much beyond the floor, but she had the impression of a vast chamber. She sniffed the air. The smell was familiar, reminding her of something.

A granary. She had just liberated the city of Sanction. Her men, busy securing the city, had come upon a granary. She had gone to inspect it, and this was the smell or close to it. In the Sanction warehouse, the grain had been recently put up and the smell was overwhelming. Here the smell was faint and mingled with mildew, but Mina was certain she had found the granary of the fortress of Storm's Keep.

The location made sense, for it was close to the dock where the grain would be unloaded from the ship. Somewhere at the top of the cliff there must be an opening, a chute down which they would have poured the grain. The granary would be empty now. It had been forty years since the Keep had been abandoned. Hundreds of generations of rats would have feasted off any stores the knights had left behind.

Not that any of that mattered. What mattered was that she had found a way to slip inside the fortress, a way to take Krell by surprise.

"Chemosh," said Mina in sudden understanding.

His name had been on her lips when she found the crack in the wall. She had not asked for his help, but he had granted it, and her heart beat fast with the knowledge that he wanted her to succeed. She eyed the crack in the wall. It was narrow, but she was slender. She could just possibly squeeze through it, although not while wearing the cuirass. She would have to take it off and that would leave her without any armor when she came to face the death knight.

Mina hesitated. She looked up at the endless stairs, where, at the top, Krell was waiting. She looked into the granary—smooth, dry floor, a secret way inside the main part of the Keep. She had only to cast off the cuirass, marked with the symbol of Takhisis.

Mina understood. "That is what you ask of me," she said softly to the listening god. "You want me to cast off my last vestige of faith in the goddess. Put all my faith and trust in you."

Balancing precariously on the stairs, her chill fingers shaking, Mina tugged and pulled at the wet leather thongs that held the cuirass in place.

Krell cursed himself for an idiot to allow himself to be seen like that. He cursed Mina, too, wondering what crazy notion had flown into the woman's head to cause her to look up instead of down, cause her to look straight at him.

"Zeboim," Krell muttered, and he cursed the goddess, a curse he uttered almost every hour of every tortured day.

He could no longer count on taking Mina by surprise. She would be ready for him, and while he didn't really think that she could cause him any harm, he was mindful of the fact that this was the woman who had brought down Lord Soth, one of the most formidable undead beings in all the history of Krynn.

It is better to overestimate the enemy than underestimate him had been one of Ariakan's dictums.

"I'll wait for her at the top of the Black Stair," Krell determined. "She'll be worn out, too tired to put up much of a fight."

He did not want to fight her. He wanted to capture her alive. He always captured his prey alive—when possible. One hapless thief, drawn to Storm's Keep by the rumor of the Dark Knights' abandoned treasure, had been so terrified at the sight of Krell that he'd dropped dead at the death knight's feet, a severe disappointment to Krell.

He had confidence in Mina, however. She was young, strong, and courageous. She would provide him with a good contest. She might survive for days.

Krell was about to leave Mt. Ambition and head back to Storm's Keep when he heard a sound that would have stopped his heart if he'd had one.

From down below came a woman's terrified scream and the clanging, clattering of metal armor falling onto sharp rocks.

Krell dashed to the end of the promontory, peered over the edge. He cursed again and smashed his fist into a boulder, cracking it from top to bottom.

The Black Stairs were empty. At the base of the cliff, almost lost to sight in the frothing, bubbling water, Krell could see floating in the sea a black cuirass, adorned with a lightning-struck skull.

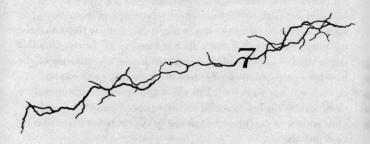

7

*H*er scream echoing back from the cliff face, Mina watched the black cuirass and helm strike the rocks below and go bounding off into the water. Her vision obscured by the gray half-light of the storm, she could not see at this distance that the armor had been empty when it plummeted off the stairs and now it was lost to sight in the lashing waves. She hoped that Krell's vision was no better.

Mina sucked in her breath and squeezed her body through the crack in the rock wall. Even without the cuirass, she barely made it, and for one frightening moment, she was wedged tight. A desperate wriggle freed her and she dropped lightly to the floor. She paused to catch her breath, wait for her eyes to adjust to the darkness, and think how good it was to have her feet on a firm, level plane. How good it was to be out of the chill wind and away from the salt spray.

Mina dried her hands as best she could on the tail of her shirt, rubbing them to restore the circulation. She had no armor and no weapon. She had tossed not only the cuirass and helm into the ocean, but also, after a moment's hesitation, she'd thrown away the morning star—thrown away the eager, innocent child who had gone searching for the gods and found them.

Mina had believed in Takhisis, obeyed her commands, endured her punishment, done the goddess's bidding without question. She had kept her faith in Takhisis when everything had started to go wrong, fighting against the doubt that gnawed at her like rats in the grain. By the end, her doubts had eaten up all her stores, so that when her faith should have been strongest, when she should have been prepared to sacrifice herself for the sake of the goddess, all that was left was chaff. Mina had known wrenching sorrow then, sorrow for her loss, and she experienced something of the same sorrow as she threw the last vestiges of her belief in the One God into the sea.

Innocence was gone. Unquestioning faith was gone. Thus she had dared to ask Chemosh, "What will you give me?" Though she had now given him proof that she belonged to him, she would not be his puppet to dance at his command, nor yet his slave to grovel at his feet. Standing alone in the darkness of Storm's Keep, Mina listened. She was not listening for the voice of the god to tell her what to do. She listened to her own voice, to her own counsel.

The Age of Mortals. Perhaps this is what the wise meant, what Chemosh meant. A partnership between god and man. It was an interesting premise.

The dim light of gray day made its way through the crack in the wall and poked through other, smaller gaps. As her eyes grew accustomed to the shadows, Mina could see most of the chamber. It was, as she had guessed, a room meant for storage, not only for grain but for other supplies.

A few wooden boxes and crates stood on the floor, their lids pried off, the contents spilled. Mina could picture the knights, in their eager haste to leave Storm's Keep to begin their conquest of Ansalon, ripping open crates to see what they contained, making certain they left behind nothing of value. She glanced at the boxes as she passed them, heading toward an iron-banded door located at the end of the room. She noticed some dust-covered, rusted tools, such as blacksmiths used, and a few bolts of woolen cloth, now moth-eaten and mildewed. There had been rumors for years that the knights had left behind stores of treasure. The rumors made sense, for the knights would not have flown to battle on dragonback carrying chests of steel coins. But if so, the treasure was not here. As she walked, her boots crunched on dried rat dung and half-eaten kernels, all that was left of the might of the Dark Knights of Takhisis.

Mina picked up a prybar. If the door to the granary was locked, she would need a tool to force the lock open. She hoped she would not have to resort to that. Krell must think her dead, killed in her fall off the stairs, and she didn't want to do anything to rouse his suspicions. Although she didn't know for sure, she guessed that the death knight still retained his power of hearing and even above the keening of the wind—the wail of a goddess's grief and fury—Krell might be able to detect the sound of someone beating at an iron lock with an iron bar.

When Mina reached the door, she put her hand on the handle and gave a gentle push. To her relief, the door swung open. Not surprising, when she considered it. Why bother to lock the door on an empty storage room?

The door opened into a hall, with the same paved stone floor and rough-hewn walls. The hall was much darker than the storage room. No cracks in the walls. She had no torch and no way to light one. She would have to feel her way.

Mina summoned from memory the map of the fortress that she left safely stowed in the boat. Prior to setting out on this adventure, she had traveled to the city of Palanthas to pay a visit to the city's famed library. There she had asked one of the Aesthetics for a map of Storm's Keep. Thinking she was a reckless treasure seeker, the earnest young Aesthetic had tried very hard to dissuade her from risking her life in such a foolhardy adventure. She had insisted, and by the rules of the library, which stated that all knowledge was available to anyone who sought it, he had brought her the requested map—a map that had been drawn by Lord Ariakan himself.

The granary had not been marked on the map. Ariakan had

included only those areas he considered important—meeting rooms, barracks, housing, etc. Mina had only the vaguest idea where she was, and that came mainly from knowledge of where she wasn't.

The inlet was on the south side of the island, which meant that she had entered the granary from the south, and was currently facing east. Since the granary was built adjacent to the stairs, she did not think it likely that the hall would extend to the south, for that was a dead end. She turned north as she exited, shutting the granary door behind her.

It was not likely Krell would come down here, but if he did, he would not find the door standing open, indicating someone had been snooping about. But by shutting the door, she shut off all the dim light from the granary, leaving her in complete darkness. She could see nothing in front of her or on either side. She shuffled her feet along the floor in an effort to avoid stumbling over some unseen obstacle. She hoped that she would not have to go far in the darkness.

She had not taken many steps when she noticed that the floor began to rise steeply.

"A ramp," she said to herself, envisioning slaves pushing wheelbarrows filled with grain.

She continued up the ramp and walked straight into a door that started to swing open when her boot hit it. Her heart lurching, she grabbed for the door and held it shut. She'd caught a brief glimpse of what lay beyond that door—a courtyard, open to view. For all she knew, Krell might be out in that courtyard, taking an afternoon stroll.

If it was afternoon. Mina had lost all sense of time, and that was something else to worry about. She did not want to be caught alone with Krell on Storm's Keep when night fell. Opening the door a crack, she peered out.

The parade ground, paved with cobblestones, was empty. It was vast and Mina recognized it from the map. The parade ground lay in the shadow of a tall tower, and now Mina knew exactly where she was. By its shape and location, the tower was the Central Tower, a massive structure that housed the main meeting rooms, dining halls, servant quarters. Lord Ariakan had his chambers in that Tower. There was also reputed to be a chamber that had led directly to the plane on which Takhisis had once dwelt. Not far from that was the Tower of the Lily, where the elite Knights of the Lily had their barracks, and at the opposite end of the fortress stood the Tower of the Skull, home to the arcane wing of the Dark Knights. Scattered about among the three were a number of outbuildings.

The flat, two-dimensional map Mina had viewed in the library of Palanthas had not conveyed the immensity of the fortress. She had not realized, on setting out, how big it was or how much ground it covered. And she had no idea in which building Krell had taken up residence. Gazing across the windswept expanse of the parade ground, Mina began to wonder if her idea of sneaking into the fort had been a good one.

"I could spend days wandering about this place searching for him," she realized. "No food and no water. Not daring to sleep for fear Krell might murder me."

All things considered, it might have been better for her to have taken her chances and confronted him on the stairs.

Mina shook her head, shook away doubt. "Chemosh brought me here. He will not forsake me."

Her confidence bolstered, Mina gave the door a shove and started to step out of the door and walk across the parade ground.

And there was Krell, emerging from behind a wall, coming from the direction of the cliffs where she had last seen him.

Mina froze, not daring to move or breathe.

Krell walked right past her, not six feet away from her. If she had left her hiding place an eyeblink earlier, she would have blundered into him.

The death knight was hideous to look upon. The burning torment of his accursed life blazed red from the shadows of the eye slits of his ram's skull helm. She knew that if he took off that helm, he would be more hideous still, for there was nothing beneath it. Nothing except the hole cut out of existence where his life had been, and that hole was blacker than the darkness inside a sealed tomb buried in a forgotten crypt.

His jointed and faceted armor—decorated with the skull and the lily—was stained with the blood Zeboim had drained from him over many days of torture. His blood glistened red, fresh as the day he'd shed it in screaming agony. The lashing rain never washed the blood away. He left bloody footprints as he walked.

He wore a sword that clanked at his side, but his most potent weapon was fear. He would use fear to grind her spirit into quivering pulp, as he would use his fists to grind her flesh and bones.

The fear that roiled off him in waves struck Mina, and she quailed and cowered beneath it. When she had faced the other death knight, Lord Soth, she had been armored with the power of the One God. She had carried in her hand the weapon of the One God. Soth had no power over her. He'd been buried beneath the rubble of his fortress.

Mina wore holy armor no longer. Chemosh had asked her to cast away her armor as a proof of her faith. She must face the formidable death knight in a rain-soaked shirt of wool that clung damply to her slender body, seeming to emphasize to her the fact that she was made of soft and quivering flesh and he was made of steel and death.

Fear paralyzed her. She could not move, but she hunkered down in the doorway, her stomach clenching, her leg muscles twitching in painful spasms. If Krell but turned his head, he would see her trembling in the doorway, craven as a gully dwarf. He would come raging at her and she would cower helplessly before him.

Mina shut her eyes, averted her gaze. The temptation to flee was overwhelming and she fought against it.

"I walked alone in the accursed valley of Neraka," she said through gritted teeth. "I endured the trials of the Dark Queen. Takhisis held me in her arms, and her glory seared my flesh, yet now I tremble before this piece of excrement. Am I brave only when the god holds my hand? Is this the way to prove myself to Chemosh?"

Mina opened her eyes. She made herself look at Krell, stared at him hard. She stopped shivering. Her muscle spasms eased. She drew in a deep breath and another and relaxed.

Krell had not seen her or heard her. He walked straight ahead, cursing aloud at having lost his prey and swinging his fist in impotent rage. Whatever torment he had arranged for her, he was sorely disappointed at having missed his opportunity.

As he strode across the parade ground, his own torment beat and tore at him. The wind of the goddess's rage buffeted him. He had difficulty walking against the furious wind, and he was strong and powerfully built. Black clouds boiled and fumed overhead. Lightning bolts struck at his feet, sending up chunks of rock and once knocking Krell to his knees. The almost constant boom of thunder shook the ground.

Staggering to his feet, Krell shook his fist at the heavens. He did not tempt the goddess further, however, but ran for the Tower of the Lily at a clumsy, armor-encumbered jog-trot.

Mina waited until he was halfway across the parade ground, then she followed him. She had hoped that the goddess might relent when she appeared, that the storm might abate for her. She was soon disabused of that notion. The moment she set foot on the parade ground, a gust of wind struck her, drove her to her hands and knees. Lancing rain pelted her with stinging, blinding force.

Zeboim was apparently not backing any favorites.

At least Krell was not inclined to stop in the midst of the cyclone to look behind to see if he was being followed. He was making for the Tower as fast as his lumbering stride could carry him.

Pushing to her feet, Mina battled her way through the storm in pursuit.

Krell was in a bad temper. The death knight was never in what one might call a good temper, but some days for Krell were better than others. Some days he was fortunate to have the living around to entertain him. Some days, if Zeboim was otherwise engaged, he could walk the parade ground and receive only a mild drenching. Today of all days, the Sea Witch must have planted herself directly overhead.

Fuming and dripping, Krell stalked into the library where he had everything set up in anticipation of his visitor, whose broken, bleeding body was now providing food for the sharks.

Krell plunked his armored self down in a chair and stared moodily at the game board and the empty chair opposite. Krell had grown sick and tired of playing khas against himself.

Krell was an avid khas player, as were most of the Knights of Takhisis. Steel Brightblade had once jested that knowledge of the game was a requirement for becoming a member of the knighthood, and in that, he had not been far wrong. Ariakan—an excellent player—believed that the intricate game taught people to consider not only their own stratagems but also those of their opponents, enabling them to anticipate their opponents' moves far in advance. Good khas players made good commanders—or so Ariakan believed.

Krell and Ariakan had spent many hours in contest over the khas board. Memories of those hours had returned full force to Krell as he had plotted his commander's assassination. Ariakan had always beaten Krell at khas.

The round khas board with its black, red, and white six-sided tiles stood in its accustomed place on a wrought iron stand before the enormous fire pit. Hand-carved jet and green jade pieces glowered at each other over the black, red, and white checkered field of battle. Krell had been in the midst of a game against himself (contests he usually won), but he had quickly cleared his game away in order to set the pieces back in their starting positions.

Now he would have to begin again. Scowling, he reached out his gauntleted hand, grasped a pawn, and moved it onto an adjacent square. He let go of the pawn and was about to stand up to move to the chair on the other side of the board when he changed his mind. He would use another opening. He reached for the pawn and was about to shift its position, when a voice—a living voice—spoke from over his shoulder.

"You can't do that," said Mina. "It's against the rules. You've taken your hand off the piece. It has to remain where you placed it."

In life or death, Ausric Krell had never been so astonished.

He whipped around to see who had spoken. A slender female, clad in sodden wet clothes, with hair that was red as his rage and eyes of amber gold stood with an iron pry bar in her hands. She was in the act of swinging the iron bar at his head.

Startled by the sight of her alive when he'd assumed she was dead, shocked at her temerity and the fact that she wasn't prostrate in terror before him, and caught off guard by the swiftness and suddenness of her attack, Krell had time for a furious snarl before the iron bar smashed into his helm.

Red hot flame lit up the perpetual darkness in which Krell lived, and then flickered out.

Krell's darkness went even darker.

Mina's blow, swung with all the pent-up force of her fear and her determination, knocked Krell's helm from his body, sent it bounding and clanking across the room to bump up against some of the corpses that he'd shoved into the corner. The armor in which his undead energy had been encased remained upright, seated in the chair, half-twisted about, one hand still extended to pick up the khas piece, the other hand raised in an ineffectual move to try to halt Mina's attack.

Mina held the bar poised for another hit, watching warily both the helm on the floor and the armor in the chair, ready to strike if the helm wobbled or the bloody armor so much as twitched.

The helm lay still. The armor did move. It might have been on display in some Palanthian noble's palace. Mina was about to breathe a shivering sigh and lower the prybar when the door blew open behind her, crashing against the stone wall with a heart-stopping bang. Mina lifted the bar and turned swiftly to face this new foe.

The gust of wind ushered in the goddess.

Zeboim seemed clad in the storm, her flowing garments in constant motion, swirling about her like the shifting winds as she entered the room. Mina dropped the iron bar and fell to her knees.

"Goddess of the Sea and Storm, I have done what I promised. Lord Ausric Krell, the traitor knight who most foully murdered your son, is destroyed."

Her head bowed, Mina glanced from beneath her lashes to see the goddess's reaction. Zeboim swept past Mina without a glance, her sea-green eyes fixed on the bloody armor, and off in the corner, the metal helm—all that remained of Ausric Krell.

Zeboim touched the armor with her fingertips, then she gave it a shove.

The armor collapsed. The mailed gauntlets fell to the floor. The cuirass sagged sideways in the chair. The greaves toppled to the left and right. His two boots remained standing, stationary, in place. Zeboim walked over to the helm. She thrust out a delicate foot, nudging the helm disdainfully with her toe. The ram's skull helm rocked a little, then settled. The empty eye sockets, dark as death, stared at nothing.

Mina remained on her knees, her head lowered, her arms crossed in humble supplication across her breast. The wind that was the goddess's escort was chill and raw, and Mina shivered uncontrollably. She kept watch on the goddess out of the corner of her eye.

"You did this, worm?" Zeboim demanded. "Alone?"

"Yes, Majesty," Mina answered humbly.

"I don't believe it." Zeboim looked swiftly about the room, as if certain there must be an army hidden away in the bookshelves or a mighty warrior tucked into a cupboard. Not finding anything except rats, the goddess looked back at Mina. "Still, you were Mommy's pet. There must be something more to you than appears on the surface."

The goddess's voice softened, warmed to springtime, a ripple of breath over sun-drenched water. "Have you chosen a new god to follow, child?"

Before it had been "worm." Now it was "child." Mina hid her smile. She had foreseen this question, and she was prepared with her answer. Keeping her eyes lowered, Mina answered, "My loyalty and my faith are with the dead."

Zeboim frowned, displeased. "Bah! Takhisis can do nothing for you now. Faith such as yours should be rewarded."

"I ask for no reward," Mina replied. "I seek only to serve."

"You are a liar, child, but such an amusing liar that I'll let it pass."

Mina glanced up at the goddess with a twinge of concern. Had Zeboim seen into her heart?

"The weak-minded among the pantheon might be deceived by your show of piety, but I am not," Zeboim continued disdainfully. "All mortals want a reward in return for their faith. No one ever does something for nothing."

Mina breathed easier.

"Come now, child," Zeboim continued in wheedling tones, "you risked your life to destroy that maggot Krell. What is the real reason? And don't tell me you did it because his treachery offended your fine sense of honor."

Mina lifted her eyes to meet the gray-green eyes of the goddess. "I *would* like to have something, if it's not too much to ask, Majesty."

"I thought so!" Zeboim was smug. "What do you want, child? A sea chest filled with emeralds? A thousand strands of pearls?

Your own fleet of sailing ships? Or perhaps the fabled treasure of the Dark Knights that lies in the vaults below? I feel generous. Tell me your wish, and I will grant it."

"The death knight's helm, My Lady," Mina replied. "That is what I want."

"His helm?" Zeboim repeated, amazed. She made a scornful gesture toward the helm that lay on the floor, near the mummified hand of one of his victims. "That heap of metal is worth next to nothing. A traveling circus might give you a few coins for it, though I doubt even they would be much interested."

"Nevertheless that is what I want," said Mina. "That is my wish."

"Take it, then, by all means," returned Zeboim, adding in a mutter, "Foolish chit. I could have made you rich beyond your dreams. I can't think what my mother saw in you."

Mina rose to her feet. Conscious of the goddess's annoyed gaze upon her, she walked past the khas board, past the toppled suit of armor, past the two chairs to the far corner. The ram's skull helm lay on the floor. Mina cast a glance at Zeboim. The goddess's ever-changing eyes had gone gray as the stone walls of the Keep. The restless winds stirred her hair and clothes.

"She hoped to ensnare me," Mina said to herself, as she turned away. "Keep me in her debt by lavishing wealth upon me. I did not lie. My loyalty and my faith are with the dead, just not the dead she was thinking about."

Mina picked up the helm, examined it curiously. The horns of the ram curled back from the hideous ram's skull that formed the visor. Each knight was free to choose his own symbol to use in the design of his armor. Mina found it intriguing that Krell had chosen a ram. He must have felt the need to prove something. She lifted the heavy helm and thrust it awkwardly under her arm. The tips of the horns and the jagged steel edges pricked her flesh uncomfortably.

"Anything else?" Zeboim asked caustically. "Perhaps you'd like one of his boots as a souvenir?"

"I thank you, Lady," said Mina, pretending not to notice the sarcasm. She made a bow. "I revere you and honor you."

Zeboim snorted. Tossing her head, she regarded Mina from slit eyes. "There is something else you want, I'll be bound."

Mina sensed a trap. She cast about in her mind, wondering what Zeboim was after.

"Safe passage off this blasted rock?" the goddess suggested.

Mina bit her lip. Perhaps she had gone too far. The goddess of the waves could very easily drown her.

"Yes, Majesty," she replied in her most humble tones. "Though perhaps that is more than I deserve."

"Save your groveling for someone who appreciates it," Zeboim snapped pettishly. "I begin to regret granting you my favor. I think I shall miss tormenting Krell."

"You granted me no favors, Lady," Mina said to herself, not aloud. She waited tensely to hear the goddess's verdict. Not even Chemosh could protect her once she set sail upon the sea that was Zeboim's province.

The goddess cast Mina and the helm one final, disdainful, sneering glance. Then she turned on her heel, leaving the library. The wind of her anger howled and tore at Mina, buffeted her with bruising force, striking at her until she dropped to her knees to avoid the blows. She crouched on the floor, her head bowed, as the wind blasted her, clutching the helm in her arms.

And then all went calm. The wind gave a final, irritated hiss, and then fell to nothing.

Mina sighed deeply. This was the goddess's answer, or at least so she hoped. She stood up too fast and staggered, almost falling again. The encounters with the death knight and the goddess had drained both her body and her spirit. She was parched with thirst, and though there was rainwater aplenty standing in puddles that were almost as deep and wide as ponds, the water had an oily look to it and smelled of blood. She would not have drunk it for all the strands of pearls in the world. And she had yet to return to the Black Stairs, climb down those broken, slippery steps to where her little boat waited, then make the journey across the sea—the heaving bosom of an angry goddess.

She started to walk wearily toward the door. At least the storm had abated. The rain now fell in a muttering drizzle. The wind was calm, though now it whipped up and then in vicious little gusts.

"You have done well, Mina," said Chemosh. "I am pleased."

Mina lifted her head, looked around, hoping that the god was here on Storm's Keep with her. He was nowhere in sight and she realized immediately that she'd been silly to think he might have come. Zeboim would still be watching her and his presence would have given all away.

"I am glad to have pleased you, my lord," said Mina softly, warm with the glow of his praise.

"Zeboim will keep her promise and calm the seas for you. She admires you. She still has hopes of winning you over."

"Never, my lord," said Mina firmly.

"I know that, but she does not; therefore, do not tempt her patience long. You have Krell's helm?"

"Yes, Lord. I have it with me, as you ordered."

"Keep it safe."

"Yes, Lord."

"God speed you to my arms, Mina," said Chemosh.

She felt a touch upon her cheek—his kiss brushed against her skin. Mina pressed her hand to her cheek, closed her eyes, and reveled in the warmth. When she opened her eyes, she had renewed strength, as if she had both eaten and drunk.

Mindful of the helm, she stripped a ragged cloak from one of the many corpses that littered the room and bound the cloak around the helm, holding it in place with a leather belt she took off another victim. Toting the helm in its bundle, she left the Tower of the Lily and crossed the parade ground, heading for the Black Stairs and her little sail boat.

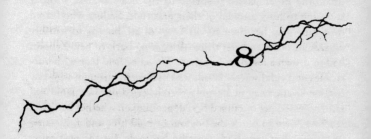

*F*rom her vantage point in the heavens, Zeboim watched Mina's boat bob across the sun-glinting water of the sea, steering toward a rock-bound and desolate strip of coastline. A restless goddess, a cruel goddess, Zeboim could have raised up a wave to capsize the small craft or summoned a sea dragon to devour it, or done any number of things to torment or kill the mortal. This would be nothing to her. She sometimes sank entire ships filled with living souls, sending passengers and sailors to terrifying death by drowning or watching them suffer for days on end, huddled in tiny life boats until they died of thirst and exposure or were devoured by sharks.

Zeboim took delight in their desperate pleas. She loved to listen to them cry out to her. They promised her anything if she would only spare their lives. Sometimes she ignored them, let them die. Other times she heeded their prayers and saved them. Her actions were not based on mere caprice, as was often the accusation leveled against her by mortals and the other gods. Zeboim was a calculating, clever goddess, who knew how to play to an audience.

Dead sailors did not leave gifts at her altars or fill the heavens with songs of praise for her. But sailors who escaped death by drowning never passed a shrine to the Sea Goddess without stopping to leave a token of their gratitude. Sailors who feared drowning gave her the best offerings of all, hoping to win her regard. In order to keep them all coming back to her, Zeboim had to drown a few now and then. The same held true with hurricanes and tidal waves, floods and cyclones. The man who saw his son swept away in a raging torrent cried out her name and either blessed her or cursed her, depending on whether her hand reached down to pluck the boy out or hold him under. Blessing or curses, they were both meat on her table, for the next rainy season, that man would be in her shrine, begging her to spare the lives of his other children.

As for determining who should live and who must die, Zeboim was a bit whimsical on this score. She might well drown the ship owner who had paid for the building of her new shrine and keep alive the cabin boy, who had given a gift of a bent pfennig and then only because his mother had made him. She would drown her own priests, just to keep everyone on their toes.

In regard to Mina, the young woman intrigued the goddess. True, Zeboim had disparaged her during their conversations together. But that had been for show; Zeboim never gave a mortal power by appearing to favor one above another.

Although Zeboim had despised Takhisis, Zeboim had to admit that her mother had a talent for finding good servants and this Mina was bold and intelligent, courageous and faithful, clearly a prize among mortals. Zeboim wanted Mina to worship her, and as she watched the boat make a safe landing and Mina depart from it, lugging with her the bundle in which she had wrapped up the helm of the death knight, the goddess toyed with various plans to try to win her.

It seemed that Zeboim had made a propitious start. The shrine of the Sea Goddess was the first place Mina went upon landing to give thanks for a safe voyage. Mina's prayer was polite and properly respectful, and although Zeboim would have preferred more groveling and maybe even a few heartfelt tears, she was satisfied. She wrapped herself in storm clouds, and having nothing more interesting to do, she went back to Storm's Keep to drag Krell's soul from whatever immortal plane it was on (perhaps he was fondly imagining he could hide from her), and return him to his prison.

A gust of wind and a flash of lightning heralded her arrival in the Tower of the Lily. She crossed her arms over her chest and stared down at the empty armor with a malicious smile.

"No doubt your miserable soul is running about in circles, trying to find your way out of this accursed existence, Krell. Perhaps you think you'll escape me this time. You are not be so lucky. My reach is long." Zeboim suited her action to her words. Extending her arm, she reached inside the armor.

"I have but to grab you by the short hairs and drag you back—"

Zeboim withdrew her hand, peered down it, expecting to see Krell's soul, cringing and whimpering, writhing in her grasp.

Her hand was empty.

Zeboim stared into the immortal plane, searching for Krell's soul.

The plane was empty.

Zeboim smote the metal armor with her hand. It disintegrated into fragments of metal no larger than a dust mote. Feverishly she stirred the fragments.

The armor was empty. Nothing lurking inside trying to hide from her wrath.

Swift as hurricane winds, Zeboim whirled through the Keep, searching every crack and crevice. She was tempted to tear the fortress apart, stone by stone, but she would only be wasting her time. She realized the truth. She knew it the moment she touched that empty armor. She was loathe to admit it.

Krell was gone. He had escaped her.

Zeboim saw Mina kneeling, heard her words.

My loyalty and my faith are with the dead.

"Ah, you clever little bitch." Zeboim swore savagely. "You conniving, thieving, clever little bitch. 'My faith is with the dead.' You did not mean my mother. You meant Chemosh!"

She spoke the name in a blast of rage that caused the seas to seethe and boil and froth. Storm winds raged, rivers overflowed their banks. Zeboim's rage shook the very foundations of the Abyss, where Chemosh felt her fury and smiled.

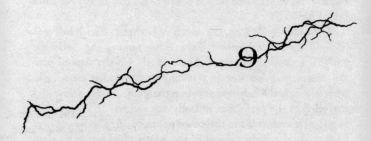

$\mathcal{C}$hemosh paced the world, waiting for Mina to return to him. He tried to interest himself in what was transpiring in the world, for events were unfolding that would have an effect on his plans and ambitions. He watched the build-up of the minotaur forces in Silvanesti with concern. Sargonnas was setting himself up to take over the leadership of the pantheon of Darkness and there did not appear to be much that could stop him now. Chemosh had some ideas in regard to that, but he was not yet ready to put those into motion. Patience. That was the key. Haste makes waste.

He dropped by for a glimpse of Mishakal, for he had recently added her to his list of gods who threatened his ambition. He would not have believed it, but the goddess who had once been known for her gentle, unassuming ways had lately become quite militant. She was starting to seriously annoy Chemosh, for her clerics were not limiting themselves to sitting beside sick-beds but were harrassing his clerics, pulling down his temples, and slaying his zombies. True, Chemosh didn't much like zombies, but they were his and killing them was an affront to himself. He would soon take care of that as well. He would present Mishakal and her do-gooder clerics with a dark mystery they would be hard-pressed to solve, provided Mina turned out to be all that he believed and hoped her to be.

The other gods were not much of a threat. Kiri-Jolith was focused on re-establishing his worship among the Solamnic Knights and other war-minded individuals. Chislev danced with the unicorns in her forests, rejoicing in having her trees back. Majere watched a lady-bug crawl up the stem of a dandelion and marveled at the perfection of both bug and weed. The gods of magic were embroiled in their own politics and in bickering over what to do about the scourge of sorcery that had reared its playful head in their well-ordered world. The gods of neutrality were going about being firmly neutral and uncommited to anything, for fear that so much as a sneeze would tip the delicate balance in favor of one side or another.

Something was going to tip it and it wouldn't be a sneeze. Mina was the golden weight in the hand of the Lord of Death, the golden weight that would drop onto the scales of balance and completely overturn them.

Chemosh had not been at all certain that Mina would succeed at the task he had set for her. He knew that she was an extraordinary mortal, but she was mortal and she was human into the bargain—an often unsatisfactory combination. He was pleasantly surprised when she stepped out of the small sail boat, carrying the bundle with the helm in her arms. More than surprised, he was admiring. Eons had passed since he had last viewed a mortal with anything akin to admiration.

Their appointed meeting place was an ancient temple dedicated to his worship off the coast of Solamnia. He had been waiting for her there, careful to keep out of sight, for Zeboim would be watching Mina for as long as she sailed upon the sea and perhaps even after she landed. Thus he had directed Mina to keep Zeboim off-guard by paying a visit to her shrine.

The temple in which he met her had once been a mausoleum, designed and built by a grieving noble lady for her noble husband.

The family name, emblazoned across the front of the mausoleum, had eroded, as had the coat of arms. The hall had fallen into ruin. Nothing was left of it except the foundation, for the materials used in its construction had been hauled off by the local residents to use in rebuilding homes damaged in the First Cataclysm. The mausoleum remained intact, however, and in relatively good condition. None dare touch it, for legend had it that one could still hear the grief-stricken wail of the bereaved widow and see her ghostly figure weeping on the marble stairs.

Built of black marble, the mausoleum was almost a small hall. Four ornately carved spires stood at each corner of a sharply pointed roof, surrounded by delicate wrought iron filigree. A columned portico at the top of the famed marble stairs sheltered an immense bronze door. Inside the mausoleum, two rows of slender columns stood like sentinels on either side of the enormous marble tomb bearing the family coat of arms and replete with the outstanding moments of the man's life carved in raised relief all around the base.

The noble lady had built an altar at the far end of the mausoleum and dedicated it to Chemosh. Here she had come to pray daily to the God of Death, swearing never to leave this place until he restored her husband to her. Since the husband's soul had already gone on, Chemosh was unable to answer her prayer. He did, however, see to it that she kept her vow. Chemosh had returned to the world to find her ghost still there, still weeping on the stairs. He'd forgotten how annoying he found her blubbering and he freed her at last, sending her off to join her husband.

He wondered if he wasn't becoming a bit of a romantic.

He entered the temple, looked around. The mausoleum was well-constructed. The roof did not leak; the building was dry and neither musty nor dank. There was only one body inside and he had remained decently interred. No stray shin bones or skulls cluttering up the place. Chemosh's followers, undeterred by the ghost, had moved into the mausoleum during the War of the Lance and had remained here up until the theft of the world deprived them of their god. He was pleased to note that they had been an unusually tidy lot, cleaning up after their rites, so there was no melted candle wax upon the altar cloth, no blood stains on the floor, no fragments of bone left on the dais.

Chemosh found some evidence that someone—either one of those new, misguided users of necromancy or grave robbers—had recently been inside. Someone had tried to pry the lid off the tomb using a crow bar. The marble lid was extremely heavy and the attempt had failed. They had raided his altar, too, carrying off a pair of golden candlesticks and a ruby-encrusted chalice, both of which he distinctly remembered, for he kept track of all his sacred artifacts.

"No thief would have dared tempt my wrath in the old days," Chemosh said, frowning in ire. "Thanks to our late and unlamented Queen, no one has any respect for the gods these days. That will change. One day soon, when mortals speak the name of Chemosh, they will speak it with respect, with reverence and awe. They will speak it with fear."

"My lord Chemosh." Mina spoke his name, but not with fear. With love and reverence.

Chemosh opened the bronze door to find her standing on the marble stairs. She was wet, bedraggled, her hands bloodied and bruised, weary to the point of dropping. Her amber eyes glowed in the warm red light of Lunitari. Bowing to him, Mina held out to him the helm of the death knight, Ausric Krell.

"As you commanded, my lord," she said.

"Come inside. Away from prying eyes."

Taking hold of Mina, he drew her inside the mausoleum and shut the great bronze doors.

"How cold your hand is. Cold as death," he said, and was pleased to see her smile at his little jest. "And you are soaked to the skin. Here. We will warm you."

He was eager to find out if his enchantment had worked and if he had indeed managed to capture Krell, but he was concerned about Mina, who could barely walk for shivering. He snapped his fingers and a fire sprang up from a brazier on the altar. Mina approached it gratefully, holding her hands to the warmth.

The sodden fabric of her cambric shirt clung to her body, flowing over the fullness of her breasts that were pale and smooth as the marble of the altar. He watched her breasts quiver with her shivering, rise and dip with her breathing. His eyes moved to the hollow of her throat, a tempting shadow of darkness in the firelight, to her face, the curve of her lips, the strong chin, the remarkable amber eyes.

Chemosh was surprised to feel his own heart beat faster, his own breath catch. Gods had fallen in love with mortals before now; Zeboim had been one of them and she had even sunk so far as to give birth to a half-mortal child. Chemosh had never understood how one could be attracted to a mortal, with their limited minds and butterfly lives, and he did not understand himself now. He had intended his seduction of Mina to be strictly business, at least as far as he was concerned. He would make love to her and ensnare her, force her to become dependent on him. He was now half-amused by his own feelings of desire and half-annoyed. Desire was an indication of weakness on his part. He had to conquer it, get back to the business of becoming king.

Mina felt his gaze upon her. She turned to look at him and she must have seen his thoughts in his eyes, for she smiled at him, the amber warm and melting.

Chemosh wrenched his thoughts and his gaze away from her. Business before pleasure. He placed the helm upon the altar and stared eagerly inside. He could see, in the shadows of the Abyss, the small and shriveled soul of Ausric Krell.

A raging gust of wind smote the mausoleum, lashed the trees and tore the leaves from their limbs. Thunder pounded the temple in frustration. Fury lit the night skies and tears of rage drowned the stars.

Inside the mausoleum, all was warm and snug. Chemosh held the spirit between his thumb and forefinger and watched Krell squirm, like a mouse caught by the tail.

"Do you pledge me your loyalty, Krell?" Chemosh demanded.

"I do, my lord." Krell's voice came from far away, sounded tinny and frantic. "I do!"

"And you will do whatever I ask of you? Obey my orders without question?"

"Anything, lord," Krell swore, "so long as you keep me out of the clutches of the Sea Witch."

"Then from this moment on, Ausric Krell," said Chemosh solemnly, dropping the spirit upon the altar, "you are mine. Zeboim has no hold upon you. She has no way to find you, for you are hidden safely within my darkness."

All this time, he was aware of Mina watching him, her amber eyes wide with awe and admiration. He was pleased to have impressed her, until it occurred to him that he was behaving just like a school boy, showing off for some giggling girl.

He gave an irritated wave of his hand and Ausric Krell, wearing the armor of his curse, stood before the altar. His red eyes, glowing like banked coals, flicked about suspiciously, taking in his surroundings.

"No tricks, Krell, as you see," Chemosh stated, adding in grating tones. "You could at least say 'thank you'."

Krell knelt down ponderously, clanking and rattling, onto one knee.

"My lord, I do thank you. I am in your debt."

"Yes, you are, Krell. And don't ever forget it."

"What is your lordship's command?"

Chemosh's thoughts kept straying to Mina. He was beginning to find the death knight an intolerable nuisance.

"I have no commands for you yet," said Chemosh. "I have a plan in mind, in which you will play a part, but the time is not yet right. You have leave to go."

"Yes, my lord." Krell bowed and started for the door. Halfway there, he halted and turned around, confused. "Go where, my lord?" •

"Wherever you want, Krell," said Chemosh impatiently. His eyes were on Mina, as hers were on him.

"I can go anywhere?" Krell wanted to make absolutely certain. "The goddess cannot touch me?"

"No, but the god can," said Chemosh, losing patience. "Go wherever you want, Krell. Commit what mayhem you will. Just don't do it here."

"I will, my lord!' Krell gave another bow. "Then, my lord, if you have no further need for me—"

"Get out, Krell."

"I await your call. Until then, I take my leave. Farewell, my lord."

Krell clanked and rattled his way out of the mausoleum. Chemosh slammed shut the bronze door behind him and locked it.

"I thought you had done something quite clever in capturing that wretch, Mina. I see now that I could have sent a gully dwarf to fetch him." Chemosh smiled at her, to show he was teasing, and reached out his hands.

Mina clasped her hands in his, moved near to him. "And what is to be my reward, Lord?"

Her amber eyes shone; her hair was red-gold flame. Her hands tightened over his, and he could feel the smoothness of the skin sliding over the hardness of bone. He could hear the rush of the pulsing blood in her veins and see the throb of her life in the hollow of her neck. He gathered her close, reveling in her warmth, the warmth of life, the warmth of mortality.

"How will I serve my lord?" Mina asked.

"Like this," he said and took her in his arms.

He kissed her lips. He kissed the hollow of her neck. He stripped the shirt from her body, and holding her tightly, pressed his lips on her breast, above her heart.

His kiss seared her flesh, which began to blacken beneath his touch. Mina cried out. Her body stiffened and she writhed in pain and struggled in his arms. He held her fast, held her close. And then, slowly, he withdrew.

She shuddered, sighed. Her eyes opened. She looked at him, deep into his eyes. Then, wincing, she looked down at her breast.

His mark was on her, the imprint of his lips, burned into her flesh.

"You are mine, Mina," said Chemosh.

The kiss had burned through flesh and bone, struck to her heart. She felt stirring within her the power he had just granted her and she leaned toward him, her lips parted, wanting his kiss again and again.

"I am yours, Lord."

Desire ached in him, and he no longer questioned it. He would take her, make her his own, but he needed to make certain she understood.

"You will not be a slave to me, as you were for Takhisis."

Chemosh caressed her neck, ran his hand over the imprint left by his kiss. Her flesh was charred and starting to blister where his lips had touched her. He traced the black kiss with his finger.

"You will be my High Priestess, Mina. You will go forth into the world and gain followers for me, followers who are young and strong and beautiful as yourself. I will be their god, but you will be their master. You will wield power over them, absolute power, the power of life and death."

"What inducements can I offer them, my lord? The young do not like to think of death . . ."

"You will give them a gift from me. A gift of rare value, one that mankind has wanted since the beginning of time."

"I will do all you ask, lord, with pleasure," said Mina. Her breath came fast.

Chemosh brushed back the red hair with his hand. The silken strands tangled around his fingers. Her lips were warm and eager, her flesh warm and yielding at his touch.

He crushed her body against his. She gave herself to him with passionate abandon, and he no longer wondered how a god could find pleasure in the arms of a mortal. He wondered only that it had taken him this long to make the discovery.

BOOK II

ASHES

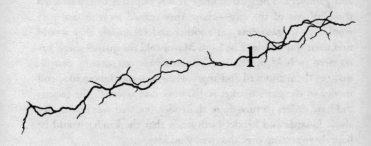

The black palanquin arrived at the city of Staughton early on the morning of the festival known as Spring Dawning. Festivities included a fair, a feast, and the annual Flower Dance. One of the most popular holidays of the calendar, the celebration of Spring Dawning, drew crowds of people to Staughton every year. Even though the day was as yet nothing more than a warm, red streak on the horizon, the gates leading into the walled city, located in the north of Abanasinia, were already jammed with people.

The lines moved fairly swiftly, for the guards were in a good humor, as were most of those in the crowd. Spring Dawning marked the end of cold, dark winter and the return of the sun. The festival was a raucous holiday celebrating life. There would be tippling and dancing and laughter and mild mayhem. The celebrants would wake the next day with aching heads, fuzzy memories, and vague feelings of guilt, which meant that they must have had a wonderful time. Babies born nine months from this night were known as "spring dawning" babies and were considered lucky. There were always a number of hastily made weddings performed after this holiday.

The very nature of the festival attracted all the ne'er-do-wells from miles around—pickpockets, thieves, con artists, whores, and gamblers. The guards knew it was hopeless to try to keep them all out of the city—those they turned away at one gate would try to gain entry at another and eventually they would find their way inside. The Lord Mayor told the guards there was no need to hold up the line by extensively questioning people, making them annoyed and angry when he wanted them to spend money in the city's market stalls, inns, and taverns. The guards did have orders to turn away all kender, but that was mainly for show. Guards and kender both knew that the kender would be happily swarming over the city by midday.

The winter had been a mild one in this part of Abanasinia, and what with the mild winter and the death of the fearsome Overlord Beryl, there was much to celebrate. Some suggested they should also be celebrating the return of the gods, but most of the city's inhabitants were ambivalent about that. Staughton had always viewed itself as a righteous city. The people missed the gods when they left the first time during the First Cataclysm, but life went on, and the people grew used to the gods not being around. Then the gods came back and the people were glad to see them return and life went on with the gods much as it had without. The gods left again, during the Second Cataclysm, and this time people were so busy, what with life going on, that they barely noticed. Now the gods were back again and everyone said they were pleased, but really it was all so tiresome, having to close the temples, then open them, close them, and then open them. Meanwhile, life went on.

Staughton was a small town of about two hundred people at the time of the First Cataclysm. It had grown and prospered in the centuries since. Its population numbered around six thousand now and it had overlapped its walls twice, causing them to be torn down, pushed out, and rebuilt. There was the inner part known as Old City and the outer ring known as New City and yet another addition of the city that as yet had no official title but was referred to locally as "newer." All parts of the city were cleaned up in honor of the day and decorated with bunting and spring flowers. The young people woke early, eager for the fun to start. This was their day to frolic, a day when mamas and papas went conveniently blind to stolen kisses and midnight assignations.

This was the day and this was the mood of the city and its people when the black palanquin hove into view, moving slowly and majestically up the road toward the city. It attracted immediate attention. Those standing in line who first saw it stared in astonishment, then tugged on the sleeves of those standing ahead of them, telling them to turn to look. Soon the entire line of people waiting to enter the city were craning their necks and exclaiming in wonder at the sight.

The palanquin did not join the line but advanced up the road toward the gate. The people stood to one side to let the palanquin pass. An awed and uneasy silence fell on the crowd. No one, from noble knight to itinerant beggar, had seen anything like it.

The curtains that covered the palanquin were of black silk that swung gently with the motion of the bearers. The frame was black, trimmed in gleaming gold skulls. The bearers attracted the most attention: four human females, each standing well over six feet tall and muscular as men. Each woman was identical in appearance to the other and all were beautiful. They wore diaphanous black robes which clung enticingly to their bodies, so that it seemed one could almost see through the thin fabric, that flowed and rippled as they walked. The bearers looked neither to the left nor the right, not even when some drunken youths called out to them. They strode forward, their heavy burden balanced easily on their shoulders, their faces set and cool and without expression.

Those who managed to look past the bearers stared into the palanquin, trying to see the person inside. Heavy black curtains, weighted down with gold bead fringe, blocked the view.

As the palanquin moved past, one man—a cleric of Kiri Jolith—recognized the golden skulls on the side.

"Take care, my friends," he called out, rushing forward to grab hold of some boisterous children, who were running along behind the palanquin. "Those skulls are symbols of Chemosh!"

Immediately the word flew up and down the line of people that the person in the palanquin was a priest of the Lord of Death. Some people shuddered and averted their eyes, but most were intrigued. No feeling of dread emanated from the palanquin; rather, the sweet fragrance of spicy perfume wafted from the swaying curtains.

The cleric of Kiri Jolith, whose name was Lleu, saw that the people were curious, not frightened, and he was uneasy, uncertain what to do. Clerics of all the gods had been waiting for Chemosh to try to grab the reins of power from Sargonnas. For a year, ever since the return of the gods, the clerics had been speculating as to what bold move he would make. Now it seemed that Chemosh was at last on the march. Lleu could see many in the crowd watching him expectantly, hoping he would make a scene. He kept quiet as the strange bearers strode past him, though he did stare at the curtains intently, trying to see who was inside.

After the palanquin passed, he left his place in line to follow discreetly after it, walking along the fringes of the crowd. When the palanquin reached the gate, the person inside would have to make himself known to the guards and Lleu intended to get a look at him.

Many others had the same idea, however, and the crowd surged forward, filling in behind the palanquin, as people jostled with one another to try to obtain a good view. The guards, having heard the rumors that this had something to do with Chemosh, had sent a runner post haste for the sheriff to ask for orders. The sheriff arrived on horseback to take charge of the situation and question this person himself. A hushed silence settled over the crowd as the palanquin arrived at the gate, and everyone waited to hear from the mysterious occupant.

The sheriff took one look at the palanquin and the females who bore it and scratched his chin, clearly at a loss.

"My lord sheriff," Lleu said quietly, "if I could be of help—"

"Brother Lleu, I'm glad you're back!" exclaimed the sheriff, relieved. He leaned down from the saddle for a quick conference. "Do you think this is a priest of Chemosh?"

"That is my guess, sir," said Lleu. "Priest or priestess." He eyed the palanquin. "The golden skulls are undoubtedly those of Chemosh."

"What do I do?" The sheriff was a big, stalwart man accustomed to handling tavern brawls and highwaymen, not six-foot-tall females, whose eyes didn't move, hauling a palanquin containing a mysterious traveler. "Do I send them packing?"

Lleu was tempted to say yes. The arrival of Chemosh boded well for no one, of that he was convinced. The sheriff had the power to deny entrance to anyone for any reason.

"Chemosh is a god of evil. I think you would be well within your province to—"

"—to do what?" called out a woman, her voice quivering with indignation "Forbid the priest of Chemosh from entering our city? I suppose this means you will be burning my shrine and turning me out next!"

Lleu sighed deeply. The woman wore the green and blue robes of a priestess of Zeboim. The city of Staughton was built on the banks of a river. Zeboim was one of the city's more popular goddesses, especially during the rainy season. If the sheriff denied access to a representative of one of the gods of darkness, rumors would fly about that Zeboim would be the next to go.

"Permit them to enter," Lleu said, adding loudly for the crowd to hear, "The gods of light promote free will. We do not tell people what they can and cannot believe."

"Are you sure?" asked the sheriff, frowning. "I don't want any trouble."

"That is my advice, sir," said Lleu. "The final decision is, of course, up to you."

The sheriff looked from Lleu to the priestess of Zeboim to the palanquin. None of them gave him much help. Zeboim's priestess watched with narrowed eyes. Lleu had said all he had to say. The palanquin stood at the gate, the bearers patiently waiting.

The sheriff stepped forward to address the unseen occupant.

"State your name and the nature of your business in our fair city," he said briskly.

The crowd held its collective breath.

For a moment, there was no response. Then a hand—a female hand—put aside the curtains. The hand was shapely. Jewels, red as blood, flashed on slender fingers. Lleu caught a glimpse of the woman inside the black palanquin. His mouth gaped, and his eyes widened.

He had never before seen such a woman. She was young, not yet twenty. Her hair was auburn, the color of leaves in the autumn, and it was elaborately arranged beneath a black and golden headdress. Her eyes were amber, luminous, radiant, warm, as if all the world was cold and her eyes the only warmth left to a man. She wore a black dress of some sheer fabric that hinted at everything beneath it and gave away nothing. She moved with studied grace and there was a look of knowing in those eyes, a knowledge of secrets no other mortal possessed.

She was disturbing. Dangerous. Lleu wanted to turn on his heel and walk disdainfully away, yet he stared, entranced, unable to move.

"My name is Mina," she said. "I have come to your city for the same purpose as have all these good people." She gestured, to indicate the crowd. "To share in the celebration of springtime."

"Mina!" Lleu gasped. "I know that name."

Kiri-Jolith is a militant god, a god of honor and war, patron god of the Knights of Solamnia. Lleu was not a knight, nor was he a Solamnic, but he had traveled to Solamnia to study with the knights when he had decided to dedicate himself to Kiri-Jolith. He had heard from them the stories of the War of Souls, heard their tales of a young woman named Mina, who had led her armies of darkness to one amazing victory after another, including the destruction of the great Dragon Overlord, Malys.

"I have heard of you. You are a follower of Takhisis," Lleu said harshly.

"The goddess who saved the world from the terror of the Dragon Overlords. The goddess who was most foully betrayed and destroyed," Mina said. A shadow darkened the amber eyes. "I honor her memory, but I now follow a different god."

"Chemosh," said Lleu in accusing tones.

"Chemosh," said Mina, and she lowered her eyes in reverence.

"Lord of Death!" Lleu added, challenging.

"Lord of Endless Life," Mina returned.

"So that is what he is calling himself these days," Lleu said scornfully.

"Come visit me to find out," Mina offered.

Her voice was warm as her eyes, and Lleu was suddenly conscious of the crowd gathered around him, their ears stretched to hear every word. They all looked at him now, wondering if he would accept her invitation and he realized, to his chagrin, that he'd been led into a trap. If he refused, they would think he was afraid to take on Chemosh and they would immediately jump to the conclusion that this must be a powerful god, yet Lleu did not want to talk to this woman. He did not want to be in her presence.

"I have only just returned from a long absence," Lleu said, temporizing. "I have much work to do. If I can find the time, perhaps I will stop by for a theological discussion with you. I think it would be quite interesting."

"So do I," said Mina softly, and he had the feeling she wasn't talking about theology.

Lleu could think of nothing to say in answer. He inclined his head politely and pushed his way through the crowd, pretending not to hear the snickers and gibes. He hoped fervently that the sheriff would refuse to admit the woman. Going straight to his temple, he stood before the statue of Kiri-Jolith and found solace and comfort in the stern, implacable face of the warrior-god. He grew calm, and after giving thanks to the god, he was able to go ahead with the work that had piled up during his absence.

The sheriff, lost in amber eyes, gave Mina admittance to the city, along with the name of the finest inn.

"I thank you, sir," she said. "Would you have any objection if I spoke to the people? I won't cause you any trouble. I promise that."

The sheriff found himself curious as to what she had to say. "Make it brief," he told her.

She thanked him and then asked her bearers to lower the palanquin to the ground.

The bearers did so. Mina parted the curtains and stepped out.

The crowd, most of whom had not been able to see her prior to this, marveled aloud at the sight. She stood before them in her cobweb thin black dress, her perfume drifting on a light spring breeze. She raised her hands for silence.

"I am Mina, High Priestess of Chemosh," she called out in ringing tones, the same that had once echoed across the battlefield. "He comes to the world with a new message, a message of endless life. I look forward to sharing his message with all of you while I am visiting in your fair city."

Mina returned to her palanquin. She paid the sheriff the tax required of all vehicles for admittance into the city and closed the curtain. The bearers lifted up the palanquin and carried her through the gates. The crowd watched in awed silence until the black palanquin was lost to sight. Then tongues began to wag.

All could agree on one thing—this promised to be a most interesting Spring Dawning.

2

Spring Dawning in Staughton proved to be far more interesting than anyone had anticipated. Word soon spread through the city that a miracle had occurred at the hostelry. As word spread, people began leaving the fair grounds and hastening to see for themselves.

One of the groomsmen was an eyewitness and he was now the center of attention, urged to tell and retell his story for the benefit of those who had arrived late.

According to the groomsman, who was reputed to be a sober and responsible individual, he had been returning from the hostelry's stables when the black palanquin was carried into the courtyard. The four bearers lowered the palanquin to the ground. Mina stepped out of it. The bearers removed a fancifully carved wooden chest from the palanquin, and at Mina's behest, carried it to her room. Mina entered the hostelry and was not seen again, though the groomsman lingered in the courtyard on purpose, hoping to catch another glimpse of her. The four female bearers returned to the palanquin. They took up their positions at the front and back of the palanquin and stood there, unmoving.

A kender immediately descended on the bearers and began badgering them with questions. The bearers refused to answer, maintaining a dignified silence. They were so silent, in fact, and so completely oblivious of the kender—when by now any normal person would have given him a box on the ears—that he poked one of the bearers in the ribs.

The kender gasped and poked the woman again.

"It's solid rock!" the kender cried shrilly. "The lady's turned to stone!"

The groomsman immediately assumed the kender was lying. Further investigation revealed otherwise. The four female bearers were four black marble statues. The black palanquin was a black marble palanquin. People swarmed to the hostelry to see the wondrous sight, doing additional wonders for the innkeeper's business in ale and dwarf spirits.

Despite a torrential rainstorm, the hostelry's courtyard was soon packed with people, with the crowds overflowing into adjacent streets. The people began chanting "Mina, Mina!" and when, after about two hours, Mina appeared at one of the upper story windows, the crowd went wild, cheering and exhorting her to speak.

Throwing open one of the lead-paned glass windows, Mina gave a brief talk, explaining that Chemosh had returned to the world with new and stronger powers than before. She was constantly interrupted by rumbles of thunder and cracklings of lightning, but she persisted and the crowd hung on every word. Chemosh was no longer interested in going about cemeteries raising up corpses, she told them. He was interested in life and the living, and he had a special gift to offer anyone who would follow him. All his faithful would receive life unending.

"You will never grow older than you are this day," Mina promised. "You will never be sick. You will never know fear or cold or hunger. You will be immune to disease. You will never taste the bitterness of death."

"I'll become a follower!" jeered one youth, one of the inn's best customers in the dwarf spirit line. "But only if you come down here and show me the way."

The crowd laughed. Mina smiled at him.

"I am the High Priestess of Chemosh, here to bring the message of the god to his people," she said in pleasant tones. "If you are serious in becoming one of his followers, Chemosh will see into your heart and he will send someone to you in his name."

She shut the window and faded back into the room, out of sight. The crowd waited a moment to see if she would return, then some went home to dry out, while others went over to poke and pinch the statues or watch those who trying unsuccessfully to chip at them with hammer and chisel.

Of course, the first thing people did was to rush word of the stone statues to Lleu, the cleric of Kiri-Jolith.

Lleu didn't believe it.

"It's some third-rate illusionist trick," he said, scoffing. "Rolf the groomsman is gullible as they come. I don't believe it." He rose from his desk, where he had been writing a letter to his superior in Solanthus, detailing his concerns about Chemosh. "I'll go expose this charlatan for what she is."

"It's no trick, Lleu," said Marta, cleric of Zeboim, entering the study. "I've seen it. Solid stone they are. Black as Chemosh's heart."

"Are you sure?" Lleu demanded.

Marta nodded gloomily, and Lleu sat back down again. Marta may have been a cleric for a goddess who was cruel and capricious, but the cleric herself was honest, level-headed, and not given to flights of fancy.

"What do we do?" he asked.

"I don't know," said Marta. "My goddess is not happy." An enormous clap of thunder that knocked several books from the shelves testified to Zeboim's perturbed state of mind. "But if we go gawking at the statues like every other person in this city, we will only be lending credence to this miracle. I say we ignore it."

"You're right," said Lleu. "We should ignore it. This Mina will be gone in a day or two. The people will forget about it and go on to some other wonder—a two-headed calf or some such thing."

He winced as another horrific thunder bolt shook the ground.

"I only wish I could convince her Holiness of that," Marta muttered, glancing toward the rain-soaked heavens. Shaking her head, she left the temple to return to her own.

Lleu knew his advice was sound, but he found he could not go back to work. He paced about the temple, confused and at odds with himself. Every time he passed the statue of the god, Lleu looked at that stern and implacable face and wished he possessed such determination and force of will. He had thought that once he did. He was distraught to find that perhaps he didn't.

He was still pacing when there came a knock at the temple door. The cleric opened it to find one of the potboys from the hostelry.

"I have a message for Father Lleu," said the boy.

"I am he," said Lleu.

The boy held out a scroll tied up with a black ribbon and sealed with black wax.

Lleu frowned. He was tempted to slam the door in the boy's face, then realized that word would go around that he was afraid. He was young and insecure. He hadn't been in Staughton that long and he was working hard to establish himself and his religion in a city that only marginally cared. He took the scroll.

"You have leave to go," he told the boy.

"I'm to stay, Father, in case there's a reply."

Lleu was about to say that there would be no reply, that he had nothing to say to a High Priestess of Chemosh, but again, he thought of how that would look. He tore off the black ribbon, broke the seal, and hastily read through the missive.

I look forward to our discussion. I will be at leisure to receive you at the hour of moon rise.

In the name of Chemosh

Mina

"Tell the High Priestess Mina that I would like very much to come to talk theology with her, but that I have pressing matters of my own temple to which I must attend," Lleu said. "Thank her for thinking of me."

"I'd reconsider if I were you, Father," said the potboy with a wink. "She's a looker."

"The High Priestess is a cleric and she is your elder," said Lleu, glowering. "As am I. You owe both of us more respect."

"Yes, Father," said potboy, chastened. He scuttled off.

Lleu returned to the altar. The cleric looked again at the face of Kiri-Jolith, this time for reassurance.

The god regarded him with a cold eye. Lleu could almost hear the voice. "I want no cowards in my service."

Lleu did not think he was being cowardly. He was being sensible. He had no need to bandy words with this woman and he certainly had no interest in Chemosh.

He went back to his study to finish his letter.

The quill sputtered. He spilled the ink. At last he gave up. Staring out at the pouring rain that beat on the roof of the temple like a drummer summoning all true knights to battle, Lleu tried to divest himself of thoughts of amber eyes.

At the hour of moonrise, Lleu stood outside the hostelry. He stared at the marble statues, which shimmered with a ghostly light in the silver moonshine of Solinari. Zeboim had worn herself out, apparently, and taken her fit of pique elsewhere, for the storm had at last abated, the clouds gone, sulking off.

Lleu found the statues profoundly disturbing. He longed to touch one but feared there might still be people watching. He shivered, for the spring night was chill and damp, and looked around. Sounds of laughter and revelry reached him from the fair grounds. There was free ale and a pig roast at the fair grounds and most of the citizenry were attending the festivities. The hostelry was quiet.

Lleu stretched out his hand to touch one of the statues.

The door to the inn opened and he quickly snatched his hand back.

Mina stood in the entrance, a slender figure of darkness against a blaze of firelight.

"Come in," she said. "I'm glad you changed your mind."

She did not look like a high priestess. She had changed out of the flowing, tantalizing dress and removed her golden and black headdress. She wore a soft black gown that was open at the front, tied together at her waist with a belt of gold cord. Her auburn hair was simply braided and coiled around her head, held in place by a jeweled pin made of amber. The scent of myrrh hung in the air.

"I can't stay," said Lleu.

"Of course not," Mina said in understanding tones.

She stepped aside so that he could enter.

The common room was deserted. Mina turned away from Lleu and started to ascend the stairs.

"Where are you going?" Lleu demanded.

Mina turned to face him. "I have ordered a light supper. I've asked that it be served to me in my private room. Have you dined? Will you join me?"

Lleu flushed. "No, thank you. I think perhaps I will return to the temple. I have work to do . . ."

Mina walked over to him, rested her hand on his forearm, and smiled at him, a friendly smile, ingenuous. "What is your name?"

He hesitated, fearing that even giving her that much information might somehow entrap him.

Finally he answered, "I am Lleu Mason."

"I am Mina, but you know that. You came here for a theological discussion, and the common room of an inn is hardly a suitable place to debate serious matters, do you think?"

Lleu Mason was a young man in his early twenties. He had blonde hair that he wore in the manner of Kiri-Jolith's clerics—

shoulder length, with a central part and straight-cut bangs. His eyes were brown and intense with a restless, seeking look about them. He was well-built, with the muscles of a soldier, not a scholar, which was not surprising. Kiri-Jolith's clerics trained alongside the knights they served and were notable among clerics in Ansalon for being skilled in the use of the long sword. His grandfather had been a mason, which is how he came by his name.

He looked at Mina. He looked around the inn, though he didn't see much of it. He smiled faintly.

"No, not very suitable." Lleu drew in a deep breath. "I will come upstairs with you."

Mina walked again up the stairs. This time he followed after her. He was gravely courteous, moved to precede her down the hallway and opened the door to the room for her. This was a private dining chamber, with a table and chairs and a fire on the hearth. The table was laid. A servant stood obsequiously in the background. Lleu held Mina's chair and then took his place across from her.

The meal was good, with roasted meats and bread followed by a sweet. They spoke little during the meal, for the servant was present. When they were finished, Mina dismissed him. They shared a jug of wine, neither drinking much, only sipping at it as they drew their chairs over to the fire.

They talked about Lleu's family. His elder brother, now thirty-five, had become a master mason, joining his father in the family business. Lleu was the youngest and had no interest in masonry. He dreamed of becoming a soldier and had traveled to Solamnia for that purpose. Once there, he was introduced to the worship of Kiri-Jolith and realized that his true calling was to serve the god.

"You might say the church runs in our family," he added with a smile. "My grandmother was a cleric of Paladine and my middle brother is a monk dedicated to the worship of Majere."

"Indeed?" said Mina, interested. "What does your brother think of your becoming a cleric of Kiri-Jolith?"

"I have no idea. His monastery is located in some isolated place and the monks rarely leave it. We have neither seen nor heard from my brother in many years."

"For many years." Mina was puzzled. "How could that be? The gods, including Majere, returned to the world only a little over a year ago."

Lleu shrugged. "According to what I am told, some of these monasteries are so isolated that the monks knew nothing of what was transpiring in the world. They maintained their lifestyle of meditation and prayer despite the fact that they had no god to pray to. Such a life would suit my brother. He was always dour and withdrawn, given to roaming the hills alone. He is ten years my senior, so I never knew him very well."

Lleu, forgetting himself, had moved his chair nearer to her. He relaxed as the meal progressed, disarmed by Mina's warmth and her interest in him. "But that is enough talk of me. Tell me of yourself, Mina. There was a time when the whole world talked of you."

"I went in search of a god," Mina replied, staring into the fire. "I found god. I kept my faith in my god until the end. There is not much more to be said."

"Except that now you follow a new god," said Lleu.

"Not a new god. A very old one. Old as time."

"But . . . Chemosh." Lleu grimaced. As he gazed at her, he was consumed with admiration. "You are so young and so beautiful, Mina. I have never seen a woman as lovely. Chemosh is a god of rotting corpses and moldy old bones. Don't shake your head. You cannot deny it."

"I do deny it," said Mina calmly. She reached out, took hold of his hand. Her touch made his blood burn. "Do you fear death, Lleu?"

"I . . . yes, I guess I do," he answered. He did not want to think of death at this moment. He was thinking very much of life.

"A cleric of Kiri-Jolith is not supposed to fear death, are you?"

"No, we are not." He grew uncomfortable and tried to withdraw from her touch.

Mina pressed his hand sympathetically, and almost unknowingly, he tightened his grip.

"What does your god tell you of death and the after-life?"

"That when we die, we embark upon the next part of our soul's journey, that death is a door that leads to further knowledge of ourselves."

"Do you believe this?"

"I want to," he said. His hand clenched. "I really want to. I have wrestled with this question ever since I became a cleric. They tell me to have faith, but . . ."

He shook his head. He stared into the fire, brooding, still clasping her hand. He turned to her abruptly.

"You are not afraid of death."

"I am not," said Mina, smiling, "because I will never die. Chemosh has promised me life unending."

Lleu stared at her. "How can he make such a promise? I don't understand."

"Chemosh is a god. His powers are limitless."

"He is the Lord of Death. He goes to battlefields, raises up unburied bodies and forces them to do his bidding—"

"That was in the old days. Times have changed. This is the Age of Mortals. An age for the living. He has no use for skeletal remains. He wants followers who are like you and me, Lleu. Young and strong and full of life. Life that will never end. Life that brings pleasure such as this."

She closed her eyes and leaned toward him. Her lips parted, inviting. He kissed her, tentatively at first, and then passion took him. She was soft and yielding, and before he knew what he was doing or quite how he was doing it, his hands were beneath her robes, fondling warm, naked flesh. He groaned softly, and his kisses hardened.

"My bedroom is next door," she whispered, her lips brushing his.

"This is wrong," Lleu said, yet he could not tear himself from her.

Mina put her arms around him, pressed her body against his. "This is life," she said to him.

She drew him into her bedchamber.

Their passion lasted all through the night. They loved and slept and woke to love again. Lleu had never known love-making such as this, never known such transports of joy. He had never felt so much alive and he wanted his feeling to last forever. He fell asleep in her arms, that thought in his mind. He woke to the dawn—spring dawning. He found Mina beside him, propped up on one elbow, gazing down at him, her hand running gently through his hair on his chest.

He raised up to kiss her, but she drew back.

"What of Chemosh?" Mina asked. "Have you thought of all I have been telling you?"

"You are right, Mina. It does make sense that a god would want his followers to live forever," Lleu admitted, "but what must I do to obtain this blessing? I've heard tales of blood sacrifices and other rites—"

Mina smiled at him. She ran her hand over his bare flesh. "That is what they are—only tales. All you have to do is give yourself to the god. Say, 'I pledge my faith to Chemosh.' "

"That is all?"

"That is all. You may even return to the worship of Kiri-Jolith, if you want. Chemosh is not jealous. He is understanding."

"And I will live forever? And love you forever?" He stole a swift kiss.

"From this day, you will not age," Mina promised. "You will never suffer pain or know hunger or fall ill. This I promise you."

"Then I have nothing to lose." Lleu smiled up at her. "I pledge my faith to Chemosh."

He put his arm around her, drew her down to him. Mina pressed her lips against his breast, above his heart. He shivered in delight, then his body shuddered.

His eyes flew open. Pain seared through him, terrible pain, and he stared at her in horror. He struggled, tried to free himself, but she held him pinned down, her kiss sucking out his life. His heart thudded erratically. Her lips seemed to feed off it. Pain wrenched and twisted him. He gave a stifled cry and clutched at her spasmodically. He writhed in agony. His heart stopped, then everything stopped.

Lleu's head lay rigid on the pillow. His eyes stared at nothing. His face was frozen in an expression of unnamed horror.

Chemosh stood beside the bed.

"My lord," said Mina. "I bring you your first follower."

"Well done, Mina," he said. Bending down, leaning across the body of the young man, he kissed her on the lips. His hand caressed her neck, smoothed her hair. "Well done."

She drew away from him, covering her nakedness with her gown.

"What is it, Mina?" he asked. "What is the matter? You've killed before, in the name of Takhisis. Are you now turned suddenly squeamish?"

Mina glanced at the corpse of the young man. "You promised him life, not death." She looked up at Chemosh and her amber eyes were shadowed. "You promised me power over life and death, my lord. If I wanted merely to commit murder, I could go to any dark alley—"

"You have no faith in me, Mina?"

Mina was silent a moment, gathering her courage. She knew he might be furious with her, but she had to take the risk.

"A god betrayed me once. You asked me to prove myself to you. It is now your turn to prove yourself to me, my lord."

She waited, tensely, for his rage to break over her. He said nothing, and after a moment, she dared look up at him.

He was smiling down on her. "As I told you, Mina. You will

not be my slave. I will prove myself to you. You will have what I promised. Put your hand on the young man's heart."

Mina did as he told her. She placed her hand on the cooling flesh, over the burst heart, over the imprint of her lips, burned black into the flesh.

"The heart will never beat again," Chemosh intoned, "but life will flow through this body. My life. Endless life. Kiss him, Mina."

Mina placed her lips on the burned imprint of her kiss. The heart of the young man remained still, but he drew in a deep breath, the breath of the god. At Mina's touch, his chest rose and fell.

"All will be as I promised him, Mina. He cannot die, for he is already dead. His life will go on unending. I ask only one thing of him in return. He must bring me more followers. There, my love, have I proven myself to you?"

Mina looked at Lleu, who was stirring, stretching, waking. The knowledge came to her that she had not only taken life, she had restored it. She had the power to give everyone in the world life unending. Her power . . . and that of the god.

She reached out her hand to Chemosh, who clasped her hand in his own. "We will change the world, my lord!"

She had only one question, one lingering doubt. She placed her hand over her own breast, where the mark of Chemosh was black on her white skin. "My lord, my heart still beats. My blood is still warm and so is my flesh. You did not take my life—"

Chemosh did not tell her that it was her life that he loved about her. Her warm, beating heart, her hot, pulsing blood. Nor did he tell her that the gift of unending life she was bestowing on these mortals was not as bright and shiny as it appeared on the surface. He could have given it to her, but then he would lose her and he was not ready to give her up. Not yet. Perhaps, some day, when he had grown weary of her.

"I am surrounded by the dead, Mina," he said, by way of excuse. "Day in, day out. Like that fool Krell, who will not leave me in peace, but is constantly pestering me. You are a 'breath of life' for me, Mina."

He laughed at his jest, gave Mina a parting kiss, and was gone.

Mina slipped out of the bed. She picked up a comb and ran the comb through her tangled hair, began to slowly and carefully work out the knots.

She heard a rustle behind her. Glancing over her shoulder, she saw Lleu sitting up amid the bed clothes. He looked confused and clutched at his heart, wincing as if in remembered pain.

Mina watched him, and combed her hair.

Lleu's expression cleared. His eyes widened. He looked around again, as if seeing everything anew. He climbed out of bed, walked over to her, bent down and kissed her neck.

"Thank you, Mina," he said fervently.

He wanted to make love to her again. He tried to kiss her. Laying down the comb, she turned to face him and put aside his seeking hands.

"Not me, Lleu," she said. "Others."

She looked into his eyes that were bright and alert, no longer wondering, no longer restless. She traced a finger over the kiss burned into his skin. "Do you understand?"

"I understand. And I thank you for this gift."

Lleu caught hold of her hand, kissed it. His skin felt cool to the touch. Not deathly chill, but cooler than usual, as if he'd come from some chill place such as a shaded grove or a cavern. In all other respects, he appeared normal.

""Will I see you again, Mina?" he asked eagerly, as he dressed himself in the robes of a cleric of Kiri-Jolith.

"Perhaps," Mina answered, shrugging. "Do not count upon it. I have my duty to Chemosh, as do you."

He frowned, disappointed. "Mina . . ."

She kept her back to him. Her fingernails tapped impatiently.

"Praise Chemosh," he said, after a moment, and went on his way.

She heard his boots clatter on the stairs, heard him give the innkeeper a boisterous greeting.

Mina picked up the comb and began to patiently ease the tangles from her auburn hair. Chemosh's words lingered with her, as did his kiss.

He had promised her power over life and death and he had fulfilled his promise. He had kept faith with her.

"Praise Chemosh," she said softly.

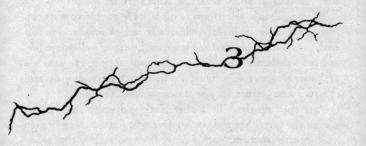

3

Rhys sat amid the tall grass at the bottom of the hill, his staff cradled loosely in his arms, his thoughts drifting skyward, up where the white clouds scudded across the clear blue sky. Spread out on the hill above him, the sheep placidly grazed. Grasshoppers buzzed in the grass around him. Butterflies fluttered from buttercup to buttercup. Rhys sat so still that occasionally the butterflies landed on him, fooled by the burnt-orange color of his home-spun robes.

Rhys was mindful of the sheep, for he was their shepherd, but he did not keep close watch on them. There was no need. His dog, Atta, lay on her belly some distance from him. Her head on her paws, she watched the sheep intently, noting every move each made. Atta saw three starting to stray from the flock, wandering off on a course that would soon take them over the hill, out of her sight. Her head raised. Her ears lifted. Her body tensed. She cocked an eye at her master, to see if Rhys had noticed.

Rhys had seen the errant sheep, but he pretended he didn't. He continued to sit at his ease, listening to the song of sparrow and goldfinch, watching a caterpillar crawl up a blade of grass, his thoughts with his god.

Atta's body quivered. She gave a low, warning growl. The sheep were almost at the top of the hill. Rhys relented.

Rhys rose easily, effortlessly to his feet. He was thirty years old. His years showed on his face, which was dark-skinned and weathered, but not on his body. Daily exercise, his rigorous outdoor life, and his simple diet made him strong, lean, supple. He wore his dark hair long, in a single braid down his back. Extending his arm in a sweeping gesture, he gave the command, "Go bye."

Atta sped up the hillside, her black and white body a blur against the green. She did not head straight for the sheep or even look directly at them. Such a move from an animal that sheep equate with a wolf would have panicked them. Facing away from the sheep, watching them out of the corner of her eyes, Atta flanked the sheep on the right, causing them to veer left, back toward the herd.

Rhys put his fingers to his mouth, gave a piercing whistle. The dog was too far away to hear his voice, but the shrill whistle carried clearly. Atta flopped onto her belly, keeping her eyes on the sheep, waiting for the next command.

Rhys made a fist of his hand, held it between the sun and the horizon line. One fist for every hour between now and sunset. Time to think about returning his flock to the pens in order to be back for supper and the ritual training exercises. He gave another shrill whistle—long, short. This was "away," the command that sent her to her left.

Atta herded the sheep down the hill, back toward where Rhys stood with his staff. She kept her body in a straight line with the shepherd, balancing his movements with her own, the sheep between the two of them. If Rhys moved left, she moved right. If he moved right, she moved left. Her duty was to keep the sheep in motion, facing the correct direction, making certain they stayed together, and do all this without sending them into a panic-stricken run.

The flock was about half-way down the hillside when Rhys spotted a sheep left behind. It had wandered into a stand of tall grass and he hadn't noticed it. Rhys whistled again, a different command, one that meant "Lie down."

Atta slowed her pace. The command was not meant to be taken literally, although sometimes the dog would actually lie down on her belly. In this instance, she came to a halt. The flock slowed their pace. Atta fixed them with her mesmeric brown eyes, holding them, and they stopped.

Rhys whistled again, another different signal. "Turn back," he commanded.

Certain that the flock would remain where she left them, Atta turned and sped up the hill. She spotted the lone sheep and got it moving, heading back to the flock. Once it was apparent that the sheep would rejoin the herd, Atta urged her flock on toward Rhys.

All was going well until a ram took it into his woolly head to defy Atta. The ram, which was far heavier and several times larger than the small dog, turned around, stamped his hoof, and refused to budge.

Atta crouched, froze in place. She stared at the sheep, her eyes intent. If the ram remained stubborn, she might rush in to give him a nip on the nose, but that rarely happened. The ram lowered his head. Atta began to creep forward at a moving crouch, her eyes fixed on the ram. After a moment's tense confrontation, the ram suddenly gave way before the dog's mesmerizing stare and whipped around to join the herd. Atta started them off once again.

Rhys felt the blessings of the god swell within him. The green hillside, the blue sky, the white clouds, white sheep, the black and white dog flying over the grass, the darting swallows, a spiraling hawk, grasshoppers jumping up on his robes; the bright, hot, sinking sun; the feel of grass beneath his calloused bare feet: all was Rhys and he was all. All was Majere's and the god was all.

The blood flowing warm through his body, his staff lightly thumping the ground, Rhys moved without haste. He enjoyed the day, enjoyed the view, enjoyed his time alone in the hills. He enjoyed going back to his home again in the evening. The granite walls of the monastery stood on a hilltop opposite him and inside those walls was brotherhood, order, quiet contentment.

His routine this day had been exactly the same as that of countless days previous. Majere willing, tomorrow would be no different. Rhys and the other monks of the Order of Majere rose in the dark hour before dawn. They spent an hour in meditation and prayer to Majere, then went out into the stone courtyard to perform the ritual exercises that warmed and stretched the body. After this, they ate a breakfast of meat or fish, served with bread and goat's milk cheese, with goat's milk to drink. Lunch—cheese and bread—was eaten in the fields or wherever they happened to be. Supper was onion soup, hot and nourishing, served with meat or fish, bread, and a mix of garden greens and fresh vegetables in the summer, apples and dried fruit and nuts in the winter.

After breakfast, the monks went to their daily tasks. These varied by season. In the summer, they worked in the fields, tended to the sheep, pigs, and chickens, and made repairs to the buildings. Fall was harvest and laying in stores, salting down meat so that it would keep through the long months of cold and snow ahead, packing apples in wooden barrels. Winter was a time for indoor work: carding and combing wool, weaving cloth, cutting and sewing clothes; doing leather work; concocting potions for the sick. Winter was also a time for the mind: writing, teaching, learning, discoursing, discussing, speculating. Majere taught that the mind of the monk must be as quick and supple as the body.

Evenings, no matter what the time of year, were spent in the ritual practice of unarmed combat known as "merciful discipline." The monks of Majere recognized that the world is a dangerous place and although they practiced and followed Majere's precepts of peace and brotherhood for all mankind, they understood that peace must sometimes be maintained with force, and that to protect their own lives and those of others, they must be as ready to fight as to pray. Every night—rain or shine, snow or blazing sun—the monks gathered in their outdoor courtyard for training. They fought by waning sunlight in the summer, in darkness or by torchlight in the winter. All were required to attend practice, from the eldest—the Master, who had seen eighty years—to the youngest. The only excuse for missing nightly training was illness.

Stripped naked to the waist, their bare feet slipping on the ice-rimed ground in the winter or the mud in the summer, the monks spent long hours training both body and mind in disciplined combat. They were not permitted to use blades or arrows or any other type of steel weapon, for Majere commanded that his monks must not take life unless innocent lives were in peril and then only when all other options had been tried and failed.

Rhys's favored weapon was the emmide—a staff that was much like a quarter staff, only longer and narrower. The word, emmide, was elven in derivation; the elves used such a staff to knock fruit from the trees. He had become a master of the art of fighting with the emmide, so much so that he now taught others.

Rhys was content with his ordered life, deeply content, now that Majere had returned to them. He could see himself at eighty years of age—the same age as the Master—looking much the same as the Master: grizzled hair, weather-beaten skin stretched taunt over muscles and sinew and bone, face deeply lined, eyes dark and placid with the wisdom of the god. Rhys never planned to leave this place where he had come to know himself and make peace with himself. He never wanted to go back into the world.

The world was inside him.

Rhys arrived at the sheep pen. The sheep trotted docilely past him and into the fold, with Atta right behind them.

"That'll do," said Rhys to the dog.

This was the command that freed her of her charge. Atta wriggled all over in pleasure and came trotting up to him, her tongue lolling, eyes bright. He gave her reward—a pat on her head and a playful fondling of her ears.

Rhys shut the sheep in the pen for the night. Atta joined the other herding dogs, brothers and sisters and cousins, who greeted her with sniffs and wagging tails. She settled down near the sheep fold to gnaw bones and doze, all the while keeping watch on the flock. Resting or sleeping, the dogs served as the guards through the night. Wolves and wildcats were not much of a problem during the summer months, when food was plentiful in the wild. The winter time was the most dangerous. Often the monks were roused from their sleep by the furious barking of the dogs. The monks would rush from their beds to drive the predators away with flaming torches.

Lingering by the sheep pen, watching a mother dog hold down a squealing pup firmly with her paw while she licked him all over, Rhys gradually became aware that something was different. Something had changed. The tranquility of the monastery had been disturbed. Rhys could not have said how he knew this, except that he had lived here so long that he could sense even the most subtle differences in the feel of the place. He left the sheep fold, circled around the outbuildings: the forge, the baker's large oven, the privies, and storage sheds, and walked within sight of the monastery proper.

The monastery had been built by the monks of Majere hundreds of years ago, and it had changed little during all that time. Simple in design, more like a fortress than a temple, the two story building had been raised by the hands of the monks themselves, constructed of stone they had dug from a nearby quarry. The main building contained the sleeping quarters for the monks on the top story, with a communal dining hall, warming room, infirmary, and kitchen on the bottom level. Each monk had his own cell, furnished only with a straw mattress. Each cell had a window that was open to the air year-round. There were no doors on the cells or any of the rooms. The main building did have a door at the entrance, though Rhys often wondered why they bothered, for it was never locked.

The monks had no fear of being robbed. Even kender would pass the monastery by with a shrug and a yawn. Everyone knew that the monks of Majere had no treasure vaults—not so much as a single pfennig, for they were not permitted to handle money. They had no possessions, nothing worth stealing unless you were a wolf with a taste for mutton.

Walking around the building to the entrance door, Rhys came upon a strange wagon parked outside. It had just arrived, apparently, for its team of draft horses were being unhitched and led off for food and rest and a rub-down by two of the younger monks.

Unhitching the horses was a bad sign, Rhys thought, for that meant the intruders would be staying. He turned on his heel and left, heading back to the monastery. He had no desire to meet these visitors. He was not in the least curious about them. He had no reason to think that these folk had anything to do with him and thus he was startled when he heard a voice call out to him.

"Brother Rhys! Stay a moment. You are summoned to the Master."

Rhys halted, looking back toward the wagon. The two novice monks, who were leading the horses to the shed, bowed as they passed him, for he was a weapons master, known as a Master of Discipline. He bowed in response then went on. He and the monk who had called to him—who was the Master of the House— bowed to each other simultaneously, to reflect their equal status.

"The visitors are here to see you, Brother," said the monk. "They are with the Master now. You are to join them."

Rhys nodded his understanding. He had questions, naturally, but the monks refrained from all unnecessary speech and, since his questions would soon be answered, there was no need to engage in conversation. The two monks bowed again, and Rhys entered the monastery, while the Master of the House, who was in charge of the daily household affairs of the monastery, went on about his duties.

The head of the monastery was known simply as the Master. He had an office off the common area. The office was not private, for it also served as the monastery library and the school room. The windowless room was furnished with several wooden desks of simple, solid construction, and wooden stools. Shelves filled with books and scrolls lined the walls. The room smelled of leather and vellum and ink and the oil that the monks rubbed into the wood of the desks.

The Master was the eldest of the monks. Eighty years of age, he had lived in the monastery for over sixty of those years, having joined at the age of sixteen. Although he answered to the Prophet of Majere, who was the head of all the monks of Majere throughout the continent of Ansalon, the Master had only met the Prophet once, twenty years ago, on the day he had been confirmed as Master.

Twice a year, the Master made a written report on the affairs of the monastery, a letter that was carried to the Prophet by one of the monks. The Prophet sent back a letter acknowledging receipt of the report, and that was the only exchange the two would have until the next letter. There were no comings and goings between monasteries, no exchange of news between one monastery and the next. So isolated were the monasteries that monks in one often had little knowledge of where another was located. Traveling monks were permitted to stay at a monastery, but most chose not to, for when they went out into the world—usually on a personal, spiritual journey, they were commanded to walk among the people.

The monks of Majere were not interested in news of their fellow monks. They had no interest in the politics of any nation, took no sides in any war or conflict. (Because of this, they were often asked to be peace negotiators or to sit in judgment on disputes.) The yearly reports made by the Master were often little more than a notation of deaths among the brethren, a record of those who had newly joined, and a record of those who had gone out into the world. There would also be a brief description of the weather and how it had affected the crops or the harvest, and any additions or changes made to the monastery's buildings.

Change and upheavals in the outside world had such small effect on the monastery that a letter written by a Master from a monastery in 4000 PC would read similar to one penned by a Master from the same monastery centuries later.

Rhys arrived in the office to find three people in the room with the Master—a middle-aged man and woman, who looked distressed and uncomfortable; and a young man, wearing the robes of a cleric of Kiri-Jolith, who was smiling, at ease. Rhys paused in the doorway. He had the impression that there was something familiar about these people, that he knew them. Rhys waited in silence for the Master to notice him.

The Master's long gray hair fell over his shoulders. His face was wrinkled as a winter apple, with high cheek bones, strong jaw and prominent nose. His eyes were dark and penetrating. He was a Master of Discipline and there was not a monk in the monastery, including Rhys, who could best him in combat.

The Master was listening patiently to the middle-aged man, who was talking so fast that Rhys could not make out the jumble of words. The woman stood silently by, nodding her head in agreement, and sometimes casting an anxious glance at the young man. The older man's voice and way of speaking was also familiar to Rhys. Finally, the Master glanced his way and Rhys bowed. The Master's eyes flickered in response. He continued to give his full attention to his visitors.

At last the elder man paused for breath. The woman dabbed at her eyes. The young man yawned and looked bored. The Master turned to Rhys.

"Honored One," Rhys said, bowing deeply to the Master. He bowed again to the strangers. "Fellow travelers."

"These are your parents," said the Master without preamble, answering the question Rhys had not asked. "And this is your younger brother, Lleu."

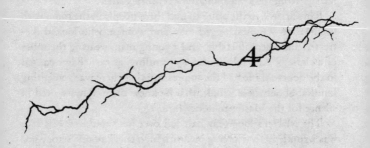

Rhys turned his calm gaze upon them. "Father, Mother," he said politely. "Lleu." He bowed again.

His father's name was Petar, his mother's Brandwyn. His brother, Lleu, was a little child when he left home.

His father's face flushed red in anger. "After fifteen years, is that all you have to say to your own parents?"

"Hush, Petar," soothed his mother, resting her hand on her husband's arm. "What should Rhys say? We are strangers to him."

She smiled tenuously at Rhys. She was not angry, like his father, only weary from the journey, and distraught over whatever troubles had brought her all this distance to seek out a son she barely remembered, a son she had never understood.

Bran, her first born, had been her darling. Little Lleu, her pet. Rhys was the middle child who never quite fit in. He was the quiet child, the child who was "different." He even looked different, with his dark eyes and black hair and slender, wiry body; a stark contrast to his blonde, big-boned brothers.

His father glanced at Rhys from beneath lowering brows. Rhys met his gaze steadily and his father lowered his eyes. Petar Mason, who was gray-haired now, but who had been a tow-head in his youth, had never been comfortable around Rhys. Although Petar adored his wife, perhaps there was some lingering doubt inside him, maybe not even recognized, that this middle son, who was so very different from the other two, was not actually his progeny. Rhys was obviously his mother's son, for he took after her side of the family. His uncles were all dark, wiry men. He had nothing in him of his father. For all that, his mother found it difficult to love the child, who rarely spoke, never laughed.

Rhys held no animosity toward his parents. He understood. He'd always understood. He waited in patient silence for them to explain the reason for their visit. The Master also waited in silence, for he had said all that was necessary. Rhys's mother looked anxiously at his father, who was flustered, unnerved. The silence grew uncomfortable, at least for the visitors. The monks sometimes went for days without speaking, and neither the Master nor Rhys were bothered. It was his younger brother who finally spoke.

"They want to talk about me, Rhys," Lleu said in an easy, overly familiar tone that was jarring. "And they can't do that with me here. I'll go take a walk around the grounds. With your permission, of course," he added, turning with a grin to the Master. "Though I don't suppose you lot have much to hide. Any chance of your Bug God finding me a glass of dwarf spirits?"

"Lleu!" exclaimed his father, aghast.

"Guess not." Lleu winked at Rhys and sauntered out of the library, whistling a bawdy tune.

Rhys and the Master exchanged glances. Majere was known as the Mantis God by some, for the praying mantis was sacred to Majere and used by the god as his symbol, the mantis appearing to be always in the aspect of prayer, keeping still and quiet, but with the capacity to swiftly attack its prey. The young man was, by his attire, a cleric of Kiri-Jolith. He was certainly not acting like a cleric of Kiri-Jolith, who was stern and serious and would not countenance such sacrelige as referring to Majere as the "Bug God."

"I am sorry, Master," said Petar, the red color in his face deepening, except that now it was from embarrassment, not anger. He wiped his face with his sleeve. "No son of mine was brought up to speak to clergy in that tone. You know that, Rhys."

Rhys did know it. His father, whose mother had been a cleric of Paladine, had always been deeply respectful of the gods and any man of god. Even in the days when the gods were gone, Petar had taught his boys to keep them in their hearts.

"Lleu's changed, Rhys," said Brandwyn, her voice trembling. "That's why we came here. We . . . we don't know him anymore! He spends his time in the taverns, drinking and carousing and hanging out with a group of young ruffians and whores. Forgive me, Father," she added, blushing, "for speaking of such things."

The Master's dark eyes flickered with amusement. "We monks of Majere take vows of chastity, but we are not ignorant of life. We understand what goes on between a man and a woman, and in most instances, we approve of it. We would soon run out of monks otherwise."

Rhys's parents did not seem to know what to make of this speech. They found it vaguely shocking.

"Your son is, by his attire, a cleric of Kiri-Jolith," the Master observed.

"Not for long," Petar said heavily. "The clerics cast him out. He broke too many of their laws. He should not be wearing those robes now, but he seems to take pleasure in making a fool of himself."

"We don't know what to do," Brandwyn added with a catch in her throat. "We thought maybe Rhys could talk to him . . ."

"I doubt I will have much influence on a brother who obviously has no memory of me," said Rhys mildly.

"It can't hurt," said his father, starting to grow angry again.

"Please, Rhys," his mother begged. "We are desperate. We have nowhere else to turn!"

"Of course, I will speak to him," said Rhys gently. "I just

wanted to warn you not to expect too much. But I will do more than speak to him. I will pray for him."

His parents looked relieved, hopeful. The Master offered them a room for the night and invited them to share the monks' simple evening meal. His parents accepted gratefully and went to the room to rest, worn out from the trip and their anxiety.

Rhys was about to depart in search of his brother, when he felt a touch upon his spirit, as clear to him as a touch on the arm.

"Yes, Master?" he said.

"Lleu is his own shadow," said the Master.

Rhys was startled, troubled. "What do you mean, Honored One?"

"I don't know," said the Master, his brow puckering. "I am not certain. I have never seen the like. I must think this over." He turned his gaze on Rhys, and it was serious, penetrating. "Speak to him, Brother, by all means. But be careful."

"He is a young man and full of high spirits, Master," said Rhys. "The life of a cleric is not for everyone."

"There is more to it than that," the Master cautioned. "Much more. Be careful, Rhys," he said, and it was unusual for him to speak Rhys's name. "I will be at my prayers, if you have need of me."

The Master sat down, legs crossed, on the floor of the office. Resting his hands on his knees, he closed his eyes. A look of peaceful repose came over the old man's face. He was with the god.

Majere had no formal places of worship, no temples filled with pews, no altars. The world is the temple of Majere, the sky his grand vaulted ceiling, the grassy hills his pews, the trees his altars. One did not seek the god inside a formal setting but looked inward, wherever one was.

Rhys left the Master to his prayers and went out to find his brother. He saw no sign of him, but hearing the dogs barking, Rhys headed in that direction. As he rounded the corner of the storage shed, the sheep fold came into view and there was his brother.

The sheep were all huddled together at the far end of the pen. Atta stood between Lleu and the sheep. The dog's ears were back, her tail moving slowly side to side, legs rigid, teeth bared.

"Foul beast!" Lleu cursed at her. "Get out of my way!"

He aimed a savage kick at the dog. Atta made a light leap sideways, easily avoiding the man's boot. Furious, Lleu struck at her with his hand.

Atta snapped and Lleu let out a yelp. He jerked his hand away, staring angrily at a red slash that ran across the back.

"Atta, lie down," Rhys ordered.

To his astonishment, Atta remained standing, brown eyes fixed on Lleu. The dog growled. Her lip curled.

"Atta, down!" Rhys said again, sternly.

Atta dropped onto her belly. She knew by his unusually loud tone that Rhys was displeased. The dog cast her master a pleading glance as though to say, "You wouldn't be angry if you understood." She shifted her watchful gaze back to Lleu.

"That demon dog attacked me!" Lleu yelled, his face twisted in a scowl. He held one hand over his injured hand, cradled it. "The beast is vicious. It should have its throat cut."

"The dog's job is to protect the sheep. You should not have been bothering them, nor should you have tried to kick her or hit her. That nip was a warning. Not an attack."

Lleu glowered at the dog, then muttered something and looked away. Atta continued to watch him warily, and the other dogs were roused and stood on the alert, hackles raised. The mother dog snapped at her pups, who wanted to play, letting them know that this was a time to be serious. Rhys found the reaction of the dogs odd. One would have thought the wolf was on the prowl.

He shook his head. This was not a propitious beginning to a confiding conversation between two brothers.

"Let me take a look at where she bit you," Rhys offered. "The infirmarer has salve we can put on it to keep it from putrefying, although generally dog bites heal quite cleanly. More cleanly than human bites."

"It's nothing," said Lleu in sulky tones. He continued to press his hand over the wound.

"Her teeth are sharp," said Rhys. "The cut must be bleeding."

"No, really. It's just a scratch. I overreacted." Lleu thrust his hands into the sleeves of the clerical robes he no longer had a right to wear. He added, with a grimace, "I suppose Father sent you out to lecture me on my sins."

"If he did, he will be disappointed. It is not up to me to tell another how to live his life. I will give advice, if my council is sought, but that is all."

"Well, then, brother, your council is not sought," said Lleu.

Rhys shrugged, accepting.

"What do you fellows do for fun around here?" Lleu asked, casting a restless glance around the compound. "Where's the wine cellar? You monkish types all make your own wine, or so I hear. Let's go split a bottle."

"What wine we do make we use for medicinal purposes," said Rhys, adding, as Lleu rolled his eyes in disgust, "I seem to remember that you enjoyed hearing tales of battle and warriors when you were small. As a cleric of Kiri-Jolith, you are a trained warrior. Perhaps you would be interested in learning some of our methods of combat?"

Lleu's face brightened. "I have heard that you monks have an unorthodox style. You don't use weapons, just your hands. Is that true?"

"In a way," said Rhys. "Come with me to the fields. I will demonstrate."

He made a gesture to Atta, dismissing her from duty, sending her back to join the pack. Lleu joined him and they headed for the compound. Rhys heard the soft patter of feet behind him and turned his head.

Atta was following him. Again, she had disobeyed his command.

Rhys halted. He said no word, only frowned, so that she could see by his expression that he was not pleased. He made an emphatic gesture, pointing at the pen.

Atta held her ground. Her brown eyes met his. She knew she was disobeying him. She was asking him to trust her.

Rhys recalled another instance when he and Atta had been searching for a lost sheep in the midst of a thick fog. He had ordered her to go down hill, thinking the animal would take the easiest route. Atta had refused, stubbornly insisted on going up the hill. He had trusted her and she had been right.

Lleu was laughing. "Who's trained who?" he asked with a sly grin.

Rhys glanced at Lleu, recalled the Master's remark. *Lleu is his own shadow.* Rhys still did not understand, but perhaps Atta could see more clearly through the fog than he.

Rhys made the gesture that brought the dog to heel. He reached down and touched Atta lightly on the head, letting her know all was well.

She thrust her nose into his palm, then fell back a pace, trotting along quietly at his heel.

"You wear a sword, I see," Rhys said to his brother. "Are you skilled in its use?"

Lleu launched into an enthusiastic account of training with the Solamnic knights. Rhys watched his brother talk, observing him closely, only half-listening to his words, trying to see what the Master and Atta saw. He realized, as they walked, that he had already sensed something was wrong with Lleu. Otherwise, he would not have been taking him to the fields to show him the art of benevolent discipline. Rhys could have taken his brother to the practice yard, where the monks trained, but he'd chosen not to.

The practice yard was not a sacred place, except as all places are sacred to Majere, nor was it secret. Yet Rhys felt more at ease with his brother out in the open, away from the monastery. Shadow or not, Lleu was a disturbing influence, one that perhaps would be dissipated in the freshening breeze, beneath the clear sky.

"It is true that we do not use weapons made of steel," Rhys

explained, in answer to the earlier question. "We do use weapons, however, those that nature and Majere provide."

"Such as?" Lleu challenged.

"This, for example." Rhys indicated his emmide.

"A stick?" Lleu cast a scathing glance at the long, slender wooden shaft. "Against a sword? Not a chance in the Abyss!"

"Let us try," said Rhys. He gestured to the long sword his brother wore at his side. "Draw your weapon and come at me."

"This is hardly fair . . ." Lleu protested. He gestured to the two of them. "We're the same height, but I outweigh you. I'm bigger through the shoulders, more muscular. I might hurt you."

"I will risk it," said Rhys.

Dark-avised, slender, he did not carry any spare flesh. He was bone and sinew and muscle, whereas he could see the tell-tale signs left on his brother by his dissipated life. Lleu's muscle were flaccid, his face an unhealthy, pasty color.

"All right, then, brother." Lleu grinned. "But never say I didn't warn you—especially when I slice your arm off."

Relaxed and confident, Lleu drew his long sword and took up a warrior's stance, the blade in his right hand. Atta had been lying on the ground in the shade of a tree. Seeing the man about to attack her master, she growled and rose to her feet.

"Atta, sit," Rhys commanded. "All is well," he added in reassurance.

Atta sat, but she obviously wasn't happy, for she did not doze, as she would have done if he'd been out here practicing fighting technique with another monk. She remained awake, alert, her gaze fixed on her master. Rhys turned his attention back to his brother. Seeing Lleu holding the sword, Rhys recollected the dog bite. He looked with concern at his brother's hand, hoping it wasn't giving him too much pain.

Lleu had struck at Atta with his right hand, the hand holding the weapon. Rhys could see quite clearly the marks made by Atta's teeth. The dog had not bitten the man hard, just enough to make him think twice about accosting her. Still the wound looked deep, though it had not bled much, apparently, for there were no blood-stains on the skin or on the sleeve of his robe. Rhys could not see the wound well, for his brother's hand kept moving, but he noted that it had a peculiar appearance, more like a bruise than a slash, for the wound was a strange color of bluish purple.

Rhys was so puzzled by this that he kept staring at the wound, rather than watching his brother, and he was taken by surprise when Lleu made a sudden rush at him, bringing the sword down in a slashing motion, meant to cleave through helm or skull and finish the fight in a hurry.

Lleu threw all his strength in the blow. Rhys, holding the emmide in both hands, lifted the staff above his head to meet the sword. The blade struck the emmide. The staff held, though the impact of the shattering strike jarred Rhys's arms and sent vibrations resonating throughout his body. He could feel the force of the blow in his teeth. Rhys had misjudged his brother, apparently. Those muscles were not so flabby as they appeared.

Lleu's face twisted in a snarl. His arm muscles bulged, his eyes gleamed. He had expected his blade to chop the fragile stick into kindling and he was angry and frustrated that his attack had been thwarted. He lifted the sword over his head, intending to strike at the staff again.

Rhys lashed out with his bare feet; first one, then the other, striking Lleu in the solar plexus.

Lleu groaned and crumpled, dropping his sword.

Rhys stepped back, waiting for his brother to recover.

"You hit me with your feet!" Lleu gasped, slowly straightening, massaging his gut.

"I did," said Rhys.

"But . . ." Lleu floundered. "That's not fair!"

"Perhaps not in a knight's tourney," Rhys agreed politely. "But if I am fighting for my life, I will use every weapon at my disposal. Pick up your sword. Have another go at me if you like."

Lleu snatched up his blade and flung himself at Rhys. The sword's blade flashed red in the waning sunlight. Lleu thrust and stabbed, fighting with more force than skill, for he was a cleric, who had only lately come to swordsmanship, not a knight who had been in training most of his life.

Rhys was not in any danger. He could have ended the fight almost before it started with a jab to the gut, a thump to the head, or another well-placed kick. He did not want to hurt his brother, but he soon saw that Lleu was under no such constraint. Lleu was outraged, wounded in both pride and body. Patiently, Rhys parried Lleu's blows, which were becoming increasingly wild and desperate, and watched for his chance.

Ducking beneath one of Lleu's arcing slashes, Rhys thrust the emmide between Lleu's legs, tripping him. His brother came down hard on his backside. He held onto his sword, but a twitch of the emmide sent the weapon flying through the air to land in the grass near Atta.

Lleu cursed and scrambled to his feet.

"Atta, guard," Rhys commanded, pointing at the sword.

The dog jumped to her feet, positioned herself in front of the weapon.

Lleu's hand darted to his belt. Pulling a knife, he lunged at the dog.

Rhys seized hold of the hand gripping the knife and squeezed Lleu's forearm, pressing his fingers deep into the soft parts of the wrist.

Lleu's hand went suddenly limp. The knife fell to the ground.

Rhys bent down, picked up the knife, and thrust it into his own belt.

"The paralysis is only temporary," Rhys advised his brother, who was staring at his hand in dumb-founded astonishment. "The feeling will return to your fingers in a few minutes. This was a friendly contest. Or so I thought."

Lleu scowled, then looked ashamed. Nursing his useless hand, he backed off, away from the dog.

"I just meant to scare the flea-bitten cur, that's all. I wouldn't have hurt it."

"That much is true," Rhys said. "You would not have harmed Atta. You would now be lying on the ground with your throat torn out."

"I got carried away, that's all," Lleu continued. "I forgot where I was, thought I was on the field of battle." He added stiffly, "May I have my sword and my knife back? I promise I'll restrain myself."

Rhys handed over the knife. Retrieving the sword from the watchful dog, he gave it to his brother, who took hold of it with his left hand. Lleu eyed it, frowning. "I still think I should have cut through that stick of yours. Damn blade must be dull. I'll have it sharpened when I return home."

"There is nothing wrong with the blade," said Rhys.

"Bah! Of course, there is!" Lleu said, scoffing. "You can't tell me that twig stood up to a long sword!"

"This 'twig' has gone up against countless swords for five hundred years," Rhys replied. "See these tiny nicks?" He held up the stick for Lleu to examine. "Those were made by sword and mace and all manner of steel weapons. None broke it or even harmed it much."

Lleu looked put out. "You might have told me the blasted stick was magic. No wonder I lost!"

"I didn't know it was a question of winning or losing," Rhys returned mildly. "I thought I was demonstrating a fighting technique."

"Like I said, I got carried away," Lleu muttered. He wiggled his right hand. He could the move the fingers now and he thrust his sword back into the scabbard. "I think that's enough demonstrating for today. When do you eat around here? I'm starved."

"Soon," said Rhys.

"Good. I'll go wash up. I'll see you at supper." Lleu turned away, then thought of something else and turned back. "I heard that you monks live on nothing but grass and berries. That's not true, I hope?"

"You will have a good meal," Rhys assured him.

"I'll hold you to that!" Lleu waved at him and walked off. Apparently all was forgotten, forgiven.

Lleu even paused to apologize to Atta, scratch her on the head. The dog submitted to his touch, but only after a nod from Rhys, and she shook herself all over the moment Lleu departed, as though to remove any trace of him. Trotting over to Rhys, she pressed her muzzle against his leg and looked up at him with her expressive brown eyes.

"What is it, girl?" Rhys asked, frustrated. He rubbed her behind the ears. "What have you got against him, besides the fact that he is young and feckless and thinks far too well of himself? I wish you could let me know what you are thinking. Still, there is a reason the gods made animals dumb."

Rhys's troubled gaze followed the figure of his brother, strolling over the meadow. "We could not bear to hear the truths you might tell us."

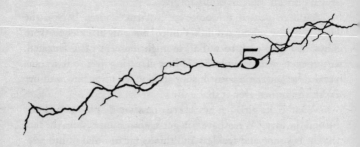

Rhys did not immediately return to the monastery. He and Atta walked to the stream that provided water for both man and beast and sat down on the grass beneath the willow trees. Atta rolled over on her side and went to sleep, worn out from the rigors of a day spent guarding first sheep and then her master. Sitting cross-legged on the bank, Rhys closed his eyes and gave himself to the god, Majere. The sighs of the wind through the willow branches and the soft evening song of the finches mingled with the chuckling laughter of the stream to soothe away worried speculation about his brother's odd behavior.

Despite the fact that he had not lectured his brother and instantly turned his life around, as his father had hoped would happen, Rhys did not feel he had failed. The monks of Majere do not view life in terms of success and failure. One does not fail at a task. One merely does not succeed. And since one is always striving for success, so long as one continues striving, one can never truly fail.

Nor did Rhys resent his parents thrusting this responsibility upon him—a son they had likely given no thought to for fifteen years. He could see they were desperate. He did feel badly in that he was going to have to tell them there was nothing he could do. He would speak to the Master first, of course, but Rhys knew what the elderly monk would tell him. Lleu was an adult. He had chosen his own path to walk. He might be persuaded through wise counsel and example, but if that didn't change him, no one had the right to bar his way or shove him off the path or force him to shift direction, even if that path was self-destructive. Lleu had to make the choice to change, otherwise he would soon be back on the same road. So Majere taught, and so the monks believed.

The bell rang, announcing the supper hour. Rhys did not move. Monks were required to be present at breakfast, where any business relating to the monastery was discussed. The supper hour was informal and those who preferred to continue to meditate or work were permitted to do so. Rhys knew he should attend, but he was loathe to leave his peaceful solitude.

His brother and parents would be there and they would expect him to sit with them. The meeting would be an uncomfortable one. They would want to talk to him about his brother, but they would feel reluctant to discuss Lleu in the presence of the other monks. And so their conversation would be limited to family matters: his father's business concerns, his mother's news of the birth of her latest grandchild. Since Rhys knew nothing about any of this, and truthfully did not care, he would have nothing to contribute. They would not be particularly interested in his life. Talk would falter and eventually die off into strained silence.

"I am better employed here," Rhys said to himself.

Rhys remained with his god, the two of them joined, the mind of the human freeing itself from the body to touch the mind of the deity, a touch the Master likened to the tiny, flailing hand of a newborn babe finding and tightly clutching at one finger of the enormous hand of his father. Rhys presented his concerns about Lleu to Majere, allowing his many questions to sift through his mind and that of the god, hoping to find answers, hoping to find some way to help.

He sank so deeply into his meditative state that he lost all track of time. Gradually, a nagging twinge, like the beginnings of a toothache, became annoying enough that he was forced to pay attention to it. Feeling true reluctance and sadness at being forced to return to the world of men, he parted from the god. He opened his eyes, sensing that something was wrong.

At first, he could not think what. Everything seemed right enough. The sun had set, darkness had fallen. Atta slept peacefully on the grass. No barking dogs, no alarm from sheep fold or barn, no smell of smoke that would have indicated a fire. Yet something was wrong.

Rhys jumped to his feet, his sudden movement startling Atta, who flopped over onto her belly, ears pricked, eyes wide.

Then Rhys knew. The bell for the weapons practice had not rung.

Rhys doubted himself a moment. His inner clock might well have been thrown off by his deep meditative state. Yet a glance at the position of the moon and the stars confirmed his reckoning. In all the fifteen years he'd lived at the monastery and in all the years the monastery had been in existence, the bell for practice had rung nightly at the same hour without fail.

Fear gripped Rhys. Routine was an important part of the discipline practiced by the monks. A break in routine might be commonplace anywhere else. A break in the monk's routine was shattering, catastrophic. Rhys picked up his emmide and he and Atta returned to the monastery at a run. He had well-developed night vision from having to practice with his weapons in pitch darkness during the winter months, and he knew every inch of ground. He could have—and once did—find his way back home through a dense fog in the blackest night. This evening, Solinari's silver light brightened the dark sky and the stars added their own pale radiance. He could see the way clearly.

He almost ordered Atta back to the sheep fold. He decided, as the command was on his lips, to keep her with him, at least until he knew what was wrong.

He arrived back at the monastery grounds to find all peaceful and quiet—a bad sign. The monks should have been in the compound, either listening to one of the masters as he demonstrated a technique or practicing with their partners. He should be hearing the sound of thwacks from emmide and quarter staff, the grunts of exertion, the thuds as one partner felled another. And all the time, the voices of the masters chiding, correcting, praising.

Rhys looked swiftly about. Yellow light streamed from the windows of the dining hall where the monks took their meals. That in itself was all wrong. At this time of the night, the lights were doused, the tables scrubbed down, wooden trenchers and crockery, kettles and pans cleaned and ready for tomorrow's breakfast. Rhys headed in that direction, hoping for some logical explanation. The thought came to him that the Master might be talking to his family and that he might have kept the other monks from their practice because he required their assistance. Such an occurrence was completely out of the norm, but not out of the realm of possibility.

The main door led to the monastery's common room. Rhys saw through the windows that it was dark, as it would be this time of night. He shoved open the door and was about to enter when Atta made a strange sound—a kind of frightened whimper. Rhys looked down at her, concerned. The two had worked together for five years and he'd never heard her make that sound. She stared into the darkened room. Her body shivered and she whimpered again.

Something terrible lay ahead. Not outlaws or marauders or thieves. Not a bear bumbling into the building, as had once happened. The dog would know how to react to that. This was something she didn't understand, and it was terrifying.

He took a slow and cautious step inside.

All was quiet. No voice rose and fell in wise counsel. No voices could be heard at all. A foul smell, as of a sick room, hung in the air.

Rhys's instinct was to rush in to see what had happened. Discipline and training overrode this impulse. He had no way of knowing what lay ahead. He gestured to Atta to "walk up" and she slowed her pace, dropped into a crouch, and crept along at his side. Rhys gripped his emmide and moved stealthily into the common room, his bare feet making no sound.

The common room opened into the dining hall. Lights shone from within and, although he could see nothing except the end of a bench, he could hear a faint sound, an odd sound, a kind of muttering mumble. He could not make out words, if words there were.

He eased ahead cautiously, listening and keeping watch on the room ahead. Atta could be trusted to warn him if someone or some thing was about to leap at him from the darkness. He had no sense of anything lurking in this room, however. Danger lay in the light, it seemed, not in the shadows. The sickening smell grew stronger.

He reached the dining hall. The stench caused him to gag and he put his hand over his nose and mouth. The mumbling voice was louder now, but it was so low that he could still not make out what it was saying, nor could he identify the person speaking. Standing just inside the entryway, so that he could see without being seen, Rhys looked into the dining hall.

He stood, appalled.

Eighteen monks lived in the monastery. Their numbers had been greater in times past, upwards of forty in the years following the War of the Lance. The monastery's population had dwindled during the Fifth Age, when there had been only five, and was only just now beginning to recover. The monks dined in brotherly companionship at a large rectangular table made of a long wooden plank arranged on wooden trestles. The monks sat on wooden benches, nine on either side.

This day, there were only seventeen monks, for Rhys had chosen to skip dinner. There had been the guests, however—Rhys's parents and his brother. They would sit with the monks at the table, share their simple repast. Twenty people, all told.

Of those twenty, nineteen were lying dead.

Rhys stared at the terrible scene in shock, his discipline shattered all to pieces, his reason scattered like leaves in a gale. He looked about in bewilderment, unable to take in the horror, unable to comprehend what had happened.

Though he could tell after one despairing glance that all were dead, he ran to the Master and knelt down beside him, placing his hand on the man's neck in a desperate hope that the faint beat of life might yet remain.

He had only to look at the elderly monk's twisted body, the frightful contortion of the facial muscles, the swollen tongue and the purged contents of his stomach to know that the Master was dead and that he had died in agony.

All the monks had died the same horrible death. Some, it seemed, had risen the moment they felt the first symptoms and tried to reach the door. Others lay near the bench where they had been seated. The bodies of all the monks were hideously contorted. The floor was foul and slimy with vomit. That and the swollen tongues revealed the cause of their death——they had been poisoned.

Rhys's parents were dead, as well. His mother lay on her back. The expression frozen on her dead face was one of sudden, horrendous knowledge. His father lay on his stomach, one arm thrust out, as though in his final moments, he had tried to seize hold of someone.

His son. His youngest son.

Lleu was alive, and to all appearances, hale and healthy. His was the voice Rhys had heard mumbling and muttering.

"Lleu!" Rhys said, his mouth dry, his throat so tight that he did not recognize the sound of his own voice.

Hearing his name, Lleu ceased to mumble. He turned to face his brother.

"You didn't come to dinner," said Lleu.

He eased himself up off the bench, stood up. His voice was

calm. He might have been in his own kitchen, chatting with a friend. Not standing in the midst of mayhem.

He's mad, Rhys thought. The horror has driven him insane.

Yet, for all that, Lleu didn't have the look of madness.

"I didn't feel like eating," said Rhys. He needed to remain calm, try to find out what was going on.

Lleu lifted a bowl of soup and held it out to his brother. "You must be hungry. You had better have some dinner."

Rhys's heart constricted. He knew in that moment what had happened, just as his mother and father had known before they died. But the why of it was as far beyond Rhys's reach as the dark face of Nuitari. Behind him, he heard Atta growl, and he put out his hand in a warding gesture, commanding her to stay where she was.

Rhys kept his gaze fixed on his brother. Lleu's robes were in disarray; he had scratches on his face and chest. Perhaps his father had managed to lay hands on his murderous son before death took him.

Lleu's chest was bare and there was a curious mark on it—the imprint of a woman's lips branded into his flesh. Rhys noted the mark as being strange, and that was all. Horror drove it out of his mind, and he forgot about it.

"You did this," said Rhys, his voice cracking. He gestured at the dead.

Lleu glanced around at the bodies, turned his gaze back to his brother. Lleu shrugged, as if to say, "Yes. So what?"

"And now you want to poison me." Rhys's hand clasped his staff so tightly that his fingers began to cramp. He forced himself to relax his grip.

Lleu considered the matter. "It's not so much a question of 'want' as 'need', brother."

"You need to poison me." Rhys worked to keep his tone cool and level. He knew now that his brother was not insane, that there was some sort of terrible rationale behind the killings. "Why? Why have you done this?"

"He would have stopped me," said Lleu. He turned his gaze to the body of the Master. "The old man there. He knew the truth. I saw it in his eyes."

Lleu looked back at Rhys. "I saw it in your eyes. All of you were going to try to stop me."

"Stop you from doing what, Lleu?" Rhys demanded.

"From bringing disciples to my god," Lleu answered.

"Kiri-Jolith?" Rhys asked in shocked disbelief.

"Not that prattling killjoy," Lleu scoffed. An expression of awe softened his face. His voice was reverent. "My lord Chemosh."

"You are a follower of the God of Death."

"I am, brother," said Lleu. He tossed the bowl of soup back down on the table and rose from the bench. "You can be one of his followers, as well."

Lleu opened his arms. "Embrace me, brother. Embrace me and embrace endless life, endless youth, endless pleasure."

"You have been deceived, Lleu."

Rhys shifted his feet, clasped his staff in both hands, and eased himself into a martial stance. Lleu was not wearing his sword; the monks would have forbade him from bringing a sword into the monastery. He was in the throes of religious ecstasy, however, and that made him dangerous.

"Chemosh does not want you to have any of that. He seeks only your destruction."

"On the contrary, I already have everything I was promised," said Lleu lightly. "Nothing can harm me."

Turning back to the table, he lifted up a soup bowl and held it for Rhys to see. "That's mine. Empty. I ate the water hemlock as did the rest of these poor fools. I had to eat it, of course, otherwise they might have been suspicious. They are dead. And I am not."

This could have been a lie, bravado, but Rhys guessed from his brother's tone and his expression that it wasn't. Lleu had spoken the truth. He'd ingested the poison and was unscathed. Rhys thought suddenly of the dog bite, the absence of blood.

Lleu tossed the bowl carelessly back onto the table. "My life is one of pleasure and ease. I know neither hunger nor thirst. Chemosh provides all. I want for nothing. You can know the same life, brother."

"I don't want that life," said Rhys. "If 'life' is what you call it."

"Then I guess you had better die," said Lleu in nonchalant tones. "Either way, Chemosh will have you. The spirits of all those who die by violence come to him."

"I have no fear of death. My soul will go to my god," Rhys replied.

"Majere?" Lleu chuckled. "He won't care. He's off somewhere watching a caterpillar crawl up a blade of grass." Lleu's tone changed, became menacing. "Majere has neither the will nor the power to stop Chemosh. Just as this old man lacked the power to stop me."

Rhys looked about at the dead, looked at the hideously contorted face of the Master, and Rhys felt a sudden stirring of rage. Lleu was right. Majere could have done something. He should have done something to prevent this. His monks had dedicated their lives to him. They had worked and sacrificed. In their hour of need, the god abandoned them. They had cried to him in their death throes, and he had turned a deaf ear.

Majere's monks were commanded to take no sides in any conflict. Perhaps the god himself was refusing to take sides in this one. Perhaps the souls of his beloved Master and his brethren were having to fight alone against the Lord of Death.

Anger twisted inside Rhys, hot and clenching and bitter-tasting. Anger at the god, anger at himself.

"I should have been here. I could have stopped this."

Rhys had pleaded as an excuse that he was with the god, but in truth, his own selfish longing for peace and quiet had kept him from being where he was needed. Because both he and Majere had failed those who put their faith in them, nineteen people were dead.

He wrestled with himself, berating himself, and at the same time, fought against the rage that made his hands itch to seize hold of his murderous brother and strangle him. Rhys was so involved in his internal struggle that he took his eyes off Lleu.

His brother was quick to take advantage. Seizing the heavy crockery bowl, he hurled it with all his might.

The bowl struck Rhys between the eyes. Pain burst in his skull, red-hot pain fringed with yellow-tinged fire, so that he couldn't think. Blood poured down his face, into his eyes, blinding him. He staggered, clutched at the table to remain standing. He had the dizzying impression of Lleu lunging for him and another impression of a black and white body hurtling past him. Rhys tasted blood in his mouth. He was falling and he stretched out his hand to stop his fall, reached out his hand to the Master . . .

A monk in orange robes stood before Rhys. The monk's face was familiar to him, though he'd never before seen it. The monk had a resemblance to the Master, and at the same time to all the other brethren of the monastery. The monk's eyes were calm and tranquil, his demeanor mild.

Rhys knew him.

"Majere . . ." Rhys whispered, awed.

The god regarded him steadily, not answering.

"Majere!" Rhys faltered. "I need your council. Tell me what I must do."

"You know what you must do, Rhys," said the god calmly. "First you must bury the dead and then you must cleanse this room of death, so that all is clean in my sight. On the morrow, you will rise with the morning sun and make your prayers to me, as usual. Then you must water the livestock and turn the cows and horses out to pasture and take the sheep to the fields. Then weed the garden . . ."

"Pray to you, Master? Pray for what? All of them died and you did nothing!"

"Pray for what you always pray for, Rhys," said the god. "Perfection of the body and the mind. Peace and tranquility and serenity . . ."

"As I bury the dead bodies of my brethren and my parents," Rhys returned angrily, "I pray to you for perfection!"

"And to accept with patience and understanding the ways of your god."

"I don't accept it!" Rhys retorted, his rage and anguish knotted inside him. "I will not accept it. Chemosh has done this. He must be stopped!"

"Others will deal with Chemosh," said Majere imperturbably. "The Lord of Death is not your concern. Look inside yourself, Rhys, and seek the darkness within your own soul. Bring that to the light before you try to wrestle with the darkness of others."

"And what of Lleu? He must be brought to justice—"

"Lleu speaks truly when he claims that Chemosh has made him invincible. You can do nothing to stop him, Rhys. Let him go."

"And so you would have me skulk here, safe inside these walls, tending to sheep and mucking out the barn while Lleu goes forth to commit more murders in the name of the Lord of Death? No, Master," said Rhys grimly. "I will not turn away and let others take on what is my responsibility."

"You have been with me fifteen years, Rhys," said Majere. "Every day, murder and worse has been done in this world. Did you seek to stop any of them? Did you search for justice for these other victims?"

"No," said Rhys. "Perhaps I should have."

"Look inside your heart, Rhys," said the god. "Is what you seek justice or vengeance?"

"I seek answers from you!" Rhys cried. "Why didn't you protect your chosen from my brother? Why did you forsake my them? Why am I alive and they are not?"

"I have my reasons, Rhys, and I do not need to share those reasons with you. Faith in me means that you accept what is."

"I cannot," said Rhys, glowering.

"Then I cannot help you," said the god.

Rhys was silent, his inward battle raging. "So be it," he said abruptly and turned away.

6

Rhys woke from a profoundly disturbing dream in which he denied his god to throbbing pain and flickering light and a rough, wet tongue licking his forehead. He opened his eyes. Atta stood over him, whining and licking his wound. He gently pushed the dog away and tried to sit up. Rhys's stomach heaved, and he was sick. He lay back down with a groan. The monks' rigorous practice session often resulted in injuries. Learning how to treat such injuries and how to bear pain was considered an important part of their training. Rhys recognized the symptoms of a cracked skull. The pain was acute and he longed to give into it, to sink back into the darkness, where he would find relief. Victims who did that, however, often did not ever wake up. Rhys might not have awakened, if it hadn't been for Atta.

He fondled her ears, mumbled something unintelligible, and was sick again. His head cleared a little and a wave of bitter memory washed over him, along with the realization of his own danger.

He sat up swiftly, gritting his teeth against the sharp pain, and looked for his brother.

The room was dark, too dark to see. Most of the thick beeswax candles had gone out. Only two remained burning and their flames wavered in the melting wax.

"I've been unconscious for hours," he murmured dazedly. "And where is Lleu?"

Blinking through the pain, trying to bring his eyes into focus, he cast a swift glance around the room but saw no sign of his brother.

Atta whined, and Rhys petted her. He tried to recall what had happened, but the last thing he remembered was his brother's charge against Majere: *He has neither the will nor the power to stop Chemosh.*

One of the candles sputtered and went out with a sizzle. Only one tiny flame remained burning. He fondled the dog's silky ears and he had no need to ask why Lleu had not murdered him while he was unconscious.

Rhys did not have to look far for his savior. Atta lay with her head in his lap, regarding him anxiously with her dark brown eyes.

Rhys had seen Atta stand guard on the sheep during an attack on the flock by a mountain lion, placing her body between those of the sheep and the lion, facing it fearlessly, brown eyes meeting and holding the cat's yellow-eyed gaze until it turned and slunk away.

He let his eyes close drowsily, petting Atta and imagining her standing over her unconscious master, glaring balefully at Lleu, her lip curled to let him see the sharp teeth that might soon be sinking into his flesh.

Lleu might be invincible, as he claimed, but he could still feel pain. The yelp he'd given when Atta bit him had been real enough. And he could still picture quite vividly what it would feel like to have those sharp teeth sinking into his throat.

Lleu had backed down and run off. Run away . . . run away home . . .

Atta barked and leapt to her feet, jolting Rhys awake.

"What's the matter?" he asked, sitting up, tense and afraid.

Atta barked again and he heard another bark, distant, coming from the sheep pen. The bark was uneasy, but it was not a warning. The other dogs could sense something was wrong. Atta kept barking and Rhys wondered grimly what she was telling them, how she would describe this horror that man had perpetrated on man.

He woke again to find that she was barking at him.

"You're right, girl. I can't do this," he muttered. "Can't sleep. Have to stay awake."

He forced himself to stand, using the bench to pull himself up. He found his emmide lying on the floor beside him, just before the flame of the final candle drowned in its own wax and went out, leaving him in moonlit darkness, surrounded by the dead.

The throbbing ache in his head made thinking difficult. He focused on the pain, and he began to mold it and shape it and press it, compact it into a ball that became smaller and smaller the more he worked on it. Then he took the small ball of pain and placed it inside a cupboard in his mind and shut the door upon it. Known as Ball of Clay, this was one of many techniques developed by the monks to deal with pain.

"Majere," he began the ritual chant without thinking. "I send my thoughts upward among the clouds—"

He stopped. The words meant nothing. They were empty, held no meaning. He looked into his heart where the god had always been and could not find him. What was there was ugly and hideous. Rhys gazed inside himself a long time. The ugliness remained, a blot on perfection.

"So be it," he said sadly.

Leaning on his staff for support, he staggered toward the door. Atta padded along beside him.

First, he needed to determine what had become of Lleu. He thought it possible that his brother was lurking somewhere around the monastery, waiting in ambush to offer up his final victim to Chemosh. Logic dictated Rhys search the stables, to see if horse or wagon was missing. He kept close watch as he went, peering intently into every shadow, pausing to listen for sounds of footsteps. He looked often at Atta. She was tense because she felt her master's tension and watchful because he was watchful. She gave no sign that anything was amiss, however.

Rhys went first to the barn, where the monks kept a few cows and the plow horses. The wagon his parents had driven was still here, parked outside. He entered the barn cautiously, his staff raised, more than half-expecting Lleu to attack him from the darkness.

He saw nothing, heard nothing. Atta buried her nose in the straw spread over the floor, but that was probably because she was not usually allowed in the barn and she was intrigued by the smells. His father's draft horses were inside their stalls. The horse that Lleu had ridden was not.

Lleu was gone, then. Gone back to his home. Gone to some other city or village or lonely farm house. Gone to create more converts of Chemosh.

Rhys stood in the barn, listening to the heavy breathing of the slumbering animals, the rustling of bats in the rafters, the hoot of an owl. He heard the night sounds and he heard, far louder, the sounds he would never hear again—the thwack of his emmide against the staff of a brother, the animated discussions in the warming room in winter, the quiet murmur of voices raised in prayer, the ringing of the bell that had divided up his day and marked out his life in long, neat furrows that had, only a few hours before, stretched into the future until Majere took his soul onto the next stage of its journey.

The furrows were jagged now and crisscrossed, one over the other in confusion, leading nowhere.

He had lost everything. He had nothing left except a duty. A duty to himself and his murdered parents and his brethren. A duty to the world that he had shunned for fifteen years and that had now come down on him with a vengeance.

"Vengeance," he repeated softly, seeing again the ugliness inside him.

Find Lleu.

Rhys left the barn, and headed back to the monastery. His head pounded. He was dizzy and sick to his stomach, and he was having trouble focusing his eyes. He dared not lie down, as he longed to do. He had to remain awake. To keep himself awake, he would keep busy and there was work to do.

Grim work. Burying the dead.

"You need help, Brother," said a voice at his shoulder.

Atta leapt straight up at the sound. Body twisting in mid-air, she landed on her feet, hackles raised, teeth bared in a snarl.

Rhys raised his emmide and whipped around to see who had spoken.

A woman stood behind him. In looks and in dress, she was extraordinary. Her hair was pale as sea foam and in constant motion, as was the green gown that rippled over her body and flowed down around her feet. She was beautiful, calm and serene as the monastery stream in midsummer, yet there was that in her gray-green eyes that told of raging floods and black ice.

She was all in darkness, yet he saw her clearly by her own inner radiance that seemed to say, "I have no need for the light of moon or stars. I am my own light, my own darkness, as I choose."

He was in the presence of a goddess and he knew, from the strands of seashells she wore in her unkempt hair, which one.

"I need no help, I thank you, Mistress of the Sea," Rhys said, thinking that it was strange that he should be conversing with a goddess as calmly he might have spoken to one of the village milkmaids.

Looking down at the broken pieces of his world in his hands, he thought suddenly that it was not so strange after all.

"I can bury my dead myself."

"I'm not talking about that," said Zeboim irritably. "I am talking about Chemosh."

Rhys knew then why she had come. He just did not know how he was to answer.

"Chemosh holds your brother in thrall," continued the goddess.

"One of the Death God's High Priestesses, a woman named Mina, cast a powerful spell on your brother."

"What kind of spell?" Rhys asked.

"I—" Zeboim paused, seeming to find it difficult to go on. The admission came out with a wrench. "I don't know," she said sullenly. "I can't find out. Whatever Chemosh is doing, he is taking great care to conceal it from the other gods. You could find out, monk; you being mortal."

"And how would I discover Chemosh's secrets better than the gods?" Rhys demanded. He put his hand to his head. The pain was seeping out of the cupboard.

"Because you are a mite, a flea, a gnat. One among millions. You can blend in with the crowd. Go here. Go there. Ask questions. The god will never notice you."

"It seems as though *you* need my help, Mistress," said Rhys wearily. "Not the other way around. Atta, come." He turned aside, resumed his walk.

The goddess was there in front of him. "If you must know, monk, I've lost her. I want you to help me find her."

Rhys stared, perplexed. His head ached so that he could scarcely think. "Her? What her?"

"Mina, of course," said Zeboim, exasperated. "The priestess who enthralled your wretch of a brother. I told you about her. Pay attention to me. Find her and you find answers."

"Thank you for the information, Mistress," said Rhys. "And now I must bury my dead."

Zeboim tilted back her head, regarded him from beneath her long lashes. A smile touched her lips. "You don't even know who this Mina is, do you, monk?"

Rhys did not answer. Turning on his heel, he left her.

"And what do you know of the undead?" Zeboim pursued him, talking relentlessly. "Of Chemosh? He is strong and powerful and dangerous. And you have no god to guide you, protect you. You are all alone. If you agreed to work for me, I can be very generous . . ."

Rhys halted. Atta, cringing, crept behind his legs.

"What is you want, Mistress?"

"Your faith, your love, your service," said Zeboim, her voice soft and low. "And get rid of the dog," she added harshly. "I don't like dogs."

Rhys had a sudden vision of Majere standing before him, regarding him with an expression that was grieving, and at the same time, understanding. Majere said no word to Rhys. The path was his to walk. The choice his to make.

Rhys reached down to touch Atta's head. "I keep the dog."

The goddess's gray eyes flashed dangerously. "Who are you to bargain with me, maggot of a monk?"

"You know the answer to that apparently, Mistress," Rhys returned tiredly "It was you who came to me. I will serve you," he added, seeing her swell with rage, like the boiling black clouds of a summer storm, "so long as your interests run the same course as my own."

"Mine do, I assure you," said Zeboim.

She placed her hands on his face and kissed him, long and lingering, on the lips.

Rhys did not flinch, though her lips stung like salt water in a fresh wound. He did not return the kiss.

Zeboim shoved him away.

"Keep the mutt, then," she said crossly. "Now, the first thing you must do is locate Mina. I want— Where are you going, monk? The highway lies in that direction."

Rhys had resumed his trek back to the monastery. "I told you. I must first bury my dead."

"You will not!" Zeboim flared. "There is no time for such foolishness. You must start upon your quest immediately!"

Rhys kept walking.

A bolt of lightning streaked down from the cloudless heavens, blinding Rhys, striking so near him that it sizzled in his blood, raised the hair on his head and arms. An enormous thunder clap exploded next to him, deafening him. The ground shook and he fell to his knees. Chunks of debris rained down around them. Atta yelped and whimpered.

Zeboim pointed to a huge crater.

"There is a hole, monk. Bury your dead."

She turned from him with a rustle of wind and a flurry of rain and was gone.

"What I have done, Atta?" Rhys groaned, pulling himself up from the ground.

By the confused look in her eyes, the dog seemed to be asking him the same question.

Rhys buried the dead in the grave provided by the goddess. He worked through the night, composing the bodies to some semblance of peace. Carrying them, one by one, from the dining hall to the gravesite. Laying them in the moist, soft earth. When all were laid to rest, he took the shovel and began to fill in the grave with dirt. The pain in his head had eased with the goddess's kiss, a blessing he had not even noticed she had granted him until after she was gone.

He was weary in body and spirit, however. No blessing could ease that. Perhaps this weariness accounted for the impression that came to him that his body was one of those in the grave. The clods were falling on top of him. He was being buried underneath them.

Night was nearly over by the time he tossed the last shovelful of dirt onto the mass grave. He said no prayers. He had forsaken Majere and he doubted that Zeboim would be interested.

He needed sleep.

Rhys turned and, summoning Atta, he went to his cell, threw himself onto his mattress, and slept.

He woke suddenly, not to the tolling of the bell, but to its aching absence.

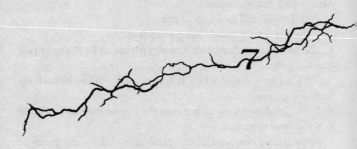

*O*nce the dead were laid to rest, Rhys had to think about the living. He could not start his journey by abandoning the livestock, leaving them to starve or fall prey to wild beasts. Their care was his responsibility now. He and Atta and the rest of the herd dogs drove the sheep and the cattle thirty miles to the nearest village, traveling the entire distance through a torrential downpour that made mud soup of the roads. Zeboim was obviously not pleased at the delay.

The last time he had walked this road was fifteen years ago, when he'd been on his way to the monastery. He had not been on it since. He had not left the monastery in fifteen years. He looked at the world to which he was returning and found it wet, sodden, gray, and not much changed. Trees were taller. Hedges were thicker. The road appeared to be more traveled than it had been, which meant that the village must be prospering. He passed a few people on the road, but they were full of their own concerns and said nothing to his greeting, although several cursed at him and his flock for blocking their way, holding them up. Rhys remembered why he'd left the world and he was sorry to be going back. Sorry, but determined.

The villagers gratefully accepted the monk's gift, although they were somewhat alarmed when Rhys told them that he was doing this because the other monks had died of disease, leaving him the sole survivor. He assured the people that there was no danger of contagion. That and the well-fed milk cows and the healthy sheep went far to persuade the villagers that they could safely accept this unlooked-for wealth.

Rhys lingered on the outskirts of the village to watch the villagers herd the sheep to the meadows. He'd given them the herd dogs as well. Atta's brothers and sisters ranged behind, keeping the flock together, guiding them up the hillside.

Atta sat at Rhys's side, watching with doleful eyes the pack into which she'd been born going off and leaving her behind. She kept looking questioningly at Rhys, waiting for him to give the command for her to rush off to join them. Rhys stroked her ears, bid her quietly, "Stay."

He had never thought of giving her up, not even at the command of the goddess. Atta had defended him when he could not defend himself. She had risked her life to protect his. There was a bond between them that he could not bear to break. He needed at least one companion in whom he could put his trust. Trusting Zeboim was out of the question.

Rhys returned to the monastery. He scrubbed the dining hall clean of all the terrible traces of the murders. This done, he scoured the kitchen. He was not certain if the poison would wash away or not and decided not to chance it. He smashed all the crockery. He hauled the pots and kettles to the stream, weighted them down with rocks and sank them in the deepest part of the water. He left no trace behind.

That final, terrible task done, he made a last tour of the buildings that were horribly, achingly silent. The monks' most valued possessions were their books, and these he locked away in a safe place until a representative from the Prophet of Majere could be found who would come to take over. Rhys would stop at the first temple of Majere to send a message to the prophet. In the meantime, he trusted that the god would watch over his own.

Rhys had no personal possessions, other than his emmide that had been a gift from the Master seven years ago. The emmide was a holy artifact, made of the wood of a holly tree, said to be sacred to Majere. Since Rhys had turned his back on the god, he did not feel right about keeping the god's gift. He left the emmide in the library with the books, propping it up against the wall. As he walked away, he felt as if he were leaving behind one of his arms.

He went to his bed, but sleep would not come to him this night, despite the fact that he was bone-tired. No ghosts of his murdered brethren haunted him. They were in his heart, however. He saw their faces before him, heard their voices. He heard, too, the impatient goddess pounding her hand on the roof. The rain fell steadily all night.

He had planned to set out before daylight, but since he couldn't sleep, he might as well start walking. He packed bread and dried meat and apples for himself and Atta in a leather scrip, slung the leather scrip over his shoulder, and then whistled for Atta.

When she did not come, he went in search of her, thinking he knew where to look.

He found her lying beside the empty sheep pen, her eyes sad, wondering.

"I know how you feel, girl," said Rhys.

He whistled again and she rose to her feet and came obediently after him.

He did not look back.

The rain ceased the moment they were on the road. A low ground fog blanketed the valley. The rising sun was an eerie red blur, its light strained through the gray mist as through a cheese cloth. Moisture dripped from the tree leaves to land with a dull plopping sound on the wet ground. All other sound was hushed and muted.

Rhys had much to think about as he walked. He gave Atta her freedom to roam, an unusual treat for the hard-working dog. She could dash into the brush in search of rabbits, bark at squirrels, frisk down the road ahead of him, come racing back with tongue lolling, her eyes bright. She did not do any of that today but trotted behind him, head down, tail drooping. He hoped she would perk up, once they were away from her familiar surroundings, away from the lingering scent of sheep and the other dogs.

When he had taken the livestock to the village he had questioned the inhabitants, asking if they had seen a cleric of Kiri-Jolith pass through recently. None of them had. Rhys did not find that surprising. The village lay north and east of the monastery, whereas the city of Staughton—Lleu's home—was located to the south. There was no reason why Lleu should not return to Staughton. He could always concoct some plausible tale to explain his parents' disappearance. Traveling these days was dangerous, particularly in Abanasinia, where lawless men roamed the countryside. Lleu had only to invent a tale of an attack by robbers, in which his parents had been killed and he himself wounded, and he would be believed.

Rhys walked along, so absorbed in his thoughts that he did not miss Atta until a cessrat skittered across his path and no dog bounded after it. He halted, called and whistled, but Atta did not appear. The thought came to him that she had gone back to her pack. That was only natural. She had made her choice, as he had made his. He had to see for himself, however, had to make certain she was safe. Turning around, his heart heavy, he almost stumbled over the goddess, who, with characteristic impetuosity, appeared with no warning to stand before him, blocking his path.

"Where are you going?" she demanded.

"I am going first to look for my dog, Mistress," he said, "and then to Staughton to search for my brother."

"Forget the dog. And forget your brother," Zeboim commanded imperiously. "I want you to seek out Mina."

"Mistress—"

"Majesty, to you, monk," Zeboim said in haughty tones.

"I am no longer a monk, Majesty."

"Yes, you are. You will be my monk. Majere can have monks. Why can't I? Of course, you will have to wear different colored robes. My monks shall wear sea-green. Now, Monk of Zeboim, what was it you were about to say?"

Rhys watched his robes change from the sacred orange of Majere to a green he presumed was reminiscent of the ocean. He had never seen the sea, so he could not judge whether it was or it wasn't. He counseled patience, then drew in a deep breath before he spoke.

"As you pointed out yesterday, I do not even know who this Mina is. I don't know anything about her. I do know my brother, however—"

"She was commander of the Dark Knights during the War of Souls. Even you secluded monks must have heard of the War of Souls," Zeboim said, seeing Rhys's blank expression.

Rhys shook his head. The monks had heard tales from travelers about a War of Souls, but they'd paid scant attention. Wars between the living were none of their concern. Neither were wars between the living and the dead.

Zeboim rolled her eyes at his ignorance. "When my honored mother, Takhisis, stole away the world, she dredged up an orphan named Mina and made her a disciple. Mina went about spreading the word of this One God, performing showy miracles, killing dragons, and leading an army of ghosts. Thus she managed to convince foolish mortals that she knew what she was talking about."

"So Mina is a disciple of Takhisis," Rhys said.

"Was." Zeboim corrected his verb tense. "When Mommy met her just reward for her treachery, Mina mourned her goddess and carried off the body. She was, by all accounts, prepared to end her miserable life, but Chemosh decided he could make use of her. He seduced her and she has now transferred her allegiance to him. Mina is the one who made your poor sap of a brother into a murderer. She's the one you must find. She is mortal and therefore the weak link in Chemosh's chain of command. Stop her and you stop him. I admit, it won't be easy," Zeboim conceded, adding grudgingly. "The chit has a certain charming way about her."

"And where do I find this Mina?" Rhys asked.

"If I knew that," Zeboim flared, "do you think I would bother with you? I would deal with her myself. Chemosh cloaks her in a darkness that not even my eyes can penetrate."

"What about other eyes? The other gods? Your father, Sargonnas—"

"That numb-skulled cow! He is too absorbed in his own concerns, as are all the others. None of the gods has the wit to see that Chemosh has developed a dangerous ambition. He means to seize my mother's crown. He plans to upset the balance and plunge Krynn into war again. I'm the only one who realizes this," Zeboim said loftily. "The only one with the courage to challenge him."

Rhys quirked an eyebrow. The idea of the cruel and calculating Zeboim as the champion of the innocent was a remarkable one. Rhys guessed uneasily there was more to it than that. This smacked of a personal vendetta between Zeboim and Chemosh. He was going to get caught in the middle, between the anvil of one and the hammer of the other. And he found it difficult to accept the fact that the gods of light were blind to this evil. He would know more, however, once he was out in the world. He remained silent, thoughtful.

"Well, Brother Rhys," Zeboim demanded, "what are you waiting for? I've told you all you need to know. Be off with you!"

"I do not now where Mina is—" Rhys began.

"You will search for her," the goddess snapped.

"—but I do know where my brother is," Rhys continued. "Or at least where he is likely to be."

"I told you to forget your brother—"

"When I find my brother," Rhys continued patiently, "I will question him about Mina. Hopefully, he will lead me to her or at least tell me where I can find her."

Zeboim opened her mouth, shut it again. "That does have a certain logic to it," she conceded grudgingly. "You may carry on with your search for your brother."

Rhys bowed his thanks.

"But you are not to waste time searching for your mutt," she added. "And I want you to make a slight detour. Since you are dealing with Chemosh, you will need someone with you who is an expert on the undead. You yourself have no such knowledge, I believe?"

Rhys had to admit he did not. The monks of Majere were concerned with life, not death.

"There is a town about twenty miles east of here. In that town is a burial ground. You will find the person you seek there. He comes every night around midnight. He is my gift to you," said Zeboim, highly pleased with herself and her magnanimity. "He will be your companion. You will need his help in dealing with your brother, as well as any other of Chemosh's followers you might encounter."

Rhys did not like the idea of a companion who was not only a crony of Zeboim but who also apparently spent his nights hanging about graveyards. Nevertheless, he did not want to argue the point. He would at least take a look at this person and perhaps ask him a few questions. Anyone with knowledge of the undead would also likely have knowledge of Chemosh.

"I thank you, Majesty."

"You are welcome. Perhaps you will think more kindly of me from now on."

As the goddess started to disappear, dissolving into the morning mists, she called to him, "I see your mutt heading back along the road. It seems you left something behind. You have my permission to wait for it."

The mists rose, burned off by the sun. Atta was walking down the path toward him. She carried something in her mouth. Rhys stared, astonished.

Atta had his staff.

The dog dropped his emmide at his feet and looked up at him, her whole back end wagging, her tongue hanging out in what was, for her, a grin.

Rhys knelt down on the path, ruffling her ears and the thick white fur on her neck and chest.

"Thank you, Atta," he said and added softly, "Thank you, Majere."

The emmide felt good in his hand, right and proper. Majere had sent it back to him—a clear message that, although he would receive no further blessings from the Mantis God, at least Rhys had Majere's forgiveness and his understanding.

Rhys rose to his feet, his emmide in his hand, his dog at his side. A day's walk would take to them to the town.

Night would introduce them to Zeboim's gift.

8

The burial ground was an old one, dating back to the founding of the town. Set apart from the town in a grove of trees, the cemetery was well-maintained, grave markers in good condition, weeds trimmed. Flowers had been planted on some of the graves and they were in bloom, their perfume scenting the darkness. Some of the graves were decorated with objects dear to the departed. A rag doll lay on one small grave.

Rhys stood in the grove, keeping to the shadows, wanting to view this mysterious personage first before speaking to him. Atta dozed at his feet, snoozing but watchful.

The night deepened, nearing the midpoint, the cross-over from one day to the next. Bats skimmed through the air, feasting on insects. Rhys gave them his grateful thanks, for the insects had been feeding on him. An owl hooted, making known this was her territory. In the distance, another answered. The graveyard was quiet, empty except for the slumbering dead.

Atta rose suddenly to her feet, ears up, body quivering, tense and alert. Rhys touched her lightly on the head and she remained quietly at his side.

A person entered the graveyard, wandering among the markers, sometimes touching them with his hand, giving each a small, familiar pat.

Rhys was taken aback. He hadn't known what to expect——a cleric of Zeboim; possibly a necromancer or even a black-robed wizard, follower of the dark god, Nuitari. In his wildest imaginings, Rhys had not foreseen this.

A kender.

Rhys's first thought was that this was Zeboim's idea of a joke, but the goddess did not strike him as the sort to indulge in a light-hearted prank, especially when she was so intent on the search for this Mina. He wondered if the kender was really the person he was supposed to meet or if his arrival was coincidental. Rhys discounted that after a moment's consideration. People did not generally flock to graveyards in the middle of the night. The kender had arrived at the appointed hour, and by the way he walked and talked, he was a frequent visitor.

"Hullo, Simon Plowman," said the kender, squatting down comfortably by a grave. "How are you tonight? Doing okay? You'll be pleased to know the wheat is up about six inches now. That apple tree you were worried about doesn't look so good, however."

The kender paused, as if waiting for a reply.

Rhys watched, mystified.

The kender heaved a dismal sigh and stood up. He moved on to the next grave, the one with the rag doll, and sat down beside it.

"Hullo, Blossom. Want to play at tiddle-winks? Maybe a game of khas? I have my board with me and all the pieces. Well, most of the pieces. I seem to have misplaced a rook."

The kender patted a large pouch he wore slung over one shoulder and looked with hopeful expectancy at the grave.

"Blossom?" he said again. "Are you here?"

He sighed dolefully and shook his head.

"It's no use," he said, talking to himself. "No one to talk to me. They've all gone."

The little fellow seemed so truly sad and heart-broken that

Rhys was moved to pity him. If this was lunacy, it had certainly taken a strange form. The kender did not appear to be insane, however. He sounded rational, and apart from looking rather thin and pinched, as if he hadn't had much to eat, he seemed healthy enough.

His hair was done up in the typical kender topknot. The tail straggled down behind him. He wore more subdued colors of clothing than was usual with kender, having on a dark vest and dark britches. (In this Rhys was mistaken. In the darkness, he mistook them for black. He would later come to find out, in the light of day, that they were a deep, but vibrant, shade of purple.)

Rhys was curious, now. He walked toward the graveyard, deliberately stepping on sticks and shuffling his feet through the leaves so that the kender would hear him coming.

Her nose twitching at the unusual smell of kender, Atta ranged alongside him.

"Hello—" Rhys began.

To his astonishment, the kender leapt to his feet and retreated behind a tall grave marker.

"Go away," said the kender. "We don't want your kind here."

"My kind?" Rhys said, pausing. "What do you mean—my kind?" He wondered if the kender had something against monks.

"The living," said the kender. He waved his hand as though he were shooing chickens. "We're all dead here. The living don't belong. Go away."

"But you are alive," said Rhys mildly.

"I'm different," said the kender. "And, no, I'm not afflicted," he added, offended, "so wipe that pity-look off your face."

Rhys remembered hearing something about afflicted kender, but he couldn't recall what and so he let that pass.

"I am not pitying you. I am curious," he said, threading his way around the grave markers. "I mean no disrespect to the honored dead, nor do I mean them any harm. I heard you talking to them—"

"I'm not crazy, either," stated the kender from behind his grave stone, "if that's what you're thinking."

"Not at all," Rhys said amiably.

He sat down comfortably near the grave marker of Simon Plowman. Opening his scrip, Rhys drew out a strip of dried meat. He broke off a share for Atta and began to chew on a piece himself. The meat was highly spiced and the pungent smell filled the night. The kender's nose wrinkled. His lips worked.

"Odd place for a picnic," the kender observed.

"Would you like some?" Rhys asked and he held out a long strip of meat.

The kender hesitated. He eyed Rhys warily. "Aren't you afraid to let me get close to you? I might steal something."

"I have naught to steal," Rhys answered with a smile. He continued to hold out the meat.

"What about the dog?" the kender asked. "Does he bite?"

"Atta is a female," Rhys answered. "And she harms only those who do harm to her or those under her protection."

He held out the meat.

Slowly, cautiously, his distrusting gaze on the dog, the kender crept out from behind the stone. He made a dart at the meat, snatched it from Rhys's hand, and devoured it hungrily.

"Thank you," he mumbled, his mouth full.

"Would you like more?" Rhys asked.

"I— Yes." The kender plopped down beside Rhys and accepted another piece of meat and a hunk of bread.

"Don't eat so fast," Rhys cautioned. "You'll give yourself a belly ache."

"I've had a belly ache for two days," said the kender. "This tastes really good."

"How long has it been since you've had a proper meal?"

The kender shrugged. "Hard telling." He put out his hand and gave Atta a gingerly pat on the head, to which Atta submitted with good grace. "You have a nice dog."

"You'll forgive me for saying this," Rhys said. "I don't mean to offend, but usually your people have little difficulty acquiring food and anything else they want."

"You mean borrowing," said the kender, growing more cheerful. He settled down comfortably beside Atta, continued to pet her. "Truth is, I'm not very good at it. I'm 'all thumbs and two left feet,' my pap used to say. I guess it's because I hang around with them all the time." He gave a nod toward the graves. "They're much easier to get on with. Not one of them ever accused me of taking anything."

"Who do you mean by 'them'?" Rhys asked. "The people who are buried here?"

The kender waved a greasy hand. "People who are buried anywhere. The living are mean. The dead are much nicer. Kinder. More understanding."

Rhys regarded the kender intently. *Since you are dealing with Chemosh, you will need someone with you who is an expert on the undead.*

"Are you saying you can communicate with the dead?"

"I'm what they call a 'nightstalker'." The kender held out his hand. "Name of Nightshade. Nightshade Pricklypear."

"I am Rhys Mason," said Rhys, taking the small hand and shaking it, "and this is Atta."

"Hi, Rhys, hi, Atta," said the kender. "I like you. I like you, too, Rhys. You're not excitable, like most humans I've met. I don't suppose you have any more of that meat left?" he added with a wistful glance at the leather scrip.

Rhys handed over the bag. He would restock his supplies in the morning. Someone in the town would need wood chopped or other chores done. Nightshade finished off the meat and most of the bread, sharing bites with Atta.

"What is a nightstalker?" Rhys asked.

"Wow! I thought everyone knew about us." Nightshade regarded Rhys with astonishment. "Where have you been hiding? Under a rock?"

"You might say that." Rhys smiled. "I am interested. Tell me."

"You know about the War of Souls?"

"I've heard mention of it."

"Well, what happened was that when Takhisis stole away the world, she blocked off all the exits, so to speak, so that anyone who died was trapped in the world. Their souls couldn't move on. Some people—mystics, mostly, usually necromancers—found out that they could communicate with these dead souls. My parents were both mystics. Not necromancers," Nightshade added hurriedly. "Necromancers are not nice people. They want to control the dead. My parents just wanted to talk to them and help them. The dead were very unhappy and lost, because they had no place to go."

Rhys regarded the kender intently. Nightshade spoke of all this in such matter-of-fact tones that Rhys found it difficult to think the kender was lying, yet the idea of the living holding conversations with the dead was a hard one to comprehend.

"I went along with my parents whenever they visited a burial ground or a cemetery or a mausoleum," Nightshade was saying. "I'd play games with them while my parents worked."

"You played games with the dead," Rhys interrupted.

Nightshade nodded. "We had a lot fun. We'd play at 'nine-men Morris', and 'duck, duck, goose, goose', and 'red rover' and 'king of the crypt'. A dead Solamnic knight taught me to play khas. A dead thief showed me how to hide a bean under three walnut shells and switch them around really fast, then have people try to guess where it's hidden. Do you want to see that one?" he asked eagerly.

"Maybe later," said Rhys politely.

Nightshade rummaged around the scrip and, not finding anything else to eat, handed it back. He leaned comfortably against the marker. Atta, seeing that no more meat was forthcoming, put her head on her paws and went to sleep.

"So now, Nightshade, you continue your parents' work?"

"I wish!" The kender heaved a gusty sigh.

"What happened?"

"Everything changed. Takhisis died. The gods came back. The souls were free to go on their journey again. And I don't have anyone left to play with."

"The dead are all leaving Krynn."

"Well, not all," Nightshade amended. "There're still your spirits, poltergeists, dopple-gangers, zombies, revenants, ghosts, skeletal warriors, phantoms, and so on. But they're harder to come by these days. Generally the necromancers and the clerics of Chemosh snap them up before I can get to them."

"Chemosh," said Rhys. "What do you know of Chemosh? Are you a follower of his?"

"Yuck, no!" Nightshade stated, shuddering. "Chemosh is a *not* a nice god. He hurts the spirits, turns them into his slaves. I don't worship any god. No offense."

"Why should I be offended?"

"Because you're a monk. I can tell by your robes, though they're sort of strange. I've never seen that odd green color before. Who is your god?"

The name of Majere came readily and easily to Rhys's lips. He paused, bit it back.

"Zeboim," he said.

"The sea goddess? Are you a sailor? I've always thought I'd like to go to sea. There must be lots and lots of bodies underneath the ocean—all those who died in shipwrecks or were swept away in storms."

"I'm not a sailor," Rhys replied, and changed the subject. "So what have you been doing with yourself since the War of Souls?"

"I travel from town to town, searching for a dead person to talk to," said the kender. "But mostly I just get thrown into jail. It's not all that bad. At least they feed you."

He was so thin and frail, and although he talked cheerfully, he seemed so unhappy that Rhys made up his mind. He still couldn't figure out if the kender was crazy or sane, lying or honest (as kender go). He figured it would be worth his while to find out, however. And he preferred not to offend his temperamental goddess, who had given him this strange gift.

"The truth is, Nightshade," said Rhys, "I was sent here to seek you out."

The kender jumped up, startling Atta from her doze. "I knew it! You're the sheriff in disguise!"

"No, no," Rhys said hastily. "I really am a monk. Zeboim was the one who sent me."

"A god looking for me?" Nightshade said, alarmed. "That's worse than the sheriff."

"Nightshade—" Rhys began.

He was too late. With a leap and a bound, the kender cleared the grave marker and took to his heels. Having spent a lifetime fleeing pursuers, the kender was fleet and agile. A good meal had given him strength. He was familiar with the surrounding territory. Rhys could never catch him. He had someone with him who could, however.

"Atta," Rhys said, "away!"

Atta was on her feet. Hearing the familiar command, she instinctively started to obey, then stopped and looked back at Rhys in perplexity.

"I will do what you say, Master, but where are the sheep?" she seemed to be asking.

"Away," he said firmly and gestured at the fleeing kender.

Atta regarded him for another second, just to make certain she understood, then she sped off, bounding through the grave yard in pursuit.

The dog used the same tactics with Nightshade that she would have used with sheep, coming up on his left flank, circling wide, not looking at him so as not to frighten him, steering around in front of him to turn him, force him back toward Rhys.

Seeing the black and white streak out of the corner of his eye, Nightshade veered from his course, heading off in another direction. Atta was there ahead of him and he was forced to turn again. She was there again and once more he had to turn.

She did not attack him. When he slowed, she slowed. When he came to a halt, she dropped to her belly, staring at him so intently with her brown eyes that he found it hard to look away. The moment he moved, she was on her feet again. Nightshade tried every dodge and dart he knew, but she was always in front of him, her lithe little body turning time and again to head him off. He could move freely only one direction and that was back the way he'd come.

Finally, panting, Nightshade climbed up on a grave marker and stood there, shivering.

"Get her away from me!" he howled.

"That'll do, Atta," said Rhys, and she relaxed and came over to him to have her head patted.

Rhys walked up to where he'd treed the kender.

"You are not in trouble, Nightshade. Quite the opposite. I am going on a quest and I need your help."

Nightshade's eyes widened. "A quest? My help? Are you sure?"

"Yes, that is why my god sent me to find you."

Rhys told the kender everything that had happened, from his brother's arrival at the monastery to the terrible crime he'd committed. Nightshade listened, fascinated, though he picked up on the wrong part of the quest. He jumped down from the grave marker and seized hold of Rhys's hand.

"We have to go back there right away!" he said, trying to tug Rhys off. "Back to where you buried your friends!'

"No," said Rhys, standing firm. "We need to search for my brother."

"But all those uneasy spirits need me," Nightshade said, pleading.

"They are with their god now," said Rhys.

"You're certain?"

"Yes," said Rhys, and he was certain. "We have to find my brother and stop him before he harms anyone else. We need to find out what Chemosh did to him to turn him from a cleric of

Kiri-Jolith to a follower of the Lord of Death. You can communicate with the dead, which might prove to be useful, and you can do so without rousing suspicion. I can't pay you anything," he added, "for we monks are forbidden to accept any reward except what we need for our survival."

"More meat like what we just ate would be fine with me. And it will be good to have a friend," Nightshade said excitedly. "A real live friend."

He glanced at Atta with trepidation. "I suppose you have to take the dog?"

"Atta makes a good guardian as well as a good companion. Don't worry." Rhys rested his hand reassuringly on the kender on the shoulder. "She's fond of you. That's why she chased after you. She didn't want you to leave."

"Really?" Nightshade looked pleased. "I thought she was herding me like I was a sheep or something. If she likes me, that's different. I like her, too."

Rhys let the darkness hide his smile. "I am staying with a farmer whose home is nearby. We'll spend the night there and get an early start in the morning."

"Farmers don't usually let me into their houses," Nightshade pointed out, falling in beside Rhys, the kender's short legs taking two strides to his one.

"I think this one will," Rhys predicted. "Once I explain to him how fond Atta is of you."

Atta was so fond of the kender that she lay across his legs all night, never letting him out of her sight.

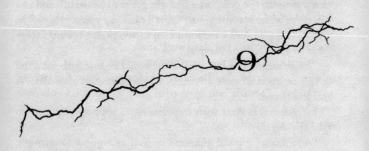

Rhys had no difficulty picking up his brother's trail. People remembered quite clearly a cleric of Kiri-Jolith who spent his nights carousing in the tavern and his days flirting with their daughters. Rhys had been grimly expecting to hear that his brother had done murder again and was surprised and relieved to hear no worse of him than he'd left town without paying his bar tab.

When Rhys asked if his brother had spoken of Chemosh, everyone looked amused and shook their heads. He'd said no word to them of any god, especially not such a dark god as Chemosh. Lleu was a pleasant and handsome young man looking for fun, and if he was a little reckless and heedless, there was no harm in that. Most thought him a good fellow and wished him well.

Rhys found this all very strange. He could not equate the picture these people were giving him of a light-hearted bounder with the cold-blooded murderer who had so ruthlessly killed nineteen people. Rhys might have doubted that he was truly on his brother's track, but everyone recognized Lleu by his physical descripion and the fact that he wore the robes of Kiri-Jolith. Clerics of that god were not plentiful in Abanasinia, where his worship was just starting to spread.

Rhys found only one man who had anything bad to say about Lleu Mason and that was a miller who had given Lleu room and board in return for a few days work at the mill.

"My daughter has not been the same since," the miller told Rhys. "I curse the day he came and curse myself for having anything to do with him. A dutiful child my Besty was before he started taking notice of her. Hard-working. She was to be married next month to the son of one of the most prosperous shop-keepers in this town. A fine match it was, but that's off now, thanks to your brother."

He shook his head dourly.

"Where is your daughter?" Rhys asked, glancing about. "If I could speak to her—"

"Gone," said the miller shortly. "I caught her sneaking home from a meeting with him in the wee hours. I gave her the whipping she deserved and locked her in her room." He shrugged. "After a few days, she managed to get out somehow and I haven't seen hide nor hair of her since. Good riddance to bad rubbish, I say."

"Did she run off with Lleu?" Rhys asked.

The miller didn't know. He didn't think so, for Lleu had departed before the daughter ran away. It was possible, the miller conceded, that she might have run off to be with him, although, in truth, she had not appeared to be that enamored of him. The miller didn't know and he obviously didn't care, except that he had lost a hard-worker and a chance for a marriage from which he stood to profit.

Rhys conceded it was possible that his brother had seduced the young woman and persuaded her to run away with him, but in that case, why hadn't they run off together? He thought it more likely that the young woman had simply fled a loveless home and the prospect of a loveless marriage. Nothing sinister about it.

Still, the matter troubled Rhys. He asked for a descripion of the girl and inquired about her, as well as about Lleu, along the road. Some had seen her, some had seen him, but none had seen them together. The last he heard of the miller's daughter, she had joined up with a caravan headed for the sea coast. His brother, it seemed, had spoken vaguely of traveling to Haven.

While Rhys talked with the living, Nightshade communicated with the dead. While Rhys visited inns and taverns, Nightshade visited crypts and cemeteries. Nightshade forbade Rhys from accompanying him, for, the kender claimed, the dead tended to be shy in the presence of the living.

"Most of the dead, that is," the kender added. "There are those who like to go about rattling bones and clanking chains and tossing chairs out of windows. I've met a few who get a kick out of reaching up from the grave and grabbing people by the ankle. They're the exception, however."

"Thank the gods," said Rhys dryly.

"I guess so." Nightshade wasn't convinced. "Those sort of dead are the interesting ones. They tend to stick around, not run off to some higher plane of existence and leave a fellow without anyone to talk to."

The "higher plane "appeared to be a popular destination, for Nightshade was having trouble communicating with the dead, or so he claimed. Those he did find could tell him nothing about Chemosh. Rhys had been skeptical of the kender's claims from the beginning and his skepticism was growing. He decided to follow the kender one night, see for himself what was going on.

Nightshade was excited this evening, for he'd heard of a battle-field nearby. Battlefields were promising, he explained, because the dead were sometimes abandoned on the field, their bodies left unburied to rot in the sun or be torn apart by vultures.

"Some spirits are good sports about it and just go ahead and depart," Nightshade explained. "But others take it personally. They hang about, waiting to vent their anger against the living. I should find someone who's eager to talk."

"Might not that be dangerous?" Rhys asked.

"Well, yes," the kender admitted. "Some of the dead develop a really nasty attitude and take it out on the first person they come across. I've had a few close calls."

"What do you do if you're attacked? How do you defend yourself? You carry no weapon."

"Spirits don't like the sight of steel," Nightshade replied. "Or maybe it's the smell of iron. I was never very clear on that. Anyhow, if I'm attacked, I just take to my heels. I'm faster than any old rattle-bones."

When darkness fell, Nightshade departed for battlefield. Rhys gave the kender a lengthy head-start, then he and Atta set off after him.

The night was clear. Solinari was on the wane and Lunitari full and bright, giving the shadows a reddish tinge. The evening air was soft and scented with the perfume of wild roses. The woodland creatures were going about their business, their rustlings and barks and howls causing Atta no end of concern.

In what he was now thinking of as his past life, Rhys would have enjoyed walking through the perfumed night. In that life, his own spirit would have been tranquil, his soul composed. He did not think he been blind to the evil in the world, to the ugliness of life. He understood that one was needed to balance the other. Or rather, he'd thought he'd understood. Now it was as if his brother's hand had torn aside a curtain to show Rhys evil he had never imagined existed. In a way, Rhys conceded, he had been blind because he'd seen only what he'd wanted to see. He would never allow that to happen again.

He had much to think about as he walked. He believed he was very close to catching up with his brother. Lleu had been in this village until two days ago. He had taken the road to Haven, a road that because of brigands and goblins was not now safe to travel. People who dared go abroad traveled in large groups for protection.

Rhys had little to fear about from bandits. "Poor as a monk" was a household expression. One glimpse of monkish robes (even those of a strange color) and thieves turned away in disgust.

Atta's low rumble caused Rhys to abandon his thoughts and turn his attention to the task ahead. They had reached the battlefield and he could see Nightshade quite clearly, the red moon smiling down on him brightly, as if Lunitari found it all quite funny.

Rhys chose a place in the shadows beneath a tree that, by its splintered branches, had been caught up in the fighting. He felt a prick from his conscience for spying on the kender, but the matter was too important, too urgent to be left to chance.

"At least I've given Nightshade the benefit of the doubt," Rhys said to Atta, as he watched the kender prowl hopefully around the battlefield. "Anyone else hearing such a tale would have hauled him off to the cells for the insane."

The battlefield was a large stretch of open ground, several acres in length and breadth. The battle had been fought only a few years previous, and although the field was now overgrown with weeds and grass, some scars of the conflict could still be seen.

Any intact armor or weapons had been looted by either the victors or the townspeople. Left behind were broken spears, rusted bits of armor, a worn boot, a torn gauntlet, splintered arrows. Rhys had no idea who had been fighting whom in the battle. Not that it mattered.

Nightshade roamed about. Once he stopped to pick up something off the ground. After examining it carefully, he dropped it into his pouch.

He glanced about, sighed dismally, then shouted out, in neighborly tones, "Hullo! Anybody home?"

No one replied. Nightshade roamed on. The night was calm, peaceful, and Rhys felt sleep start to overcome him. He shook his head to shake off the fuzziness, rubbed his eyes and drank some water from his flask. Atta tensed. Rhys could feel her body stiffen. Her ears pricked.

"What—" he began, then his voice stuck in his throat.

Nightshade had stooped to pick up a battered and dented helm. Pleased with his find, the kender put the helm on his head.

The helm was far too large, but that didn't bother Nightshade. He thunked himself on the top of the helm with his fist and endeavored to flip up the visor, which was somewhere around his chin.

He was fumbling with the visor, which was rusted, and missed seeing the ghostly apparition rising up out of the ground almost directly in front of him. Rhys saw it clearly and even then he might have doubted his senses, but he could tell from Atta's stare and her rigid muscles, taut beneath his hand, that she could see it, too.

The specter was about the height and bulk of a human male. He was clad in armor—nothing as sophisticated as a knight might wear; just a few cast-off pieces cobbled together. He wore no helm and there was a ghastly wound on his head, a gash that had cleaved through his skull. His features were twisted in a scowl. The specter reached out a ghostly hand toward the kender, who was still happily ensconced in the helm, with no inkling of the horror in front of him.

Rhys tried to call out a warning. His throat and mouth were so dry that he could make no sound. He might have sent Atta, but the dog was shivering, terrified.

"Whoo boy, it got cold all of a sudden," said Nightshade, his voice echoing inside the helm.

He managed to free the visor about that time and it popped open. "Oh, hullo, there!" he said to the specter, whose hand was inches from his face. "Sorry. I didn't know you were here. How have you been?"

At the sound of the kender's voice, the specter dropped its hand. It hovered uncertainly in front of Nightshade, as if trying to make up its mind to something.

Awed, Rhys listened and watched and tried to make some sense of what was happening. Nothing in his training, his prayers, or meditation had prepared him for this sight. He stroked Atta, soothing her and reassuring himself at the same time. It was good to touch something warm and alive.

Nightshade pulled off the helm and let it fall to the ground.

"Sorry. Was that yours?" He saw that the specter was missing about half its skull. "Oh, I guess not. You probably could have used it. So things haven't been going real well for you. Would you like to tell me about it?"

It seemed that the specter was speaking, though Rhys could not hear the voice. He could see the spectral hand making angry gestures. The spectral head would turn to look off into the distance.

Nightshade listened with calm attentiveness, his expression one of sympathy and concern.

"There's nothing here for you now," Nightshade said at last. "Your wife has married someone else by now. She had to, even though she grieved for you and missed you. There were the kids to raise and she couldn't manage the farm by herself. Your comrades lift a glass to you and say things like, 'Do you remember the time old Charley did such and such?' But they've moved on with their lives, too. You need to move on with yours. No, I'm not trying to be funny. Death is a part of life. The sort of dark and quiet part, but definitely a part. You're not doing yourself any good hanging about here, fretting about how unfair it all was."

Nightshade listened to the specter again, then said, "You could look at it that way or you could take the view that the unknown is filled with new and exciting possibilities. Anything's better than this, right? Skulking about here lost and alone. At least, give what I've said some thought. You don't happen to play khas, do you? Would you like a game before you leave?"

The specter apparently wasn't interested. The ghastly form began to dissipate like mist in the moonlight.

"Oh, I almost forgot!" Nightshade called. "Have you seen or heard anything from Chemosh lately? Chemosh. God of the Dead. You never heard of him? Well, thanks anyway. Good luck to you! Have a safe journey."

Rhys tried to pick up the shattered pieces of what he'd thought he'd known about life and death and sort them all out and reassemble them. At length, he found he couldn't and he simply threw them all away. Time to begin again. He walked over to where Nightshade was standing. The kender was eyeing the helm and eyeing his pouch, as if trying to determine if it would fit.

Hearing movement, Nightshade turned his head. His face brightened. Dropping the helm, he came dashing up to them. "Rhys! Did you see that? A specter! He was kind of a dismal specter. Most of them are livelier, so to speak. Oh, and he doesn't know anything about Chemosh. My guess is the man died before the gods came back. I hope he feels better now that's he's on the next part of his journey. What's the matter with Atta? She's not sick, is she?""

"Nightshade," said Rhys contritely, "I want to apologize."

The kender's face screwed up in a bemused wrinkle. "If you want to, Rhys, you can. I don't mind. Who are you going to apologize to?"

"You, Nightshade," said Rhys, smiling. "I doubted you and I spied on you, and I'm sorry."

"You doubted——" The kender paused. He glanced at Rhys, glanced at the dog, glanced around the empty battle field. "I see. You came after me to make sure I wasn't lying when I said I could talk to the dead."

"Yes. I'm sorry. I should have trusted you."

"That's all right," said Nightshade, though he said it with a little sigh. "I'm used to being not trusted. Comes with the territory."

"Will you forgive me?" Rhys asked.

"Did you bring any food with you?"

Rhys reached into his scrip, pulled out a hunk of cheese, and handed it to the kender.

"I forgive you," said Nightshade, taking a large and contented bite. He cocked an eye at Rhys. "It's very odd."

"It's ordinary goat cheese——"

"Not the cheese. It's quite good. No, what I mean is that it's odd that the specter didn't know Chemosh. None of the specters or ghosts or haunts I've met have been visited by him or his clerics. True, Chemosh wasn't around when that particular specter was alive, but it seems to me that if I were the Lord of Death, the first thing I would have done when I came back was to send out my clerics to do a sweep of all the battlefields and dungeons and dragon lairs, to enslave as many wandering spirits to serve me as I could find."

"Maybe the clerics just missed this one," Rhys suggested.

"I don't think so," said Nightshade. He munched his cheese with a thoughtful expression.

"What do you think is going on then?" Rhys prodded, truly interested to hear what the kender had to say. He'd developed a good deal of respect for Nightshade in the past hour.

The kender gazed out over the dark and empty field. "I think Chemosh has no need for dead slaves."

"Why is that?"

"Because he's finding slaves among the living."

"Like my brother," said Rhys, with a sudden cold feeling in the pit of his stomach. Other than their first conversation in the graveyard, when Rhys had told Nightshade about Lleu and the murders, the two had not discussed it much. The subject was not one Rhys liked to dwell on. Apparently Nightshade had been giving the matter thought, however.

Nightshade nodded. He handed back the remainder of the cheese and Rhys returned it to the scrip, much to Atta's disappointment.

"How do you suppose Chemosh is doing that?" Rhys asked.

"I don't know," Nightshade answered, "but if I'm right, it's pretty scary."

Rhys had to agree. It was very scary.

10

$\mathcal{H}$aven was a large city, the largest Rhys had visited thus far.
He and Nightshade spent days tramping from place to place,
patiently giving a descripion of his brother, searching for someone
who had seen Lleu. When they finally found a tavern owner who
remembered him, Rhys learned that his brother had not stayed
in Haven long but had almost immediately moved on. The best
guess was that he'd gone to Solace, the reasoning being that
everyone traveling through Abanasinia ended up in Solace. Rhys,
Nightshade, and Atta journeyed on.

Rhys had been to Solace with his father when he was a child
and he clearly remembered the city, famous in legend and lore for
the fact that its houses and shops were built among the branches
of enormous vallenwood trees. Its very name conjured up images
of a place where the wounded of heart and mind and body could
go to find comfort.

Rhys's childhood memories of Solace were of a town of
remarkable beauty and friendly people. He found Solace much
changed. The town had grown into a city of noise and bustle,
confusion and turmoil, roaring with a loud and raucous voice.
Rhys could honestly say that had if it not been for the legendary

Inn of the Last Home, he would not have recognized the place. And even the Inn had changed, having grown and expanded so that it now sprawled across the branches of several vallenwood trees.

Because the original dwellings had been built in the treetops, the citizens of Solace had not needed to build walls to protect their homes and businesses. That had worked well in the days when Solace was a small town. Now, however, travelers flowed in and out of the city unchecked, with no guards to ask questions. People of all sorts filled the streets: elves, dwarves, kender by the score. Rhys saw more different races in thirty seconds in Solace than he'd seen in all his thirty years.

He was astonished beyond measure to see two draconians, one male and one female, stroll down the main road with as much confidence as if they owned the place. People went out of their way to avoid the "lizard men," but no one appeared to be alarmed by their presence, except Atta, who growled and barked at them. He heard someone say they were from the draconian city of Teyr and that they were here to meet some hill dwarves to discuss trade deals.

Gully dwarves fought and scrabbled among the refuse and a goblinish face leered at Rhys from the shadows of an alleyway. The goblin vanished when a troop of guards, armed with pikes and wearing chain mail, marched down the street, accompanied by a parade of giggling small boys and girls wearing pots on their heads and carrying sticks.

Humans were the predominant race. Black-skinned humans from Ergoth mingled with crudely dressed barbarians from the Plains and richly clothed humans from Palanthas, all of them jostling and shoving each other and trading insults.

Every type of occupation was represented in Solace as well. Three wizards, two wearing red robes and one wearing black, bumped into Rhys. They were so absorbed in their argument that they never noticed him or begged his pardon. A group of actors, who referred to themselves as Gilean's Traveling Troupe, came dancing down the street, beating a drum and banging tambours, adding to the noise level. Everyone either had something to sell or was looking for something to buy, and they all were shouting about it at the top of their lungs.

While all this was happening on the streets below, Rhys looked up to see more people traveling along the swaying plank and rope bridges running from one vallenwood tree to the next, like the silken filaments of a gigantic spider web. Access to the tree levels was limited, it seemed, for he noted guards posted at various points, questioning and halting those who could not convince them that they had business up above.

As he slogged through the mud churned up by an unending stream of traffic, Rhys marveled at the changes that had come to Ansalon while he'd been hidden away in the never-changing world of the monastery. From what he'd seen, he hadn't missed much. The noise, the sights, the smells—ranging from rotting garbage to unwashed gully dwarf, from day-old fish to the scent of meat being roasted over hot coals and bread coming fresh from the baker's oven—left Rhys longing for the solitude and tranquility of the hills, the simplicity of his former life.

Atta, by her demeanor, was in agreement. She often looked up at him, her brown eyes moist with confusion, yet trusting him to guide them through it. Rhys petted her, reassuring her, if he could not reassure himself. He might be daunted by the size of Solace, by the numbers of people, but that did not change his resolve to continue to search for his brother. At least, he now knew where to look. Lleu had rarely missed stopping at a single inn or tavern along with the way.

Rhys had one other option, or so he hoped. The idea came to him when he saw a small group of black-robed clerics walking openly down the street. A city the size and disposition of Solace might well have a temple dedicated to Chemosh.

Rhys turned his steps toward the famous Inn of the Last Home, thinking that he would start by asking for information there. He had to stop once on the way to extricate Nightshade from a group of kender, who latched onto him as though he were a long-lost cousin (which, in fact, two of them claimed to be).

The famous inn where, according to legend, the Heroes of the Lance had been accustomed to meet, was filled to capacity. People stood in line, waiting to enter. As customers departed, a certain number were admitted. The line began at the foot of the long flight of stairs and extended down the street. Rhys and Nightshade took their places at the end, waiting patiently. Rhys kept watch on all those traipsing up and down the stairs, hoping one of them might be Lleu.

"Look at all these people!" exclaimed Nightshade with enthusiasm. "I'm certain to raise a few coppers here. That roasted goat meat smells wonderful, doesn't it, Atta?"

The dog sat at Rhys's side, her gaze divided between her master and Nightshade. The kender thought happily that Atta had developed a true affection for him, for she never let him out of her sight. Rhys did not disabuse his companion of this notion. Atta took to "kender-herding" quite as well as she took to herding sheep.

As he watched those leaving the Inn, Rhys listened to the chatter around him, picking up various bits of local gossip, hoping he might hear something that would lead him to Lleu. Nightshade was busy advertising his services, telling those ahead of him in line that he could put them in contact with any relative who had shuffled off this mortal coil for the bargain price of a single steel, payable upon delivery of the said relative. The watchful dog, meanwhile, kept the kender from accidentally "borrowing" any pouches, purses, knives, rings, or handkerchiefs by insinuating her body between that of Nightshade and any potential "customer."

The crowd was generally in a good humor, despite the fact that they were having to wait. That good humor suddenly deteriorated.

"Perhaps you didn't hear me the first time, gentlemen," a man stated, his voice rising. "You have no right to cut in front of me."

Rhys looked over his shoulder, as did everyone around him.

"Did you hear something, Gregor?" asked one of the men to whom this statement had been addressed.

"No, Tak," said his friend, "but I sure do smell something." He laid heavy emphasis on the word. "Must be driving a herd of swine through town today."

"Ah, you're mistaken, Gregor," said his friend in mock serious tones. "It's not swine they've let into town this day. Swine are sweet-smelling, clean, and wholesome beasts compared to this lot. They must've let in an *elf!*"

Both men laughed uproariously. By their leather aprons and brawny arms and shoulders and soot-blackened hands and faces, they were metal-workers of some kind, ironmongers or black-smiths. The man who was the butt of their joke wore the green garb of a forester. He had his cowl pulled up over his head so that no one could see his face, but there was no mistaking the lithe body and graceful movements and the soft and melodic tones of his voice.

The elf said nothing in reply. Stepping out of line, he walked around the two humans, and stepped back into line, in front of them.

"You damn grass-eater, get the hell outta my way!" The man called Gregor seized the elf by the shoulder and spun him around.

Steel flashed, and Gregor sprang backward.

The elf held a knife in his hand.

The two humans glanced at each other; then, doubling their huge fists, they came surging forward.

The elf was ready to lunge, when he suddenly found his way blocked, as Rhys stepped between the combatants. Rhys did not raise his staff, nor did he raise his voice.

"You may have my place in line, gentlemen," he said.

The men—all three—stared at him, mouths agape.

"I am near the front, at the foot of the stairs," Rhys continued pleasantly. "There, where the kender and the dog are waiting. We are next to go up. Take my place and welcome, all three of you."

Behind Rhys, the elf said vehemently, "I do not need your help, monk. I can handle these two myself."

"By spilling their blood?" Rhys asked, glancing around. "What will that accomplish?"

"Monk?" repeated one of the humans, eyeing Rhys uncertainly.

"By his weapon, he is a monk of the Mantis," said the elf. "Or Majere, as you humans know it. Though I never saw one wearing sea green robes," he added scornfully.

"Take my place, sirs," Rhys repeated, gesturing toward the stairs. "A mug of cool ale to quench a hot temper, eh?"

The two humans eyed each other. They eyed Rhys and they eyed his staff. There was no good way out of this. If they'd had the support of the crowd, they might have continued the fight. As it was, Rhys's offer had clearly captured the crowd's fancy. Perhaps these two were well-known bullies, for people were grinning at their discomfiture.

The two men lowered their fists.

"C'mon, Tak, I'm not hungry anymore," one said scathingly, turning on his heel. "The stench has killed my appetite."

"Yeah, you can drink with their kind if you want, monk," sneered the other. "I'd sooner suck down swamp water."

The elf glowered at Rhys. "That was my battle. You had no right to interfere."

He, too, walked off, heading in the opposite direction.

Rhys returned to his place in line. Several in the crowd applauded and an old woman reached out to touch his shabby, travel-stained robes "for luck." He wondered what she would think if she knew he was not truly a monk of Majere but a sworn follower of Zeboim. He realized, with an inward sigh, that it probably wouldn't make any difference. He had pleased her, pleased the crowd, as they would have been pleased by a Punch and Judy puppet show.

Rhys took his place in line, next to Nightshade, who was all agog with admiration and excitement. The kender's eager questions were interrupted by the man who regulated the flow of traffic into the inn.

"Go on up, monk," he called with a flourishing gesture, "before you drive off the rest of my customers."

Everyone laughed and the crowd cheered as Rhys, Nightshade, and Atta climbed the stairs, with Nightshade waving and leaning over the rails precariously to shout out, "Would any of you like to make contact with a loved one who has passed over? I can talk to the dead—"

Rhys took hold of the kender by the shoulder and gently guided him through the open door.

The Inn of the Last Home had achieved ever-lasting fame during the War of the Lance, for it was here that the legendary Heroes of the Lance began a quest that would end with the defeat of Takhisis, Queen of Darkness. The Inn was owned by the descendants of two of those heroes, Caramon and Tika Majere. Listening to the gossip as he'd been standing in line, Rhys had learned a considerable amount about the Inn, its owners, and Solace in general.

A daughter, Laura Majere, ran the inn. Her brother, Palin, had once been a famed sorcerer, but was now the Lord High Mayor of Solace. There was some sort of scandal involving his wife, but that was apparently resolved. Laura and Palin had a sister, Dezra. People rolled their eyes when she was mentioned. The Sheriff of Solace was a friend of Palin's, a former Solamnic knight named Gerard. He was a popular sheriff, it seemed, with a reputation for being tough, but fair-minded. He had a thankless job, as far as most of the gossipers were concerned, for Solace had grown far too fast for its own good. In addition, it was located near the border of what had once been the elven kingdom of Qualinesti. The dragon Beryl had driven the elves from their homes and Qualinesti was now a wild, lawless and uncivilized no-man's land, refuge to roving bands of outlaws and goblins.

The Inn of the Last Home had undergone a number of changes down through the years. Those who recalled it from the days of the War of Lance would not have recognized it now. The inn had been destroyed at least twice by dragons (maybe more times, there was an argument on that score) and besides being rebuilt had undergone a series of expansions and renovations. The famous bar, made from the vallenwood tree, was still there. The fireplace beside which the infamous mage Raistlin Majere once sat had been shifted to a different location to make room for more tables. An additional wing had been built to accommodate the growing crowds of travelers. The kitchen was no longer where it had once been but was in a different place entirely. The food was still as good—better, some said—and the ale was still spoken of in near reverent terms by ale-connoisseurs all over Ansalon.

Upon entering, Rhys was impressed by the atmosphere of the inn, which was merry without being boisterous or rowdy. The busy barmaids found time to laugh and exchange friendly barbs with the regulars. A broom-wielding gully dwarf kept the floor spotless. The long wood plank tables where the customers sat were clean and neat.

Nightshade immediately launched into his spiel. The kender spoke extremely fast, knowing from experience, that he rarely got far before he was summarily stifled. "I can talk to dead people," he announced in a loud voice that carried clearly over the laugher and the shouting and the clanking of pewter and crockery. "Anyone here have loved ones who have died recently? If so, I can talk to them for you. Are they happy being dead? I can tell you. Have you been searching for Uncle Wat's will? I can find out from his spirit where he left it. Did you forget to tell your late husband how much you loved him? I can pass on your regards . . ."

Some customers ignored him completely. Others regarded the kender with expressions that ranged from grinning amusement to shock and indignation. A few were starting to look seriously offended.

"Atta, away," ordered Rhys quietly, and the dog leapt into action.

Trotting over to the kender, Atta pressed her body against his legs, so that he had no choice but to back up or tumble over her.

"Atta, nice dog," said Nightshade, patting her head distractedly. "I'll play with you some other time. I have to work now, you see—"

He tried to circle around the dog, tried to step over her. Atta dodged and wove, and all the while continued to force the kender backward until she had him wedged neatly into a corner, with a table and chairs hemming him in on two sides and the patient dog in front.

Atta dropped down on her belly. If Nightshade moved a muscle, she was back on her feet. She did not growl, was not menacing. She just made certain the kender stayed put.

As the patrons of the Inn watched this in awe, a barmaid hastened over, offering to guide Rhys to a table.

"Thank you, no," he said. "I came for information, that is all. I am looking for someone—"

The barmaid interrupted him. "I know that the monks of Majere take vows of poverty. It's all right. You're a guest of the Inn this day. There's food and drink for you and mats in the common room for you and your friend."

She cast a glance in the direction of Atta and Nightshade, but whether by "friend" she meant the dog or the kender was left open.

"I thank you, mistress, but I cannot accept your offer, which is kind, but does not apply in my case. I am not a monk of Majere. As I said, I am searching for someone and I thought perhaps he had been here. His name is Lleu—"

"Is there a problem, Marta?"

A large man with a shock of straw-colored hair and a face that might have been called ugly, but for its strength of character and a genial smile, came up to where Rhys and the barmaid were talking. The man was clad in a leather vest. He wore a sword at his hip and a gold chain around his neck, all of the finest quality.

"The monk here has refused our hospitality, Sheriff," said the barmaid.

"I cannot accept her charity, my lord," said Rhys. "It would be given under false pretenses. I am not a monk of Majere."

The man held out his hand.

"Gerard, Sheriff of Solace," he said, smiling. He cast an admiring glance at the dog and the penned-up kender. "I don't suppose you're looking for work, Brother, but if you are, I'd be glad to take you on. I saw the way you handled yourself out there in the line this morning, and that kender-herding dog of yours is worth its weight in steel."

"My name is Rhys Mason. Thank you for the offer, but I must decline." Rhys paused, then said mildly, "If you were watching what was happening between those men and the elf, my lord Sheriff, why did not you intervene?"

Gerard grinned ruefully. "If I rushed around trying to stop every knife fight that took place in Solace, Brother, I'd never do anything else. I spend my time on more important matters, such as trying to keep the town from being raided, looted, and burned to the ground. Gregor and Tak are the local bullies. If things had gotten out of hand, I would have come down to settle those boys. You had the situation under control, or so it looked from my end. Therefore, Brother, you, the dog, and the kender will be my guests for supper. It's the least I can do for you, seeing as how you did my work for me this day."

Rhys felt he could accept this offer and he did so. "That'll do, Atta," he called, and the dog jumped up and returned to his side.

Nightshade was on his way over to join Rhys when the kender was accosted by a plump, middle-aged woman, wearing a black shawl over her head, who said she wanted to talk to him. The two sat down and were soon deep in conversation; the kender looking extremely sympathetic, the woman dabbing her eyes with the hem of her shawl.

"She's a recent widow," said Gerard, frowning at the kender. "I wouldn't want anyone to take advantage of her grief, Brother."

"The kender is what is called a 'nightstalker', my lord," Rhys explained. "He can actually do what he says he can do—speak to the dead."

Gerard was skeptical. "Truly? I've heard of his sort before. Didn't know they actually existed. Figured it was just another tale the little buggers made up to make nuisances of themselves."

"I can vouch for Nightshade, my lord Sheriff," said Rhys, smiling. "He is not your typical light-fingered kender. He is able to communicate with the dead. I've seen him do it. Unless, of course, the spirits have moved on, in which case he can impart that information. Perhaps he can be of comfort to the widow."

Gerard eyed the kender. "I knew a kender once," he said quietly, speaking more to himself than to Rhys. "He wasn't your typical kender either. I'll give this one a chance, Brother, especially if you'll vouch for him."

A moment later, Nightshade came hurrying over. "The widow and I are going to the burial ground to talk to her husband. She misses him most dreadfully and she wants to make sure he's doing all right without her. I'll probably be gone most of the afternoon. Where shall I meet you?"

"You can meet your friend here," said Gerard, interrupting Rhys. "You have a place in the common room to sleep tonight."

"No more sleeping in stables! That's wonderful. I'm getting really tired of the smell of horses," said Nightshade, and before Rhys could contradict the sheriff, the kender had dashed off.

Gerard eyed Rhys. "I'm holding you responsible for emptying his pockets when he comes back."

"You needn't worry about that, my lord. Nightshade's not very good at 'borrowing.' If he tries, he's so inept that he's almost always caught in the act. He is much more interested in speaking to the dead."

Gerard snorted and shook his head. Sitting across the table from Rhys, the sheriff regarded the monk curiously, more interested in him than in the kender, which, the gods knew, Solace had in abundance.

The barmaid brought over bowls of savory stew, so thick with meat and vegetables that Rhys could barely dig his spoon into it. She put down a bowl of water and a meaty bone for Atta, who accepted the treat after a glance at Rhys and suffered the barmaid to pat her head. Atta dragged her bone under the table, plopped down on top of Rhys's feet, and began to gnaw at it contentedly.

"You said you were searching for someone?" Gerard asked, leaning back in his chair, looking at Rhys with a pair of eyes that were a startling shade of blue. "I don't begin to try to keep track of everyone who comes into Solace, but I do get around. Who is it you're looking for?"

Rhys explained that he was searching for his brother. He described Lleu as wearing the robes of a cleric of Kiri-Jolith and spending his time in taverns and ale houses.

"Where are you from?"

"Staughton," Rhys answered.

The sheriff raised his eyebrows. "You've traveled a long way in search of this young man, Brother; gone to a lot of trouble. Seems to me there must more to it than a family worried about a young vagabond."

Rhys had decided to keep the truth about Lleu to himself, knowing that if he told anyone that his brother was guilty of murder, Lleu would be hunted down and slaughtered like a wild beast. Rhys found himself liking this man, Gerard, whose calm demeanor accorded well with Rhys's own. If Rhys did find Lleu, he would be obliged to hand him over to the local authorities until he could be brought to justice by the Prophet of Majere. The Prophet would be the one to determine Lleu's fate, since his crime had taken place in one of the monasteries. Rhys decided to tell the sheriff at least part of his story.

"I am sorry to say that my brother has lately become a follower of Chemosh, God of the Dead," he told Gerard. "I fear that he is the victim of some evil spell cast on him by a disciple of Chemosh. I need to find Lleu in order to have the enchantment broken, if that is possible."

"First Takhisis, now Chemosh," Gerard growled, running his hand through his hair and making it stand straight up. "Sometimes I wonder if the return of the gods was such a good thing. We were doing all right on our own—not counting the Dragon Overlords, of course. We've got trouble enough now, what with displaced elves, rumors of a goblin army build-up in southern Qualinesti, and our local robber baron, Captain Samuval. We don't need gods like Chemosh coming around to complicate matters. But then, I guess you must've figured that out for yourself, Rhys, since you're no longer a monk of Majere, eh? You're wearing monks' garb, though, so you must be a monk of some sort."

"I can see why you were hired on as sheriff, my lord," Rhys said, meeting the blue eyes and holding them. "You have the ability to interrogate a man without letting him feel like he is being interrogated."

Gerard shrugged. "No offense, Brother. I'm a good sheriff because I like people, even the rascals. This job is never boring, I can tell you that much."

He leaned his elbows on the table and studied Rhys intently. "Here you are, a monk who leads the life of a monk of Majere and follows the ways of a monk of Majere and yet claims he's not a monk of Majere. Wouldn't you find that to be of interest?"

"I find everything involving mankind to be of interest, my lord Sheriff," Rhys replied.

Gerard was about to respond, when their conversation was interrupted. One of his men entered the Inn, came up to him in haste. The two conferred in low tones together, and Gerard rose to his feet.

"Duty calls, I'm afraid. I haven't seen this brother of yours, Brother, but I'll keep an eye out for him. I can find you here, I guess?"

"Only if I can engage in some task to earn my keep," Rhys said firmly.

"See? What did I tell you! Once a monk, always a monk." Gerard grinned, shook hands again with Rhys, and left. He had gone only a few steps, when he turned back, "I almost forgot. There's an abandoned temple a few blocks off the Town Square in what we locals call 'Gods' Row.' Supposedly this temple was once dedicated to Chemosh. It's been empty since anyone here can remember, but who knows? Maybe he's moved back. Oh, and there's a tavern off the beaten path known as the Trough. It's popular with young ne'er-do-wells. You might try looking for your brother there."

"Thank you, my lord Sheriff, I will investigate both," Rhys replied, grateful for the tips.

"Good hunting," called Gerard with a wave as he departed.

Rhys ate his stew and carried his bowl back to the kitchen, where he was finally able to persuade the reluctant Laura Majere to allow him to work to pay for their room and board. Ordering Atta to a corner, where she wouldn't be underfoot, Rhys washed dishes, hauled water and wood up the kitchen stairs and chopped potatoes, destined to be used for one of the Inn's best known delicacies.

It was late afternoon by the time Rhys was finished with his chores. Nightshade had not yet returned. Rhys asked the cook directions to the Trough. He received a startled look. The cook was certain Rhys must be mistaken. Rhys persisted and eventually the cook told him, even going so far as to walk to the top of the stairs to point out the road he should take.

Before he left, Rhys took Atta to the stables and gave her the command to wait for him. She flopped down on her belly in the straw, put her head between her paws, and gazed up at him. She was not happy, but she was prepared to obey.

He had considered bringing her with him. Atta was an obedient dog, one of the best that Rhys had ever trained, but she had taken against Lleu from the very start, and after his violent attack on her master, Rhys was afraid that if the two came in contact again, Atta would not wait for her master's command but would go for Lleu's throat.

Rhys gave her a pat and some meat scraps by way of apology and to assure her she was not being punished, then he departed, heading for the Trough, which sounded just like the kind of place his brother tended to frequent.

Rhys did not go immediately to the Trough as he had planned. Discovering that God's Row was not far from the main square, he decided to visit the ruined temple on his way out of town, perhaps gaining information that might prove useful in dealing with his brother, should he chance to find him.

The end of the War of Souls brought the return of the gods, and the return of their clerics, performing miracles in the name of their gods and gaining followers. They built new temples dedicated to the various gods, and here in Solace, as in other cities, the temples tended to be clustered in the same general part of town, much as sword dealers located in Sword Street, cloth merchants in Clothier's Street, and mageware shops in Magi Alley. Some said this was so that the gods, who'd been duped once by one of their own, could keep a closer eye on each other.

Gods' Row was located near the Tomb of the Last Heroes. Rhys paused for a look at this monument, which——he was thankful to see——remained faithful to childhood's memory. Solamnic knights posted honorary guard in front of the Tomb. Kender picnicked on the lawn and celebrated their hero, the famous Tasslehoff Burrfoot. The tomb was graced with a reverence and a solemnity that Rhys found restful. After paying a moment of silent respect for the dead who slumbered within, he continued on past it to the street where the gods lived.

Gods' Row was bustling with activity, with several new temples under construction. The temple to Mishakal was the largest and most magnificent, for it was in Solace that her disciple, Goldmoon of the Que-Shu, had come bearing the miraculous blue crystal staff. Because of this, the people of Solace always claimed that the goddess took a personal interest in them. The temple to Kiri-Jolith was almost as large and stood side-by-side with Mishakal. Rhys saw several men wearing tabards that marked them as Solamnic knights emerging from this temple.

Next to these two, Rhys was nonplussed to see a temple dedicated to Majere. He had not expected to find such a temple, though, on second thought, he supposed he should have been prepared for it. Solace was a major cross-roads in the region. Locating a temple here provided the clerics of Majere with easy access to a major portion of western Ansalon.

Rhys crossed the street to walk on the opposite side of the temple, keeping to the shadows. If ordinary laymen mistook him for a monk of Majere, Majere's clerics would do the same and they would find out the truth immediately, for Rhys would not think of trying to lie to them. He might well be waylaid and questioned and brought before the temple's High Abbot for a "talk." They might have even heard about the murders from the Prophet of Majere and want to discuss that. The clerics would be well-meaning, of course, but Rhys did not want to waste time answering their questions, nor did he think he was up to the task.

Several clerics in their orange and copper robes were working in the temple garden. They paused in what they were doing to regard him curiously. He continued on his way, his gaze straight ahead.

A blast of wind, the scent of the sea, and the feel of an arm entwined through his arm announced the presence of his goddess.

"Keep close to me, monk," Zeboim ordered peremptorily. "Majere's busy-bodies will not notice you this way."

"I do not need your protection, Majesty," Rhys said, trying unsuccessfully to withdraw from her embrace. "Nor did I ask you for it."

"You never ask me for anything," Zeboim returned, "and I would be so happy to accommodate you."

She pressed up against him, so that he could feel the softness and the warmth of her.

"What a hard, firm body you have," Zeboim continued in admiring tones. "All the walking you do, I suppose. Make a scene," she added, her voice soft as a summer breeze with just a hint of thunder, "and you will spend the rest of the night discussing the good of your soul, when you might be talking to your brother."

Rhys cast her a sharp glance. "You know where Lleu is?"

"I do, and so do you," she returned with a meaningful look.

"The Trough?"

"He is there now, tossing down tumbler after tumbler of dwarf spirits. He is drinking so much, one would imagine the makers are about to go extinct. They would, if I had anything to say about it. Hairy little bastards—dwarves."

"Thank you for the information, Majesty," said Rhys, once more trying to disentangle himself. "I must go to Lleu—"

"Certainly, you must. You will. But not before you pay a visit to my shrine," said Zeboim. "It's just down the road. That is where you were bound, I presume?"

"In truth, Majesty—"

"Never tell a woman the truth, monk," Zeboim warned.

Rhys smiled. "Then, yes, that is where I was bound."

"And you have some little gift for me?" the goddess asked archly.

"My possessions consist of my scrip and my emmide," said Rhys, smiling. "Which would you like, Majesty?"

Zeboim regarded the proffered objects with disdain. "A smelly leather sack or a stick. I want neither, thank you."

They passed the temple of Majere. Seeing Rhys walking with a woman, the clerics knew he was not one of theirs and went back to the chores. Ahead was the temple to Zeboim, a modest structure made of drift wood hauled here from the shores of New Sea, decorated with sea shells. Before they reached the doorway, Zeboim halted and turned to face him.

"Your gift to your goddess will be a kiss."

Rhys took hold of her hand, and respectfully pressed it to his lips.

Zeboim slapped him across the cheek. The blow was hard, left him with burning skin and an aching jaw.

"How dare you mock me?" she demanded, seething.

"I do not mock you, Majesty," Rhys returned quietly. "I show my respect for you, as I would hope you have respect for me and the vows I have taken—vows of poverty and chastity."

"Vows to another god!" Zeboim said scornfully.

"Vows to myself, Majesty," said Rhys.

"What do I care about your silly vows? Nor do I want your respect!" Zeboim raged. "I am to be feared, adored!"

Rhys did not flinch before her, nor did he touch his stinging cheek. Zeboim grew suddenly calm, dangerously calm, as the seas will go smooth and flat before the storm.

"You are an insolent and obdurate man. I put up with you for one reason, monk. Woe betide you if you fail me!"

The goddess departed, leaving Rhys feeling as drained as if he'd come from the field of battle. Zeboim did not want a follower. She wanted to capture him, take him prisoner, force him to work for her like a chained-up galley-slave. Rhys had one weapon to use to keep her at a distance and that was discipline—discipline of body, discipline of mind. Zeboim had no understanding of this and did not know how to fight it. He infuriated her, yet he intrigued her. Rhys knew, however, that the time would come when the fickle goddess would cease to be intrigued and would give way to her fury.

At the far end of the street, Rhys could see the broken-down temple of Chemosh, the ruins of which were strewn among a patch of weeds. Rhys had no need to go there, since he now knew where to find Lleu, but he decided to pay a visit to the temple anyway. Rhys had all night to find Lleu, who would not soon leave the tavern. He turned his steps toward the temple of the God of Death.

Perhaps it was the influence of the god, or perhaps it was merely Rhys's imagination, but it seemed to him that the shadows of coming night clustered more thickly around the temple than other parts of the street. He would need a light to investigate and he had no lantern with him. He returned to the shrine of Zeboim. He saw no sign of priest or priestess. No one answered his repeated calls. Several candles, standing in holders fashioned to look like wooden boats, burned on the altar—gifts to Zeboim made in hopes that she would watch over those who sailed the seas or traveled the inland waterways.

"You said I never asked you for anything, Majesty," Rhys said to the goddess. "I ask you now. Grant me the gift of light."

Rhys removed one of the candles from the altar and carried it outdoors. A puff of wind caused the flame to waver and nearly go out, but the goddess relented, and candle in hand, Rhys went to investigate the temple of Chemosh.

Chunks of fallen stone lay upon crumbling stairs. Rhys had to climb over them to gain the door, only to find that it was blocked by a pillar. He squeezed his way inside through a crack in the wall. The temple floor was littered with debris and dust. Weeds and grass poked up through the cracks. The altar was cracked and overgrown with bind-weed. Any objects sacred to the god had been carried off either by his priests or looters or both. The prints of Rhys's bare feet were the only prints in the dust. He held the flame high, looked searchingly all around the temple. No one had been here in a long, long while.

Carrying the candle back to the shrine of Zeboim, Rhys placed it in its little wooden boat and gave his thanks to the goddess. He turned his footsteps toward the path that would take him to the Trough.

"Whatever Chemosh is doing in the world, he is not interested in building monuments," Rhys remarked to himself as he walked past the beautiful temple, all done in white marble, of Mishakal.

He found that thought disturbing, more disturbing than if he'd come upon a group of black-robed priests skulking about inside the temple walls, raising up corpses by the score. The Lord of Death was no longer hiding in the shadows. He was out in the sunlight, walking among the living, recruiting followers like the wretched Lleu.

But to what end? To what purpose?

Rhys had no idea. Once he found his brother, he hoped he would gain answers.

"Rhys, hullo!" Nightshade appeared out of the twilight, came running up to him. "They told me back at the inn where you were going so I thought I'd come with you. Where's Atta?"

"I left her at the Inn," said Rhys.

"The people are nice there," Nightshade commented. "A lot of places won't let me in, but the lady who runs the Inn—you know, the plump, pretty woman with the red hair—anyway, she told me that she's partial to kender. One of her father's best friends was a kender."

"Were you able to help the widow contact her husband?" Rhys asked.

"I tried." Nightshade shook his head. "His soul had already passed on to the next part of his journey. If you'll believe it, she was hopping mad. She said she figured he'd gone off with some floozy. I tried to explain that it didn't work that way, that his soul was off broadening its horizons. She said 'broad' was the right word for it; he'd always been one for the ladies. She's going to marry the baker and that would fix him. She didn't give me any money, but she did take me to meet the baker and he gave me a meat-pie."

The two made their way through the streets, leaving behind the bustling and busy part of Solace and entering into a part that was dark and dismal. There were no shops and only a scattering of tumble-down houses from which dim lights shone. Few people walked in this part of town by night. Occasionally they met some straggler, hurrying along the deserted street, keeping his head low and looking neither to the right nor the left, as if fearful of what he might see. Rhys was just starting to think that perhaps he'd taken a wrong turn, for it seemed they had reached the end of the civilized world, when he smelled wood smoke and saw flickering firelight streaming through a window. Loud voices raised in a bawdy song.

"I think we found it," said Nightshade.

The original Trough was long gone. It and several later incarnations of the tavern had burnt to the ground. First the kitchen had caught fire. The next time it had been the chimney. Once a band of drunken draconians had set fire to the tavern when confronted with what they considered to be an unreasonable bill, and once the owner had set fire to it himself for reasons that were never very clear. Each time it had been rebuilt, using money said to be supplied by the hill dwarves, for it was one of the few places remaining in Abanasinia where one could buy the potent liquor known as dwarf spirits.

The tavern lurked in the thick shadows of a grove of trees near the edge of the road and had few distinguishing characteristics. Even when Rhys was close to it, he could get no clear impression of the building, except that it was long and low, rickety and unstable. It did boast a single window in the front. The glass for the window must have cost more than the entire building and Rhys wondered why the owner bothered. As it turned out, the window was not there for aesthetic purposes, but so those inside could keep on an eye on those outside and if necessary make a quick dash for the back door.

Rhys placed his hand on the iron door handle, noting it had a greasy feel to it, and leaned down to say in a low voice to the kender, "I do not think you're going to find much work here. It would be best if you did not seek to offer your services for contacting the dead."

"I was thinking the same thing," Nightshade returned.

"Nor do I think this would be a good time for you to borrow anything from anyone."

"There never does seem to be a good time," Nightshade said cheerfully. "Don't worry. I'll keep my hands in my pockets."

"And," Rhys added, "if my brother is here, let me do the talking."

"I'm to be seen and not heard," said Nightshade. He looked a little daunted. "I miss Atta."

"So do I," said Rhys. He opened the door.

A fire burning sullenly in a fire pit at the back of the tavern was the only source of light, and it was smoking so much that it wasn't doing a very good job of that. Rhys peered through the murky interior of the tavern. The song fell silent in midnote when he and the kender entered, except for one drunk who was not singing the same song anyway and who droned on without pause.

Rhys saw Lleu immediately. His brother sat at a table by himself in the middle of the tavern. He was in the act of taking a swig from an earthenware jug when Rhys entered. Wiping his mouth, Lleu set the jug back on the table. He glanced at the new visitor, then glanced away, not interested.

Rhys crossed the room to the table where his brother sat. He was afraid that his brother might try to run, once he recognized him, so he spoke to him first.

"Lleu," said Rhys calmly, "do not be alarmed. I've come to talk with you. Nothing more."

Lleu looked up. "Fine with me, friend," he said with a smile that was meant to be genial but which had a strained quality to it. "Sit down and talk away."

Rhys was disconcerted. This was not the reaction he had expected. Rhys stared at Lleu, who stared right back, and Rhys realized that his brother did not recognize him. Given the shadowy, smoky atmosphere of the tavern and the fact that he was no longer wearing orange robes, this was perhaps understandable. Rhys sat down at the table with his brother. Nightshade plunked down beside him. The kender regarded Lleu with a round-eyed gaze, then glanced at Rhys and seemed about to say something. Rhys shook his head and Nightshade remembered that he was supposed to keep quiet.

"Lleu," said Rhys, "it's me, Rhys. Your brother."

Lleu cast him a bored glance, went back to his jug. "If you say so."

"Don't you recognize me, Lleu?" Rhys pressed. "You should. You tried to kill me."

"Obviously I failed," Lleu grunted. He lifted the jug, took a long pull at the liquor and set it back down again. "So you've got nothing to complain about, that I can see. Have a drink?"

Lleu held out the jug to his brother. On Rhys's refusal, Lleu offered it to the kender. "How about you, little fella?"

"Yes, thank . . . uh, no, that's all right," said Nightshade, catching Rhys's eye.

"Just as well," Lleu continued, shoving the jug away in disgust. "Damn spirits must be more than half water. This is my second jug and I can still see just one of you, monk, and just one of your little friend there. Usually after three tips, I'm seeing six of everything and pink goblins to boot."

He turned his head, yelled over his shoulder, "Hey, where's my supper?"

"You ate already," said a voice from the vicinity of the bar, that was lost in a gloom of smoky haze.

"I don't remember eating," Lleu said angrily.

"Well, you did," said the voice dourly. "Yer empty plate's sittin' in front of you."

Lleu frowned down at the table to see a battered pewter plate and a bent knife.

"Then I'm hungry again. Bring me some more of whatever that slop was."

"Not 'til you pay for the last meal you ate. And them two jugs of spirits."

"I'm good for it," Lleu snarled. "I'm a cleric of Kiri-Jolith, for gods' sake."

A snort came from out of the smoke.

"I have part of a meat pie I couldn't finish," said Nightshade, and he brought out the pie wrapped in a grease-spotted handkerchief.

Lleu snatched up the pie and devoured it hungrily, as if he'd not eaten in days. "Any more where that came from?"

"Sorry," said the kender.

"I don't know why it is," Lleu muttered. "I eat and eat and never get full. Must be the damn food in this part of the country. All tastes the same. Bland, like these dwarf spirits. No kick to 'em."

Rhys took hold of his brother's arm, gripped it hard.

"Lleu, quit talking about food and dwarf spirits. Don't you have any remorse for what you've done? For the terrible crime you committed?"

"No, he doesn't," said the kender.

"I told you to be quiet," Rhys ordered impatiently.

Nightshade leaned close to Rhys and put his hand on his arm. "You do realize he's dead, don't you?"

"Nightshade, I don't have time—"

The words froze on Rhys's tongue. He stared at his brother. Slowly, he relaxed his grip, loosened his hold on his brother's arm.

Unfazed, Lleu sat back in his chair. He picked up the jug, took another swig, and then set it back down with a thump.

"Where's my food?" he yelled.

"Ask me again and you'll get your food, all right. I'll stuff it straight up your arse."

"Nightshade, what are you talking about?" Rhys whispered. He could not take his gaze from his brother. "What do you mean, 'he's dead'."

"Just what I said," the kender replied. "He's dead as a coffin nail. He just doesn't know it yet. Would you like me to tell him? It might come as a shock—"

"Nightshade, if this is some type of jest—"

"Oh, no," Nightshade protested, appalled at the mere suggestion. "I may joke about a lot things, but not my work. I take that very seriously. All those poor spirits waiting to be set free . . ." The kender paused, cocked an eye at Rhys. "You truly can't see he's dead?"

Lleu had forgotten they were there. He stared into the smoke, every so often taking a pull from the jug, more by force of habit, seemingly, then because he took any pleasure in it.

"He is acting very strangely," Rhys conceded. "But he is breathing. His flesh is warm to the touch. He drinks and eats, he sits and talks to me—"

"Yeah, that's the odd part," said Nightshade, screwing up his face into a puzzled expression. "I've seen plenty of corpses in my life, but they were all quiet, peaceful sorts. This is the first time I ever saw one sitting in a tavern drinking dwarf spirits and wolfing down meat pies."

"This is not funny, Nightshade," Rhys said grimly.

"Well, it's hard to explain!" The kender was defensive. "It's like you trying to tell a blind person what the sky looks like. I can see he's dead because . . . because there's no light inside him."

"No light . . ." Rhys repeated softly. He recalled the Master's words: *Lleu is his own shadow.*

"When I look at you or those two men playing bones over in the corner, I see a kind of light coming off them. Oh, it's not much. Not bright like the fire or even a candle flame. You couldn't read a book by it, or find your way in the dark or anything like that. It's just a wavering, shimmering glow. Like the very tip tiptop of the flame before it trails off into smoke. That sort of light. When you had hold of him, did you feel a pulse? You might see if he's got one."

Rhys reached out, took hold of his brother's wrist.

"What are you doing?" Lleu asked, regarding Rhys with a frown.

"I am afraid that you are not well," Rhys said.

"That's an understatement," muttered the kender.

"I'm fine, I assure you. I never felt better. Chemosh takes care of me."

"Well?" the kender asked Rhys eagerly.

Rhys felt something that might have been a pulse but was not quite the same. It did not feel like the rush of life beneath the skin. More like turgid water moving sluggishly beneath a layer of thick ice.

"What about the eyes?" Nightshade sat forward, trying to see Lleu through the smoke.

Rhys had a better view. He looked into his brother's eyes and recoiled.

He'd seen those eyes before gazing up at him from the grave. Eyes that were empty. Eyes that had no soul behind them.

Lleu's eyes were the eyes of the dead.

He could not take this as proof, however, for he was starting to doubt his own senses. His brother looked alive, he sounded alive, his flesh felt alive to the touch. Yet, there were the Master's warning, the kender's assessment, and now that Rhys came to think of it, there was Atta's reaction to Lleu. She had taken against him from the first, confronting him with bared teeth and raised hackles. She did not want him near the sheep. She'd bitten him when he tried to lay his hands on her.

Rhys might have assumed that the Master was speaking in metaphors. He might dismiss the kender as talking nonsense. But Rhys trusted the dog. Atta had realized from the moment she saw and smelled Lleu that there was something wrong about him.

"You are right," said Rhys softly. "His eyes are those of a corpse."

Lleu shoved back his chair, stood up. "I've got to go. I'm meeting someone. A young lady." He winked and leered.

"That wouldn't be Mina, would it?" Rhys asked.

Lleu's reaction was startling. Reaching over the table, he grabbed hold of the collar of Rhys's robes and nearly dragged him from the chair.

"Where is she?" Lleu demanded, and he was panting with an ugly eagerness. "Is she around here somewhere? Tell me how to find her! Tell me!"

Rhys looked down at his brother's hands, gripping the homespun fabric. The knuckles were white with intensity. The fingers quivered.

"I have no idea where she is," Rhys said. "I was hoping you could tell me."

Lleu glared at him suspiciously. Then he let go.

"Sorry," Lleu mumbled. "I need to find her, that's all. It's all right. I'll keep looking."

Lleu flung open the door and walked out, slamming the door shut behind him. The barkeep roared out that he wanted his money, but by then, Lleu was long gone.

Rhys was on his feet. Nightshade jumped up in response.

"Where are we going?"

"After him."

"Why?"

"To see what he does, where he goes."

"Hey!" shouted the barkeep. "Are you going to pay for your friend?"

"I have no money——" Rhys began and was interrupted by the sound of steel coins ringing on the bar.

"Thanks," said the barkeep, scooping up the coins.

Rhys looked accusingly at Nightshade.

"I didn't do it," said the kender promptly.

"That's two you owe me, monk," said Zeboim's sultry voice from the smoky shadows. "Now go after him!"

Rhys and Nightshade left the tavern, silently hurrying along behind Lleu, who was heading back into Solace.

They took precautions to keep him from seeing that he was being followed, although that proved unnecessary, for he never once looked behind. He strolled jauntily down the road, his head thrown back, singing the refrain of the bawdy song.

"Nightshade," said Rhys, "I have heard that there are undead known as zombies." He felt strange, asking such a question, unreal, as if in a horrible dream. "Is it possible—"

"—that he's a zombie?" Nightshade shook his head emphatically. "You've never seen a zombie, have you? Zombies are corpses that are raised up after death. Their stench alone is enough to curl your socks. They have rotting flesh, eyeballs hanging out of the eye sockets. They shuffle when they walk because they don't know how to move their legs or feet. They're more like horrible puppets than anything else. They don't sing, I can tell you that, and they're not young and handsome.

"I'll say one thing for your brother, Rhys," Nightshade concluded solemnly. "He's the best looking dead man I ever saw in my life."

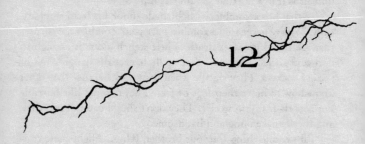

12

Rhys and Nightshade followed Lleu to one of the newer parts of Solace. In order to accommodate the numbers of people moving into the city, houses were being hastily constructed below the vallenwood trees, not up among the branches. Those who lived in these new houses were generally refugees who had fled the destruction caused by Beryl. They had lived in tents when they first arrived in Solace, but by now some of them had done well for themselves and wanted permanent dwellings.

A great many houses could be built around the bole of one of the giant trees. To save money and wood, the designer followed the elven plan of using the tree itself as one wall of the house, so that the homes resembled mushrooms sprouting out of the mud at the base of the tree. The hour was late. Most of the houses were dark, their occupants having gone to bed, but here and there a light shone from one of the windows, casting its glow into the street.

Lleu slowed his pace when he reached this part of town and ceased to sing. He walked up to one of the darkened houses and peeked in a window. Then he loitered up and down the street, casting an occasional glance at the house. Rhys and Nightshade stood in the shadows and watched and waited.

The door to the house opened a crack. A young woman in a cloak slipped out and softly and stealthily closed the door behind her. She was having trouble seeing in the darkness and looked about fearfully.

"Lleu?" she called in a tremulous tone.

"Lucy, my dove." He caught her in his arms and kissed her.

"No, no, not here!" she said breathlessly, pushing him away. "Suppose my husband were to wake up and see us?"

"Where shall we go, then?" said Lleu, holding her around the waist and nuzzling her neck. "I can't keep my hands off you."

"I know a place," she said. "Come with me."

Clinging together, laughing and giggling, the two hastened down the street. Rhys and Nightshade followed after them. Rhys was troubled, uncertain what to do. This was apparently nothing more than a midnight assignation with a young woman, perfectly normal for a young man like Lleu, except that Lleu was far from normal and the young woman was married.

Rhys should probably call a halt to this now, take hold of the young woman and drag her back to her house. There would be a scene with the husband: tears and wails, rage, a fight. The neighbors would wake. Someone would summon the authorities.

No, Rhys determined. Nothing good would come of an uproar. He would bide his time, wait until they were someplace quiet, then try to talk to Lleu.

The couple reached a secluded, cleared area amidst a grove of pine trees. From the looks of the trampled grass, this was the local meeting ground for lovers. They had barely stopped walking before Lleu had his hands all over the woman. His kissed her neck, ran his hands over her breasts, lifted up her skirts.

"He's pretty lively for a dead guy," Nightshade observed.

Rhys was uncomfortable watching this. He felt he should intervene, although what he would say was open to question. The young woman would be embarrassed and upset. Lleu would be angry. Again, there would be tears, recriminations.

The young woman sighed, panted, and clung to Lleu, pressing

his head against her bosom, running her fingers through his hair. Lleu took off her cloak and spread it on the pine needles. The two sank down onto the ground.

"We should leave," said Rhys, and he was about to turn to go when his brother's next words halted him.

"Have you thought more about what we talked about, my dearest?" Lleu asked. "About Chemosh?"

"Chemosh?" Lucy repeated vaguely. "Don't let's talk about religion now. Kiss me!"

"But I want to talk about Chemosh," Lleu said, his hand fondling her breasts.

"That old, moldy god?" Lucy sighed, pouting. "I don't see why you want to talk of gods at a time like this."

"Because it is important to me," said Lleu. His voice took on a soft tone. He kissed her on the cheek. "To us." He kissed her again. "I can't run away with you if you won't swear to worship Chemosh, as I do."

"I don't see what difference it makes," Lucy said, between her own kisses.

Lleu brushed her lips with his own. "Because, my sweet, I will live forever, as I am now—young, vibrant, handsome—"

She giggled. "You are so vain!"

"You, on the other hand, will grow old. Your hair will turn gray. Your skin will wrinkle and your teeth fall out."

"You wouldn't love me then," Lucy said, faltering.

"You will die, Lucy," Lleu said softly, stroking her cheek with his hand. "And I will be alive and healthy and needing someone to share my bed . . ."

"And if I worship Chemosh, he will keep me young and beautiful?" Lucy asked. "Forever and always?"

"Forever and always," said Lleu. "And that is how long I will love you."

"Well, then," said Lucy with a laugh, "I give my soul to Chemosh!"

"You will not regret it, my love," said Lleu.

He pulled down her bodice, exposing her breasts that were white in the moonlight. She sighed and shivered and put her hand on his head, drew him down to kiss her soft flesh. He pressed his lips against her left breast, gripped her tightly in his arms.

"Lleu," Lucy said, her tone changing. "Lleu, you're hurting me— Ah!"

She gave a piercing scream and struggled in his arms. Lleu held her fast. Her scream swelled to an agonized shriek. Her body jerked and twitched. Rhys jumped to his feet and raced toward the couple, with Nightshade dashing along behind.

"She's dying!" cried the kender. "He's killing her! Her spirit light's fading."

The young woman shuddered, her body stiffened, and then she went limp.

Rhys grasped hold of Lleu, pulled him off her and flung him aside. Kneeling down on the ground, he gathered up the body of the young woman in his arms, hoping to feel yet some spark of life.

"Too late," Lleu said coolly. He rose to his feet, looked down at the dead woman dispassionately, as upon a job well done. "She belongs to Chemosh now."

The woman was no longer breathing. Her eyes were empty and unknowing. Rhys felt for the lifebeat in her neck, found none. On her breast, burned into her flesh, was the imprint of his brother's lips.

"Majere," Rhys prayed. "She didn't know what she was saying. Have mercy on her. Restore her to life!"

Rhys shifted position slightly. The woman's head lolled to one side. Her flaccid arm slid off his knee and fell limply to the ground. Rhys listened for the voice of the god.

"Do not punish this innocent woman because of me, Lord!" Rhys begged. "Her death is my fault! I could have saved her, as I could have saved my brothers."

There came no answer. The only sound was Lleu's scornful laughter.

"Zeboim," Rhys cried, his voice harsh. "Grant this poor woman her life."

An echo of his brother's scornful laugh came back to him from out the shadows of the trees.

Rhys gently lowered the woman's body onto the ground.

"Her spirit's gone," said Nightshade. "I'm sorry, Rhys. There's nothing can be done. I'm afraid your brother may be right. Chemosh has her."

Rising to his feet, Rhys faced his brother. "I didn't want to do this, Lleu, but you have left me no choice. You are my prisoner. I'm going to take you to the authorities. You'll be charged with murder. I want you to come with me quietly. I don't want to have to hurt you, but I will, if necessary."

Lleu shrugged. "I'll come with you willingly, brother. But I think you're going to find it hard to make that charge of murder stick."

"Why is that?" Rhys asked grimly.

"Because there has been no murder," said a voice behind him, with a giggle.

Lucy scrambled to her feet and ran over to stand beside Lleu. She clasped her arms around him, pressed up against him. Her hair was disheveled, her bodice undone. Rhys could still see the mark—red and fiery—of Lleu's lips on her breast, that rose and fell with the breath of life. She regarded Rhys with mocking laughter in her eyes.

"I am alive, monk," she said. "Better than ever."

"You were dead,' said Rhys, his throat constricting. "You died in my arms."

"Maybe I did," Lucy returned archly, "but who will believe you? No one. No one in the whole wide world."

"Do you want me to come with you to the sheriff, brother?" Lleu asked. "I can introduce him to a couple of other young women I've met during my time in Solace. Women who now understand and embrace the ways of Chemosh."

Rhys was starting to understand, though the understanding was so horrendous that he found it difficult to accept.

"You are dead," he said.

"No, brother, I am one of the Beloved of Chemosh," said Lleu. He and Lucy both laughed.

"I tried to explain all to you once, Rhys, but you wouldn't listen. Now, you see it for yourself. Look at Lucy. She is beautiful, blooming, radiant. Does she look dead to you? Show him, Lucy."

The young woman advanced upon Rhys, hips swaying, her eyes half-shut, her lips parted provocatively. "Your brother is envious, Lleu. He wants me for himself."

"He's all yours, my dove," said Lleu. "Have fun—"

Lucy continued to advance, her head thrown back, her lashes half-closed, her lips parted.

"Kill her!" said Nightshade suddenly.

Rhys fell back a pace. He could not take his eyes from her, the woman who had died in his arms, and who was now fondling him with a flirtatious smile.

"Kill her and kill him, too," said Nightshade urgently.

"According to Lleu, they can't be killed," Rhys said. "Besides, there's been too much death already."

Lucy took hold of the collar of Rhys's robes, slid her hands beneath it.

"You have never lain with a woman, have you, monk? Wouldn't you like to find out what you've been missing all these years?"

Rhys thrust aside her clutching hands, shoved her away.

"You have to try to kill them," said Nightshade, relentless, "or they'll do murder again."

"A monk of Majere does not kill . . ." Rhys said softly.

"You're not a monk," Nightshade returned brutally, "and if you were, it doesn't matter. They're already dead!"

"I can't be sure of that." Rhys shook his head.

"Yes, you can! Look in her eyes, Rhys! Look in her eyes!"

Rhys looked into the girl's eyes. He saw not emptiness, as he had seen in his brother's eyes, but something more terrible. He had seen such a look once before and he tried to recall where.

Then it came to him—the eyes of a starving wolf. Driven by hunger, desperate to feed, the animal's need overrode every other instinct, including fear. Rhys had been armed with two flaming torches. Atta tore at the wolf's flank with her teeth. The wolf had gone straight for Rhys's throat . . .

He saw the truth of the kender's words in Lucy's eyes. She would kill again to satisfy that desperate need. Again and again . . .

Rhys lifted the emmide and jabbed it straight into the girl's forehead. Her head snapped back and he heard, quite clearly, the neck bone crack. She slumped to the ground, her head twisted at an odd angle. Rhys whipped around to face his brother.

Lleu lounged against a tree, his arms folded across his chest, watching the proceedings with a smile.

Rhys gripped the staff and started to advance on his brother.

"Look out! Behind you!" Nightshade's voice rose shrilly.

Rhys turned, stared, horrified.

Lucy walked toward him, hips swaying, lips parted, hands outstretched.

"Chemosh will have your soul," she said to him, laughing, lilting. Her head was at an odd angle from where he'd broken her neck. With a twist and a jerk, she righted it and kept coming. "Whether you will it or not."

He could hear, behind him, the scraping of Lleu's sword sliding from its scabbard. Rhys faced Lucy, holding her at bay with the emmide, his eyes watching her while his ears kept track of Lleu's movements. Nightshade was yammering something and waving his hands, as though he was casting some sort of magic spell. Rhys wished the kender would be quiet. He heard a rustle in the grass, a crackle of brown pine needles, and Lleu's sudden, indrawn breath.

Rhys sprang sideways, twisting his body. The sword sliced the air where he had been standing.

Lleu's wild lunge carried him halfway across the clearing. Rhys smacked Lucy in the face with the emmide. The blow smashed her nose, spread it all over her face. A thin trail of blood trickled from the wound, but not the gushing torrent that should have flowed from such an injury. She cried out, more in anger than in pain, and staggered backward.

Rhys shifted about to face Lleu in time to see his brother run at him again, sword in one hand, knife in the other.

Rhys struck the sword with his staff, broke it in two. Twirling the staff rapidly so that it looked like a windmill in a high gale, he brought it down hard on Lleu's wrist, heard the snap of bone. Lleu dropped the knife. Rhys remembered clearly the last time he'd struck Lleu, he'd also cried out in pain. Lleu did not cry out now, did not even appear to notice the fact that his hand no longer functioned.

Weaponless, Lleu flung himself at his brother, grappling for his throat with one good hand, flailing at him with his broken hand, using it as a club.

His soul sick with horror, Rhys side-stepped. Lleu lurched past him, and as he went, Rhys kicked his feet out from underneath him. Lleu fell onto his stomach.

Standing over his fallen brother, Rhys drove the butt end of the staff with all his strength into Lleu's spinal column, separating the vertebrae, smashing through to the spinal cord, severing it.

Rhys fell back, on the defensive, watching his brother.

"My mystic spell didn't work!" Nightshade panted, running toward him. "I've cast that spell a hundred zillion times and it always stops undead. Usually bowls 'em over like nine pins. It didn't even faze your brother."

Lleu grimaced, as if he'd stubbed his toe, then, slowly, as though putting himself back together, he started to regain his feet. He rubbed his back, arching it.

"If you want my opinion, Rhys," the kender added, gasping for breath, "you can't do anything to kill them. Now would be a good time to run away!"

Rhys didn't answer. He was watching Lleu.

"Right now!" Nightshade urged, tugging on Rhys's sleeve.

"I told you before, Rhys," said Lleu. He reached down to his maimed hand, grabbed the wrist and snapped it back in place. "I am one of the Beloved of Chemosh. I have his gift. Life unending . . ."

"I am also Beloved of Chemosh," said Lucy. She appeared oblivious to the fact that her nose was mangled and bloodied. "I have his gift. Life unending. You can have it, too, Rhys. Give yourself to Chemosh."

The two corpses advanced on him, their eyes alight, not with life, but with the desperate need to take life.

Bile filled Rhys's mouth. His stomach clenched. He turned and fled, running through the forest, crashing into tree limbs, plunging headlong into weed patches. He stopped to be sick, and then he ran again, ran from the mocking laughter that danced among the trees, ran from the body of the girl in his arms, ran from the bodies in the mass grave at the monastery. He ran blindly, heedlessly, ran until he had no more strength and he fell to the ground, gasping and sobbing. He was sick again and again, even when there was nothing left to purge, and then he heaved up blood. At last, exhausted, he rolled over on his back and lay there, his body clenched and shaking.

Here Nightshade found him.

Although the kender had recommended running away, he hadn't been prepared for Rhys to act on his advice in quite such a sudden manner. Caught off guard, Nightshade made a slow start. The hungry eyes of the two Beloved of Chemosh turning in his direction put an extra spring in the kender's step. He couldn't see Rhys, but he could hear him tearing and slashing his way through the forest. Kender have excellent night vision, much better than humans, and Nightshade soon came across Rhys, lying on the forest floor, eyes closed, breathing labored.

"Now don't you go dying on me," the kender ordered, squatting down beside his friend.

He laid his hand on Rhys's forehead and felt it warm. His

breathing was harsh and rasping from his raw throat, but strong. Nightshade recited a little singsong chant he'd learned from his parents and stroked the monk's hair soothingly, much the way the kender petted Atta.

Rhys sighed deeply. His body relaxed. He opened his eyes and, seeing Nightshade bending over him, gave a wan smile.

"How are you feeling?" Nightshade asked anxiously.

"Much better," Rhys said. His stomach had ceased to churn, his raw throat felt warm and soothed, as if he'd drunk a honey posset. "You have hidden talents, seemingly."

"Just a little healing spell I picked up from my parents," Nightshade replied modestly. "It comes in handy sometimes— mending broken bones and stopping bleeding and making fevers go away. I can't do anything major, not like bringing back the dead—" He gulped, bit his lip. "Oops. Sorry. Didn't mean to mention that."

Rhys rose swiftly to his feet. "How long was I unconscious?"

"Not long. You might have waited for me, you know?"

"I wasn't thinking," Rhys said softly. "I couldn't think of anything except how horrible—" He shook his head. "Are they coming after us?"

Nightshade glanced back over his shoulder. "I don't know. I guess not. I don't hear them, do you?"

Rhys shook his head. "I wish I could."

"You *want* them to chase after us? They want to kill us! Give us to Chemosh!"

"Yes, I know. But if they were coming after us, it would mean that they fear us. As it is—" He shrugged. "They don't care what happens to us. That's disturbing."

"I see," said Nightshade solemnly. "They know there's nothing we can do to stop them. And they're right. My magic had no effect on them. And that's never happened to me before. Well, not since I was a little kender and just starting out. Maybe if we had a holy weapon—"

"The emmide is a holy weapon blessed by the god. Majere gave it to me, a parting gift." Rhys tightened his grip on the staff. He could see Atta prancing with it in her mouth and he felt a momentary warmth in the midst of the chill darkness. "Even though the wielder of the staff may not be blessed by Majere, the weapon is. And you as you saw, it could not slay my brother or even slow him down much. As Lleu said, he's not afraid that we might tell someone that he is a murderer. Who would believe us?"

"I guess you're right," said Nightshade. "I never thought about it that way. So what do we do?"

"I don't know. I can't think rationally any more." Rhys looked around. "I have no idea where we are or how to get back to the Inn. Do you?"

"Not much," said Nightshade cheerfully. "But I see lights over in that direction. Don't you?"

"No, but then I do not have a kender's eyes." Rhys put his hand on Nightshade's shoulder. "You lead the way. Thank you for your help, my friend."

"You're welcome," said Nightshade. He sounded dispirited, though, not his usual cheerful self. He started walking, but he wasn't watching where he was going and he almost immediately stepped into a hole.

"Ouch," he said and rubbed his ankle.

"Are you all right?"

"Yeah, I guess."

"What's the matter?"

"There's something I need to tell you, Rhys."

"Yes, what is it?"

"You're not going to like it," Nightshade warned.

Rhys sighed. "Can it wait until morning?

"I suppose it could. Except . . . well, it might be important."

"Go ahead then."

"I saw more people like your brother and Lucy. I mean, like those things that used to be your brother and Lucy. I saw them today, in Solace."

The kender's face was a white glimmer in Solinari's light.

"How many?" Rhys asked, despairing.

"Two. Both of them young women. Pretty, too. But dead. Dead as dead can be." Nightshade shook his head sadly. "I would have told you before, except I didn't know what I was seeing. Not until I saw your brother in the tavern. Then I knew. Those women were just like him—no spirit light shining from them, yet they were walking about as happy as you please, talking, laughing . . ."

Rhys thought back to the miller's daughter, who had taken up with Lleu, then run away from her home. How many more young women had Lleu seduced, murdered, and given their souls to Chemosh? Rhys saw again the terrible hunger in Lucy's eyes. How many young men would these women seduce in their turn? Seduce and murder. The Beloved of Chemosh.

"No one knows what they are about, because no one knows they are dead," he said to himself, as the awful perfection of the god's scheme struck him.

Rhys knew the truth of the matter, but as he had told the kender, who would believe him? How could he convince anyone? Nightshade could always tell what he saw, but kender were not known for their veracity. Rhys might seize hold of Lucy, truss her up and drag her before the magistrates, demand that they look into her eyes. Rhys could envision their reaction. He would be the one arrested, locked up as a raving lunatic.

Death had a new face and that face was young and beautiful; Death's body whole and strong.

Rhys could shout this to the world.

And no one would believe him.

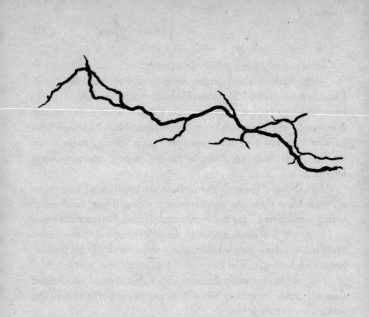

BOOK III

BELOVED
OF
CHEMOSH

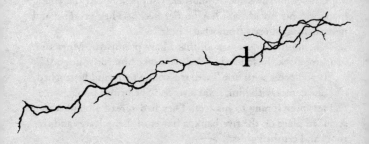

Mina ran her fingers through the man's fair hair. He had soft, fine hair, like that of a child. The bangs were cut short and fell over his forehead, and she brushed it out of the way to see his eyes. She could not recall his name. She never remembered their names. She remembered the eyes, however, remembered the seeking, the yearning, and wondering. Pain, sometimes, unhappiness, anger, frustration. Adoration, of course. They all adored her. The young man seized her hand and kissed her fingers.

During the War of Souls, her soldiers had adored her. They adored her as she led them to death. Adored her as she knelt over them and prayed for them, sent their souls into the vast river of the lost. She saw the fear in their eyes, fear of the unknown.

So much fear. The fear of life, of living. She had the power to take away the fear. Take away the unknown. At her kiss, the spirit left the body, tottered a short distance, arms extended to Chemosh, as a babe totters to its mother. Chemosh sent the spirit back to the body, bathed, cleansed, stripped of all uncomfortable feeling. No love, no guilt, no anguish, no jealousy . . .

"You will be beloved of Chemosh," she said to the young man, his lips warm on her open palm. "You will have unending life.

An end to pain. You will never know cold or hunger."

"One god's the same as another, I suppose," said the young man, and his breath was hot on her neck. "They promise and never deliver, at least from what I hear."

"Chemosh will give you all that I have promised," Mina said, brushing back the fair hair. "Will you take him for your god?"

"If you come with him," said the young man, and he laughed.

"She comes with him," said a voice. "She brings him."

Her lover sprang to his feet. They had spread a blanket in a secluded place on the riverbank, a bower of damp leaves and tree roots and crushed grass.

"Who are you?" the young man demanded of the handsome, elegantly dressed god who seemed to have sprung from the earth, for he had heard no sound of his approach.

"Chemosh," he answered, and as the young man's jaw dropped, the god reached out his hand and touched the young man on his chest, over his heart. "And you are mine."

The young man gasped in pain and clutched his chest. His body shuddered. He sank to his knees. His eyes stared at the god, as the light slowly faded from them. He pitched forward on his face and lay still. Chemosh stepped over the body. He looked at Mina, his expression dark and frowning.

"I do not like this," he said.

"How have I displeased you, my lord?" asked Mina. She rose with dignity to face him. "I do all that you require of me."

What she had said was perfectly true and that only made Chemosh angrier; that and the fact that he did not understand why he should be angry with at her at all.

"You are a High Priestess of the Lord of Death," Chemosh stated. "It is not fitting that these yokels should paw at you with their coarse, ham-fisted hands. You seem to take great pleasure in their pawing and mauling, however. Perhaps I do wrong to stop you."

"My gentle lord," said Mina, moving close to him, looking up at him. Her amber eyes, liquid and golden, poured over him.

"You command me to bring these young ones to you. I obey your commands."

She moved closer still, so that he could feel her warmth, smell the fragrance of her hair and the scent of her flesh that was still soft and pliable with desire.

"The hands that touch me are your hands," she said to him. "The lips that kiss mine are your own. None other."

Chemosh took her in his arms and kissed her hard, brutally, venting his anger on her, who was the cause of it, though he could not say precisely why. Mina returned his kiss, fierce and desperate, as on the field of battle, when all the turmoil of the fight fades away and leaves the two combatants, locked together in a precious moment that will live until one of them dies.

"My lord . . ." Mina breathed. "Would you have me grant him your blessing?"

She gestured to the body of the young man that lay upon the blanket beside the river bank.

"I will deal with it," he said and, bending down, he placed his hand on the young man's still breast.

The eyes of the corpse opened. He had green eyes and fair blonde hair. He looked to Chemosh and he knew the Lord of the Dead, and there was reverence in his gaze. He rose to his feet and bowed.

"You are one of my Beloved," Chemosh said to the young man. "Travel east, into the morning of your new life. And, as you go, find others who will swear to worship me and bring them to my service."

"Yes, lord." The young man made another low bow to Chemosh, who brushed him off with a wave of his hand.

The young man's eyes stole to Mina, who smiled on him, a smile that didn't know his name. Chemosh's brows lowered, and the young man turned and ran away.

"If you can wrench your mind from your conquest, perhaps we can get back to business," Chemosh said. He knew he was being unjust. Mina was doing nothing more than he had instructed her to do. He couldn't help himself, however.

"You are in an ill humor this day, my lord," said Mina, entwining her hands over his arm. "What has happened to cast this dark shadow over you?"

"You would not understand," he said shortly, pushing her hands aside. "You are a mortal."

"A mortal who has touched the mind of a god."

Chemosh looked at her sharply. If she was smiling, smug and triumphant, he would slay her where she stood.

He saw her serious, unknowing. She loved him, adored him.

He sighed deeply, reassured.

"It is Sargonnas. The horned god puffs and struts about heaven as if he were the king of us all." Chemosh fumed as he walked, pacing back and forth along the river bank. "He flaunts his victories in Silvanesti, brags that he has crushed the elves, laughs at how he has cozened the ogres into believing that his minotaur are their allies. He boasts that he and his cows will soon be the unchallenged rulers of the eastern third of Ansalon."

"Mere braggadocio, my lord," said Mina dismissively.

"No," said Chemosh. "The bull-god may be a boorish churl, but he has a crude sort of honor and does not lie." Chemosh halted in his pacing, turned to face Mina. "It is time for us to put our plan into action."

"Surely, it is early yet, my lord," Mina protested. "The numbers of our Beloved grow, but there are not near enough and they are mostly in the west of Ansalon, not the east."

Chemosh shook his head. "We cannot wait. Sargonnas gains in strength daily and the other gods are either blind to his ambition or too preoccupied with their own concerns to see the danger. If he wins the east, do they truly believe he will be content with that? After centuries of being trapped on their isles, the minotaur have finally gained a foothold upon the main continent. He seeks to rule not only the east, but all the world and heaven into the bargain."

Chemosh clenched his fist. "I am the only one who is in a position to challenge him. I must act now before he grows stronger still. Where is that fool, Krell?" He glanced about, as though the death knight might be hiding under a rock.

"Committing mayhem somewhere, I suppose, my lord," said Mina. "I have not kept track of him."

"Nor have I. I will summon him to meet us in the Abyss. You must leave this plane for a time, Mina. Leave your work that is so dear to you."

He cast a scathing glance at the rumpled blanket, the imprint of two intertwined bodies still fresh upon it.

"You are dear to me, my lord," said Mina softly. "My work is just that—my work."

Chemosh saw his reflection in her amber eyes. He saw no other. He took hold of her hands and pressed them to his lips. "Forgive me. I am not myself."

"Perhaps that is the problem, my lord," said Mina.

He paused, thinking this over. "Maybe you are right. I am not even sure what 'myself' is these days. It was easier when Takhisis and Paladine held sway in heaven. We knew our places then. We may not have liked it. We may have railed against them and chafed beneath the yoke, but there was order and stability in heaven and in the world. There is something to be said for peace and security, after all. I could sleep with both eyes closed instead of keeping one always open, always on the lookout for someone sneaking up behind me."

"So you lose a few eons of sleep, Lord," said Mina. "It will all be worth it, when you are the ruler and the others bow to you."

"How did you gain such wisdom?" Chemosh took her in his arms, held her close, and pressed his lips against her neck. "I have made a decision. No longer will rough mortals fawn over you. No more clumsy mortal lips will bruise your flesh. You are loved of a god. Your body, your soul, are mine, Mina."

"They have always been, my lord," she said, shivering in his embrace.

Darkness closed over Chemosh, enfolded him and surrounded her, carried them both to a deeper, thicker, warmer darkness, lit with the single candle flame of ecstasy.

"And will always be."

Chemosh returned to the Abyss to find it dark and dreary. He had no one but himself to blame. He could have lit the Abyss bright as heaven, filled it with chandeliers and candelabra, glowing lamps, and glimmering lanterns. He could have peopled it, furnished it, added song and dance. In eons past he had done so. Not now. He loathed his dwelling place too much to try to change it. He wanted, needed, to be among the living. And now was the time to start to put his plan to gain his heart's desire into action.

He waited impatiently for Krell and was pleased to hear at last the clank and rattle of the death knight, clumping his way through the Abyss, making heavy going of it, as though he were slogging through the thick mud of a battle field. His eyes were two pinpoints of red. Small and set close together, they reminded Chemosh of the eyes of a demonic pig.

Longing for something better to look upon, Chemosh shifted his gaze to Mina. She was dressed in black, a silken gown that flowed over the curves of her body like the touch of his hands. Her breasts rose and fell with her breathing. He could see the faint quiver of the pulse of life beating in the hollow of her throat. He suddenly wished Krell a thousand miles away, but he could not indulge himself, not yet.

"So, Krell, here you are at last," said Chemosh briskly. "Sorry to call you away from slaughtering gully dwarves or whatever it was you found to amuse yourself, but I have a task for you."

"I was not slaughtering gully dwarves," returned Krell sullenly. "There's no pleasure in that, no fight in the little beasts. They simply squeal like rabbits and then fall down and piss themselves."

"It was a jest, Krell. Were you always this stupid or did death have a bad effect on you?"

"I was never one for jests, my lord," said Krell, adding stiffly,

"And you should know where I was. It was you who sent me. I was following your orders, bringing new recruits to you."

"Indeed?" Chemosh put the tips of his fingers together, tapped them gently. "And is that going well?"

"Very well, my lord." Krell rocked back on his heels, pleased with himself. "I think you will find my recruits far more satisfactory than others."

He cast a glance at Mina. She had rescued him, freed him from the tormenting goddess and his rock-bound prison, but he hated her, for all that.

"At least my recruits are trustworthy," Mina returned. "They aren't likely to betray their master."

Krell clenched his fists and took a step toward her.

Mina rose from her chair to face him. Her skin was pale, her eyes glinting gold. She was fearless, beautiful in her courage, radiant in her anger. Chemosh allowed himself a moment's pleasure, then wrenched himself back to business.

"Mina, I think you should leave us."

Mina cast a distrustful glance at Krell. "My lord, I do not like—"

"Mina," Chemosh said. "I gave you an order. I told you to leave."

Mina seemed inclined to argue. One glance at the god's dark and glowering face, however, and she subsided. She gathered up her long skirts and departed.

"You need to keep her in line," Krell advised. "She's getting a bit above herself. As bad as a wife. You should just kill her. She'd be less trouble dead than alive."

Chemosh rounded on the knight. The light in the eyes of the god was fell, a light darker than the darkness. What little there was left of the death knight shriveled up inside his armor.

"Do not forget that you are mine now, Krell," said Chemosh softly, "and that, with a flick of my finger, I can reduce you to a pile of bird droppings."

"Yes, my lord," said Krell, subdued. "Sorry, my lord."

Chemosh summoned a chair, summoned another chair, summoned a table, and placed it between the two of them.

"Sit down, Krell," he said testily. "I understand that you are fond of the game of khas."

"Maybe I am, my lord," said Krell warily, suspecting a trap.

He glared hard at the chair, which had materialized out of the darkness of the Abyss. When he thought Chemosh wasn't looking, Krell gave the chair a surreptitious poke with his finger.

"Sit, Krell," Chemosh repeated coldly. "I like eyes—even pig's eyes—on a level with mine."

The death knight lowered his armor-encased nothingness ponderously into the chair.

Chemosh waved his hand, and a single point of light shone down upon a khas board.

"What do you think of these pieces, Krell?" Chemosh asked casually. "I had them specially made. They're carved out of bone."

Krell was about to say he didn't give a damn if they were carved out of horse manure, but then he caught Chemosh's eye. With a gloved forefinger and thumb, Krell picked up one of the pawns, carved to resemble a goblin, and made a show of admiring it.

"Nice workmanship, my lord. Is it elven?"

"No," said Chemosh. "Goblin. These pieces are elven." He gestured to the two elf clerics.

"I didn't know goblins could carve as well as this," Krell remarked, pinching the goblin by the neck as he peered at it intently.

Chemosh sighed deeply. Even the life of a god was too short to deal with someone as thick-headed as Ausric Krell.

"It isn't carved at all, you dull-witted lunk head. When I said it was made of bone, I meant that it is— Oh, never mind. That's a goblin you're holding. A dead one, shrunken down."

"Ha, ha!" Krell laughed heartily. "That's a good one. And these are dead elves?" He gave one of the clerics a poke. "And is this a dead kender—"

"Enough, Krell!" Chemosh drew in a deep breath, then continued as patiently as he could. "I am about to launch my campaign."

The god placed his elbows on the table, on either side of the khas board, and leaned over it, as though contemplating a move.

"The action I plan to take will, of necessity, attract the attention of the other gods. Only one poses a significant threat to me. Only one could be a serious hindrance. In fact, she has already started to seriously annoy me."

He fixed his eye upon Krell, to make certain he was attending.

"Yes, my lord." Krell looked less stupid now. Campaign, battle—these were things he understood.

"The goddess who concerns me is Zeboim," Chemosh said.

Krell grunted.

"She has come across a follower—a disenfranchised monk of Majere—who has stumbled upon the secret of the Beloved of Chemosh. He has told Zeboim, and she is threatening to expose me unless I return you to Storm's Keep."

"You're not going to do that, are you, my lord?" Krell asked nervously.

Reaching out his hand, Chemosh picked up one of the pieces from the side of darkness—the piece known as the knight. He fondled the piece, twisted it in his hand.

"As a matter of fact, I am. Wait!" He raised a hand, as Krell squealed in irate protest. "Hear me out. What do you think of this move, Krell?"

He slowly and deliberately placed the piece in front of the black queen.

"You can't make such a move, my lord," Krell rumbled. "It's against the rules."

"It is, Krell," Chemosh conceded. "Against all the rules. Pick up that piece. Take a good look at it. What do you make of it?"

Krell lifted up the piece and peered at it through the eye slits of his helm. "It is a knight riding a dragon."

"Describe it further," Chemosh prompted.

"The knight is a Dark Knight of Takhisis," Krell stated, after closer perusal. "He has the symbol of the lily and the skull on his armor."

"Most observant, Krell," remarked Chemosh.

Krell was pleased, not recognizing the sarcasm. "He is wearing a cape and a helm, and he rides a blue dragon."

"Is there anything at all familiar about this knight, Krell?" Chemosh asked.

Krell held the piece practically to his nose. The red eyes flared.

"Lord Ariakan!" Krell stared at the piece, incredulous. "Down to the last detail!"

"Indeed," said Chemosh. "Lord Ariakan, beloved son of Zeboim. Your task is to guard that khas piece, Krell. Keep it safe and follow my orders to the letter. For this is how we will keep the Sea Queen penned up on her side of the board, completely and utterly helpless."

The death knight's red eyes fixed on the piece, and flickered, dubious. "I don't understand you, my lord. Why should the goddess care about a khas piece? Even if it does look like her son—"

"Because it *is* her son, Krell," said Chemosh. He leaned back in his chair, put his elbows on the arms, and placed the tips of his fingers together.

Krell's hand twitched and he nearly dropped the piece. He set it down hastily and drew back away from it.

"You can touch him, Krell. He won't bite you. Well, he would bite you, if he could get hold of you. But he can't."

"Ariakan is dead," Krell said. "His mother took away his body—"

"Oh, yes, he's quite dead," Chemosh agreed complacently. "He died, by your treachery, and his soul came to me, as do all the souls of the dead. Most pass through my hands as fleeting as sparks rising to the heavens, on the way to the continuation of their journey. Others, such as yourself, Krell, are bound to this world in punishment."

Krell growled, a rumble in the coffin of his armor.

"Still others, like my lord Ariakan, refuse to leave. Sometimes they cannot bear to part from a loved one. Sometimes they cannot bear to part from someone they hate. Those souls are mine."

Krell's red eyes flickered, then understanding dawned. He threw back his helmed head and gave a great guffaw that echoed throughout the Abyss.

"Ariakan's thirst for vengeance against me keeps him trapped here. Now that is a fine jest, my lord. One I can appreciate."

"I am glad you are so easily amused, Krell. Now, if you can stop gloating for a moment, here are your orders."

"I am all attention, my lord."

Krell listened to orders carefully, then asked a few questions that actually bordered on the intelligent.

Satisfied that this part of his plan would proceed, Chemosh dismissed the death knight.

"I trust you will not mind returning to Storm's Keep, Krell?"

"Not so long as I am free to depart when I want to, my lord," said the death knight. "I can leave once my duty's done?"

"Of course, Krell."

The death knight picked up the khas piece, stared at it a moment, sniggered, then stuffed it into his glove. "Truth to tell, I've kind of missed the place."

"Keep that khas piece safe," Chemosh warned.

"I will not let it out of my sight," Krell returned with a chuckle. "On that you can count, my lord."

Krell stalked off, still laughing to himself.

"Mina," said Chemosh, displeased, "were you spying on me?"

"Not spying, my lord," said Mina, coming to him from the darkness. "I was concerned. I do not trust that fiend. He betrayed his lord once. He will do so again."

"I assure you that I am capable of dealing with him, Mina," said Chemosh coldly.

"I know, my lord. I am sorry." Mina moved close to him. She

slid her arms around him, nestled near him. Her head rested on his breast.

He could feel her warmth, smell the perfume of her hair that brushed against his skin.

She will be less trouble to you dead than alive.

It was, after all, a consideration.

"Why are you concerned about Zeboim, my lord?" Mina asked, unaware of his thoughts. "I know that there is this monk who has been nosing about, but all you would have to do is to give me leave to deal with him——"

"The monk is a nuisance," said Chemosh. "Nothing more. I threw him onto the pile just to let the goddess know that I know what she has been up to. And also to distract her from my true purpose."

"And what is that, my lord?"

"We are going on a hunt for buried treasure, Mina," said Chemosh. "The richest cache of treasure known to man or gods."

Mina stared, perplexed. "What need do you have of treasure? Wealth is as dust to you."

"The treasure I seek does not consist of such paltry things as steel coins, or gold crowns, silver necklaces, or emerald gewgaws," Chemosh returned, scoffing. "The treasure I seek is made of material far more valuable. It is made of—myself."

She gazed at him, looked long into his eyes. "I think I understand, my lord. The treasure is——"

He laid his finger on her lips. "Not a word, Mina. Not yet. We do not know who may be listening."

"May I ask where this treasure lies, my lord?"

He took her in his arms, folded her in his embrace, and said softly, "The Blood Sea. That is where we will go, you and I, once certain prying eyes are closed and pricking ears shut."

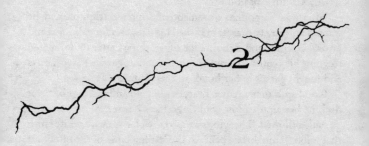

Lord Ausric Krell loathed Storm's Keep. He had been elated to be free of the place, had sworn he would never more set foot upon it, unless it be to demolish it, yet when he found himself standing once more upon the wind and wave-swept stones of the courtyard, he felt true pleasure. He had left a prisoner, sneaking out in ignominy, and now he was lord and master.

He laughed out loud to hear the puny plashing waves breaking on the rocks. Leaning over the edge of the cliff, he made a rude gesture at the sea, shouted out an obscenity. He laughed again and strode with brisk steps back across the courtyard, heading for the Tower of Lilies and the library. Zeboim would soon realize he had returned and he had to have everything in readiness.

Zeboim was in the Blood Sea, assisting her father, Sargonnas, when she heard Krell's curse. The minotaur were launching a grand expeditionary force to firmly clinch their hold on Silvanesti. A fleet of ships—battle ships, supply ships, troop transports and ships filled with immigrants—were leaving the minotaur isles, setting sail for Ansalon.

This was Sargonnas's moment of supreme triumph and he wanted nothing to mar it. He asked his daughter for calm seas and favorable winds and Zeboim, having nothing better to do, agreed to grant his request. In return, the minotaur gave her lavish gifts and fought games in her honor in their Circus.

Blood spilt in her name. Bracelets of gold and earrings of silver decking her altars. How could a goddess refuse?

Sails billowed. The winds capped the blue sea with white froth that bubbled and broke beneath the leaping bows of the minotaur vessels. The minotaur sailors sang songs and danced on the rolling decks. Zeboim danced with them upon the sparkling water.

And then came Krell's voice rolling across the world.

He cursed her name. He cursed her wind and water. He cursed her, and then he laughed.

Turning her far-seeing eyes his direction, Zeboim saw Krell standing on a cliff atop Storm's Keep.

The goddess did not stop to think. She did not ask herself how he came to be there or why he felt so bold as to be able to challenge her. Swift as raging flood waters sweeping down out of the mountains, Zeboim swept through the heavens and broke upon Storm's Keep in a torrent of fury that lashed the seas and caused them to rise up and crash over the cliffs.

Zeboim sensed Krell's foul presence in the Tower of Lilies. She smote the heavy door that led to the Tower, splintered it, and with a wave of her hand, sent the wreckage flying to the four corners of the compass. She blew through the chill stone corridors, so that they were awash in sea water, to find Krell sitting at his ease in a chair in the library.

The goddess was always too impatient to be observant of details, which were meaningless to her anyway. Zeboim saw nothing except the death knight. She was suddenly, dangerously calm, as the seas before the hurricane, when, the sailors say, the wind "eats" the waves.

"So, Krell," said Zeboim, soft and menacing, "Chemosh has tired of you at last and thrown you back upon the refuse heap."

"Really, now, Madame," said Krell, leaning back comfortably in his chair and crossing his legs. "You should not speak of this fine fortress that you yourself built for your beloved son—the late and most lamented Lord Ariakan—as a refuse heap."

Zeboim crossed the room in a bound. Lightning flared in the skies, and thunder cracked. The air sizzled with her anger. She loomed over him, roaring and sparking.

"How dare you sully his name by speaking it! The last time you did that, I cut out your tongue with my knife and watched you choke on your own blood. I will give you back your tongue, just so I have the pleasure of cutting it out—"

She raised her hand.

"Careful, Madame," said Krell imperturbably. "Do not do anything to jostle the khas board. I am in the middle of a game."

"To the Abyss with your game!" Zeboim reached down to seize hold of the board and upend it, scatter the pieces, stamp on them, pulverize them. "And to the Abyss with you, Ausric Krell! This time I will utterly and finally destroy you!"

"I would not do that, Madame," Krell said coolly. "I would not touch that khas board if I were you. If you do, you will regret it."

The tone of his voice—sneering and smug—and a cunning yellow glow in the heart of the red-flame eyes gave the goddess pause. She did not understand what was happening, and a little belatedly, she asked herself the questions that she should have asked before she came to Storm's Keep.

Why had Krell returned voluntarily to his prison? She had assumed that Chemosh had abandoned the death knight, banishing him back to this fortress. Now that she was paying attention, she sensed the presence of the Lord of Death. Chemosh held his hand protectively over Krell, as Krell was holding his hand protectively over the khas board. Krell was acting with Chemosh's blessing—a blessing that made Krell daring enough to curse her, defy her.

Why? What was Chemosh's game? Zeboim did not think it was khas. Struggling to regain at least a semblance of composure, she dug her nails into her palms and bit off the words that would have reduced Ausric Krell to a sizzling heap of molten metal.

"What are you talking about, Krell?" Zeboim demanded. "Why should I give a damn about this khas board or any other khas board, for that matter?"

She spoke disdainfully but, when she thought Krell wasn't looking, she sneaked a swift, uneasy glance at the board. It seemed ordinary enough as far as khas boards went. Zeboim had never liked khas. She did not like any games, for that matter. Games meant competition, and competition meant that someone won and someone lost. The idea that she might lose at anything was so supremely laughable that it was not worthy of consideration.

"This is a very valuable khas board, Madame. Your son, my lord Ariakan, had it specially made for him. Why don't you sit down and finish the game with me," Krell invited. He gestured at the board. "You take the dark pieces. It is your move."

Zeboim tossed her head and sea foam flicked about the room. "I have no intention—"

"It is your move, Madame," repeated Ausric Krell, and the red eyes flickered with amusement.

The presence of Chemosh was very strong. Zeboim was tempted to call out to him, then decided that she would not give him the satisfaction. She did not like the fact that Krell kept speaking of her son. Fear stirred in her, irrational fear.

Chemosh had always been a shadowy god, least known to her of any of the gods, keeping to himself, making no friends, forging no alliances. After the return of the gods to the world, Chemosh had grown even more secretive, retiring to deeper, darker shadows. The heat of his ambition could be felt throughout heaven, however, spewing forth steam, causing small tremors, like the molten lava boiling in the dark depths of a mountain.

"I know nothing about this game," Zeboim said dismissively. "I do not know what pieces to play and I truly do not care."

"Might I suggest a move, Madame?"

Krell was being officiously polite, but she heard laughter gurgle in his hollow armor. Her hands itched to seize hold of that armor and rend it open. She clasped her hands together to restrain herself.

Krell leaned over the board. His thick, gloved finger pointed. "Do you see the knight on the blue dragon? The one standing next to the figure of the queen? I'm going to take that piece with my rook unless you make a move to stop me."

The placement of the pieces on the hexes on the board meant nothing to her. The pieces were scattered all about, with some standing on hexes on one side of the board and some standing on hexes on the other; some facing their rulers and others turned away. The knight to which Krell pointed appeared to be in the thick of some type of action, for he and the queen he served were surrounded by other pieces. As was most natural to her, Zeboim concentrated on the queen.

She studied the piece intently and suddenly her eyes widened. She was the queen, standing upon a conch shell, her sea green dress foaming around her ankles, her face carved in delicate detail.

Zeboim's heart melted. Her son had obviously had this carved in tribute to her. She clasped the piece fondly, loathe to set it down.

"Now that you have picked up the piece, Madame, you must move it," said Krell. "You might place it on this hex over here. That way, I will not be able to threaten your son."

Zeboim was still at a loss to know what was going on. "I will play along with your silly game for only so long, Krell," she warned.

As she started to place the piece where he had indicated, his words suddenly smote her.

That way, I will not be able to threaten your son.

Zeboim dropped the queen. It rolled around on the khas board, knocking over a pawn or two, and finally came to rest at the feet of the black king. The goddess snatched up the knight on the blue dragon. She saw immediately the likeness to Ariakan.

The storm winds dropped. The storm clouds lowered. The ocean waters swirled, lapped ominously upon the rocks of Storm's Keep. She turned the khas piece of her son in her hand.

"A fine likeness," she said diffidently.

"Indeed it is," said Krell in mock serious tones. "I think the sculptor captured Lord Ariakan perfectly. The face is so expressive, especially about the eyes. You can look into them and see his very soul . . ."

The clouds of Zeboim's confusion parted, shredded by a chill wind of terror. She had loved Ariakan, adored him, doted on him. His death left a void that all creation could not fill. She looked at the eyes of the khas piece and the eyes of the piece looked back at her, raging, furious, helpless . . .

Zeboim gave a hollow cry. "Chemosh!" She stared wildly about the room. "Chemosh!" she repeated, her voice rising to a howl of fury and fear and dismay. "Free my son! Free him! Now! This moment! Or I'll—"

"You'll what?" said Krell.

Reaching out his hand, he plucked the figure of Lord Ariakan from Zeboim's shaking fingers. "Threaten all you want, Madame. Bluster and blaze. You can do nothing."

He placed the piece back onto the khas board. The figure of the goddess lay at the feet of the black king, and now she could see that the king was done in the likeness of the Lord of Death. Zeboim stared at it, her throat closing, so that she could barely speak.

"What does Chemosh want of me?" she asked in low, tight tones.

"He wants the seas calm. The winds dead. The waves flat. He wants a certain monk to stop making a pest of himself. Beyond that, no matter what happens anywhere in the world—or beneath it—you will take no action. You will, in short, do nothing, because there is nothing you can do, not without endangering your dear son."

"What is Chemosh plotting?" Zeboim demanded in smothered tones.

Krell shrugged his shoulders. Picking up the figure of the queen, he moved her off the board and set her to one side, away from the battle. Then he picked up the figure of the knight. He held the knight in his hand, the head pinched between his thumb and forefinger.

"Do you agree, Madame?"

Zeboim cast the figure a tormented glance. "Chemosh must promise to free my son."

"Oh, yes," Krell replied. "He promises. On the day of his triumph, King Chemosh will set free the soul of Lord Ariakan. You have his word."

"King Chemosh!" Zeboim gave a bitter laugh. "That will never happen!"

"For the sake of your son, Madame, you should pray that it does," said Krell. "Do you agree?" His gloved fist engulfed the khas piece, hiding it from her sight.

"I agree!" Zeboim cried, unable to think of anything except the tormented eyes of her son. "I agree."

"Good," said Krell. He placed the knight back on the board, stood it in front of the black king. "And now I want to get back to my game. You have leave to go, Madame."

Zeboim's fury pulsed in her temples, throbbed in her breast, came near to choking her. All over the world, the skies went dark. Seas and rivers began to rise. Ships rocked precariously on turbulent waters. People cried out that Zeboim's wrath was soon to be unleashed, bringing hurricanes, typhoons, tornadoes, floods, death and ruin. They stared up into the swirling, boiling clouds and waited in terror for the violence of the goddess to break over them.

Zeboim searched the heavens for help. She cried to her father, Sargonnas, but he had ears only for his minotaur. She sought her twin brother, Nuitari, god of the dark moon, but he was nowhere to be found.

They could do nothing, anyway, she realized. She could do nothing.

The goddess gave a deep, shuddering moan. Small droplets of rain fell from the skies. The clouds disintegrated into ragged wisps. The wind died to nothing, not so much as a whisper. The ocean waters went flat.

On Storm's Keep, the waves licked meekly at the rocks. The thunder clouds rolled away and the sun shone brightly, so brightly that Krell, who wasn't used to it, found the light annoying and he was forced to leave his khas game to close the shutters.

*T*he ships of the minotaur expeditionary force crawled like bugs over a sea that was flat as a mill pond. The rowers of the enormous triremes labored ceaselessly, day and night, until many collapsed of exhaustion. Food and water had to be rationed. Crew and passengers began to sicken and to die. All over the world, ships languished on lifeless oceans. Sailors everywhere prayed to Zeboim for relief. None came. In desperation, some turned to other gods to intercede with Zeboim on their behalf.

Sargonnas, especially, would have been glad to do so. His armies were due to make landfall in Silvanesti in mid-summer, to take advantage of the fine weather to fortify defenses, conquer new lands, build new homes for the immigrants. As slowly as his ships were moving, they might arrive in time to celebrate Yule.

Those that arrived at all . . .

In a rage, the horned god stomped through the heavens in search of his daughter. He had no idea what perverse whim had seized Zeboim, but her latest tantrum-throwing snit had to end. His plans for the conquest of both the mortal world and the plane of heaven were being thrown into jeopardy.

Sargonnas searched the seas and the rivers, the streams and

creeks. He searched among the clouds that no longer boiled and churned but gathered in a gray mass that lay thick and weeping upon the quiet seas. He shredded the mists and tore apart the fog and thundered her name.

Zeboim did not answer. She had vanished and none of the other gods, even the far-seeing Zivilyn, knew where she had gone.

Rhys was also searching for Zeboim. Though much humbler than the gods, he searched for her with equal zeal and so far with equal luck.

Rhys and Nightshade remained in Solace for several days, pursuing their investigations of the robust, life-loving dead. Rhys kept close watch upon his brother, while Nightshade roamed the town, searching for other living corpses. Their numbers were growing. The kender noticed more every day. All of them laughing, talking, drinking, carousing. All of them dark, empty, lifeless shells of flesh.

"Yesterday morning I saw one of them flirting with a young man," Nightshade told Rhys. "This morning I saw him again."

Rhys cast the kender a questioning glance.

"There was nothing I could do, Rhys," Nightshade protested, helpless. "I tried to warn him about hanging about that sort of woman. He told me to mind my own business and if he caught me snooping about again he'd beat me to a pulp and stuff me into one of my own pouches."

"We have to do something to stop these 'Beloved of Chemosh,' " Rhys said. "I've managed to prevent my brother from killing several times—more by scaring away the victim than by doing anything to him. He refuses to talk to me, when he remembers me at all, which is rare. He apparently has no memory of me trying to kill him or, if he does, he isn't holding a grudge, for when I confront him, he merely laughs and walks off. And I can't be around him day and night. He has no need for sleep. I do."

He looked in bitter frustrated at Lleu, who was sauntering jauntily down the main street of Solace, his hat tipped back, as if to feel the morning sunshine on his face, except that it was drizzling rain. It had been drizzling rain for days now, and Solace was a sea of mud and sodden, grumpy inhabitants.

Lleu hummed as he went along. Once he'd sung a dance tune. Then he hummed snatches and fragments of it. Now his humming was no longer recognizable, off-key and jarring, as if he'd forgotten the song, which, Rhys thought, he probably had. Just as he forgot from one moment to the next if he'd eaten or drunk. Just as he forgot Rhys. Just as he forgot his victims the moment he'd slain them.

"Rhys," said Nightshade suddenly, tugging on Rhys's wet sleeve. "Look! Where's he going?"

Rhys had been absorbed in his thoughts that were as gloomy as the day, not paying attention. He had assumed that Lleu would be returning to the Trough, which was where he spent his time when he wasn't making deadly love to some doomed young woman. Rhys peered through the desultory rain to see that Lleu had veered off in a different direction. He was walking toward the main highway.

"I think he's leaving town," said Nightshade.

"I think you're right," said Rhys, stopping so fast that he took Atta by surprise. She pattered on a few steps before she realized that she'd lost her master. She turned around, fixed him with a hurt look, as though to say he could have given her some notice, before she shook off the rainwater and came trotting back.

"Come to think of it," said Nightshade. "I didn't see any of the Beloved when I went through the market this morning and there were none in the Inn, either. There's usually always one or two hanging about there."

"They're moving on," said Rhys. "I went to visit the parents of poor Lucy. I was hoping to talk to her, but they said that she had disappeared and so had her husband. Look at how Lleu has moved from town to town. Perhaps, after the Beloved of Chemosh fulfill their mission in one place, they are ordered to move on to the next and the next after that. That way, no one becomes suspicious, as they might if they stayed around too long. And they are all traveling east."

"How do you know that?" Nightshade asked.

"I don't, for certain," Rhys admitted, "except that all this time Lleu has been traveling in that direction. It's as if something is drawing him . . ."

"Someone," Nightshade corrected darkly.

"Chemosh, yes," said Rhys. "For what reason, I wonder? What purpose?"

Nightshade shrugged. He saw no point in continually asking questions that couldn't be answered and he came back to the practical.

"Are we going after him?"

"Yes," said Rhys, resuming walking. "We are."

Nightshade heaved a dismal sigh. "This is not really getting us anywhere you know. Going from one place to the next, watching your brother eat twenty meals a day and drink enough dwarf spirits to choke a kobold—"

"There's nothing else to be done," Rhys returned, frustrated. "The goddess is no help. I've asked her to assist me in finding this Mina and in trying to discover what Chemosh is plotting. Zeboim won't answer my prayers. I went to her shrine and found that it was closed, the door locked. I think she's deliberately avoiding me."

"So we just follow your brother and hope he leads us somewhere? Somewhere besides the next tavern, that is."

"That's right," said Rhys.

Nightshade shook his head and trudged on. They had traveled only about a quarter of a mile, however, when they heard shouting and the sound of hoof beats.

Rhys stepped to the side of the road. One of the city guard reigned in his horse next to them.

Nightshade flung his hands in the air. "I didn't take it," he said promptly, "or if I did, I'll give it back."

The guardsman ignored the kender. "Are you Rhys Mason?"

"I am," Rhys replied.

"You're wanted back in Solace. The sheriff sent me to fetch you."

Rhys looked after the figure of his brother, disappearing into the fog and rain. Whatever Gerard wanted with him, it must be urgent for him to send one of his men.

Rhys turned his steps back toward Solace. Nightshade fell in alongside him.

"The sheriff didn't say anything about wanting kender," said the guardsman, glowering.

"He is with me," said Rhys calmly, placing his hand on Nightshade's shoulder.

The guardsman hesitated a moment, watched to make certain that they were on their way, then galloped back to report.

"What do you suppose the sheriff wants," Nightshade asked, "since it's not me?"

Rhys shook his head. "I have no idea. Perhaps it has something to do with one of the murder victims."

"But no one knows they're murdered except us."

"Perhaps he has found out somehow."

"That would be good, wouldn't it? At least then we wouldn't be alone anymore."

"Yes," said Rhys, thinking suddenly how very much alone he felt, a single mortal, standing in opposition to a god. "That would be very good."

They found Gerard waiting impatiently for them at the bottom of the steps leading up to the Inn of the Last Home. He shook hands with Rhys and even gave Nightshade a friendly nod.

"Thanks for coming, Brother," said Gerard. "I'd like a private word with you, if you don't mind."

He took Rhys to one side, said in low tones, "Do you think that kender-herding dog of yours could keep an eye on your little friend for an hour or so? I want you to come to the prison with me. It's about a prisoner I've got there."

"I would like Nightshade to accompany me," said Rhys, thinking that if this was one of the Beloved of Chemosh, he would need the kender's help. "He has special talents—"

"I do, you know," said Nightshade modestly.

Both men turned and found the kender standing right behind them. Gerard glared at him.

"Oh, by private, I guess you meant private," Nightshade said. "Anyway, I was just going to add that I don't mind staying with Atta, Rhys. I've already seen the Solace prison, and while it's very nice," he added hurriedly for Gerard's benefit, "it's not some place I want to visit again."

"Laura will give him a meal," Gerard offered. "And the dog, too."

The meal cinched the deal, as far as Nightshade was concerned. "You don't need me. You pretty much know what to look for," he said in an undertone to Rhys. "The eyes. It's all in the eyes."

Rhys sent Atta with Nightshade, telling the kender to keep an eye on the dog and commanding the dog, with a quiet word and a gesture, to keep an eye on the kender.

Gerard walked off, and Rhys fell into step alongside him. The two traveled in silence through the streets of Solace. It was now about mid-morning, and despite the rain, the streets were crowded. People called out respectful and friendly greetings to Gerard, who answered with a cheerful wave or nod. Idlers took themselves off at his approach, or if he came upon them too quickly, ducked their heads in guilty nods. Strangers eyed him either boldly or furtively. Gerard took note of everyone, Rhys noticed. He could almost see the man storing up their images in his head for future reference.

"You're not much of a one for talking, are you, Brother," Gerard said.

Rhys, seeing no reason to reply, did not.

Gerard smiled. "Anyone else would be pelting me with questions by now."

"I did not think you would answer them," Rhys said mildly, "so I saw no reason to ask them."

"You're right there. Though it's more that I *can't* answer them than I wouldn't."

Gerard wiped rain water from his face.

"That's our prison, over there. Solace outgrew the old prison, more's the pity, and so we built this one. It was just finished a month ago. I hear Lleu Mason left town this morning," Gerard added in the same conversational tone. "You were leaving to go after him?"

"I was, yes," said Rhys.

"Lleu appeared to behave himself while he was here," Gerard said, casting a swift, intense glance at Rhys. "Your brother seems kind of peculiar, but no one made any complaints about him."

"What would you say, Sheriff, if I told you that my brother was a murderer?" Rhys asked. His staff thumped the ground, sending up little spurts of mud and water every time it struck. "That he killed a young woman in Solace night before last."

Gerard put out his hand, caught Rhys by the shoulder, and spun him around. The sheriff's face was red, his blue eyes flaring.

"What? What woman? What in hell do you mean by telling me this now, Brother? What do you mean letting him get away? By the gods, I'll hang you in his place—"

"The woman's name is Lucy," said Rhys. "Lucy Wheelwright."

Gerard stared at him. "Lucy Wheelwright? Why, Brother, you're daft. I saw her alive and well as you are this morning. She and her husband. I asked them what they were doing up so early, and she said they were off to one of the neighboring villages in the east to visit a cousin."

Gerard's gaze narrowed, hardened. "Is this some sort of

joke, Brother? Because if so, it isn't funny."

"I apologize if I upset you, Sheriff," Rhys said quietly. "I merely posed it as a hypothetical question."

Gerard eyed Rhys. "Don't do it again. You nearly got yourself throttled. Here we are. Not much to look at it, but it gets the job done."

Rhys barely glanced at the building that was located on the outskirts of the city. It looked more like a military barracks than it did a prison, and in this, Rhys recognized the hand of Gerard, the former Solamnic knight.

Gerard led the way inside the structure that was made of wood covered with plaster. Numerous small iron-barred windows, no larger than man's fist, dotted the walls. There was only one door, only one way in or out, and it was guarded twenty-four hours a day. Gerard nodded to the guards as he led Rhys into the prison.

"One of the prisoners has asked to see you," said Gerard.

"Asked to see me?" Rhys repeated, startled. "I don't understand."

"Me neither," muttered Gerard. He was still in a bad humor, still annoyed by Rhys's earlier pronouncement. "Especially as this person is also a stranger here in Solace. Asked for you by name. I sent over to the Inn, but you'd already left."

Taking a key from the jailer, Gerard led Rhys down a long corridor lined with doors on either side. The prison had the usual prison stench, though it was cleaner than most Rhys had seen. One large open cell was filled entirely with kender, who waved merrily as the sheriff passed by and called out in cheerful tones to ask when they would be set free. Gerard growled something unintelligible and continued down the corridor past more large open cells that he termed holding pens.

"Places where drunks can sleep it off, couples can get over their spats, con artists can cool their heels."

Rounding a corner, he entered a corridor lined with wooden doors.

"These are our private cells," he said. "For the more dangerous prisoners."

He thrust a key into the iron padlock on a cell door, turned the lock, and as the door opened, he added, "And the lunatics."

A ray of sunshine slanted through the small window, leaving most of the cell in shadow. At first Rhys saw nothing in the cell except a bed, a slop bucket, and a stool. He was about to tell Gerard that the cell was empty, then he heard a rustling sound. Huddled in a corner of the cell, crouched in the darkest part of the cell, was a dark and shapeless bundle of clothes that he assumed held a person. He could not tell for certain, for he could not see a face.

"I am Rhys," he said, stepping inside the cell. He did not feel fear, only pity for the person's obvious misery. "The sheriff says that you asked to see me."

"Tell him to leave us," said the person in a muffled voice, the face still hidden. "And close the door."

"Nothing doing," said Gerard firmly. "Like I said—crazy."

He rolled his eyes and wiggled his fingers around his temples.

"I am capable of taking care of myself, Sheriff," said Rhys with a faint smile. "Please . . ."

"Well, all right," Gerard said reluctantly. "But five minutes. That's it. I'll be down the corridor. If you need me, yell."

Gerard shut the cell door behind him. The room grew darker. The air was stuffy and smelled of rain. Rhys propped his staff against the wall, then ventured closer to the prisoner. He knelt down beside the shapeless bundle.

"What can I do to help?" he asked gently.

A beautiful and shapely hand slid out of the bundle of black robes. The hand grasped hold of Rhys's arm. Sharp nails dug into his flesh. Sea green eyes glittered, and a voice hissed from the shadows of the cowl.

"Slay Ausric Krell," said Zeboim, hissing the name in venomous hatred, "and save my son."

4

Zeboim's eyes shone with a wild and lurid light. Her face was deathly pale, her cheeks marred by bloody scratches, as though she had clawed herself. Her lips were cracked and rimed with a white powder, like sea salt or perhaps the salt of her tears.

"Majesty?" Rhys said, bewildered. "What are you doing in this place? In prison? Are you . . . are you ill?"

He knew that was a stupid question, but the situation was so bizarre and unreal that he was having trouble ordering his thoughts and he said the first thing that came into his head.

"Gods, why do I bother with you mortals!" cried Zeboim. She gave him a shove that flung him off-balance, sent him toppling sideways. Then, casting her cowl over her head, she hid her face in her hands and began to sob.

Rhys gazed grimly at the goddess. He did not know which he was more inclined to do—comfort her or shake her until her immortal teeth rattled.

"What are you doing here, Majesty, in a prison cell?" he asked.

No answer. The goddess sobbed stormily.

He tried again. "Why did you send for me?"

"Because I need your help, damn it!" she cried in tear-muffled tones.

"And I need yours, Majesty," Rhys said. "I have discovered some profoundly disturbing things about these followers of Chemosh. I have prayed to you countless times in the past few days and you have not answered me. All of these disciples are dead. They appear to be alive, but they are not. They go out among the living and trick innocent young people into proclaiming their loyalty to Chemosh, and then they murder—"

"Chemosh!" Zeboim raised her swollen and tear-streaked face to glare at him. "Chemosh is behind this, you know. That steel-plated idiot Krell could not have come up with this on his own. Not that it matters. Not that any of it matters. My son. He is all that matters."

"Majesty, please try to control yourself—"

Zeboim sprang up suddenly, seized hold of Rhys's arms, clutched at him with both hands. "You must save him, monk! They'll destroy him, otherwise. I can do nothing . . ." Her voice rose to a shriek. "You must save him!"

"Are you all right, Brother?" Gerard called, his voice echoing down the long corridor.

"All is well, Sheriff," Rhys returned hastily. "Give me just a few more moments."

He took hold of Zeboim's hands, pressed them tightly. He spoke to her in soothing tones, his voice low and firm. "You need to explain to me what is the matter, Majesty. I cannot help you if I don't know what you are talking about. We don't have much time."

Zeboim drew in a sobbing breath. "You are right, monk. I will be calm. I promise. I have to be. I must be."

She began to pace about the prison cell, beating her hands together as she spoke.

"My son, Lord Ariakan. Yes, I know he's dead," she added, forestalling the question on Rhys's lips. "My son died long ago in the Chaos War." Her hands clenched to fists. "He died due to the treachery, the perfidy of a man he trusted. A man he had raised up from the muck—"

"Majesty, please . . ." Rhys prompted quietly.

Zeboim passed a hand over her brow, distracted.

"When my son died, I thought . . . I assumed that his spirit would continue on to the next stage of the soul's journey. Instead"—she struggled for breath—"instead Chemosh kept his spirit, imprisoned it. He's held my son captive all these long years."

Zeboim's voice dropped, low and throbbing with fear. "Now he has given the spirit of my son to the death knight who betrayed him. A death knight named Ausric Krell"—she choked on the name, as though it were a foul taste in her mouth—"is threatening to destroy my son's spirit, to cast him into oblivion. Of course, Krell is acting under orders from Chemosh."

"I assume, then, Majesty, that Chemosh is holding your son's spirit hostage so that you will do something for him in return. What does he want you to do?"

"First, I am to stop you," said Zeboim. "Chemosh finds you annoying."

"I don't know why," Rhys said bitterly. "I'm not a threat to him or likely to be one, the way things are going."

"Further, I am not to interfere with any of Chemosh's plots and schemes. I have no idea what those may be," the goddess added, "but I'm not to do anything to thwart him."

"So Chemosh is plotting something . . ." Rhys murmured.

"Oh, yes," said Zeboim with a vicious snap. "He is plotting something grand, of that you may certain. And whatever it is, he fears me. He fears that I will stop him, which I would!"

"And he fears me, it seems," Rhys added.

"You?" Zeboim laughed, then said grudgingly, "Well, yes, I suppose he does. I am to rid myself of you and the kender, but that is not what is important. My son is important. I can do nothing to help him. If a drop of rain so much as falls on his helm, Krell will destroy my son's soul. But you, monk . . ."

Zeboim sidled closer. Taking hold of Rhys's hands, she stroked, carressed him. "You could go to Storm's Keep. Krell wouldn't suspect you."

"Majesty," protested Rhys, taken aback, "I can hardly get in the middle of a battle between two gods—"

"You are already in the middle," Zeboim retorted angrily, shoving him away. "Chemosh commands that I get rid of you. Do you think he means that I am to send you back to your monastery with a pat on the ass and orders to be a good little boy?"

Rhys stood in the prison cell, his gaze fixed on the goddess.

Zeboim settled her robes around her, smoothed her disheveled hair. "You will go to Storm's Keep. I will transport you through the ethers, don't worry about that. You will need to make up some excuse for your presence there so that Krell won't be suspicious. He has less brains than a mollusk, so that won't be hard. Perhaps you will say you are sent by me to negotiate. Yes, Krell will like that. He's easily bored and he enjoys tormenting his victims. It is too bad you are not more charming, entertaining. He likes to be entertained."

"And how do you propose I rescue your son, Majesty, if I am to be tortured and killed?" Rhys asked. "You say this Krell is a death knight. That means that his power is only slightly less than that of a god—"

Zeboim waved that consideration away. "You serve me. I will grant you all the power you need."

"You haven't thus far," Rhys stated coolly.

She cast him an angry glance. "I will. Don't worry. As to how you save my son"—she shrugged—"that is up to you. You are clever, for a human. You will think of a way."

Rhys sank down on the bed, tried to organize his scattered thoughts. That was proving difficult, since he could not believe that he was having this conversation.

"Where is Krell holding your son? I assume there are dungeons . . ."

"He is not being held in a dungeon," said Zeboim, her hands

twisting together. "His spirit is imprisoned inside"——she drew in a seething breath, barely able to speak for her rage——"inside a khas piece!"

"A khas piece," Rhys repeated, stunned. "Are you certain?"

"Of course I am certain! I saw it! Krell flaunted it before me, bragged that he played with it nightly."

"Which piece is it?"

"One of the two black knights."

"Is there any way you can tell them apart?"

"Yes," she said in scathing tones, "one is my son. It looks just like him."

"Having never had the honor of meeting your son," Rhys said carefully, "I do not know what he looks like. If you could give me something more to go on——"

"He is riding a blue dragon. But then, the other was also riding a blue dragon. I don't know!" Zeboim tore at her hair with her hands. "I can't think! Leave me alone. Just take yourself off and rescue him—— Wait a moment. The pieces are real. Real corpses. Shrunken. Except for the one that was me, of course. And the king. That was Chemosh."

Rhys rubbed his forehead. This was devolving into a strange and terrible dream.

"It is Chemosh's idea of a jest," Zeboim said by way of explanation. "He means to humiliate me. See here, monk, is this really important? We're wasting time——"

"You are asking me to go on a hopeless venture, Majesty. Any information you can give me, however insignificant it seems to you, might help."

Zeboim heaved an exasperated sigh. "Very well. Let me try to think back. The White Queen and King are elves. The Black Queen is . . . is me. The Black King is Chemosh." She ground the name with her teeth.

"The two White clerics are monks of Majere." Zeboim arched a brow at him. "Fancy that! The two Black Robe clerics are dwarves. The two White knights are elves riding silver dragons.

The pawns on the side of darkness are goblins. The pawns on the side of light are kender. As I said, Chemosh created this to humiliate me. My gallant son, doing battle against the likes of monks and kender . . ."

There came a thunderous knock on the door. Gerard's voice boomed, "Time's up, Brother."

"Just one moment," Rhys called. Rising to his feet, he turned to Zeboim. "Let us understand each other, Majesty. Either I go to Storm's Keep and rescue your son or you will slay me——"

"I will do it, monk," said Zeboim, calm as the eye of the storm. "Never think I won't."

Wrapping herself in her dark and tattered robes, she sat down on the bed and stared at the wall across from her.

Rhys bent near her, said to her softly, "You know, Majesty, my death would be quicker, easier if I told you just to kill me now."

Zeboim looked up at him with her sea-green eyes. "It might be, or it might not. Whether it would or it wouldn't, you're not taking into account your friend the kender, nor all those doomed young people, like your brother, murdered in the name of Chemosh. Nor all those thousands of sailors on board ships stranded in the middle of flat and listless seas. Sailors who will surely die——"

Gerard banged on the door again. A key rattled in the lock.

Rhys straightened. "I understand, Majesty," he said with the calm of one who can either be calm or break down and weep.

"I thought you might," Zeboim said in languid tones. "Let me know your decision."

"Where will you be, Majesty?"

Lying on the bed, the goddess gathered her robes around her, drew her cowl over her head, and turned her face to the wall. "Here. Where no one can find me."

"Time's up," said Gerard, entering the cell. "How'd everything go?" he asked in a low voice.

"Well enough," said Rhys.

Gerard cast a look at the bundle of clothes on the bed, then ushered Rhys out the door. He locked it behind him and the two walked down the corridor. When they were out of ear-shot of the prisoner, Gerard halted.

"What do I about the crazy woman?" he asked in a low tone. "Should I let her go?"

Rhys did not answer. In truth, he hadn't heard the question. He was thinking about what he had to do and trying to figure out some way to do it and survive.

Gerard ran his hand through his hair. "As if I didn't have enough trouble, now some evil curse has been cast on Crystalmir Lake—"

"What's that?" Rhys asked, startled. "What about the lake?"

"Can't you smell it?" Gerard wrinkled his nose. "It stinks to high heaven. Fish dying by the hundreds. Washed up on the shores over night. Rotting in the sun. Our people depend on the water from that lake and now everyone's afraid to go near it. They say it's cursed. What with that and a crazy woman on my hands—"

"Sheriff," Rhys interrupted. "I have a favor to ask you. I am planning to go away for a little while and I need someone to take care of Atta. Would you look after her?"

"Will she herd kender for me?" Gerard asked, his eyes brightening.

Rhys smiled. "I will teach you the commands. And I will find a way to pay for her board and keep."

"If she herds kender as good for me as she does for you, she'll more than pay for herself," Gerard held out his hand. "You got yourself a deal, Brother. Where is it you're going?"

Rhys did not answer. "And you will continue to care for her if I don't come back?"

Gerard eyed him intently. "Why wouldn't you be coming back?"

"The gods alone know our fate, Sheriff," said Rhys.

"You can trust me, Brother. Whatever trouble you're in—"

"I know that, Sheriff," said Rhys gratefully. "That's why I have asked you to care for Atta."

"Very well, Brother. I won't pry into your business. And don't worry about the dog. I'll take good care of her."

As the two continued on down the corridor, Gerard had another thought, an alarming one, to judge by his tone.

"What about that kender? You're not going to ask me to keep him, too, are you, Brother?"

"No," Rhys replied. "Nightshade will be coming with me."

5

"A death knight," said Nightshade.

"According to the goddess, yes," Rhys answered.

"We're supposed to go to Storm's Keep and confront a death knight and rescue the goddess's son's spirit, which is trapped in a khas piece. From a death knight."

Rhys nodded his head in silent confirmation.

"Have you been drinking?" Nightshade asked seriously.

"No," said Rhys, smiling.

"Did you get hit on the head? Run over by a wagon? Stepped on by a mule? Fall down a flight of stairs—"

"I'm in my right mind," Rhys assured him. "At least, I think I am. I know this sounds unbelievable—"

"Whoo-boy!" Nightshade exclaimed with a whistle.

"But here is the proof."

He and the kender stood on the road several hundred yards from the shores of Crystalmir Lake. The name came from the lake's deep blue crystalline water. The name was a misnomer now. The water was a sickening shade of yellow green and smelled of decaying eggs. Untold numbers of fish lay on the shore, dead or dying. Even from this distance, with the wind blowing away from them, the smell was appalling.

Nightshade held his nose. "Yeah, I guess you're right. You know that I'll never be able to eat fish again," he added in aggrieved tones.

The two of them walked back toward Solace, passing the crowds of people who had turned out to see the fish-kill. Everyone had a theory, from outlaws poisoning the lake to wizards casting a curse on it. Fear tainted the air as badly as the smell of dead fish.

"I've been thinking, Rhys," Nightshade said, as they headed back into town. "I'm not very trustworthy and I'm not at all good in a fight. If you don't want to take me with you, my feelings won't be hurt. I'll be glad to stay with the sheriff to help care for Atta."

He put his hand on Atta's head, petting her. She permitted this, although her gaze was intent on Rhys.

He smiled at Nightshade's generous offer. "I know this is dangerous. I would not ask you risk your life, my friend, but I truly do need you. I won't be able to tell for certain which khas piece contains the knight's soul—"

"The goddess told you it was the black knight," Nightshade interrupted.

"My mother had a saying," said Rhys wryly. " 'Consider the source.' "

Nightshade sighed. "Yeah, I guess you're right."

"In this case, our source is not very reliable. She might be lying to us. Krell might have lied to her. Krell might switch the spirit from one piece to another. For my plan to work, I must know which piece holds the knight's soul. You are the only one who can tell me. Besides," Rhys added with a smile, "I thought kender were adventurous, filled with curiosity, utterly without fear."

"I'm a kender," Nightshade said. "I'm not stupid. This is stupid."

Rhys was inclined to agree. "We don't have much choice, my friend. Zeboim has made it quite clear that if we don't attempt this, she will kill us."

"So instead the death knight kills us. I don't see that we've gained a lot, except maybe a trip to Storm's Keep, and we probably won't live long enough to enjoy that. You know, Rhys, most people wouldn't trust a kender with such an important mission. And I must say that I can't blame them. Kender cannot be counted upon. I'd leave me behind if I were you."

"I have always found you to be emminently trustworthy, Nightshade," Rhys replied.

"You have?" Nightshade was taken aback. He sighed. "Then I guess I should try to live up to that."

"I think you should."

" 'Live' being the optimal word." Nightshade stressed this point.

"Look at it this way. At least we've accomplished something," Rhys pointed out. "We've attracted the god's attention."

"Something people with any sense would avoid," Nightshade said crossly. "My dad had a saying. 'Never attract a god's attention.' "

"Your father said that? Really?" Rhys cocked an eye at the kender.

"Well, he would have if he'd thought about it." Nightshade stopped in the middle of the road to argue the point. "How do we even get to Storm's Keep, Rhys? I don't know anything about boats. Do you? Good! Then that's how we get out of this. We can't go to Storm's Keep if we can't get there. The goddess must see the logic in that—"

"The goddess will send us on the winds of the storm, I suppose. I have only to let her know we're ready."

Nightshade rolled his eyes. Atta, seeing her master downcast and unhappy, gave his hand a gentle lick. He stroked her head, rubbed her beneath the jowls, smoothed her ears. She crowded close to him, looking up at him sadly, wishing she could make everything right.

"She'll miss us," said Nightshade in a choked voice.

"Yes," said Rhys quietly, "she will."

He rested his hand on the kender's shoulder. "All your life you have worked to save lost spirits, Nightshade. Think of this as something you were born to do—your greatest challenge."

Nightshade pondered this. "That's true. I guess I will be saving a soul. But if that's true for me, Rhys, what about you? What were you born to do?"

"Like all men," Rhys said simply, "I was born to die."

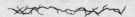

Later that morning, outside the Inn of the Last Home, Rhys knelt down in front of Atta and placed his hand on the dog's head, almost as if he were bestowing a benediction. "You are to be a good girl, Atta, and mind Gerard. He is your new master now. You work for him."

Atta gazed up at Rhys. She could hear the sorrow in his voice, but she didn't understand it. She would never understand, never know why he had abandoned her. He stood up. It took him a moment to speak.

"You should take her away now, Sheriff," he said.

"Come, Atta," said Gerard, issuing the command Rhys had taught him. "Come with me."

Atta looked at Rhys. "Go with Gerard, Atta," said Rhys, and he motioned with his hand, sending the dog away.

Atta looked at him one more time, then, her head and tail drooping, she obeyed. She allowed Gerard to lead her off. He returned, shaking his head.

"I took her back to the Inn. I hope she'll be all right. Laura offered her some food, but she wouldn't take it."

"She's a sensible animal," said Rhys. "Give her work to keep her occupied and she'll soon come around."

"She'll get plenty of work what with all the kender we have flocking here to see the fish kill. So you two are off. When do you leave?" Gerard asked.

"Nightshade and I have to pay a visit to the prisoner first," said Rhys, "and then we'll be going."

"The prisoner?" Gerard was astonished. "The crazy woman? You're going to see her again?"

"I assume she is still there," Rhys said.

"Oh, yes. I don't seem to be able to get rid of her. What do you want to see her for, Brother?" Gerard asked with unabashed curiosity.

"She seems to think that I can be of some help to her," said Rhys.

"And the kender? Is he helping her, too?"

"I'm a cheering influence," said Nightshade.

"You don't need to accompany us, Sheriff," Rhys added. "We just need your permission to enter her cell."

"I think I'd better come along," said Gerard. "Just to make sure nothing happens to you. Any of you."

Rhys and Nightshade exchanged glances.

"We need to speak to her in private," said Rhys. "The matter is confidential. Spiritual in nature."

"I didn't think you were a monk of Majere anymore," Gerard said, giving Rhys a shrewd look.

"That does not mean that I can no longer assist those who are troubled," Rhys replied. "Please, Sheriff. Just a few moments with her alone."

"Very well," said Gerard. "I don't see how you can get into too much trouble locked up in a prison cell."

"A lot he knows," Nightshade said gloomily.

Inside the prison, Nightshade had to stop to say a word to the kender. Rhys was concerned to hear Nightshade bidding them what appeared to be a final farewell. When he reached into his pouches, prepared to distribute all his worldly wealth—the kender's version of a last will and testament—Rhys seized hold of Nightshade by the collar and hauled him off.

Gerard gestured at the cell door. "She's hasn't moved from the bed," he reported. "She won't eat. Sends back the food untasted. You have visitors, Mistress," he called out, unlocking the door.

"It's about time," said Zeboim, sitting up on the bed.

She drew back her cowl. Sea green eyes glittered.

Rhys gave Nightshade a shove, propelled the kender into the cell, and followed after him.

Gerard shut the cell door and inserted the key into the lock. He did not turn it but left the key where it was. He paused a moment, listening. The three kept their voices low, and anyhow, he'd promised he'd give them privacy.

Shaking his head, Gerard walked off to spend a few moments visiting with the jailer.

"How long you going to give them, Sheriff?" asked the jailer.

"The usual. Five minutes."

A small hourglass stood on the desk. The jailer upended it, much to the fascination of the kender, who stuck heads, arms, hands, and feet between the bars in order to try to get a clearer view of the proceedings, all the while pelting Gerard with questions, the number one being how many grains of sand were in the glass and offering, since he didn't know, to make a quick count.

Gerard listened to the jailor's complaints about the kender, which he made on a daily basis, and watched the sand trickle through the hourglass and listened expectantly for sounds of trouble from down the corridor.

All was quiet, however. When the last grain dropped through the narrow neck, Gerard shouted, "Time's up" and tromped off down the corridor.

He turned the key in the door and shoved it opened. He stopped, stared.

The crazy woman lay on the bed, her cowl over her head, her face to the wall. No one else was with her.

No monk. No kender.

The cell door had been locked. He'd had to unlock it to let himself in. There was only one way out of the corridor and that was past him and no one had passed him.

"Hey, you!" he said to the crazy woman, shaking her by the shoulder. "Where are they?"

The woman made a slight gesture with her hand, as if brushing away an insect. Gerard flew backward out of the cell and into the corridor, where he smashed up against the wall.

"Do not touch me, mortal!" the woman said. "Never touch me."

The cell door slammed shut with a bang.

Gerard picked himself up. He'd hit his head on the wall and there would be a giant bruise on his shoulder in the morning. Grimacing at the pain, he stood staring at the cell door. Rubbing his shoulder, he turned and tromped down the corridor.

"Let the kender loose," he called.

The kender began to whoop and holler. Their shrill cries could have cracked solid stone. Gerard winced at the racket.

"Just do it," he ordered the jailer. "And be quick about it. Don't worry, Smythe. I have a wonderful dog who'll help me keep them in line. The dog needs something to do. She's missing her master."

The jailer opened the cell door and the kender streamed out joyfully into the bright light of freedom. Gerard cast a glance at the prison cell at the end of the corridor.

"I think she may be missing her master a long, long time," he added somberly.

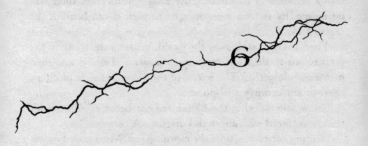

6

*T*he Maelstrom of the Blood Sea of Istar. Once sailors spoke of it in hushed tones, when they spoke of it at all. Once the Maelstrom was a spiral of destruction, a swirling maw of red death that caught ships in its teeth and swallowed them whole. Once out of that maw, you could hear the thunder of the voices of the gods.

"Look on this, mortals, and know our might."

When the Kingpriest of Istar dared, in his arrogance, to deem himself a god, and the people of Istar bowed to him, the true gods of Krynn cast down a fiery mountain upon Istar, destroying the city and carrying it far beneath the sea. The waters of the ocean turned a reddish brown color. The wise claimed that this color came from the sandy soil on the ocean floor. Most people believed that the red stain was from the blood of those who had died in the Cataclysm. Whatever the cause, the color gave the sea its name. It henceforth became known as the Blood Sea.

The gods created a maelstrom over the site of the disaster. The immense, blood-tinged whirlpool was meant to keep away those who might disturb the final resting place of the dead and to serve as a constant reminder to mortals of the power and majesty of the gods. Feared and respected by sailors, the Maelstrom was a horrific, awesome sight, its swirling red waters disappearing into a hell-hole of darkness. Once caught in its coils, there was no escape. Its victims were dragged to their doom beneath the raging seas.

Then Takhisis stole away the world. Without the wrath of the gods to stir it, the Maelstrom spun slower and slower and then it stopped altogether. The waters of the Blood Sea were placid as those of any country mill-pond.

"Now look at what the Blood Sea has become." Chemosh's voice was tinged with anger and disgust. "A cesspool."

Shading her eyes against the morning sun, Mina stared out to where Chemosh pointed, to what had been one of the wonders of Krynn, a sight both terrifying and magnificent.

The Maelstrom had kept the memory and the warning of Istar alive. Now the once-infamous waters of the Blood Sea crept listlessly onto gritty sand beaches littered with filth and refuse. Remnants of broken packing crates and slime-covered planking, rotting nets, fish heads and shattered bottles, crushed shells, and splintered masts floated on top of the oily water, the trash rocking sluggishly back and forth with the slogging of the sea. Only the old-timers remembered the Maelstrom and what lay beneath it—the ruins of a city, a people, a time.

"The Age of Mortals," Chemosh sneered. He nudged a dead jelly fish with the toe of his boot. "This is their legacy. The awe and fear and respect for the gods is gone, and what is left in its stead? Mortal refuse and litter."

"One could say that the gods have only themselves to blame," Mina remarked.

"Perhaps you forget that you are speaking to one of those gods," Chemosh returned, his dark eyes glittering.

"I am sorry, my lord," said Mina. "Forgive me, but I sometimes do forget . . ." She halted, not quite certain where that sentence might lead.

"Forget that I am a god?" he asked angrily.

"My lord, forgive me—"

"Do not apologize, Mina," said Chemosh. The sea breeze tousled his long, dark hair, blowing it back from his face. He gazed out to sea, seeing what had once been, seeing what now was. He sighed deeply. "The fault is mine. I come to you as a mortal. I love you as a mortal. I want you to think of me as mortal. This aspect of me is only one of many. The others you would not particularly like," he added dryly.

He reached out his hand to her and she took it. He drew her close, and they stood together upon the shore, the wind mingling their hair, black and red, shadow and flame.

"You spoke the truth," he said. "We gods are to blame. Although we did not steal away the world, we gave Takhisis the opportunity to do so. Each of us was so absorbed in our little part of creation, we locked ourselves up in our own little shops, sitting on our little stools with our little feet twined around the rungs, peering down at our work like a short-sighted tailor, plying our needles at some small piece of the universe. And when we woke one day to find that our Queen had run away with the world, what did we do? Did we grab up our flaming swords and sweep through the heavens, scattering the stars to search for her? No. We ran out of our little shops all amazed and frightened and wrung our hands and cried, 'Alack-a-day! The world is gone. Whatever shall we do!'"

His voice hardened. "I have often thought that if my own army had been arrayed outside her palace gates, my own forces ready to storm her walls, Queen Takhisis might have thought twice. As it was, I was lazy. I was content to make do with what I had. All that has changed. I will not make the same mistake again."

"I have made you sorrowful, my lord," said Mina, hearing the regret and harsh bitterness in his voice. "I am sorry. This was meant to be a joyous day. A day of new beginnings."

Chemosh took hold of Mina's hand and brought it to his lips and kissed her fingers. Her heart beat fast and her breath came short. He could rouse her to desire with a touch, a look.

"You spoke the truth, Mina. No one else, not even one of the other gods, would dare say such a thing to me. Most lack the capacity to see it. You are so young, Mina. You are not yet one and twenty. Where do you find such wisdom? Not from your late Queen, I think," Chemosh added sardonically.

Mina gave this consideration, gazing out upon a sea that was flat but not particularly calm. The water stirred restlessly, back and forth, reminding her of someone endlessly, nervously pacing.

"I saw it in the eyes of the dying," she said. "Not those who now give their souls to you, my lord. Those who once gave their souls to me."

The Battle of Beckart's Cut. The Solamnic knights broke out of Sanction, broke the siege of that city by the Dark Knights of Takhisis, then known, ignominiously, as the Knights of Neraka. The knights and soldiers of Neraka turned and fled as the Solamnics poured out of the fortress. The Neraka command crumbling, Mina took charge. She ordered her troops to slay those who were fleeing, ordered them to kill their comrades, kill friends, brothers. Inspired by the light of golden glowing amber, they obeyed her. The bodies piled up high, choking the pass. Here, the Solamnic charge ground to a halt, brought to a stop by a dam made of broken bone and bloody flesh. The day was Mina's. She'd turned a rout into victory. She walked the field of battle, held the hands of those who were dying by her command, and she prayed over them, giving their souls to Takhisis.

"Except that the souls didn't come to Takhisis," said Mina softly to the sea that had rocked her as a child. "The souls came to me. Like flowers, I plucked them and gathered them to my heart, holding them close, even as I spoke her name."

She turned to Chemosh. "That is my truth, my lord. I didn't know it for a long time. I shouted, 'For the glory of Takhisis' and I prayed to her every day and every night. But when the troops chanted my name, when they shouted, 'Mina, Mina,' I did not correct them. I smiled."

She was silent, watching the waves wander aimlessly to the shore, watched them deposit filth at her feet.

"Once more mankind will fear the gods," said Chemosh, "or at least one of them. Down there"—he pointed beneath the filth, the debris, the garbage—"down there lies the beginning of my rise as King of the Pantheon. I am going to tell you a story, Mina. Below the sea lies a graveyard, the largest in the world, and this is the tale of those who are buried beneath the waves. . . ."

My story begins in the Age of Dreams, when a powerful wizard known as Kharro the Red determined that the Orders of Magic needed safe havens where wizards could meet together, study together, work together. They needed places where they could safely store spell books and artifacts. He proposed that the wizards build Towers of High Sorcery, strongholds of magic.

Kharro sent mages throughout Ansalon to locate sites on which to build these new Towers. The White Robes, under the leadership of a wizardess named Asanta, chose as their location a poor fishing village known as Istar.

The Black Robes and the Red chose large and prosperous cities in which to build the Towers. Kharro summoned Asanta to Wayreth and demanded to know the reason for her choice. Asanta was a seer. She saw the future of Istar and predicted that one day its glory would eclipse all other cities on Ansalon. The White Robes were given permission to start work upon the Tower, and forty years later, Asanta led the incantation that raised the Tower of High Sorcery of Istar.

Asanta had been given a glimpse of Istar's rise. She did not foresee its fall. Not even we gods could foresee that.

For many decades, the wizards of the Tower of Istar ruled benevolently over the people of that small village and were instrumental in its rapid growth. Soon Istar was no longer a village but a thriving, prosperous city. Not long after that, it became an empire.

As Istar grew, so did the power of its clerics, particularly those of Mishakal and Paladine. Eventually one of these clerics rose to prominence in the government of Istar. He proclaimed himself ruler, calling himself by the title of Kingpriest. From this point on, the influence of the wizards began to wane and that of the clerics to grow.

An uneasy alliance continued to exist between the church and the Robes, though distrust was building on both sides. A white-robed wizard named Mawort, the Master of the Tower of Istar, managed to keep peace between the two factions.

The Conclave of Wizards viewed Mawort as the Kingpriest's pawn, and when he died, they appointed a Red Robe to take over as Master of the Tower, hoping by this to reestablish the independence of the wizards and have greater influence on Istarian politics.

The Kingpriest was furious, the citizens of Istar outraged. Distrust of the wizards deepened to hatred. Treachery and mischance caused open warfare to break out between the Kingpriest, his followers, and the wizards. Thus began the Lost Battles, so named for no one came out the winner.

The Kingpriest declared holy war on the wizards of Ansalon. The wizards retreated into their strongholds, threatening to destroy the Towers and their environs if they were attacked. The Kingpriest did not heed the warning and attacked the Tower at Daltigoth. Knowing that they must go down to defeat, the wizards fulfilled their promise and destroyed the Tower. A great many innocent lives were lost in the destruction. The wizards were saddened by this, but they believed that they had actually saved lives, for many more thousands would have died had the wizards' powerful spell books and artifacts fallen into the hands of those who would misuse them.

Shocked by this calamity and fearing that the wizards might next destroy the Tower of Istar, the Kingpriest offered to negotiate a peaceful settlement. The wizards would agree to abandon the Towers of Istar and Palanthas. In return, they would be granted safe haven in the Tower of Wayreth. The Conclave argued long and bitterly, but eventually they realized that they had no choice. The Kingpriest was immensely powerful and seemed to have the blessing of the gods on his side. They agreed to his terms.

A month after the Lost Battles, the Highmage emerged from the Tower of Istar, the last wizard to leave. She sealed its gates and ceded it to the Kingpriest.

The Kingpriest was not certain what to do with the Tower and for months it remained locked and empty. Then, following the advice of his counselor, Quarath of Silvanesti, he turned the Tower into a trophy room, displaying artifacts seized from those accused of heresy and the worship evil gods.

Over the next two decades, hundreds of idols, icons, artifacts, and holy relics were brought to the Tower which was renamed *Solio Febalas*—the Hall of Sacrilege. Many of my own artifacts were taken there, for, of course, my followers were among the first to be persecuted. Being in communication with the spirits of the dead, I heard from them about the Kingpriest's ambitious plans to ascend to godhood himself. He would do this by upsetting the balance, destroying the power of the gods of darkness and neutrality. Then he would usurp the power of the gods of light.

I tried to warn the other gods that they were next. The day would come when their own holy relicts would be inside the Hall of Sacrilege. They shrugged and laughed it off.

They did not laugh long, however. Soon the mild and inoffensive clerics of Chislev were being hauled from their forests and imprisoned or killed. The icons of Majere showed up in the Kingpriest's trophy case. Gilean joined me in warning that the balance of the world was being tilted and some of the gods of light added their voices to ours. The Kingpriest targeted them for persecution next, and by the end, even the healer Mishakal's symbol was found hanging in shame in the Hall of Sacrilege.

The Kingpriest announced to the world that he was wiser than the gods. He was more powerful than the gods. He proclaimed himself to be a god and demanded that he should be worshipped as a god. It was then that we true gods cast the fiery mountain on Istar.

The earth trembled at our wrath. Quakes leveled the city and split the Tower of High Sorcery of Istar in half. Fire gutted it, destroying the Hall of Sacrilege. The Tower fell into ruins which were carried down to the bottom of the Blood Sea along with the rest of that doomed city.

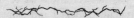

"There lies the Tower to this day," Chemosh concluded, "and inside those ruins lie many of the world's most powerful holy relics and artifacts."

"Wishful thinking, I am afraid, my lord," said Mina. "They could not have survived such terrible destruction."

"I don't know about the other gods"—Chemosh smiled cunningly—"but I made sure that my own artifacts were safe. And I have no doubt that the others did the same."

"You sound very certain, my lord."

"I am certain. I have proof. Soon after Istar's destruction, I went searching for the Tower, only to find that the Gods of Magic had hidden it from sight. Zeboim is Nuitari's twin sister and cousin to the other gods of Magic. They went to her and convinced her to use the powerful turbulence of the maelstrom to bury the Tower far beneath the ocean floor, so that no eyes— mortal or immortal—should ever discover it.

" 'Now,' I asked myself, 'why should the gods of Magic go to all this trouble to hide a ton of charred and blasted rubble? Unless there is something inside the rubble that they do not want any of us to find . . .' "

"Your holy artifacts," said Mina.

"Precisely."

"And now that the Maelstrom has subsided, you can go in search of them."

"Not only can I go in search of them, I can search without fear of interruption. If I had so much as dipped a toe into the surf, Zeboim would have known it. She would have raced from the far corners of the heavens to stop me. As it is, she is nowhere to be found this fine day. I may do what I like in her ocean—piss in it, if I want—and she does not dare protest."

Chemosh clasped Mina's hand, entwined her fingers with his. "Together, Mina, you and I will seek out the fabled and long-lost ruins of the Hall of Sacrilege. Think of it, my love! Hundreds of holy artifacts down there, some dating back to the Age of Dreams, imbued with godly power that is unimagined in this 'Age of Mortals.' And unattainable. There are artifacts belonging to Takhisis down there. Though she is gone, her power lives within them still.

"Artifacts of Morgion, Hiddukel, Sargonnas. Artifacts belonging to Paladine and Mishakal. I plan to distribute these powerful relics among the Beloved, who are traveling across Ansalon, on their way here to receive them. When that is accomplished, my followers will be the most formidable and powerful in all the world. I will then be in a position to challenge the other gods for rulership of the heavens and the world."

"I would go with you to ends of that world, my lord, and I would gladly see the wonders that live in the ocean depths, but as I forget you are a god, you forget that I am not," Mina said, smiling. "I can swim, but not very well. As for holding my breath—"

Chemosh laughed. "You do not need to swim, Mina. Or hold your breath. You will walk with me upon the ocean floor as you walk upon the floor of our bedchamber. You will breathe the water as you breathe the air. The weight of the water will sit as lightly on your shoulders as a fur mantle."

"Then you will transform me into a god, my lord," said Mina, teasing.

Chemosh's laughter ceased. The expression in his eyes was deep and fathomless, darker than the sea-depths.

"I cannot do that, Mina," he said. "At least, not yet."

Mina felt a sudden jolt of fear, a bone-jellying terror such as she had experienced standing on the treacherous broken stairs of Storm's Keep, staring down far below at the jagged, razor-edged rocks and the foaming, hungry water. Her throat closed; her heart shivered. She wanted, suddenly, to turn and flee, to run away. She had never felt terror like this, not when the fierce dragon Malys was diving down on her from the blood-raining skies, not when Queen Takhisis, mortal mad, was striding toward her, intent on tearing out her life.

Mina took a step backward, but Chemosh had hold of her.

"What is it, Mina? What's wrong?"

"I don't want to be a god, my lord!" she cried, struggling, trying to free herself from his grasp.

"You wanted power, Mina, power over life and death—"

"But not like that! You forget, my lord," she said in hollow tones, "that I have touched the mind of a god. I have seen into that mind, seen the immensity, the emptiness, the loneliness! I cannot bear it—"

The words froze on her lips. She looked at Chemosh in terror. She, who had betrayed his innermost secrets.

"I *was* lonely, Mina," he said softly. "I *was* empty. And then, I found you."

His arms enfolded her. He pressed her to him, body to body, mortal flesh to god's flesh made mortal. He put his mouth on her mouth, his lips eager and warm. He drew her down into the sand, his kisses spreading like treacle over her fear, hiding her terror beneath his sweetness that was thick in her mouth. She was consumed in his love until only the memory of her fear remained and his caresses soon burned that away.

The tide rose, as they lay among the sand dunes. The waves lapped over their feet, then their ankles. The sea water stole up and around them, smooth and soft as silken sheets. The waves covered Mina's shoulders. Her red hair stuck to her wet flesh. She tasted salt in her mouth and she coughed.

Chemosh took hold of her. "The next kiss I give you, Mina, will take away your mortal's breath. You will feel suffocated for an instant, but an instant only. I will breathe into your lungs the breath of the gods. For as long as you are beneath the water, my breath will sustain you. The water will be to you as the air is now."

"I understand, my lord," Mina replied. Her hair swirled in the water, flame dipped in blood.

"I am not sure you do, Mina," said Chemosh, regarding her intently. "The water is as air to you. That means, the air will be as water. Once I do this, if you come to the surface, you will drown."

In answer, she touched her lips to his, closed her eyes, and held him fast. He seized her, crushed her to him, and putting his mouth over hers, he drew the air from her body, sucked the life from her lungs.

The water rose over her head. Mina could not breathe. She gasped for the air, but water flowed in her mouth. She choked, strangled. Chemosh held her fast. She tried not to struggle, but she couldn't help it. Her body's instinct to survive overrode her heart. She fought to wrench herself free of the god's grip, but he was too strong. His fingers dug into her flesh and muscle and bone, his legs pinned her down beneath the water.

"He is killing me," she thought. "He lied to me . . ."

Her heart throbbed, her chest burned. Hideous star-bursts obscured her vision. She writhed in his grip and gasped and water flowed into her lungs and into her body as the sea rose higher and higher, gently rocking her. She was too tired to fight, so she closed her eyes and gave herself to the blood-tinged darkness.

7

Mina woke to a world that had never known sunlight, a world of heavy, eternal night.

Sea water pressed on her, surrounded her, enveloped and encompassed her. It pushed her and pulled her, constantly in motion. There was no up, no down. Nothing beneath her feet or above her head to orient her. She was adrift, alone.

Mina could breathe the water as well as she had once breathed air; at least she tried telling herself she could. She felt smothered, half-suffocated. Panic fluttered inside her. She was suddenly afraid she might be trapped here in the squeezing, fluid darkness forever. Her impulse was to swim to the surface, but she forced herself to abandon that idea. She had no idea where the surface was, and flailing about in the water, she might sink deeper, not rise.

She could not call out to Chemosh. She could not cry out or scream. The water swallowed up her voice. She forced the panic down, tried to remain calm, relax.

"I have walked the dark places of Krynn," Mina told herself. "I have walked the dark places of the mind of a god. I am not alone . . ."

A hand touched hers. She clasped the hand thankfully, held it fast.

"Not afraid, were you?" Chemosh said, half-teasing, half-serious. "You can talk, Mina. Remember, the water is for you as air. Speak. I'll hear your words."

"I was going to say that if I was afraid, it is only because fear is the curse of mortals, my lord," said Mina.

"That is true," said Chemosh, his tone grown grim. "Fear gives mortals good instincts."

"Is something wrong, my lord?"

"There is a stirring, an energy that was not here when I came here before only a year ago. It may have nothing to do with our treasure-hunt, yet I do not like it. It has the smell of a god about it."

"Zeboim?" Mina asked.

Chemosh shook his head. "I thought as much, and I returned to the surface. No storm clouds gather, no lashing winds howl. The sea is so flat that birds are starting to build nests on the water. No, whatever is amiss is down here; Zeboim is not to blame."

"What other gods might be at work in the sea, Lord?"

"Habbakuk holds sway over the sea creatures. I do not worry about him, however. He is indolent and lazy, as one might expect of a god who spends his time among fish."

He paused, listening. Mina listened, too, but despite what Chemosh said, her ears were stopped up with water. She could hear nothing except the sound of her own pulsing blood and the voice of the god.

"I don't hear anything," he said at last, and he sounded perplexed, "yet the feeling persists. Perhaps it is only my imagination. Come, let us find that which we seek. The ruins are not far."

He walked through the water as though he walked on dry land. Mina tried to imitate him, but found walking difficult. She ended up half-swimming, half-walking, propelling herself forward with broad strokes of her arms, kicking with her legs. The fathomless darkness began to grow lighter; she and Chemosh were rising nearer to the surface, to the sunlight.

He halted again, his expression dour. He looked at her, looked at the filmy, silky gown she wore. "I should never have allowed you to come down here unarmed with no armor to protect you. I will send you back—"

"Do not send me away, my lord. I am armored in my faith in you. My love for you is my weapon."

Chemosh drew her near. Her hair floated free in the water, shifting about her head and shoulders in sensuous waves. Her amber eyes seemed luminescent, the blood-red water lending them an orange hue, so that they had a fiery glow.

"It is no wonder I chose you as my High Priestess, Mina," said Chemosh. "Yet I will give you something more substantial than faith to protect your mortal body, and a weapon more capable of doing damage.

He dove down into the darkness, plunging down to the bottom of the ocean. In a few moments he returned, carrying a human skeleton.

"Not very pretty, but it's functional. You will not feel squeamish wearing a man's ribcage, will you, Mina?"

"The armor Takhisis gave me was wet with the blood of a man who dared to mock her," Mina replied. "Will you be my squire, my lord?"

"Just this once," he said with a smile, and he began to fasten the bony armor to her body. "Does this fit? If it does not, I can find something that will. We have an unlimited supply of skeletons."

"The fit is perfect, my lord."

Her cuirass was a man's breastbone and ribs. Collarbones protected her shoulders, shin bones her legs, and arm bones her arms. Chemosh welded them together with his power, strengthened them with his might. When he had dressed her, he eyed her accouterments and was satisfied.

"And now, your helm," he said.

"Not a skull, my lord," Mina protested. "I do not want to look like Krell."

"God forbid!" Chemosh said dryly. "No, Mina. Here is your helm."

He took her head in his two hands, kissed her on the forehead, on her cheeks, her chin and, finally, on her mouth.

"There, you are protected." He hesitated, keeping hold of her. His grip on her tightened. "Mina," he said softly, "I—"

"What, my lord?" she asked.

"Nothing," he said abruptly. He drew back from her, away from her touch, her amber eyes.

"Have I displeased you, my lord?" Mina asked, troubled.

"No," he said, and he repeated, "No."

He looked at her, at her body, warm and yielding and soft, clasped in the ghastly armor of a dead man's bones, and it was the Lord of Death who shuddered.

He snatched the bones off her, tearing them from her and casting them back into the sea.

"It really did not bother me, my lord," Mina protested.

"It bothered me," he said and turned away abruptly.

They drifted through the sunlit depths, searching for the ruins of the Tower.

Whatever power Chemosh sensed down here was growing, not diminishing, or so Mina judged by his increasingly dark expression. He did not speak to her. He did not look at her.

She tried to remain focused, to watch for danger. She found it difficult, however. She was in a different world, a world of strange and exotic beauty, and she was constantly distracted. Fish swam past her, darted around her, some eyeing her curiously, some completely ignoring her. Shelves of pink-tinged coral rose up from the ocean floor, home to a veritable forest of strange-looking plants and beings that appeared to be plants but weren't, as she discovered when she touched what she thought was a flower and it lashed out at her, stung her. The colors of everything—fish and plants—were brighter, more vivid and vibrant than any colors she had seen on land.

She forgot the danger and gave herself over to the enchantment.

Schools of silver fish flipped and spun in quicksilver unity. Tiny fish darted at her, nibbled at her hands. Others hid from sight, disappearing into coral doorways and diving through coral windows.

Suddenly, Chemosh hissed a warning. Catching hold of her, he dragged her into the shadows of green and undulating branches.

"What is it?" she asked softly.

"Look! Look there!" he said, disbelieving, and furious.

A building with walls of smooth, glistening crystal thrust up from the ocean floor. The crystalline structure caught the drowned shafts of sunlight and made them captive, so that the building gleamed with shimmering panes of watery light. A dome of black marble topped the building. Atop the dome, a circlet made of burnished red-gold twined with silver flashed in the sunlight. The center of the circlet was jet black, as if a hole had been opened up in the sea to reveal the emptiness of the universe.

"What is that place, my lord?" Mina asked, awed.

"The desecrated, burned-out, meteor-struck, fire-gutted, rubble-strewn Tower of High Sorcery of Istar," said Chemosh, adding, with a curse, "Somehow, some way, it has been rebuilt."

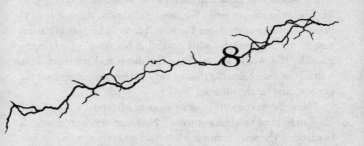

8

*O*ne moment Rhys and Nightshade were in Zeboim's cell, patiently arguing with the goddess, trying to make her see reason. The next moment, between the space of one breath and the next, one word and the next, one rant and the next, Rhys was standing on crumbling flagstone in the middle of an island fortress, with the lingering echo of a raging sea roaring in his head. Having grown weary of his argument, Zeboim had brought it to an end.

Rhys had never been to the Storm's Keep. He had heard tales of it, but he had paid scant attention to the stories. He was not one who yearned for adventure. He did not join the younger monks, who thrilled to hear ghost stories told round the fire on a winter's night. More often than not, he left that cozy fire to go walking alone across the frozen hills, rejoicing in the cold, glittering beauty of the frost-rimed stars.

The bodies of those young monks lay beneath the earth. Their ghosts, it was to be hoped, were roaming free among those very stars. He had set out to solve the mystery of their deaths. Knowing how, he had yet to discover why. His search had brought him here. Looking back on the road that he had traveled, he could not see it for all the bends and twists and turns it had taken.

If he had obeyed Majere and remained at the monastery to seek perfection of body and mind, what would he be doing now? He knew the answer well. The hour was sunset. Almost time to bring the sheep down from the hills. He would be sitting at his ease in the tall grass, his staff cradled in his arms, Atta lying by his side. She would be watching the sheep and watching him, waiting for the command that would send her skimming over the grass, racing up the hillside.

The scene was peaceful, but he was not. His spirit was troubled, plagued by doubt and inner turmoil. No longer was he free to walk out among the stars at night. He would go every evening to visit the mass grave and he would feel, as he gazed down at the new grass starting to cover it, that he had failed his brethren, failed his family, failed mankind. Rhys looked at what might have been and the image faded away. If he should die in this dread place—as seemed most likely—his spirit would go forth on the next stage of the journey content in the knowledge that he had done right, though it had turned out all wrong.

A gaudy sunset washed the sky with reds and golds and purples, splashing the gray walls of Storm's Keep with lurid color. Rhys's first incongruous thought was that the fortress was ill-named. No storms raged on Storm's Keep. The sky was empty, save for a single, solitary wisp of white cloud that ran away swiftly, afraid of being caught. No breeze stirred on land or water. The sea sloshed sullenly against the cliffs. Wavelets slobbered at the bottoms of the jagged rocks, fawning, caressing them.

Rhys studied his surroundings, looking them over long and intently—the formidable towers jutting up into the garish sky, the parade ground on which he stood, the various outbuildings scattered amid the rocks. And beyond and all around him, the sea, avidly watching his every move.

His every move. His and his alone. The kender was nowhere in sight. Rhys sighed and shook his head. He'd tried to explain to Zeboim that the presence of the kender was essential to his plan. He had thought he'd convinced her—of that, at least, if nothing else. Perhaps the kender had tumbled out of the ethers onto a different part of the isle. Perhaps . . .

"Nightshade?" Rhys called softly.

A outraged squeal answered. The squeal came from the leather scrip that hung on Rhys's belt, and after a moment's startled amazement, he breathed easier. Zeboim had acted on his plan with her usual impetuosity, just not bothering to tell him she'd done so.

"Rhys!" Nightshade wailed, his voice muffled by the scrip in which he was ensconced, "what happened? Where am I? It's pitch dark in here and it stinks of goat cheese!"

"Keep quiet, my friend," Rhys ordered and he placed his hand reassuringly over the scrip.

The scrip obediently fell silent, though he could feel it quivering against his thigh. He gave the kender a soothing pat.

"You're inside my scrip. The scrip and I are on Storm's Keep."

The scrip gave a lurch.

"Nightshade," said Rhys, "you must keep perfectly still. Our lives depend on it."

"Sorry, Rhys," squeaked the kender. "I'm just a little surprised, that's all. This was all so sudden!" He shrieked the last word.

"I know," Rhys said, striving to keep his tone calm. "I didn't expect to make this journey, either. But we're here now, and we have to carry on with our plan as we discussed it. Can you do that?"

"Yes, Rhys. I lost control there for a moment. It's kind of a shock, you know, finding yourself three inches tall and stuck in a sack that smells of goat cheese and then discovering you've dropped in on a death knight." Nightshade sounded bitter.

"I understand," said Rhys, glad that the kender could not see his smile.

"I'm over all that now, though," Nightshade added after a pause to catch his breath. "You can count on me."

"Good." Rhys glanced about again. "I have no idea where we

are or where we are supposed to go. Zeboim sent us off before I could ask her."

The towers of a massive fortress rose from the cliffs. The buildings all appeared to have been carved from the island as a sculptor carves his work from the marble block, leaving the base rough-hewn, the top smooth and shaped and crafted. Rhys had the eerie sensation that he was standing on the very topmost point of a jagged splinter of earth, with the rest of the world falling away all around him. On his hillside, he had always felt himself to be at one with a benevolent universe. Here he felt himself alone, isolated and abandoned, in a universe that didn't give a damn.

The flagstones of the parade ground radiated the heat of the afternoon sun into the air. Sweat trickled down Rhys's neck and his chest. The kender, he thought, must be suffocating. Rhys opened the scrip slightly to let in more air.

"Keep quiet," he reiterated. "And keep still."

Two enormous towers that must be the fortress's main buildings stood at one end of the island. Rhys would have to traverse the length of the parade ground to reach them. Gazing up at the myriad windows in the tall towers, Rhys realized the death knight, Ausric Krell, might be standing, watching him.

He thought back to the conversation that had taken place in the prison cell just moments before he'd so unexpectedly set off on this journey.

Majesty, Nightshade and I require your help if we are to survive this encounter with this death knight. You promised me you would grant me your holy power——

I changed my mind, monk. I have thought it over. What you ask is too dangerous for my son. If you fail, Ariakan will still be in Chemosh's possession. If he even suspected that I helped you, he would retaliate against my poor son.

Mistress, without your aid, we cannot proceed——

Bah! Your plan is a good one, as good as any plan could be, given the circumstances. You might succeed. If you do, you have nothing to worry about. If not, death won't matter to you. Because of your sacrifice, you will be assured of a peaceful afterlife. Majere could hardly deny you that, whereas my poor son—

Majesty—

It was then that Zeboim had ended the argument.

Now he stood on Storm's Keep, forced to face a death knight with only his staff for a weapon and a miniature kender for a companion, with no god to give him aid. Gazing out at the sullen waves and the empty, darkening sky, Rhys gripped his staff, which had been a sorrowful last gift from Majere, and said a prayer. He did not know to whom he was praying, if anyone—perhaps to the sea, perhaps to the endless sky. He asked for no spells, no holy magic, no godly powers. Useless to ask. No one would answer.

"Give me strength," he prayed, and with that, he started to walk toward the fortress to find the death knight.

He had taken only a few steps when a shadow fell over him from behind. The shadow was cold as despair, dark as fear. He could hear, behind him, the creak of leather and the rattle of armor and the sound of breathing, which was not the sound of the living breathing, but the hissing, rasping sound of the undead trying to remember what it was to breathe. The stench of decay, of death, filled his nose and mouth. Between the stench and the horror, he was so sickened that for a moment he feared he might pass out.

Rhys gripped his staff hard. His spiritual self went forth to do battle. Fear was the death knight's most potent weapon. He had to defeat fear or fall where he stood. His spirit fought with the fear, soul seeking to overcome the weakness inherent to flesh. The struggle was brief, sharp. Rhys had trained for this all his days in the monastery. He could not call upon Majere to aid him, but he could call upon the lessons of Majere. Spirit won. His soul triumphed. The sick feeling passed. The hot prickling sensation in his limbs eased, though his hand clutching the staff had gone numb.

Master of himself, he maintained that mastery and turned with unhurried calm to look fear in the face.

At the sight of the death knight, Rhys's resolve came close to crumbling. Krell stood near Rhys, looming over him. Looking into the eye slits of the helm, Rhys saw the accursed light of undeath, light that was as fierce and fiery as the sun, yet could not illuminate the darkness of the being trapped inside the blood-stained armor. Rhys steeled himself to look past the flaring light at that being.

It was not daunting. It was mean and shriveled.

Krell's small red eyes peered at Rhys. "Before I kill you, Mantis Monk, I will give you a chance to tell me what you're doing on my island. Your explanation should be amusing."

"You are mistaken, sir. I am not a monk of Majere. I came to speak for Zeboim, to negotiate for the soul of her son."

"You're dressed like a monk," Krell leered, sneering.

"Appearances can be deceiving," Rhys returned. "You, sir, are dressed like a knight."

Krell glared. He had the feeling he'd been insulted, but he wasn't sure. "Never mind. I'll have the last laugh, monk. Days of laughter, so long as you don't up and die on me too soon, like so many of the bastards."

Krell rocked back on his heels, rocked forward, his hands hooked through his belt.

"Zeboim wants to negotiate, does she? Very well. Here are my terms, monk: you will entertain me as do all my 'guests' by playing khas with me. If, by chance, you beat me, I will reward you by cutting your throat." He added, just in case Rhys did not understand, "Killing you swiftly, you see."

Rhys nodded, kept a tight grip on the staff. So far, so good. All was going as planned.

"If you do not beat me—and I warn you that I am an expert player—I will give you another chance. I am not such a bad fellow, after all. I'll give you chance after chance to beat me. We will play one game after another after another."

Krell made a motion with his gloved hand. "The game board is set up in the library. A rather long walk, but at least you can enjoy this unusually pleasant weather we're experiencing. You might want to take a good last look at the sunset."

Krell chuckled, a hideous sound, his amusement echoing hollowly in the empty armor. He stomped off, gleefully rubbing his hands in anticipation of the game. Half-way across the courtyard, he came to a halt, turned to face Rhys.

"Did I mention that for every khas piece you lose, monk, I will break one of your bones?" Krell laughed outright. "I start with the small bones—fingers and toes. Then I will break your ribs, one by one. After that maybe a collar bone, a wrist or an elbow. Then I start on the legs—a shin bone, thigh bone, pelvis. I leave your spine until the end. By that time, you'll be begging me to slay you. I told you I find this game entertaining! I'm going off to set up the board now. Don't keep me waiting. I do so long to hear what Zeboim has to offer me in exchange for her son."

The death knight strode off. Rhys stood unmoving, gazing after him.

"Oh, Rhys!" Nightshade cried, appalled.

"Not so loud. How good a khas player are you?" Rhys asked quietly.

"Not that good," Nightshade answered, his voice quavering. "We'll be forced to give up pieces, Rhys. It's the only way to play the game. I'm sorry. I'll try to find Ariakan quickly."

"Just do the best you can, my friend," said Rhys, and gripping his staff, he started walking toward the tower.

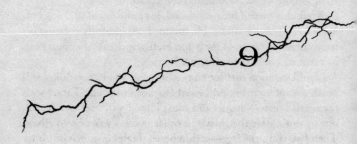

Krell rose from his seat as Rhys entered the library. Bowing with a mocking show of polite welcome, the death knight ushered Rhys to a chair placed near a small table on which the khas board was all arranged. The room was chill and oppressive and smelled of rotting flesh. Krell irritably kicked aside several bones that littered the floor.

"Excuse the mess. Former khas players," he said to Rhys.

Leg bones, arm bones, collar bones, fingers and toes, skulls— all cracked or shattered, some in several places. Krell casually trod a few underfoot, crushing them to dust.

He settled his ponderous armored body in his chair and indicated with another wave that Rhys was to sit down. The round khas board stood in between the two players; the shrunken bodies that were the khas pieces stood on the black and white and red hexes, two opposing armies facing each other across a checkered battlefield.

Seating himself, Rhys appeared to have lost his nerve. His customary calm deserted him. He was shivering, his hands shaking so that the staff slipped from his sweaty palms and fell to the floor. He sought to remove the scrip from his belt and dropped it as well. Rhys bent to pick up the scrip.

"Leave it," Krell growled. "Get on with the game."

Rhys mopped sweat from his forehead with the sleeve of his robe. As he sank, trembling, into his seat, his knee jerked, striking the khas board and upending it. The board fell off its stand. The pieces slid to the floor and scattered in all directions.

"You clumsy oaf!" Krell snarled. The death knight leaned down to pick up the khas pieces, going after one in particular that he snatched up hurriedly.

Rhys could not get a good look at it, for Krell closed his gloved hand over it.

"You pick up the rest, monk," Krell grunted. "And if any of those pieces are damaged, I'm going to break two of your bones for every piece you lose. Be quick about it."

Rhys crawled on the floor, on his hands and knees, scrabbling to pick up the pieces, some of which had rolled to far parts of the room.

"There are twenty-seven bones in the human hand," stated Krell, returning the pieces he'd picked up to the khas board. "I start with the forefinger of the right hand and work my way along. You missed a pawn, one of the kender. It's over by the fire pit."

Rhys picked up the last piece—a kender pawn—and placed it on the board.

"What are you doing, monk?" Krell demanded.

Rhys's hand on the kender froze. He could feel Nightshade quivering beneath his fingers.

"Pawns don't go there." Krell said in disgust. "That hex is where you put the rook. The pawn goes here."

"I am sorry," Rhys said, and he moved Nightshade to the indicated hex. "I know very little about the game."

Krell shook his head. "And here I was hoping you would live to entertain me for a week at least. Still," the death knight added cheerfully, "there are twenty-six bones in the human foot. You'll last at least a day or two. You have first move."

Rhys resumed his seat. Placing his foot firmly on the kender pawn he'd switched out for Nightshade, he shoved the pawn beneath his chair.

Rhys took hold of Nightshade, who stood stiff and straight as the rest of the pawns, and advanced the kender one square. Then Rhys hesitated. He could not recall if he was supposed to move one square or two on his opening gambit. Nightshade apparently sensed his dilemma, for he gave a little wriggle. Rhys advanced him another square then sank back in his chair. The trembling and shaking had been an act, but the sweat on his brow was real. He mopped it again with the sleeve of his robe.

Krell advanced a goblin pawn two squares on the opposite side of the board.

"Your move, monk."

Rhys looked at the board and tried hard to remember his lessons in khas, given to him by Nightshade the night before. They had a game plan in mind, the object being to move Nightshade close enough to the dark knight pieces so that he could find out which was Ariakan. Nightshade explained all the contingencies—what to move if Krell moved this, what to move if Krell moved that. Unfortunately, Rhys had proved a poor pupil.

"You have to think like a warrior, Rhys," Nightshade had said to him at one point in exasperation, "not like a shepherd!"

"I am a shepherd," Rhys had returned, smiling.

"Well, stop thinking like one. You can't protect all your pieces. You have to sacrifice some of them to win."

"I don't have to win," Rhys had pointed out. "I just have to stay in the game long enough for you to accomplish your mission."

What neither of them had counted on were broken bones.

Rhys put his hand on a pawn and glanced at Nightshade. The kender stiffened in his place, very slightly shook his head. Rhys lifted his hand off the piece.

"Hah, monk!" Krell rumbled, leaning forward with a rattle of armor. "You touched the piece. You have to move it."

Nightshade's shoulders slumped. Rhys moved the pawn. He'd

barely taken his hand off it before Krell swooped down. Seizing one of his pieces, he slid it across the board and knocked over Rhys's pawn. Krell triumphantly moved the pawn to his side of the table.

"My turn again," said Krell.

Rising up out of his chair, his small red eyes flaring with anticipation, the death knight seized hold of Rhys's hand.

Rhys gasped and shuddered beneath the death knight's touch, which seared his flesh with the white-hot hatred the accursed dead bear the living.

The monks of Majere are trained to withstand pain without complaint, using many disciplines, including one called Frost Fire. Through the use of consistent practice and mediation, the monk is able to completely banish minor pains, so that they are no longer felt, and can reduce debilitating pain to a level where the monk can continue to function. The "fire" is rimed with ice, the monk envisioning hoar-frost settling over the pain, so that it subsides beneath the freezing cold that numbs the affected part of the body.

Rhys had counted upon using this discipline to be able overcome the pain of the shattered bones, at least for a while. Meditation and discipline were no match for thhe death knight's touch. Rhys had once tipped over a lantern, spilling flaming oil on his bare legs. His flesh blistered and bubbled, the pain so severe he'd almost passed out. Krell's touch was like flaming oil being poured through Rhys's veins. He could not help himself. He cried out in agony, his body jerking spasmodically in Krell's hold.

Grabbing hold of Rhys's index finger on his right hand, Krell gave it an expert twist. The bone snapped at the knuckle. Rhys moaned. A wave of sickening heat and dizziness swept over him.

Krell released him and sauntered back to his chair.

Rhys sank back, fighting faintness, sucking in the deep breaths used to clear his mind and enter the Frost Fire state. He was having difficulty. The broken finger was discolored and starting to swell. The flesh where Krell had touched it was a ghastly shade of white, like that of a corpse. Rhys was weak and unsteady. The khas pieces wavered in his vision, the room swam.

"If you give way now, all is lost," he told himself, wavering on the verge of unconsciousness. "This behavior is unforgivable. The Master would be bitterly disappointed. Were all these past years a lie?"

Rhys closed his eyes and he was back on the hills, sitting in the grass, watching the clouds drift across the sky, mirroring the white woolly sheep roaming the hillside. Slowly he began to regain mastery, his spirit triumphing over his wounded body.

Nursing his broken finger, he returned his attention to the khas board. Nightshade's lessons came back to him and he lifted his hand—his injured hand—and made his move.

"I'm impressed, monk," said Krell, regarding Rhys with grudging admiration. "Most humans usually pass out on me and I have to wait for them to come around."

Rhys barely heard him. His next move would advance Nightshade, but it meant sacrificing another piece.

Krell made his move and gave a nod to Rhys.

Rhys pretended to study the board, all the while composing his spirit, bracing himself for what must come next. He placed his hand on the khas piece, glanced at Nightshade.

The kender had gone quite pale, so that he was now barely distinguishable from the rest of the shrunken kender corpses. Nightshade knew what was coming as well as Rhys, but it had to be done. He gave a small nod.

Rhys picked up the piece, moved it, set it down, and after only a slight hesitation, removed his hand from it. He heard Krell chortle with pleasure, heard him knock over one of his pieces, heard the death knight rise ponderously to his feet.

The chill shadow of the death knight fell over him.

For one horrible minute, Nightshade knew he was going to faint. He'd heard quite clearly the rending, snapping sound of that first bone breaking, and Rhys's agonized moan, and the soft-hearted kender had gone unpleasantly hot all over. Only the terrible thought of himself—a khas piece—suddenly slumping over in a dead faint on his black hex (a move not found in any rule book) kept Nightshade on his feet. Wobbly but determined, he pressed on with his end of the mission.

Nightshade was an unusual kender in that he was not fond of adventure. His parents considered this a lamentable trait and sought to reason with him, to no avail. His father maintained sadly that this lack of true kender spirit probably came from the fact that Nightshade chummed around with dead people all the time. Some dead have such a negative view of life.

Thus far, this adventure had gone a long way to confirming Nightshade's bad opinion.

From the beginning, he had not been keen on Rhys's plan to reduce him to the size of khas piece. In a world of tall people, Nightshade considered that he was short enough already. He further did not like the idea of being dependent on Zeboim to shrink him in the first place and in the second place to bring him back from being shrunken. Rhys had assured Nightshade that he would have Zeboim swear on whatever it was goddesses swore upon that she would perform as required. Unfortunately, the goddess had whipped the spell on the kender before they'd had a chance to conclude this important term in the negotiations. Nightshade had been standing beside Rhys in the goddess's prison cell, and the next thing he knew he was inside a smelly leather pouch, sweating and recalling with a pang that he'd skipped breakfast.

He'd wanted out of that pouch until the death knight showed up, and then he'd wanted only to crawl inside the pouch's seams. He supposed he was as brave as any kender living, but even his famous Uncle Tas had, according to legend, been afraid of a death knight.

After that, there had been no time for fear. After Rhys

dropped the scrip, Nightshade had only seconds to crawl out of the pouch and roll away before the death knight could spot him. Then there was the business of trying to hold stiff and unmoving as Rhys picked him up—gently as he could—and stood him on the khas board. In the worry and anxiety over all that, he hadn't had time to be intimidated by the death knight.

When that flurry of activity was over, however, Nightshade had quite a good view of Krell, for he was forced to stand facing the death knight, who was every bit as loathsome as the kender had pictured.

Nightshade wondered if anyone would notice if he shut his eyes. A covert glance showed him that all the other kender on the board had his or her eyes wide open.

"Of course, they're corpses—lucky bastards," Nightshade muttered in his throat.

Krell did not appear too observant, but he might notice. Nightshade was forced to stare straight at the death knight. Nightshade might not have been able to withstand the awful sight but that he suddenly caught a glimpse of Krell's spirit. Krell was big and ugly and terrifying. His spirit, by contrast, was small and ugly and craven. In the spirit department, Nightshade could have taken on Krell, thrown him to the ground, and sat on his head. This knowledge made Nightshade feel immensely better and he was starting to think that they just might get out of this alive—something he hadn't really expected—when Krell broke Rhys's first finger, and Nightshade had nearly collapsed.

"The sooner you finish your part of the job," Nightshade told himself to keep himself from passing out, "the sooner you and Rhys can get out of here."

Nightshade gulped, blinked away his tears, and proceeded to do what he'd been sent here to do—find out which of the khas pieces contained the spirit of Lord Ariakan.

When he'd heard that all the khas pieces were shrunken corpses, Nightshade had been concerned that he'd be over-whelmed with the spirits of the dead. Fortunately, the spirits of the dead had long since departed, leaving their tormented bodies behind. Nightshade felt the presence of only one spirit, but that spirit was angry enough for twenty.

Ordinarily Nightshade could have used such strong emotions as he felt resonate from the spirit to determine which khas piece was which. Unfortunately, the rage cascading over the khas board was so very strong that it made distinguishing between the pieces impossible. Anger and the fierce desire for vengeance was every-where and could have come from any one of the pieces.

Zeboim had insisted that her son was trapped in one of the two dark knights, each riding a blue dragon—for that was what Krell had told her. Nightshade thought this likely, though he could not discount the possibility that Krell had lied. He looked over the heads of the goblin pieces standing opposite him and peered around the corpse of a black-robed wizard to get a good look at both knight pieces to see if he could note anything about them that might help him decide.

He rather hoped one might quiver in indignation, or give a vicious snort, or poke another piece with his spear . . .

Nothing. The knight pieces stood as rigid and unmoving as—well—corpses.

There was only one way to find out. He would make himself known to the spirit and ask it to please reveal itself.

Nightshade generally talked to spirits in a normal tone of voice; they tended to like that, it made them feel at home. Speaking aloud was not an option here. While Krell didn't look any too bright, even he was bound to be suspicious of a talking khas piece. Nightshade could, if he had to, speak to spirits on their own plane in a voice akin to theirs, something he sometimes had to do with very shy spirits.

Unfortunately, being undead himself, Krell existed on both planes—the mortal and the spiritual—and he might overhear the kender. Nightshade decided he had to take the risk. He couldn't let Rhys endure any more torture.

Nightshade looked intently at Krell and his spirit. The death knight appeared to be entirely engrossed in both the game and in torturing Rhys. Krell seemed pretty well entrenched in the mortal plane, as was his small, ugly little spirit.

"Excuse me," Nightshade called out in a polite whisper, trying to watch both knight pieces and Krell, "I'm looking for Lord Ariakan. Could you make yourself known, please?"

He waited expectantly, but no one answered his summons. The rushing tide of fury did not abate, however. Ariakan was here, the kender was sure of it.

Nightshade was being ignored.

Out of the corner of his eyes, Nightshade saw Rhys's wounded hand hovering over the khas board. Nightshade looked up fearfully to see what Rhys was going to do. They had worked out several strategies with the goal of advancing Nightshade across the board toward the knight pieces. He tensed to see the fingers come down and gave a small, relieved sigh when Rhys made the correct move. Nightshade sighed again, more deeply and sorrowfully. Rhys would sacrifice a piece in this move. Krell would break another bone. Nightshade decided to get firm.

"Lord Ariakan—" he began more loudly, taking a no-nonsense tone.

"Shut up," said a voice, cold and sepulchral.

"Oh, there you are!" Nightshade focused on the dark knight piece standing on his side of the board. "I'm glad I found you. We've come to rescue you. My friend and I." He could not turn around, but he swiveled his eyes and gave a very small jerk of his head toward Rhys.

The fury lessened a modicum. Nightshade now had the spirit's full attention.

"A kender and a monk of Majere here to rescue me from Chemosh?" Ariakan gave a bitter laugh. "Not likely."

"I am a kender. I admit that. But Rhys is no longer a monk of Majere. Well, he is, but he isn't, if you take my meaning, my lord, which you probably don't, because I don't understand it very well myself. And it wasn't our idea to come. Your mother sent us."

"My mother!" Ariakan snorted. "Now it all makes sense."

"I think she's trying to help," Nightshade offered.

Ariakan snorted again.

Behind him, Nightshade heard the snap of another bone. Rhys moaned and then fell silent, so silent that for a moment Nightshade feared his friend had lost consciousness. Then he heard harsh breathing and saw Rhys's hand move over the board.

Jagged-edged bone protruded from the flesh. Blood splattered down on the khas board. The kender gulped, his heart wrung for his friend's suffering.

"Now that you know we're here to save you, my lord," said Nightshade, desperately hurrying things along, "here's our plan—"

"You're wasting your time. I'm not leaving," returned Ariakan fiercely, "not until I've torn out the liver of this traitor with my bare hands and fed it to him in small bites."

"He doesn't have a liver," Nightshade said crossly. "Not anymore. And I'd just like to say that it is this sort of bad attitude that's kept you in prison all these years. Now. Here is the plan. Rhys will capture you"—Nightshade stated this confidently, though he had misgivings on this score—"and move you to his side of the board. I'll distract Krell. Rhys will pocket you and we'll escape and carry you back safely to your goddess mother. All you have to do is—"

"I do not want to be rescued," said Ariakan. "If you try, I will raise holy hell. Even Krell can't fail to notice. I'm afraid you've wasted your time. And your lives."

"He definitely takes after his mother," Nightshade muttered. "Poor Rhys," he added, wincing as he heard his friend draw in a halting breath. "He can't take much more. Oh, no! There he goes. About to move the wrong piece!"

Nightshade gave a violent jerk of his head and rolled his eyes and, fortunately, Rhys took the hint. His hand—he was using his left hand now—shifted from the queen to a rook. Nightshade heaved a deep sigh and cast a glance at Krell.

"That should give him something to think about," said the kender in satisfaction.

The death knight was impressed by the move. Krell leaned over the board, started to move a piece, thought better of it. Drumming his gloved fingers on the chair's carved wooden arm, he sat back and stared at the board.

Nightshade stole a glance at Rhys. The monk was very pale, his face covered with a sheen of sweat. He sat with his right hand cradled in his left. His robes were spattered with his own blood. He made no sound, did not groan, though the pain must have been excruciating. Every so often, Nightshade heard that soft, sharp intake of breath.

Kender are by nature easy-going folk, willing to let bygones be bygones, live and let live, turn the other cheek, never judge a book by its cover or cry over spilt milk. But sometimes they get mad. And anyone on Krynn can tell you that there is nothing in the world quite as dangerous as a kender with his dander up.

"Here we are," Nightshade said to himself, "risking our lives to rescue this knight, only to find out the steel-plated jackass refuses to be rescued. Well," he stated grimly, "we'll see about that!"

No kender "borrowing" required. No artful sleight-of-hand, no sly maneuvering. Just a crude snatch-and-grab. Nightshade didn't have any way to alert Rhys to the change of plans. He could only hope that his partner would take the hint, which—after all—was going to be an extremely broad one.

Krell reached out his gloved hand to make a move. As Nightshade had anticipated, the death knight was about to pick up the dark knight piece. He was going to move Lord Ariakan.

Nightshade lowered his head like a bull he'd seen at a fair and charged.

Some part of Rhys was cognizant of the khas board and the pieces on it and what was going on in the game. Another part of him was not. That part of him was on the hillside, bare feet cool in the dew-sparkled green grass, the sun warm on his shoulders. He was finding it increasingly hard to stay on the hillside, though.

Jagged flashes of agony disrupted his meditative state. Every time Krell laid his cold and fleshless hand upon Rhys, the horrible touch further depleted his strength and his will.

According to their plan, he had several more moves to go. He would have to lose more pieces.

Night had fallen outside. Through the window, Rhys could see the flicker of lightning on the horizon; Zeboim waiting impatiently for news.

Inside, no fire burned, no candle flared. The board was illuminated by the red glow of Krell's eyes. Rhys tried to focus . . . but he was finding it impossible to make sense of a game that had never made sense. Trying to remember what piece he was supposed to move, he was alarmed to see the black hexes rise up from the board and float a good three inches off the surface. Rhys blinked his eyes and drew in a deep breath, and the black hexes returned to their normal position.

Krell's fingers drummed on the chair. He leaned forward, his hand reaching for one of the dark knight pieces.

When Nightshade first broke into a run, Rhys feared his eyes were again deceiving him. He stared at the khas piece, willing it to return to normal.

Krell gave a startled grunt and Rhys realized that he wasn't seeing things. Nightshade had taken the game into his own hands. The pawn was making his own move.

Dodging in and out among the khas pieces, Nightshade barreled across the board and launched himself straight at the dark knight khas piece. The kender wrapped both arms around the legs of the blue dragon and kept going.

Pawn and knight tumbled off the board.

"Here now," Krell said sternly. "That's against the rules."

Rhys could not see the khas pieces, but he could hear them land on the floor, one with a clatter and the other with a yelp.

Krell gave a low rumble of anger. His red eyes turned on Rhys.

Snatching up his staff, holding it in both hands, Rhys rose from his chair and drove the staff with all his might into the center of the death knight's helm, hitting Krell between the fiery eyes.

Rhys hoped that the jab in the heavy steel helm would distract the death knight, slow him long enough for Rhys to find Nightshade and Lord Ariakan. Rhys did not anticipate doing any damage to Krell.

But the staff was holy, blessed by Majere, the last gift of the god to his lost sheep.

Acting on its own accord, the staff flew out of Rhys's hands. As he stared, amazed, the staff altered form, changing into an enormous mantis, the insect sacred to the god Majere.

The mantis was ten feet tall, with bulbous eyes and a green shell body, and six huge green legs. The huge praying mantis grasped the death knight's head with its spiny forelegs. The mantis clamped its mandibles over Krell's cringing spirit and began to feed off him, the jaws of the god tearing through the armor to reach the accursed soul beneath.

Caught in the grip of the gigantic insect, Krell screamed in horror, his coward's heart shriveling.

Rhys whispered a quick prayer of thanksgiving to the god and knelt down swiftly to recover the khas piece and the kender. He found them easily enough, for Nightshade was jumping up and down and waving his arms and shrieking. Rhys picked up Nightshade.

"He doesn't want to be rescued!" the kender yelled.

Rhys thrust Nightshade into the leather scrip, then picked up the dark knight khas piece. The pewter was hot to the touch, as though it had just come molten from the fire.

Rhys glanced at Krell, grappling with the god, and guessed that Ariakan's vengeance-thirsting soul would continue to remain bound to this world for a long time to come.

Her son's spirit was Zeboim's concern. Rhys deposited the khas piece into the pouch, wincing at the kender's yelp as Nightshade came into contact with the blazing metal. Rhys had no time to help. Krell was starting to recover from the first horrific shock of the mantis's attack and was now fighting back, slugging the insect's green body with his fists, kicking it savagely, trying to fling it off him. Rhys had to make good their escape while Krell and the mantis were still battling. Rhys hoped that the mantis would destroy Krell, but he dared not stay around to see the final outcome.

He turned to run. He'd only taken a few steps when he realized he wouldn't be able to run far. He was too weak.

Gasping for breath, sick and dizzy, he staggered into the night. His legs trembled, his feet stumbled on the uneven cobblestones and he tripped over a broken stone. He was so weak he could not recover his balance. He fell forward onto his hands and knees. He tried to keep going. All he could do was pant. He was sick. He was exhausted. He was finished. He lacked the strength to run anymore, and behind him, he heard fell heavy footfalls and Krell roaring in fury.

Rhys looked up at the starlit heavens.

"Zeboim," he cried, his breath torn and ragged. "Your son is safe in my possession. It is up to you now."

The sea rose. Gray clouds, massed on the horizon, waited for the command to attack. Rhys also waited, confident that at any moment the goddess would carry them off this island.

A single stroke of lightning zinged from sky to ground. Striking the top of the tower, the bolt blasted off a great chunk of rock. Thunder rumbled, distant and far away. Rhys stood in the courtyard, the kender and the khas piece in his pouch.

The death knight's heavy boots pounded closer.

The mantis's horrific attack had scared Krell witless. No mortal could inflict pain on a death knight, but a god could and Krell knew agony and terror as the insect's mandibles chomped down on his soul, as the hideous, bulbous eyes reflected back the nothingness of the death knight's cursed existence.

Krell had always detested bugs.

He managed to land a few panic-stricken punches against the mantis and those were enough to dislodge it. Krell yanked his sword from its sheathe and thrust the blade into the insect's body. Green blood oozed. The mantis's jaws clicked horribly. Its spiny claws lashed out at him.

Krell slashed wildly at the mantis, hitting it again and again. He struck blindly, flailing away at it, not aware of what he was hitting, only wanting the horrible bug dead, dead, dead. It took him a few moments to realize he was stabbing thin air.

Krell halted, looked fearfully around.

The mantis was gone. The monk's staff was there, lying on the floor. Krell lifted his foot, prepared to stomp on the staff and grind it to splinters. He held his foot poised in the air. Suppose he touched it and the bug came back? Slowly, Krell lowered his foot to the floor and edged away. Keeping as far from the staff as possible, he circled warily around it.

Krell peered under the table. The knight piece was not there, nor was the kender.

Krell looked at the board. The other knight piece remained, standing on its hex. He snatched it up, stared at it hopefully, then flung it from him with a bitter curse.

The death's knight's view of the theft having been blocked by a giant mantis trying to eat his head, Krell had not actually seen Rhys run off with the khas piece. But the death knight had no problem figuring out what had happened. He set off in pursuit of the monk, spurred on by the dreadful knowledge of what Chemosh would do to him if he lost Ariakan.

Krell dashed into the courtyard. He could see Rhys some distance away, running for his life. He could also see storm clouds, gray and menacing, gathering overhead. A bolt of lightning struck one of the towers. The next bolt, he had the feeling, would be aimed at him.

"Don't you lay a hand on me, Zeboim!" Krell bellowed, desperately dissembling. "Your monk stole the wrong khas piece. Your son is still in my possession. If you do anything to help this thief escape, Chemosh will melt down your pretty pewter boy and hammer his soul into oblivion!"

Lightning flickered from cloud to cloud; thunder gave a low, ominous growl. The wind rose, the skies grew darker and still darker. A few spatters of rain fell, along with a couple of hail stones.

And that was all.

Krell chuckled and, rubbing his hands, he went after the monk.

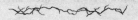

Rhys heard Krell's bellow and his heart sank.

"Zeboim!" Rhys called urgently. "He's lying. I have your son! Take us away from here!"

Lightning flickered. The rumble of thunder was muted. The clouds swirling about overhead were confused, unsure. The death knight raced across the parade ground. His fists clenched, his red eyes flaring, Krell advanced, incensed. When he caught Rhys, he would do more than break a few fingers.

"Majesty," Rhys prayed, "We risked our lives for you. Now is time for you to risk something for us."

Rain drizzled down in desultory ploppings all around him. The wind sighed and gave up. The clouds began to retreat.

"Very well, Majesty," said Rhys. He yanked the scrip from his belt. "Forgive me for what I'm about to do, but you've left me no choice."

Grasping the pouch in his one good hand, Rhys looked around, getting his bearings, judging distance. This would be his last move, use up all his remaining strength. He broke into his final sprint.

The heavens opened. The rain fell heavily, pounding at him. Rhys ignored the goddess's warning. She could bluster and blow and threaten all she wanted. She dared not do anything drastic to him, for he might, in truth, have her son in his possession.

Zeboim tried blowing him off his feet. Rhys picked himself up and kept on running. She threw hail stones at his face. He flung up his arm to protect his eyes and kept going.

Krell pounded after him. The death knight's footfalls shook the ground.

Rhys slipped and stumbled, his strength flagging. He did not have far to go, however. The parade ground ended in a jumble of rocks, and beyond that, the sea.

Krell saw the danger and his pace increased.

"Stop him, Zeboim," Krell shouted angrily. "If you don't, you'll be sorry!"

Rhys thrust the scrip containing the kender and the khas piece into the bosom of his robe and climbed out onto the jagged rocks that were wet and slick from the rain. He slipped, had to use both hands to steady himself, and he sobbed in agony from the pain of his broken fingers.

He could hear Krell's hissing breath behind him and feel his rage. Rhys pressed on.

His strength was gone by the time he reached the island's edge. He didn't need it by then, anyway. He had only one more step to take and that would not require much energy.

Rhys looked down. He stood at the top of a sheer cliff. Below him—far below him—the sea heaved and swelled and crashed up against the rock face. The goddess's anger and fear lit the night until it was as bright as day. Rhys noted small details—the swirling foam, the green sweep of algae trialing off a glistening rock, floating on the surface like the hair of a drowned man.

Rhys looked out over the ocean to the horizon, shrouded in mist and driving rain.

Krell had reached the rocks and was blundering his way through them, cursing and swearing and waving his sword.

Moving carefully, so as not to slip, Rhys climbed up onto a promontory extending out over the sea. He stood poised, his soul calm.

"Hold on, Nightshade," Rhys said. "This is going to get a little rough."

"Rhys!" the kender wailed, terrified. "What are you doing? I can't see!"

"Just as well."

Rhys lifted his face to heaven.

"Zeboim, we are in your hands."

He stood as though on the green hill, the sheep flowing over it in a mass of white, Atta poised at his side, looking into his face, her tail wagging, waiting eagerly for the command.

"Atta, come bye," Rhys said and jumped.

*N*ight seeped from the Blood Sea's depths, spreading ink-like through the water, drifting gently toward the surface. Mina gazed upward, watching the last vestige of flickering sunlight shimmer on the water's surface. Then it vanished, and she was in utter darkness.

During the hours they had spent waiting and watching the tower in the Blood Sea, she and Chemosh had seen no one enter it, no one leave. The sea creatures swam past the crystal walls as carelessly as they swam past the coral reef or the hulk of a wrecked ship lying on the ocean floors. Fish brushed up against the walls, traveling up and down the smooth surface, either finding food or entranced by their own reflections. None appeared afraid of the Tower, though Mina did notice that the sea creatures avoided the strange circlet of red-yellow gold and silver at the top. None would come near the dark hole in the center.

With the coming of night beneath the waves, Chemosh watched to see if any lights appeared in the Tower.

"There were windows in the Tower of Istar," he recalled, "though you could not see them by day. All you could see was the smooth, sheer, crystal walls. When night fell, however, the wizards in their chambers would light their lamps. The Tower would gleam with pinpoints of fire. The people of Istar used to say that the wizards had captured the stars and brought them to the city for her own regal glory."

"The Tower must be deserted, my lord," said Mina. She fumbled for his hand in the darkness, glad to feel his touch, hear the sound of his voice. The darkness was so absolute she was beginning to doubt her own reality. She needed to know he was with her. "There seems nothing sinister about it. The fish go right up to it."

"Fish are not noted for their intelligence, no matter what Habakkuk says to the contrary. Still, as you say, we've seen no one come near the place. Let us investigate." He released her hand from his grasp and was gone.

"My lord," Mina called, reaching out to him. "My mortal eyes are blind in this murk. I cannot see you. I cannot see myself! More to the point, I cannot see where I am going. Is there some way you can light my path?"

"Those who can see can also be seen," said Chemosh. "I prefer to remain cloaked in darkness."

"Then you must guide me, Lord, as the dog guides a blind beggar."

Chemosh grasped her hand and pulled her swiftly through the water, making no difference between it and air. The water flowed past Mina, washing over her body. Once, tentacles brushed her arm and she jerked away. The tentacled creature did not pursue her. Perhaps she tasted bad. If Chemosh noticed the creature, he paid no attention. He pressed forward, eager and impatient.

As they drew nearer the Tower, Mina became aware that the walls were shining with a faint phosphorescence, greenish blue in color. The eerie light covered the crystal walls, giving the Tower a ghostly appearance.

"Wait here for me," Chemosh said, letting go her hand.

Mina floated in the darkness, watched as the god drew near the Tower. He ran his hands over the smooth surface of the walls and peered through the crystal walls, trying to see inside.

The crystal reflected his own image back to him.

Chemosh craned his neck. He looked up and he looked down and around. He shook his head, profoundly perplexed.

"There are no windows," he said to Mina. "No doors. No way inside that I can see, yet there must be. The entrance is hidden, that is all."

He moved along the walls, searching with his hands as well as his eyes. She could see his silhouette, black against the green phosphorous glow. She kept him in sight as long as she could, and then he disappeared, drifting around a corner of the building.

Mina was alone, utterly alone, as if she stood on the brink of Chaos.

She was parched with thirst and hungry. The hunger she could endure; she'd gone without food on many long marches with her army. Thirst was a different matter. She wondered how she could be thirsty, when her mouth was filled with water, except that the water tasted of salt and the salt was increasing her thirst. She did not know how long she could survive without drinking, before the need for water would become critical and she would have to admit to Chemosh that she could no longer go on. She would have to remind him, once again, that she was mortal.

Chemosh returned suddenly, looming out of the darkness.

"Admittedly, it has been many centuries since I last saw this Tower, yet something about it did not look right to me. I have figured out what is wrong. At least one third of it remains buried beneath the ocean floor. That includes the entrance presumably. In the old days, a single door led inside the Tower and now that door is buried in the sand. I can find no other way—"

Chemosh halted, staring. "Do you see that?"

"I see it, my lord," said Mina, "but I am not sure I believe it."

Deep inside the Tower, lights winked on. First one. Then another. Small globules of white-blue light appeared in different levels of the Tower—some far above them, near the top; others down below. Some of the lights seemed to be shining from deep within the Tower's interior, others closer to the crystal walls.

"It is as I remember," said Chemosh. "Stars held captive."

The lights were like starlight, cold and sharp-edged. They illuminated nothing, gave off no warmth, no radiance. Mina watched one closely. "Look there, my lord," she said, pointing.

"What is it?" Chemosh demanded.

"One of the lights went out and then came back," said Mina. "As if something or someone had walked in front of it."

"Where? Which light?"

"Up there, about two levels. My lord," Mina added, "you can enter the Tower. You are a god. These walls, no matter if they are solid or illusion, cannot stop you."

"Yes," he said, "but you cannot."

"You must go in, my lord," said Mina. "I will wait for you outside. When you find an entrance, you will come for me."

"I don't like to leave you alone," he said, yet he was tempted.

"I will call you if I have need."

"And I will come, though I am at the ends of the universe. Wait for me here. I won't be long."

He swam toward the crystal wall, swam through the crystal wall. The darkness, warm and smothering, pressed down on her.

Mina kept watch on the star-like lights, focusing on them and not on her thirst, which was becoming acute. She counted eight lights scattered all over the tower, with no two on the same level, if there were levels. None of them blinked on or off but burned steadily.

She missed Chemosh, missed his voice. The silence was thick and heavy as the darkness. Suddenly, quite near her, a ninth light flared.

This light was different from the others. It was yellow in color and seemed warmer, brighter.

"I can stay here, thinking of nothing except the unbearable silence and the taste of cool water on my tongue, or I can go discover the source of this light."

Mina pushed herself through the water, half-swimming, half-crawling, moving slowly and stealthily toward the strange light.

As she drew near, she saw that it was not a single point of light, as she had first supposed, but multiple lights, like a cluster of candles. She realized that the lights looked different—warmer, brighter—because they were outside the walls. She could see the light mirrored on the crystal surface. She drew nearer, curious.

The series of lights hung in the water as though strung together, like small lanterns hung on a rope. The lights were lined up in a row, jagged and irregular, which bobbed and drifted and gently swayed with the underwater currents.

"Strange," said Mina to herself. "It looks like some sort of net—"

Her danger flashed before her in that instant. She tried to flee, but movement beneath the water was agonizingly slow and sluggish. The lights started to spin rapidly, dazzling her, so that she was blinded and confused. A net of heavy rope whipped out from the center of the whirling lights and, before she could escape it, settled over her.

She fought desperately to free herself from the entangling folds of heavy rope that fell over her head and shoulders, wrapped around her arms and hands and thrashing legs. She tried to lift the folds of the net, put it aside, shove it off her, but the lights were so bright that she could not see what she was doing.

The net drew in around her, tighter and tighter, until her arms were squeezed up against her chest, her feet and legs trussed up so that she could not move.

She could see and feel the net being dragged through the water with her inside, moving rapidly toward the crystal wall. The net did not stop when it reached the wall and it seemed that she must smash into the crystal. She closed her eyes and braced herself for the shattering impact.

A sensation of numbing cold, as if she'd fallen into bone-chilling water, was all that happened. Gasping from the shock, she opened her eyes to see that she had passed through a kind of porthole that had swirled opened to admit her and was now spiraling shut behind her.

The net's movement ceased. Mina hung suspended in the water. Still entangled in the net, she could not easily turn her head and she had only a limited view of her surroundings. From what she could see, she was in some type of small, well-lighted chamber filled with sea water.

Two faces peered at her through a crystal pane.

"Fishermen," Mina realized suddenly, recalling how the fishermen on Schallsea Isle would use lights at night to lure fish to their nets. "And I am their catch."

She could not get a good look at her captors, for the net began to revolve and she was losing sight of them. The two were apparently as shocked to see her as she had been to see them. They began speaking to each other—she was able to see their mouths move, though she could not hear what they were saying.

It was then she noticed the surface of the water over her head ripple, as though air were being blown into the chamber. Looking up, she saw that the water level was starting to sink. The fishermen were pumping the water out of the room, replacing it with air.

The water is as air to you . . . the air will be as water.

Mina recalled Chemosh's warning about the spell he had cast over her, a warning she had not taken very seriously at the time, for she had not imagined that the two of them would be separated.

The water level was falling rapidly.

Mina pushed at the net with her hands and kicked her feet, trying frantically to free herself. Her efforts were futile, only caused the net to spin wildly.

She tried to draw attention to her plight, doing her best to shake her head, pointing upward.

The faces in the window watched her struggles with avid interest. Either they did not understand or they did not care.

Mina had not forgotten Chemosh's admonition to call him if she were in trouble. She had been too startled to do so when she first was caught in the net, and then too busy trying to free herself. After that, she had been too proud. He was constantly reminding her that she was weak as all mortals are weak. She wanted to prove herself to him, as she had proven herself at Storm's Keep. Common sense dictated that she seek his help now.

Mina would not yell out his name in a panic, however. Though she died in this moment, her pride would not allow to beg him.

"Chemosh," Mina said softly, to herself, to the memory of his dark eyes and his burning touch, "Chemosh, I am in need. The inhabitants of this Tower have caught me in some sort of net."

The top of her head broke through the surface of the water. She could feel the air on her scalp. Soon she would be exposed to the air.

"Chemosh," she prayed swiftly, as the water level continued to drop, "if you do not come to me soon, I will die, for they are depriving me of the water I need to breathe."

Silence. If the god heard her, he did not answer.

The water level fell to her shoulders. She dared not draw in a breath. She held the water in her lungs as long as she could, until her lungs burned and ached. When the pain became too great, she opened her mouth. Water spewed down her chin. She tried to breathe, but she was like a landed fish. She gasped for life, her mouth opening and closing.

"Chemosh," she said, as the light began to fade, "I come to you. I am not afraid. I embrace death. For now I will no longer be mortal . . ."

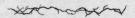

The net and its captive hit the floor. Eagerly, the two wizards turned the handle to the door of the air lock and hastened inside, the skirts of their black robes sloshing through the ankle-deep water. The two leaned down for a better look at their catch.

The woman lay on her back, enmeshed in the net, her eyes wide open, mouth gasping, her lips blue. Her hands and feet twitched spasmodically.

"You were right," said one wizard to the other, his tone one of academic interest. "She is drowning in air."

*liding through the crystalline Tower walls, Chemosh found himself in a room intended for use as a library in some future point of time. The room was in disarray, but shelves, lining the walls, were undoubtedly meant to hold books. Scroll cases stood empty in the center of the room, along with several writing desks, an assortment of wooden stools and numerous high-backed leather chairs, all jumbled together. A few books stood on the shelves, but most remained in boxes and wooden crates.

"I seemed to have arrived on moving day," Chemosh commented.

Walking over to a shelf, he picked up one of the dusty volumes that had toppled over on its side. The book was bound in black leather with no writing on the cover. A series of glyphs inscribed on the spine bore the book's title, or so Chemosh supposed. He could not read them, was not interested in reading them. He recognized them for what they were——words of the language of magic.

"So . . ." he murmured. "As I suspected."

Dropping the book onto the floor, he looked about for something on which to wipe his hands.

Chemosh continued to poke around, peering into crates, lifting the lids on boxes. He found nothing of any interest to him, however, and he left the library by way of a door at the far end. He entered a narrow corridor that curved off to his left and right. He looked down one way and then down the other, saw nothing that aroused his curiosity. He strolled off to his right, glancing into open doors as he passed. He found empty rooms, destined to be living quarters or school rooms. Again, nothing of interest, unless you counted it as interesting that someone was obviously preparing for a crowd.

Chemosh had never before walked the halls of one of the Towers of High Sorcery. The provinces of the gods of magic, the Towers are home to wizards and their laboratories, their spellbooks and artifacts, all of which are jealously guarded, off-limits to all outsiders. That includes gods.

Especially gods.

Prior to the rise of Istar, Chemosh had never felt any inclination to enter one of the Towers. Let the wizards keep their little secrets. So long as they didn't interfere with his clerics, his clerics did not interfere with wizards. Then came the Kingpriest and suddenly the world—and heaven—changed.

When the Kingpriest tossed the wizards of Istar out on their ears and then filled up the Tower with holy artifacts, stolen from the ruins of demolished temples, the gods were incensed. Several of the more militant, including Chemosh, proposed storming the Tower of Istar and removing their artifacts by force. The proposal was debated in heaven and eventually discarded; the idea being that this would take away the free will of the creatures they had created. Mankind must deal with mankind. The gods would not intervene, not unless it became clear to them that the foundation of the universe itself was threatened. Chemosh wanted his artifacts returned to him, but he wanted the destruction of the Kingpriest and Istar more, and so he went along with the others. He agreed to wait and see.

Mankind dropped the ball. They went along with the Kingpriest, supported him. The universe gave a dangerous lurch. The gods had to act.

They rained down destruction on the world. Clerics vanished. The Age of Despair began. The gods kept apart, remained aloof, waiting for the people to return to them. Chemosh might have secured his artifacts then, but he was hip-deep in a dark and secret conspiracy meant to return Queen Takhisis to the world. He dared not do anything that might draw attention to their plot. When the War of the Lance started and the other gods were preoccupied, Chemosh entered the Blood Sea to search for the Tower. It was gone, buried deep beneath the shifting sands of the ocean floor.

Now the Tower had been rebuilt and he had no doubt that his artifacts and those of the other gods must be somewhere inside. They had not been destroyed. He could sense his own power emanating from those he had blessed and in some instances forged. His essence was quite faint, not strong enough to help him locate his holy relics, but it was there—a whiff of death amidst the roses.

Chemosh irritably rubbed a smudge of dust off the sleeve of his coat. He was thinking over what to do, whether it would be worth his while to institute a search.

A quiet voice, soft with threat and malice, broke the silence. "What are you doing in my Tower, Lord of Death?"

A gibbous head, pale as corpse light, hung disembodied in the darkness. Lidless eyes were darker than the dark; thick full lips pushed in and out.

"Nuitari," said Chemosh. "I guessed I might find you hanging about here somewhere. I haven't seen much of you lately. Now I know why. You've been busy."

Nuitari glided silently forward. His pallid hands slipped from out the folds of the sleeves of his velvet black robes. The long, delicate fingers were in constant motion, rippling, grasping like the tentacles of a jelly fish.

"I asked a question—what are you doing here, Lord of Death?" Nuitari repeated.

"I was out for a stroll—"

"At the bottom of the Blood Sea?"

"—and I happened to pass by. I couldn't help but notice the improvements you've made to the neighborhood." Chemosh glanced languidly about. "Nice place you've got here. Mind if I take a look around?"

"Yes, I mind," said Nuitari. The lidless eyes never blinked. "I think you had better leave."

"I will," said Chemosh, pleasantly, "as soon as you return my artifacts."

"I have no idea what you are talking about."

"Then let me refresh your memory. I am here to recover the artifacts that were stolen from me by the Kingpriest and secreted in this Tower."

"Ah, *those* artifacts. I fear that you must go home empty-handed. They were all most regrettably destroyed, burned to ashes in the fire that consumed the Tower."

"Why is it I don't believe you?" Chemosh asked. "Perhaps because you are a consummate liar."

"Those artifacts were destroyed," repeated Nuitari. He slid his restless hands inside the sleeves of his robes.

"I wonder"—Chemosh eyed Nuitari intently—"do your cousins, Solinari and Lunitari, know about this little construction project of yours? Two Towers of High Sorcery remain in the world—the Tower at Wayreth and the Tower of Palanthas that is hidden in Nightlund. The three of you share custody of those Towers. My guess is you're not sharing custody of this one. Taking advantage of the confusion when we returned to the world, you decided to strike out on your own. Your cousins will find out eventually, but only after you've moved in your Black Robes and all their spellbooks and paraphernalia so that it would be difficult for anyone to dislodge you. I doubt your cousins will be very happy."

Nuitari remained silent, the lidless eyes dark and impassive.

"And what about the other gods?" Chemosh continued, expanding on his subject. "Kiri-Jolith? Gilean? Mishakal? And your father, Sargonnas? Now, there's a god who will be very interested in hearing about your new Tower—especially since it's located underneath the sea route his ships take to Ansalon. Why, I'll bet the horned god sleeps easier at night, secure in the knowledge that a bunch of Black-Robe wizards who have always despised him are working their dark arts beneath the keels of his ships. Then there's Zeboim, your dear sister? Should I go on?"

Nuitari's thick, full lips curled in a sneer. Although Zeboim and Nuitari were twins, sister and brother despised each other as they despised the parent gods who had given them life.

"None of the other gods knows, do they?" Chemosh concluded. "You've kept this a secret from us all."

"I do not see that it is any of your business," Nuitari responded, the lidless eyes narrowing.

Chemosh shrugged. "Personally, I don't care what you do, Nuitari. Build Towers to your heart's content. Build them in every ocean from here to Taladas. Build them on the dark moon, if you've a mind. Oops, bad joke." He grinned. "I won't say a word to anyone if you give me back my artifacts.

"After all," Chemosh added with a deprecating gesture, "they are holy artifacts, sacred relicts, blessed by my touch. They're of no use to you or your wizards. They could, in fact, be quite deadly if any of your Black Robes was so foolish as to try to mess with them. You might as well hand them over."

"Ah, but they *are* useful to me," Nuitari said coolly. "Their purchasing power alone is worth something, as you have just proven by making an offer for them."

Nuitari raised a thin, pale finger, emphasizing a point. "Always provided that such artifacts exist, which, so far as I know, they do not."

"So far as you know?" It was Chemosh's turn to sneer and Nuitari's turn to shrug.

"I have been extremely busy. I haven't time to look about. Now, my lord, much as I've enjoyed our conversation, you really should leave."

"Oh, I intend to," said Chemosh. "My first stop will be heaven, where the other gods will be fascinated to hear about what a busy boy you've been. First, though, since I've come all this way, I'll have a look around."

"Some other time, perhaps," Nuitari returned, "when I am at leisure to entertain you."

"No need to put yourself out, God of the Dark Moon." Chemosh made a graceful gesture. "I'll just stroll around on my own. Who knows? I might happen to stumble across my holy relics. If so, I'll just take them along with me. Get them out of your way."

"You waste your time," said Nuitari.

He motioned to a large wooden chest that stood on the floor. The chest was oblong, about as long as a human is tall, and made of roughhewn oak planks. The chest had two silver handles, one on either end, and a golden latch in front to facilitate raising the lid. No lock, no key. Runes were burned into the wood on the sides.

"Try to open it," suggested Nuitari.

Chemosh, playing along, put his hand to the handle in front. The chest began to glow with a faint reddish radiance. The lid would not budge. Nuitari flicked his pallid hand at one of the closed doors. It, too, began to give off the same reddish glow.

"Wizard-locked," said Nuitari.

"God-opened," Chemosh returned.

He struck the chest with his hand. The oak planks split apart. The silver handles clanged onto the floor, burying the golden latch in a pile of oak kindling. The books inside the chest spilled out onto the floor at the feet of the Lord of Death.

"So much for your wizard locks. Shall I kick in the door next? I warn you, Nuitari, I will find my artifacts if I have to break apart all the boxes and doors in this Tower, so be reasonable. It will be far less work for your carpenters if you just hand over my artifacts—"

"Your mortal is dying," said Nuitari.

Chemosh paused in what he was saying, realizing, in the instant of pausing, that he had made a mistake. He should have said immediately and impatiently, "What mortal?" as if he had no idea what Nuitari was talking about and could care less.

He did say those words, but it was too late. He'd given himself away.

Nuitari smiled. "This mortal," he said and he held out his hand.

Something lay wriggling on his palm. The image was blurry and Chemosh thought at first it was some sort of sea creature, for it was wet and flopped about inside a net like a new-caught fish.

Then he saw that it was Mina.

Her eyes bulged in her head. Her mouth gaped, gasping. She writhed in agony, trying desperately to find air. Her blue-tinged lips formed a word.

"Chemosh . . ."

He was ready with his response and he spoke it calmly enough, though he could not wrench his gaze from her.

"I have so many mortals in my service and all of them dying— for such is the lot of mortals—that I have no idea who she is."

"She prays to you. Do you not hear her?"

"I am a god," said Chemosh carelessly. "Countless pray to me."

"Yet her prayers are special to you, I think," Nuitari said, cocking his head.

Mina's voice echoed from the darkness.

Chemosh . . . I come to you. I am not afraid. I embrace death. For now I will no longer be mortal.

"Such devout love and faith," said Nuitari. "Imagine the surprise of my wizards when, while fishing for tuna, they catch instead a beautiful young woman. And imagine their surprise to find that she breathes water and drowns in air."

The spell had only to be reversed and Mina would live. Chemosh had to locate her, though. She was somewhere in this Tower, but the Tower was immense and she had only seconds left. She was losing consciousness, her body shuddering.

"She is one mortal, nothing more. I can have a hundred, a thousand if I wanted them," he told himself, even as he cast forth tendrils of his power, searching for her. "She is a burden to me. I am inside the Tower. I can take what I came for and Nuitari cannot not stop me."

He could not find her. A shroud of darkness surrounded her, hid her from him.

"She dies," said Nuitari.

"Let her," said Chemosh.

"Are you certain, my lord?" Nuitari displayed Mina in his palm, placed his other hand over her, holding her suspended in time. "Look at her, Lord of Death. Your Mina is a magnificent woman. More than one god envies you, to have such a mortal in your service . . ."

"She will be mine in death as she was in life," Chemosh returned, off-handedly.

"Not quite the same," said Nuitari dryly.

Chemosh chose to ignore the salacious innuendo. "In death, her soul will come to me. You cannot stop that."

"I wouldn't dream of trying," said Nuitari.

Mina's eyes flickered open. Her dying gaze found Chemosh. She held out her hand to him, not in supplication. In farewell.

Chemosh stood with his arms at his side. His fists, hidden by the lace on his cuffs, were clenched.

Nuitari closed his fingers over her.

Blood seeped from between the god's fingers. The red drops fell to the floor, fell slowly at first, one after the other. Then the drops were a trickle, the trickle a torrent. The god's hand was suffused with blood. He opened it . . .

Chemosh turned away.

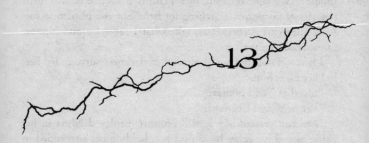

13

Across the continent of Ansalon, the Beloved of Chemosh walked the land. Young men and young women, healthy, strong, beautiful, dead. Murderers all, they walked about openly, fearing no law, no justice. Followers of Chemosh, they basked in the sunlight and avoided graveyards. Beloved of Chemosh, they brought him new followers nightly, killing with impunity, seducing their victims with sweet kisses and sweeter promises: unending life, unfading looks, forever young. All they asked in exchange was a pledge to Chemosh, a few simple words, spoken carelessly; the lethal kiss, the mark of lips burned on flesh, a new-risen corpse.

As time went by, the Beloved discovered that unending life was not all they had earned. They began to lose the memory of who they were, what they had done, where they had been. Their memories were replaced by a compulsion to kill, a compulsion to find new converts. If they failed in this, if a night passed and they had not delivered that fatal kiss, the god let them know of his disappointment. They saw in their dead minds his face, his eyes watching them. They felt, in their dead bodies, his ire, which burned in their dead flesh, growing more painful day by day. Only when his Beloved came to him with offerings of new converts did he ease their torment.

And so the Beloved of Chemosh roamed Ansalon, drifting from village to city, from farm to forest, always traveling east, the morning sun on their faces, to meet their god.

A god who was not on hand to receive them.

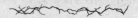

The Lord of Death left Nuitari's presence with every intention of searching through the whole blasted Tower, from spire to basement, pillar to post, for his holy artifacts. He opened a door and there was Mina.

For now I will no longer be mortal.

He slammed shut that door, opened another. She met him there.

More useful to you dead . . .

Mina was in every room he entered. She walked with him through the corridors of the Tower. Her amber eyes gazed at him from the darkness. Her voice, her last prayer, whispered over and over. The sound of blood falling, drop by drop, onto the floor at Nuitari's feet, thudded in his breast like the beating of a mortal heart.

"This is madness," Chemosh said to himself angrily. "I am a god. She a mortal. She is dead. What of it? Mortals die every day, thousands at a time. She is dead. Her mortal weaknesses die with her. Her spirit will be mine for eternity, if I want it. I can banish it if I don't. Far more practical . . ."

He caught himself staring into an empty crate for the heavens knew how long, not seeing that it was empty, seeing only Mina's face, staring back at him. He realized that he was wasting his time.

"Nuitari took me by surprise. I had not expected to find the Tower rebuilt. I did not expect to find the God of the Dark Moon taking up habitation here. Small wonder that I am distracted. I need time to think how to combat him. Time to plan, come up with a strategy."

Chemosh grew calmer, thinking this through.

"I will leave now, but I will return," he promised the moon-faced god.

He walked through the crystal walls, through the shifting ocean depths, through the ethers heading back to the darkness of the Abyss.

Darkness that was empty and silent.

So very silent. So very empty.

"Her spirit will be here," he said to himself. "Perhaps she will choose to go on to the next stage of her life's journey. Perhaps she will leave me, abandon me, as I abandoned her."

He started to go to the place where the souls passed from this world to Beyond, walking through the door that would lead to them to wherever it was they needed to go in order to fulfill the soul's quest. He went there to receive Mina's soul.

Or watch it walk away from him.

He stopped. He could not go there, either. He did not know where to go and in the end, he went nowhere.

Chemosh lay in his bed, their bed.

He could still smell her scent. He could see the depression in the pillow where she lay her head. He found a strand of glistening red hair and he picked it up and wound it around and around his finger. He ran his hand over the sheet, smoothing it, and he was running his hand over the soft, smooth skin, delighting in the feel of her warm and yielding flesh.

Delighting in the life. For she brought life to him.

He had once said to her: "When I am with you, that is the time I come closest to mortality. I see you lie back upon the pillow, and your body is covered with a fine sheen of sweat, and you are flushed and languorous. Your heart beats fast, the blood pulses beneath your skin. I feel life in you, Mina."

All that was gone.

He lay on the empty bed and stared into the darkness. His plans were all thrown into disarray. The "Beloved" were roaming Ansalon, their deadly kisses bringing more and more converts to his worship, converts who would obey his least command. He would have a powerful force at his disposal. He was not now certain what he would do with them.

He had meant for Mina to lead them.

Chemosh closed his eyes in agony and, when he opened them again, she stood before him.

"My lord," she said.

"You came to me," he said.

"Of course, my lord," she said. "I pledged you my faith, my love."

He reached out to her.

The amber eyes were ashes. Her lips dust. Her voice was the ghost of a voice. Her touch ghostly chill.

Chemosh rolled over on the bed, away from her.

No mortal, not even a dead one, should see a god weep.

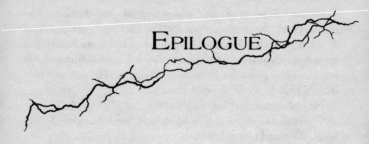

*F*ar distant from the Abyss, in the former Tower of High Sorcery at Istar—which had been renamed the Tower of the Blood Sea—Nuitari, god of dark magic, was closeted in one of the tower rooms with two of his wizards.

The three stood staring with rapt intensity into a large silver bowl of unique shape and design. Made to resemble the coiled body of a dragon, the base of the bowl was the dragon's body winding around and around upon itself, ending in a tail. The dragon's head, mouth agape, formed the bowl. Four dragon legs were the base, supporting the body. When the gaping mouth was filled with dragon's blood (blood that had to be taken from a willing dragon) the bowl had the ability to reveal to those who looked into it what was transpiring, not in the world—that was of little interest to Nuitari—but in heaven.

The theft of the world by one of their own had caused profound changes in all the gods, some for the better, others for much the worse. The three cousins, gods of magic, had always been allies, if they had not always been friends. Their love and dedication to the magic formed a bond between them that was strong enough to accept differences of philosophy in regard to how the magic should be used and promulgated. They had always come together to make decisions in regard to the magic. They had worked together to raise up the Towers of High Sorcery. They had grieved together to see the Towers fall.

Nuitari still felt a bond with his cousins. He had joined with them to bring back godly magic to the world and he was a staunch—even ruthless—supporter of their desire to put an end to the practice of sorcery. But the relationship between the cousins had changed. Takhisis's treachery had left Nuitari suspicious of everyone, including his cousins.

Nuitari had never trusted Takhisis's ambition. He had many times worked against his own mother, particularly when her interests and his own clashed. Even he had not been prepared for her betrayal. Her theft of Krynn had caught him flat-footed, made him look the fool. She had left him to search the universe for his lost world as a child searches the house for a lost marble.

His anger at his mother for her betrayal and at himself for being blind to her perfidy was a smoldering fire in him. Never again would he put faith in anyone. From now on, Nuitari would look out for Nuitari. He would raise up a fortress for himself and his followers, one that he alone would control. From the safety of that fortress he would keep close watch on his fellow gods and do what he could to thwart their plans and ambitions.

The ruins of the Tower of Istar had long rested beneath the Blood Sea. Most of the gods had fondly supposed the Tower completely destroyed. The gods of magic knew better. Following the Cataclysm, they had acted swiftly to make certain that the holy artifacts and relics in the Tower were protected. In order to keep these safe and secret, they buried the ruins of the Tower beneath a mountain of sand and coral. Sometime, in the far, far distant future, when the tale of Istar was nothing more than a fable used to frighten children into eating their vegetables, the gods of magic would restore the Tower, recover the lost artifacts, and give them back to the gods who had forged and blessed them.

Takhisis shattered those plans. When the gods finally recovered the world, they became absorbed in the pressing need to reestablish magic and quash sorcery. Solinari and Lunitari were dedicated to this cause and oblivious to all others. Nuitari was there to lend his aid when called upon. When he wasn't needed, he was beneath the Blood Sea, working for himself. He raised up the ruins of the Tower of Istar and rebuilt them to his own design. He recovered the stolen artifacts and relics. He brought these to a secret vault hidden beneath the Tower that he termed the Chamber of Relics. He sealed this chamber with powerful magical locks and posted a guardian—a sea dragon, a fierce, cunning creature known as Midori.

Thus far, none of the gods knew about his Tower. They were so busy building new temples and recruiting new followers that none thought of peering down beneath the ocean. He trusted their ignorance would continue for some time, long enough for him to firmly entrench himself and his followers. The only two who were a serious threat to him were his twin sister Zeboim and the god of sea life, Habakkuk.

Fortunately, Zeboim had gone off on one of her tangents— something to do with a death knight she'd cursed. As for Habakkuk, he was embroiled in a bitter battle with a Dragon Overlord who'd taken up residence in the seas on the opposite side of globe, a distraction brought about by Nuitari's partner, the sea dragon Midori.

Nuitari had not thought he had anything to worry about from any other god and he'd been surprised and extremely displeased to find Chemosh coolly walking the halls of his Tower. The God's Eye revealed Chemosh's growing ambition.

The God's Eye revealed Mina.

Like all the gods, Nuitari was an admirer. He toyed with the idea of seeking her out, making her one of his own followers. The fact that she was his mother's creation put an end to that notion. Nuitari wanted nothing to do with anything his mother had touched, and so he had left her to Chemosh.

A good thing, too. Chemosh's weakness for this particular mortal had been his undoing. Even though Nuitari had not expected Chemosh to actually let Mina die, the god of the Unseen Moon had been quick to see how this could work to his advantage.

Peering into the Dragon-sight bowl, Nuitari saw the Lord of Death prostrate on his bed, beaten down, defeated, alone, with only the ghost of Mina to offer help, support.

The ghost of Mina. Nuitari's thick, full lips smacked.

"A remarkable illusion," he said to his wizards. "You have fooled even a god. Admittedly, a god who was ready to be fooled, but still—good work."

"Thank you, my lord."

"My lord, thank you."

The two Black Robes bowed respectfully.

"Can you sustain this illusion for as long as I require it?" Nuitari asked.

"So long as we have the live model from which to work, my lord, yes, we can sustain it."

The wizards and the god turned to look into the prison cell which they had conjured up on the spot. The cell's walls were clear crystal and inside they could see Mina—wet and bedraggled and very much alive—pacing, back and forth.

"She can hear me?" Nuitari asked.

"Yes, my lord. She can hear and see us. We can see her, though we cannot hear her."

"No one can hear her? Not her voice? Not her prayers?"

"No one, my lord."

"That is well. Mina," called out Nuitari, "I don't believe I have had a chance to welcome you to my home. I trust your stay will be a long and pleasant one. Pleasant for us, though not, I fear, for you. By the way, you have not thanked me for saving your life."

Mina ceased her restless pacing. Striding over to the wall, she glared at him defiantly, her amber eyes flaring. She called out to him—he could see her mouth moving.

"I am not a reader of lips, but I don't believe she is expressing her gratitude, my lord," observed one of the Black Robes.

"No, I don't believe she is." Nuitari smiled broadly and bowed mockingly.

No one could hear Mina's curses, not even the gods. She struck her hands against the wall that was smooth and clear as ice. She struck it again and again, hoping to find a crack, a crevice, a flaw.

Nuitari was admiring. "She is truly magnificent, as I said to Chemosh. Notice this, gentlemen. She has no fear. She is weak from her ordeal, half-dead, yet she would like nothing better than to find a way to get at you two and rip out your hearts. Use her as you will, but guard her well."

"Trust us, my lord," said both Black Robes.

Nuitari turned from Mina back to the God's Eye bowl to see the illusion of Mina standing beside Chemosh, gazing down upon him in wistful sorrow.

"Look at that." Nuitari made a disdainful gesture, indicating the misery of the god. "Chemosh is convinced that his lover is dead, that nothing remains to him but her spirit. He weeps. How pitiful. How sad." Nuitari chuckled. "How very useful for us."

"I must admit, my lord," said one of the wizards, "I had some reservations about this plan of yours. I would not have thought it possible to deceive a god."

Nuitari's thoughts went to his mother.

"Only one who is weak," said Nuitari grimly. "And then only once."

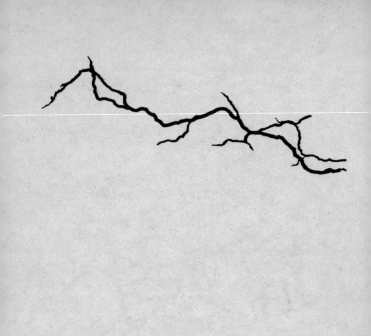

Appendix

Tower of the Blood Sea

by Jaleigh Johnson

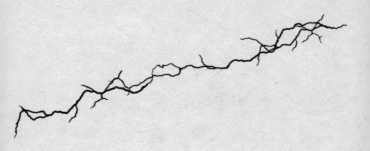

Note: For more detailed information on the various topics presented in this Appendix, readers are referred to: *The DRAGONLANCE Campaign Setting*, published by Wizards of the Coast; *The Towers of High Sorcery*, a DRAGONLANCE d20 System Supplement, published by Sovereign Press; and The Kingpriest Trilogy, written by Chris Pierson, published by Wizards of the Coast.

*O*nce a powerful bastion of knowledge and magic, the Tower of High Sorcery in the city of Istar rose to glory, then suffered an ignominious defeat at the hands of religious zealotry. The structure was almost completely destroyed during the Cataclysm and lay buried in darkness while the waters of the Maelstrom churned around it. Now the Tower has been rebuilt in secret, a stronghold for Nuitari the Black, and it has acquired a new name—the Tower of the Blood Sea.

HISTORY

The mighty wizard Kharro the Red sent members of the Conclave to find locations ideal for the construction of the Towers of High Sorcery, places where magical energies would be their strongest. A powerful White-robed wizardess named Asanta chose an insignificant town named Istar as the site of one Tower, much to Kharro's ire. It wasn't until Asanta shared her vision of Istar's future glory that the leader of the Conclave approved.

Raising the Tower became the life's work of Asanta, and as an old woman she led the powerful incantation that created the Tower from the bones of the earth. The beautiful, crystalline structure stood in strange contrast to the crude huts that surrounded it. Asanta died in peace, knowing that one day Istar would match her Tower's glory. Sadly, her foresight did not reveal to her that Istar would also be the instrument of the Tower's destruction.

The wizards who dwelled in Istar became instrumental in bringing peace and order to the surrounding lands and contributed greatly in the town's rising prosperity. For long years, they battled Istar's enemies and the forces of evil. People looked to magic as their savior, and magic always answered.

When the world was threatened by the Dark Queen, Takhisis, and her evil dragons during the Third Dragon War, the Conclave of Wizards devised a desperate plan to counter the threat. Meeting in secret in Palanthas, the wizards created the dragon orbs—powerful artifacts that would help turn the tide of battle. Unfortunately, when the armies of evil threatened Istar, the city's wizards were busy in Palanthas and were not in Istar to render aid. The city's leaders turned to the gods to save them, and it was the patriarch of the Temple of Paladine who rallied the people and called upon the god's holy powers to save them. Paladine answered, and Istar was spared. The people of Istar now began to question whether or not they could look to the Conclave of Wizards for guidance and protection.

Thanks to this victory, the church of Paladine rose to ascendance in Istar and the city's prosperity increased, so much so that Istar became the capital of a mighty empire. Its leader was the head of the church, who called himself the Kingpriest.

During this time, a conflict known as the Three-Thrones War (in which three successors vied for the throne) turned popular opinion against the wizards in the Tower of High Sorcery. The Kingpriest actually sent a force against the Tower, but he was unable to penetrate its protective grove. Bloodshed was avoided, and for generations the wizards and the priests continued to live under an unofficial, uneasy truce. Peace came to an end when a Kingpriest named Belindas Pilofiro took the throne.

Treachery, misfortune, and violence brought about a complete rupture between the wizards and the clerics. Eventually, the Kingpriest formed the Knights of the Divine Hammer and sought to attack two of the Towers of High Sorcery. Rather than allow their powerful magic to fall into the hands of those who might misuse it, the wizards themselves destroyed two of their Towers and the cities in which they stood. Terrified by such power, the Kingpriest negotiated surrender terms with the wizards.

To save their Orders, the wizards agreed to withdraw to the Tower of High Sorcery in the forest of Wayreth and to abandon the Towers of Istar and Palanthas and give them to the church.

The Kingpriest was not quite sure what to do with these trophies of his victory. He briefly entertained the idea of making the Tower of Istar his private dwelling, but eventually settled upon an idea suggested by his advisor, the Silvanesti elf cleric, Quarath. The Tower of Istar was rededicated to holding the sacred artifacts of heretical religions. The massive chamber in which the artifacts were stored was named *Solio Febalas*—the Hall of Sacrilege.

At first only the prized relics of dark and false gods adorned the hall, but the Kingpriest's zeal was great, and soon objects sacred to the gods of Neutrality were added to the storehouse as well. Eventually even artifacts of the gods of the good pantheon found their way into *Solio Febalas*.

As the power of the Kingpriest grew, so did his pride. He began to see himself as a god. At this, the gods were alarmed, and when the Kingpriest failed to heed their warnings, the gods came together to deliver their terrible punishment. Earthquakes sundered the Tower of Istar. Fire destroyed it from within. The gods threw down the fiery mountain from the heavens, and history records that the remains of the Tower of Istar were completely destroyed, along with the once-glorious city in which it stood.

THE TOWER RESTORED

The ruins of the Tower of Istar rested under the sea for many mortal generations, holding within it powerful and dangerous treasures. The gods of magic planned to eventually restore the Tower, planning to direct the Orders of High Sorcery to raise it back up from the sea. They did not believe that the world was yet ready to handle the dangerous artifacts that lay within and so these plans were destined for a distant future—one that would never come to pass.

Instead came the unexpected release of Chaos and the subsequent war that came near to destroying Krynn. Gods fought alongside mortals and the world was saved, only to be snatched away by Queen Takhisis and carried by her into another part of the universe. An Age of Mortals began, an age presumably without gods, although Takhisis was behind the scenes, working to make the world her own.

Her reign ended with the War of Souls. The gods found their lost world and the sacred constellations, moons, and planets returned to the heavens above Krynn. Takhisis was cast down from the immortal plane and slain.

The gods found a world in which sorcery and mysticism was flourishing, traditional magic almost forgotten. The Orders of High Sorcery, founded in the Age of Dreams, were now disbanded; its members were either dead or scattered. The gods went to work to reform the Orders. They forbade Dalamar the Dark from entering the Tower of High Sorcery that had once been in Palanthas, but which he had removed to Nightlund, and they left that Tower hidden until they could determine what to do with it. They set about working to ensure the future of the one habitable Tower that remained at Wayreth. In this, as they had been in the past, the gods of Magic were united.

Except for Nuitari the Black.

The god of dark magic still seethed with rage over the deception of his mother, Takhisis. He felt her betrayal keenly. Though still united with his cousins in the bonds of their magic and dedicated to magic's cause, he wished to ensure his own power and his position upon Krynn.

The shattered Tower of Istar provided him with the perfect opportunity. Working with two powerful Black-robed disciples, who were unknown to the world and to the other two gods, Nuitari cast the incantation that would not only restore the Tower but redesign it to suit Nuitari's needs. He had determined that the Tower of the Blood Sea would be a bastion of dark wizardry.

Nuitari knows that his Tower cannot be kept secret from the Conclave and the other gods forever, but he hopes to keep the fact that it has been rebuilt concealed for as long as possible, until he can build up his strength and make his Tower impregnable.

Meanwhile, the powerful, holy, and profane artifacts that were not destroyed in the Cataclysm remain hidden in a secret location inside the Tower, watched over by a powerful guardian.

DESCRIPTION

The Tower of the Blood Sea looks much like the original structure, retaining the deceptively delicate, crystalline walls. When light somehow penetrates the deep ocean water, it gives the Tower a mesmerizing beauty; its translucent and reflective surface attracts the creatures of the sea, who constantly circle its structure.

The main physical difference between the Tower of Istar and the Tower of the Blood Sea is to be found on the Tower's dome. The faceted, crystal walls of the Tower are capped by an orb of black marble, very different from the "bloody fingers" of the original design. The dome is crowned with a circlet made of red-gold intertwined with silver, with a black void at its center. The red-gold honors Lunitari, goddess of neutral magic. The silver portion gives homage to Solinari of the white moon. The black void, central to the crowning circlet, represents Nuitari, who claims the Tower as his own.

Fish, sharks, dolphins, whales, and octopi swim about the Tower, either eyeing it curiously, or not appearing to give it much notice, as if it were just another coral formation. Some fish, fooled by its translucent crystal, bump into the walls or fight with their reflections. The exception to this is the black void within the circlet atop the Tower's dome. Though the creatures of the Blood Sea might swim near the red-gold and silver circlet, they instinctively keep away from the black void, as they instinctively keep away from poisonous plants and deadly traps.

Unlike its counterparts, the Tower of the Blood Sea has many windows of clear crystal, though they are visible when a lamp is lit inside the walls. If many such lamps are lighted, the Tower resembles a field of stars sparkling in a night-black sky. Currently, due to the fact that there are only a few people inhabiting the Tower, only one or two rooms may be lit at any given time.

The central doorway into the Tower still exists, but is buried under tons of sand and debris. The servants of Nuitari created a new means of entrance and egress—a magical air lock. The wizards created a special chamber that allows them to catch fish and to come and go from the Tower. The air lock is a cylinder created between portions of the crystal wall. At the magical command, a porthole in either the inner or the outer wall starts to swirl and then becomes insubstantial. Upon speaking another phrase, the second porthole does the same. The chamber may be filled with water when the portholes are opened and can be drained when both magical portholes are closed. The portholes are cleverly disguised to appear to be part of the crystal wall. The only time the portholes are visible is when they are swirling open or closed. There are no markers or other symbols to identify their location. The wizards have designed a fish net that is decorated with lights to attract fish to their location. The rope net is concealed by illusion magic until the wizards activate it.

A large, winding stairway is the central feature of the Tower's interior, very much like the staircase found in the Tower of Nightlund. Histories report that a magical light source once glowed brightly in the center of the shaft, to light the way of those ascending or descending the stairs. That has not yet been restored and the staircase remains perilously dark. The private chambers of long-dead Istaran mages lie abandoned on the eastern side of the stairwell. Two of these rooms, located about mid-level in the Tower, have been recently cleaned and are now furnished with comfortable beds. Black robes hang in the wardrobes, and each room has a small writing desk. These are the personal living quarters of the Tower's two new occupants.

Small laboratories, work areas, and scroll archives are located on the west wall. When the Kingpriest seized the Tower and turned it into the Hall of Sacrilege, these rooms were turned into storerooms that held the minor idols, altars, and artifacts blessed by the various gods. Eventually, all the gods, with the exception of Paladine, were represented in this chamber, including the healer, Mishakal. The objects blessed by the gods of Light were stored in the chambers located in the Tower's upper stories.

Those of neutrality were placed in the central rooms, while the unholy relics of the dark gods were stored in the Tower's lower levels.

Only the most minor artifacts are still located in the storerooms. The wizards have carefully cataloged and removed those artifacts of significant power to a secret chamber located beneath the Tower—a chamber guarded by a fearsome protector.

The Hall of Audience, now empty, holds Nuitari's throne. Here he holds meetings with the two wizards he has brought to work within the hidden Tower. The Laboratory of the Highmage has also been restored to limited functionality, though currently it holds crates and boxes that have yet to be unpacked.

The Chamber of Eyes was once known throughout the Orders as the pinnacle of achievement for scrying magic. The original implements of this magic were either removed or destroyed before the Kingpriest claimed the Tower, but Nuitari has placed in their stead an item more powerful than even the Istaran mages would have dared dream—the God's Eye.

Now that one of the gods has prematurely learned of the Tower's existence, Nuitari must accelerate his plans to populate the Tower with loyal followers. He alone knows the secret of transporting wizards far beneath the depths of the Blood Sea and, although he has presumably found a way to control Chemosh, Nuitari knows that if one god has discovered his secret, others will follow. The foreboding black void located inside the circlet atop the dome is thought to be involved in the process. The only two wizards known to have survived the perilous journey have nothing to say on the subject.

Basalt Darkeye

Basalt is probably not the dark dwarf's original name, but he has used it for hundreds of years and has, by now, forgotten whatever name he was given. The dwarven wizard of the Black Robes serves the god Nuitari and is one of the two caretakers of the Tower of the Blood Sea.

Background: Basalt is a dwarf of the Theiwar clan, born in the years just after the Cataclysm. Like others of his kind, he studied magic and demonstrated great promise and unwavering devotion to the gods of magic, who granted him the power to battle his enemies. Unlike many of his clan, Basalt wanted to gain in magical power and he believed that the only way to do this was to work with others of his Order. Fifty years before the War of the Lance, Basalt left the mountain kingdoms and journeyed to Wayreth to take the Test. His Test forced him to choose between loyalty to his clan and life under the mountain or the power granted by magic. Basalt was willing to murder his cousins for the power he sought and swore his allegiance to Nuitari upon receiving the Black Robes.

Basalt sided with the Dragonarmies during the War of the Lance, although he always honored the wizards' pact to devote themselves to magic first and personal or political animosities second. He had the misfortune to be in Neraka at the end of the war and might have died during the destruction of the Temple, but for a fortuitous encounter with the powerful mage Raistlin Majere. Basalt had thought to try to rise to power by assassinating Raistlin, but he soon realized that his powers were no match for the young human mage, and fearing that Raistlin suspected his plotting, Basalt fled for his life.

Like others of the Orders of High Sorcery, Basalt was enraged by the emergence of the gray-robed Knights of the Thorn. Renegades whose powers were enhanced directly by the Dark Queen, the Thorne Knights defied the history, heritage, and traditions of the wizard orders established during the Age of Dreams. The dark dwarf eagerly joined with his fellows in attempting to combat the dark knight wizards. The war against Chaos forced everyone who lived upon Krynn, both good and evil, to become allies in a battle for survival. Basalt fought side-by-side with those wearing white and red robes against the shadow wights and daemon warriors. He was terribly wounded and very nearly died.

Basalt spent nearly a year recovering from the wounds inflicted on him by the minions of Chaos. These were nothing, however, compared to the loss of his magic that came when Takhisis stole away the world. He raged, then despaired, for he was powerless. When the "new magic" of sorcery was discovered, Basalt did not have the heart to try it. For him, true magic came from the power of the moons, and he cursed the pale orb that shone in their stead each night.

Having lost his power, Basalt became a hermit and a vagrant. He wandered Ansalon in a half-crazed state, constantly peering up in the night sky at the void in the stars where the black moon should be. The War of Souls left him untouched, a pitiful shell of his former self, worthy of neither fear nor respect. Then, a miracle happened.

One fateful night, the false moon vanished from the sky. The constellations and planets of the old gods were restored. Lunitari and Solinari shone once more, while Nuitari appeared to those who could look into his blackness and understand. Basalt felt the long-unused power course through his veins. The words of magic that he had mumbled uselessly day by day suddenly burned bright in his mind.

Basalt was among the first of the former Black Robes to realize that Nuitari had returned. He fell to his knees and cried out his praises to the dark god. Touched by his follower's loyalty, Nuitari appeared before Basalt in mortal guise to make him an offer.

A new bastion of magic was being created—a stronghold where dark magic would reign supreme. Basalt could leave the surface world and serve the god of the black moon in his new abode. Honored by the dark god's trust, Basalt left his life on land behind to move below the waves. The Tower of the Blood Sea is now his home.

Description: Basalt is an albino, which gives him a truly startling appearance for a dwarf. Both his skin and hair are bone-white; his eyes are pink, tinged with red. He has the short, stocky build of all dwarves, though his pursuit of magic makes him appear thin by dwarven standards. He tends to stand with his arms crossed, warding people away. His fiery-eyed, intense gaze gives him the appearance of glaring malevolently at those he encounters.

Basalt Darkeye: Male dark dwarf (Theiwar) Rog2/Wiz5/Black Robe 9; CR 16; Medium humanoid (dwarf); HD 2d6+14d4+64; hp 114; Init +2; Spd 20 ft.; AC 17, touch 14, flat-footed 15; Atk +13/+8 melee (1d4+4/17-20, *+3 keen dagger*); SA sneak attack +1d6, spells; SQ arcane research +4, black robe order secrets, darkvision 120 ft., dark dwarf traits, evasion, moon magic (Nuitari), trapfinding; AL NE; SV Fort +5, Ref +8, Will +13; Str 12, Dex 14, Con 19, Int 20, Wis 13, Cha 7.

Skills and Feats: Balance +6, Bluff +3, Climb +4, Concentration +21, Craft (stonemasonry) +6, Decipher Script +18, Escape Artist +6, Hide +9, Intimidate +14, Knowledge (arcana) +22, Move Silently +8, Search +11, Sleight of Hand +5, Spellcraft +24, Spot +7, Swim +4; Empower Spell, Iron Will, Magical Aptitude, Reserves of Strength, Scribe Scroll (B), Spell Focus (Necromancy) (B), Stubborn, Weapon Finesse.

Spells Prepared (4/6+1/5+1/5+1/5+1/4+1/3+1/2+1/2+1; save DC 15 + spell level): 0—daze, detect magic, ray of frost, read magic; 1st—*burning hands, cause fear*, identify (x2), *magic missile,* ray of enfeeblement* (x2); 2nd—*darkness, false life*, ghoul touch*, locate object, scare*, spectral hand*;* 3rd—*deep slumber, halt undead*, ray of exhaustion*, stonesight, vampiric touch** (x2); 4th—*animate dead*, bestow curse*, crushing despair, ethereal flame*, phantasmal killer, wall of ice;* 5th—*dominate person, empowered lightning bolt, feeblemind, fog of fear*, symbol of pain*;* 6th—*circle of death*, eyebite*, greater dispel magic, symbol of fear*;* 7th—*finger of death*, forcecage, greater arcane sight.*

* These spells belong to the school of Necromancy, which is this character's enhanced specialty. Prohibited schools: Abjuration, Conjuration, Transmutation.

Order Secrets: Magic of Darkness, Magic of Fear, Magic of Hunger, Magic of Pain.

Spellbook: As an experienced Black Robe wizard and one of Nuitari's chosen caretakers of the Tower of the Blood Sea, Basalt has access to an incredible array of spells. He has knowledge of all arcane spells listed in the *Dungeons & Dragons Player's Handbook* and in the *DRAGONLANCE Campaign Setting* (except for named spells, such as *Fistandantilus's Portal* or *Magius's Light of Truth*).

Equipment: *Bracers of armor +3, ring of protection +2, +3 keen dagger, eyes of doom, robe of bones, necklace of adaption, ring of swimming, wand of acid arrow* (22 charges).

CAELE

A savage heart beats beneath the black robes of the half-elf mage from Southern Ergoth. Ruled by his passions, which can go from icy coldness to white-hot rage in a heartbeat, Caele is unpredictable and highly dangerous.

Background: Caele never found out exactly what the relationship was between his mother, a Kagonesti elf shaman, and the Ergothian sailor who fathered him. His mother made it clear to the half-elf at an early age that any discussion of his father was forbidden. Though ostensibly part of the Kagonesti tribe, the two were never truly accepted and lived in relative isolation. Caele's early years were spent in the wild—hunting small game, climbing trees, and swimming in clear streams.

For reasons unknown to him (though possibly related to his ostracism by his Kagonesti tribesmen), Caele had what he called "black moods" come over him. During these times, he lashed out at anyone near him, taking perverse pleasure in causing pain and distress to innocent victims. When he was young, he would feel guilty over the torment of small animals or people. As he grew older, he saw that these destructive forces brought him power over others and his guilt waned, eventually vanishing altogether.

Still a young man, Caele fell in love with a young woman of his tribe, one of the rare silver-haired beauties of the Kagonesti. A secret romance between the two blossomed and Caele felt that his black moods were forever behind him. He planned to run away with his lover and start a new life. The half-elf told the maiden his plans for them at one of their secret meeting spots near the top of a waterfall. The maiden refused to go. She didn't want to leave her people, especially to run away with a half-breed.

Darkness overwhelmed Caele. He grabbed his lover and dragged her to the edge of the cliff. He ignored her screams and paid no attention to her flailing fists and scratching nails. He shoved her over the waterfall, watching dispassionately as her body smashed into the jagged rocks at the base of the falls. Caele gazed down at her for some time, until the water washed away all traces of his crime.

Although no one could prove that he had murdered the young woman, the two had been seen together and her disappearance aroused the suspicions of the tribe. Caele was termed a dark elf and forced to flee for his life. He traveled to the port towns of Northern Ergoth, earning his keep by thievery. The dark elf might have ended his days as a thief, except that he tried to rob an Ergothian sea-mage named Dunbar Mastermate, wizard of the White Robes.

The powerful and high-ranking wizard easily caught the inept young thief. Dunbar saw potential in young Caele, and hoped that compassion and understanding might bring the half-elf to the paths of light. Caele was not interested at first in learning magic, which he thought was for weaklings. A demonstration of magical power impressed him and caused him to change his mind. Scholarly pursuits did not come naturally to him, but he had talent and determination. Caele sailed the seas with Dunbar, and for a time, the sea brought peace to his troubled soul. Eventually, however, the black moods returned. He was constantly getting embroiled in fights and in arguments, until the crew took against him and threatened to maroon him.

Dunbar tried to intervene with Caele, hoping to turn the young man aside from a path leading to true darkness, but their "talks" always ended in arguments. One morning, while sailing just off the coast of Solamnia, the crew woke to find both Caele and a lifeboat missing—along with some of Dunbar's scrolls and magical accoutrements. Deciding not to pursue him, Dunbar heard nothing of Caele for many years.

The sea-mage was eventually elected head of the Order of White Robes, and took up semi-permanent residence in the Tower of High Sorcery at Wayreth. He was surprised one day to see Caele traveling through the forest, searching for the Tower, wishing to take the Test.

The Test forced Caele to relive the darkest day of his life—the murder at the falls. He was not interested in rewriting the past, nor in hearing his lover's hurtful words once more. This time he cut her throat immediately, then shoved her bleeding body over the cliff's edge. Nuitari claimed Caele for his own.

Caele grew in power rapidly under the dark light of the black moon and he rose quickly in the Order, hoping to challenge even the great Dalamar the Dark for control. Then the Summer of Chaos scorched the world. The black moon left the sky. Caele's magic was gone.

The powerless wizard went back to the sea, sailing on merchant ships. He learned that magical objects of the Fourth Age could give him temporary power and he took to searching for and stealing any he could find. His thievery did not go unnoticed. He was arrested, convicted, escaped, arrested again, escaped again. A hunted man, he was forced to leave civilization behind and retreat to the wilderness. A capable survivor, he hunted and fished, determined to go on with his life, even without the magical power that had once defined him.

Caele's powers returned with the three moons. One of the few truly powerful Black Robes left alive, Caele was sought out by Nuitari, who appeared to Caele and offered him the chance to become one of the dark god's personal wizards. Caele agreed and became the second of the two caretakers of the Tower of the Blood Sea.

Appearance: Caele is tall, lean, and muscular. He has light brown skin and dark eyes. His long, wavy hair is jet-black. He dresses in the black robes of his Order for formal occasions, but, in the wilderness, he is completely at-ease wearing a loincloth or nothing at all. He has several faded tribal tattoos on his chest and arms. His face is closed and expressionless, even when he is in one of his rages, which makes him all the more frightening.

Caele: Male half-elf (Ergothian/Kagonesti) Bar2/ Wiz5/Black Robe 10; CR 17; Medium humanoid (half-elf); HD 2d12+15d4+34; hp 92; Init +6;

Spd 40 ft.; AC 19, touch 12, flat-footed 17; Atk +11 melee (1d3+2/x2, unarmed strike); SA rage 1/day, spells; SQ half-elf traits, darkvision 30 ft., low-light vision, uncanny dodge; AL NE; SV Fort +9, Ref +6, Will +10; Str 14, Dex 15, Con 15, Int 17, Wis 8, Cha 10.

Skills and Feats: Climb +7, Concentration +21, Handle Animal +4, Intimidate +6, Jump +6, Knowledge (arcana) +22, Listen +8, Search +6, Spellcraft +24, Spot +2, Survival +7, Swim +10; Craft Wondrous Item, Empower Spell, Enlarge Spell, Improved Initiative, Scribe Scroll (B), Spell Penetration, Quicken Spell, Track.

Spells Prepared (4/5/5/5/4/4/3/2/1; save DC 13 + spell level): 0—*acid splash, detect magic, mage hand, open;* 1st—*burning hands, enlarge person, identify, summon monster I, true strike;* 2nd—*bull's strength, invisibility, protection from arrows, scorching ray, web;* 3rd—*clairvoyance, empowered magic missile, haste, lightning bolt, summon monster III;* 4th—*dimension door, globe of invulnerability (lesser), shout, stoneskin;* 5th—*baleful polymorph, prying eyes, quickened magic missile, wall of force;* 6th—*permanent image, programmed image,* [Tenser's] *transformation;* 7th—*spell turning, summon monster VII;* 8th—*prismatic wall.*

Order Secrets: Magic Betrayal, Magic of Darkness, Magic of Fear, Magic of Hunger, Magic of Pain.

Note: Caele has chosen not to take an arcane focus as a Wizard of High Sorcery.

Spellbook: As an experienced Black Robe wizard and one of Nuitari's chosen caretakers of the Tower of the Blood Sea, Caele has access to an incredible array of spells. He has knowledge of all arcane spells listed in the *Dungeons*

& *Dragons Player's Handbook* and in the *Dragonlance Campaign Setting* (except for named spells, such as *Fistandantilus's Portal* or *Magius's Light of Truth*).

Possessions: *Amulet of natural armor +4, ring of protection +3, cloak of the manta ray, boots of elvenkind, ring of elemental command (water), rod of metamagic (empower).*

THE GOD'S EYE

A powerful item created by Nuitari during the dark god's attempts to locate the lost world of Krynn during the early years of the Age of Mortals, the God's Eye is a magical scrying device that can pierce the veils of the planes of existence and see into the realms of both mortals and gods. Though the Eye did not help Nuitari locate the missing world, it becomes a valuable tool for spying during a time when he feels no one—man or god—should be trusted.

The God's Eye is a large bowl created from dragonmetal (the same silvery substance used to forge dragonlances). It is shaped like a serpentine dragon coiled about itself, its long tail forming the bowl.

Game Information

Only focused spellcasters (clerics and wizards) may use the God's Eye. If a spontaneous spellcaster (mystic, sorcerer, or bard) attempts to use the artifact, the liquid inside will boil away within seconds and nothing useful can be accomplished.

When filled with water, wine, or any other mundane liquid, the bowl functions exactly like a *crystal ball* with a caster level of 20. Anything viewed is subject to the effects of a *true seeing* spell. The DC of a Will save against the scrying attempt is 25.

The God's Eye gains its true power when the vessel is filled with the blood of a dragon. (This must be a true dragon, not a creature of the dragon type such as a draconian.) Only fresh dragon's blood will function as a catalyst. After forty-eight hours, the blood is drained of its magic and becomes inert. A minimum of 10 hit points of damage must be inflicted (either voluntarily or forcibly) to acquire the blood needed to fill the Eye. (Blood gained from a willing dragon is preferred, because it is likely to be freshest, but the dragon blood used may be obtained by any means.)

With fresh dragon's blood, the God's Eye allows the user to scry any location, on any plane of existence. A Will save is allowed to detect the scrying attempt, with a DC of 40 plus 1 for every age category of the dragon whose blood is being used. If a deity is the subject of the scrying attempt, the viewer must make a Wisdom check (DC 18) the first round or become *confused* for 2d4 rounds. A cleric gains a +2 competence bonus to the check, while a cleric of the deity being scryed gains a +4 competence bonus.

When dragon's blood is used as the catalyst, the God's Eye can also be used to cast certain spells on the location being scryed. All spells of the illusion school, as well as any Compulsion or Mind-Affecting spell, can be cast through the Eye unaffected by range (as long as the target or area is within the place being scryed). The saving throw DC of any spell cast through the Eye is increased by 1 for every age of category of the dragon whose blood is in the bowl.

Use of the God's Eye is not without risk. Any deity who discovers he or she is being scryed is not likely to be forgiving. Even the gods of good would not appreciate anyone spying on their affairs, even one of their own chosen, and, if discovered, the spy is likely to be severely punished. Obtaining the fresh dragon's blood necessary to fuel the artifact's power is also an extremely dangerous undertaking.

NEW YORK TIMES BESTSELLING AUTHOR
MARGARET WEIS
RETURNS TO
DRAGONLANCE!

THE
DARK DISCIPLE
TRILOGY

AMBER AND ASHES
Volume One
Mina, the central figure of the War of Souls saga, declares her
new faith and love in Chemosh, God of Death, and leads an evil,
vampiric cult that sweeps across Krynn. The fate of the world is
left in the hands of a pair of unlikely heroes—a wayward monk
and a kender who can communicate with the dead.

AMBER AND IRON
Volume Two
The trilogy continues to follow the mysterious warrior-woman
Mina through Krynn.

AMBER AND BLOOD
Volume Three
The Dark Disciple Trilogy draws to a bloody conclusion.

Release dates and downloads at
www.wizards.com

DRAGONLANCE and its logo are trademarks of Wizards of the Coast, Inc.
in the U.S.A. and other countries. ©2005 Wizards.

THE MINOTAUR WARS
RICHARD A. KNAAK

*A new trilogy featuring the minotaur race that
continues the story from the New York Times best-
selling War of Souls trilogy!*

NIGHT OF BLOOD
Volume One

As the War of Souls spreads, a terrible, bloody coup led by
the ambitious General Hotak and his wife, the High Priestess
Nephera, overtakes the minotaur empire. With legions of
soldiers and the unearthly magic of the Forerunners at his
command, the new emperor turns his sights towards Ansalon.
But not all his enemies lie dead...

TIDES OF BLOOD
Volume Two

Making a bold pact with the ogres, and with the assurances of
the mysterious warrior-woman Mina sweetly ringing in his
ears, the minotaur emperor Hotak decides to invade Ansalon.
But betrayal comes from the least expected quarters, and an
escaped slave called Faros, the last of the blood of the lawful
emperor, stirs up a fresh, vengeance-driven rebellion.

EMPIRE OF BLOOD
Volume Three

A new emperor sits on the throne in Nethosak, supported by
fanatical Protectors and the dark magic of the Forerunners.
Faros leads the rebellion to the capital and the temple, to a
showdown with the usurpers—and destiny.

www.wizards.com

DRAGONLANCE and its logo are trademarks of Wizards of the Coast, Inc.
in the U.S.A. and other countries. ©2005 Wizards.

THE LINSHA TRILOGY COMES TO ITS THRILLING CONCLUSION!

CITY OF THE LOST
Volume One

MARY H. HERBERT

Linsha Majere, the granddaughter of Caramon Majere, a hero of the War of the Lance, has been entrusted with a terrible secret. When the precarious order of Ansalon is shattered, she must embark on a desperate quest to save the city from an unstoppable enemy.

FLIGHT OF THE FALLEN
Volume Two

MARY H. HERBERT

As the Plains of Dust are torn asunder by invading barbarian forces, Rose Knight Linsha Majere is torn between two vows— her pledge to the Knighthood, and her pledge to guard the eggs of the dragon overlord Iyesta. To keep her honor, Linsha will have to make the ultimate sacrifice.

RETURN OF THE EXILE
Volume Three

NANCY VARIAN BERBERICK

Linsha has been taken prisoner, and the only chance she has to keep her vow and save the dragon eggs is to marry the feared leader of the Tarmak invaders. On the far-away island home of the Tarmak, she finds hope in the most unexpected place of all— among her enemies.

www.wizards.com

DRAGONLANCE and its logo are trademarks of Wizards of the Coast, Inc. in the U.S.A. and other countries. ©2005 Wizards.

THE ELVEN NATIONS TRILOGY GIFT SET

FIRSTBORN
Volume One

PAUL B. THOMPSON & TONYA C. COOK

In moments, the fate of two leaders is decided. Sithas, firstborn son of the elf monarch Sithel, is destined to inherit the crown and kingdom from his father. His twin brother Kith-Kanan, born just a few heartbeats later, must make his own destiny. Together—and apart—the princes will see their world torn asunder for the sake of power, freedom, and love.

THE KINSLAYER WARS
Volume Two

DOUGLAS NILES

Timeless and elegant, the elven realm seems unchanging. But when the dynamic human nation of Ergoth presses on the frontiers of the Silvanesti realm, the elves must awaken—and unite—to turn back the tide of human conquest. Prince Kith-Kanan, returned from exile, holds the key to victory.

THE QUALINESTI
Volume Three

PAUL B. TOMPSON & TONYA C. COOK

Wars done, the weary nations of Krynn turn to rebuilding their exhausted lands. In the mountains, a city devoted to peace, Pax Tharkas, is carved from living stone by elf and dwarf hands. In the new nation of Qualinesti corruption seeks to undermine this new beginning. A new generation of elves and humans must band together if the noble experiment of Kith-Kanan is to be preserved.

www.wizards.com

DRAGONLANCE and its logo are trademarks of Wizards of the Coast, Inc. in the U.S.A. and other countries. ©2005 Wizards.